Encircling 3

AFTERMATH

A Novel

Carl Frode Tiller

Translated from the Norwegian by
Barbara J. Haveland

Graywolf Press

First published in Norway in 2014 as *Innsirkling 3* by H. Aschehoug & Co. (W. Nygaard), Oslo.

This publication is made possible, in part, by the voters of Minnesota through a Minnesota State Arts Board Operating Support grant, thanks to a legislative appropriation from the arts and cultural heritage fund. Significant support has also been provided by Target Foundation, the McKnight Foundation, the Lannan Foundation, the Amazon Literary Partnership, and other generous contributions from foundations, corporations, and individuals. To these organizations and individuals we offer our heartfelt thanks.

MINNESOTA
STATE ARTS BOARD

CLEAN
WATER
LAND &
LEGACY
AMENDMENT

NORLA
Norwegian
Literature Abroad

This translation has been published with the financial support of NORLA.

Published by Graywolf Press
250 Third Avenue North, Suite 600
Minneapolis, Minnesota 55401

www.graywolfpress.org

Published in the United States of America
Printed in Canada

ISBN 978-1-64445-058-1

2 4 6 8 9 7 5 3 1
First Graywolf Printing, 2021

Library of Congress Control Number: 2020944393

Cover design: Scott Sorenson

Cover photo: manicproject.com

For Marita, Oline, Othilie, and Cornelia

Encircling 3

AFTERMATH

MARIUS

Trondheim, June 21st, 2006. Is that all you get?

I open the bathroom door and go back into the living room. Sounds like they've finished discussing business policy, Julie's talking about the wedding again, although I can't imagine the others are all that interested in our wedding, it's a bit embarrassing the way she goes on about it at such length and in such detail. I glance at Kjersti and Jan Olav and force a little smile as I sit down, but they don't catch it, they're focused on Julie, nodding and trying to seem interested in what she's saying. I pick up my wine glass and take a sip, glance at Kristian as I do so, he's sitting there twirling his beard, then he stops, lowers his hand discreetly and shoots his wrist out of his shirtsleeve, steals a quick peek at his watch, then raises his hand and starts twirling his beard again, his eyes on Julie.

"Luckily, though, my mom's making my wedding dress, so that's a big saving right there," Julie says, reaching out and picking up her wine glass, trying hard to look sober but not quite managing it, she's pretty drunk now, her smile is a little too big and soppy; she blinks slowly, puts her glass to her lips to take a drink, then stops, lowers her glass, and looks at Kjersti again. "She made my friend's wedding dress as well and it was lovely, really simple, but that was because she wanted a simple dress. Me, I want a long train, a veil, the works, but that's me, that's just how I am," she says with a rippling red-wine giggle. "Well, anyway, everybody loved it and wanted to know where she'd bought it. Didn't they, Marius?"

I haven't said anything for a while and my throat feels a bit dry, I'm not sure my voice will hold, so I put a hand over my mouth and give a little cough.

"Uh-huh," I say, then I cough again, look at Kjersti as I do so, she's sitting with both hands on the table, sliding her little ring up and down the lower part of her fourth finger and smiling at Julie.

"How wonderful," she says.

"Have you had any thoughts about your speech, Jan Olav?" Julie asks.

"Not yet," Jan Olav says.

"Will you be making a speech?" Kjersti says.

"Well, I *am* going to be best man."

"*You're* going to be best man?" she says. Jan Olav obviously hasn't said anything to her and she sounds as though Jan Olav is just about the last person she would have expected to be best man.

"Yeah," Jan Olav says, trying to sound as if he doesn't know why she's so surprised, but it doesn't quite work, there's a hint of irritation in his eyes and his voice, he doesn't like it that she looks and sounds so surprised, I can tell by his face, maybe it's because he's trying to spare me somehow. Kjersti's surprise suggests that Jan Olav and I aren't as close as the bridegroom and best man are supposed to be and that in turn gives the impression that I exaggerated our friendship when I asked him to be my best man, it's probably the embarrassment attached to this that he wants to spare me. I look at him for a moment, then my cheeks start to burn. Maybe Kjersti's right, maybe I did think Jan Olav and I were closer than we actually are, or at any rate closer than he thinks we are. "What?" Jan Olav says, looking at Kjersti and raising his eyebrows, like he's trying to insist that him being my best man is the most natural thing in the world, that's what that look on his face is saying, he's trying to spare me, wants me to go on believing that we're as close as I thought we were, but it's too late, it was an odd thing for me to do, to ask him to be my best man, I see that now, feel my cheeks getting hotter and hotter, my face suddenly turning red. I pick up my wine glass, take a sip, try to hide behind the glass.

"No, no . . . it's just that I haven't known Marius very long," Kjersti says. "And we've been together for a few years now, so it's easy to forget that you had a life before I came on the scene, so to speak."

"Well, believe it or not, I did," Jan Olav says, chuckling.

"But why didn't you tell me?" Kjersti says.

"Marius just called a couple of days ago to ask me. And I haven't been home much lately, we've hardly spoken to each other."

Kjersti turns to me and smiles, turns back to Jan Olav.

"But that's fantastic," she says.

"Absolutely," Jan Olav says, sounding pretty convincing, although he doesn't look at any of us, keeps his eyes lowered as he picks up his wine glass and takes a sip. Maybe he doesn't want anyone to see that he's lying, maybe that's why he's so quick to take a drink, it rather looks like it, looks as if he's trying to do much the same as I just did, he's afraid his face will betray how he really feels about being my best man, so he's trying to hide behind his wine glass.

"Thank you for a lovely dinner," Kristian says.

"Mm, yes, thank you, it was lovely," Julie says.

"You're welcome," Kjersti and Jan Olav say. Jan Olav puts down his glass and clasps his hands behind his head, tips his chair back, and sits there, looking replete. I smile at him as well as I can and he smiles back at me, there's nothing in his expression to indicate that he thinks there's anything awkward about being my best man, not at this moment anyway, on the contrary, he looks extremely relaxed, so I could be wrong, I do have a bad habit of looking for signs that all is not as it should be and that's probably what's making me think like this, it's probably just my imagination.

"That was so good," Kristian says.

"Delicious," Julie says.

Silence.

"Is something the matter, Marius?"

It's Kjersti who asks. I turn to her, don't answer straightaway, I'm not quite sure what she's talking about, so I just sit there staring at her for a moment, then I hear Kristian start to laugh, he's laughing at me now, he hasn't changed a bit, doesn't bother to hide what he thinks or feels about anyone, doesn't care whom he might offend. I turn around, he's looking at his lap, shaking his head and sniggering at how weird he thinks I am. This is exactly how it was fifteen years ago, I feel myself getting as annoyed at him as I used to do back then. He can be so insensitive sometimes, Kristian, but still, I would have thought he was above this, sitting there like that, sneering at me, especially now, when I've got Julie with me, this is only the second or third time she's met these people whom I call my best friends and now one of them is sneering and making fun of me, doesn't he realize that this might lead her to see me through his eyes, so to speak, that she might start to think I'm as weird and ridiculous as he does.

"Marius?" Kjersti says. I turn to her again, suddenly feeling the sweat breaking out on the back of my neck and my brow. I raise my hand as casually as I can, smile at Kjersti as I wipe it away. "Is something the matter?" she asks.

"No," I say, then add quickly: "Thanks for dinner. It was delicious."

She looks a little surprised.

"Good to hear it," she says, smiling warmly as she takes a sip of her wine. "I'm so glad you enjoyed it. Although it's even better with saffron," she adds, then she drums her fingers together, glancing sidelong at the table with a mock huffy look on her face, trying to tell us guests that this last comment was meant as a playful dig at Jan Olav.

"Okay, okay," Jan Olav says.

"Do we detect signs of a marital disagreement?" Kristian laughs, knocking back the last of his red wine, slipping his hand around one of the candelabra and reaching, almost coincidentally, for the wine bottle. He refills his glass and places the bottle back on the table. Julie's not the only one who's pretty drunk now, Kristian isn't entirely sober either, I can tell, he has those bleary, wine-sodden eyes and I can see the reflection of the flickering candles in them.

"No-oo, not at all," Kjersti says, raising her eyes from

the table and fixing them on the ceiling instead, still drumming her fingers.

"But I told you, they were out of saffron," Jan Olav says.

"Hmm," Kjersti says, nodding and pursing her lips as if to say Jan Olav would have to do better than that. "It's funny how they're always sold out when *you* do the shopping," she goes on. "I've never known the supermarket to be out of saffron when I go there, but *you*—you come back with turmeric every time. If I were the suspicious sort, I might think there was a connection between this and the fact that you always put less meat and more beans in chili con carne than the recipe says, but of course I don't, I know you and you're not the slightest bit stingy."

I look at Jan Olav, don't know anyone as stingy as him, he was a real tightwad when we were students anyway, and I doubt he's changed much, it doesn't look like it anyway, looks like he knows she's right on target too, because he's having a good laugh at his own expense, he and Kjersti and Kristian, they're all laughing, Julie and I are the only ones not laughing, she doesn't know Jan Olav so she doesn't know how stingy he is, she just smiles and sips her wine, suddenly looking left out.

"Hey, Jan Olav, how much does a lawyer earn these days?" Kristian asks, sitting back, putting his hand up to his beard and twirling it again.

More laughter.

"Ah, but it's not the money that matters," Kjersti says. "It's the satisfaction he gets from saving it."

"Money was tight when I was a boy, Kjersti, and the memory of that has stayed with me," Jan Olav says, spreading his hands, looking at her with his Labrador eyes and biting his lower lip to stop himself from laughing at his own droll wit. "I don't expect you to understand, of course, coming as you do from a wealthy, middle-class family, but the need to scrimp and save is deeply ingrained in me."

"*I* understand," Julie pipes up, looking across at Jan Olav, she doesn't realize that he was being ironic, she blinks and nods solemnly. "Money was tight when I was a kid as well," she says, slurring her words slightly and taking a little pause for breath between "as" and "well." "Not that we were poor, exactly, but there was little to spare. Especially after my dad was paralyzed and needed care, because then we had to manage on Mom's earnings," she adds, then she picks up her wine glass and takes a sip. I look at her, am just about to tell her that Jan Olav was being ironic, but I don't, and I won't, it would only upset her. Jan Olav and Kjersti smile at her, looking interested; fortunately they're kind enough not to point out that she's not quite following, instead they make her feel included and listen to what she says, I feel grateful for that, they're good friends. "I remember, for example, how embarrassing it was to be the only girl in the class who wore home-made clothes until I was twelve or thirteen," Julie goes on. "Nowadays, when almost everything we wear is made by child workers in Asia, most Norwegians can afford to buy clothes, but in the seventies and eighties things were expensive, right? And my mom couldn't afford to buy new clothes for us so she sewed or knitted just about everything I wore," she says, then she blinks slowly and takes another sip of her wine.

I pick up my glass and take a little drink as well, my eyes meeting Kjersti's over the rim. She smiles at me as if to say I shouldn't let this worry me.

"It didn't matter so much when I was in elementary school, lots of kids there wore homemade clothes," Julie goes on. "But when I started junior high, oh . . . oh, it was awful," she says. I look at her, struck by how much I love her. I don't know why, but there's something so pure, almost noble about the fact that she didn't detect the irony in Jan Olav's voice; the way she simply assumes that he meant what he said, the way she responds by talking seriously about her own childhood, it makes her a little less degenerate than the rest of us, somehow, a little more genuine. I look at her, I even love the way she dresses and does her makeup, everyone else here thinks there's something pathetic about her style, I know they do: the rather slapdash way she applies her lipstick, the pink eye shadow that is supposed to match her pink sweater but doesn't quite, they think it's pathetic, bordering on tasteless probably, but I love it, in fact that pathetic, slightly gauche air is exactly what I love about her, maybe because that too makes her seem that bit more genuine.

"Oh, Julie, I do love you!" I say, it just comes out and I know with every fiber of my being that I mean it and she can see that I mean it, I can tell just by looking at her, her face suddenly seems to come alive, her real face seems to break through the rather dopey, drunk mask and she beams at me.

"Aw," Kjersti says. "That calls for a toast."

And they all raise their glasses. Kristian looks as though he's trying hard not to laugh, he evidently thinks it's totally nuts to blurt out something like that when everybody can hear, but he too raises his glass.

"Cheers!" we all say.

I hold Julie's gaze as I raise my glass and drink, there's

fresh life in her eyes now too, a completely different light from a moment ago.

"So, are you from Trondheim?" Jan Olav asks, looking at Julie.

"Yep. I grew up on the east side, Lademoen," she says. "And you?"

"I'm from Oslo."

"Oh, right, whereabouts in Oslo?"

"Do you know Oslo?"

"Well, I've been working at the SAS hotel for four years, so . . ."

"I grew up in Frogner."

"Oh dear," Julie says. "That can't have been easy, growing up in such a posh part of town. I mean, when I was a kid, Lademoen was a typical working-class neighborhood and even though things were even harder for us after my dad was disabled and needed care, we weren't all *that* different from the other families there. But to have to watch every penny when everybody around you is rolling in money, that must be tough."

Jan Olav and Kjersti exchange glances.

Silence.

"I think Jan Olav was joking when he said money was tight when he was a boy," Kristian says, grinning broadly, as if to play down the misunderstanding and make the whole situation a little less awkward. Julie looks at him: his words don't really seem to sink in right away, she just sits there staring at him in amazement for a moment, then she runs her eye around the rest of us and suddenly it dawns on her that she has misunderstood and I see how stupid she feels.

"Oh, right," she says with a strained little laugh. "Silly

me." She picks up her wine glass, gives that same little laugh again as she raises it to her lips, as if to disguise the fact that she's upset, but it's no good, everyone can both hear and see that she's mortified and upset. I try to look as though this is nothing to worry about, look at her and smile, but she doesn't smile in return, she knocks back the last of her wine in one big gulp and puts down her glass, then she sits there staring at the table with a rather stiff, expressionless smile on her lips.

Silence.

Jan Olav and Kjersti exchange a quick glance, they too finding this a bit unpleasant, their eyes suddenly serious.

Then Kristian takes charge.

"Would you like a refill, Julie?" he asks, speaking loudly, in a voice that says "Come on, people, lighten up." He picks up the bottle of wine and holds it over Julie's glass, giving her a big smile.

Julie looks up at him, doesn't answer straightaway, but then she seems to brighten up, smiles back.

"Yes, please," she says, accepting Kristian's offer and seizing this chance to move on. I feel an immediate surge of happiness, look at her, and smile. She waits until Kristian has finished filling her glass, then she raises it to her lips, looking at me as she does so, but what sort of a look is that, suddenly there's contempt and anger in her eyes. I raise my brows, puzzled, the expression on my face asking what's she mad at *me* for? She holds my eye for a second, then she blinks slowly and looks away as she takes a swig of her wine, looks away in a manner that says she couldn't care less about me. I look at Jan Olav and Kjersti as they get up and start to clear the table, look at Julie again. But why's she so mad at *me*? I mean, I even told her I loved her, blurted it out in front of everyone, and I don't think anyone doubted that it came from the heart, not even Julie, I could tell she didn't. But maybe she's interpreting what I said differently now that she knows Jan Olav was joking. Not only was she the one person who didn't realize he was being ironic when he said money was tight when he was a boy, she then proceeded, in all seriousness, to relate stories of her own childhood and now, when she feels she's made a fool of herself, maybe she thinks I meant something else entirely when I said I loved her: *you're thick as two short planks, but I love you anyway*, maybe that's how she's interpreting my declaration of love, maybe that's why she's mad at me all of a sudden.

"Well, you may be thrifty, but you never stint when it comes to wine," Kristian says, looking at Jan Olav and nodding at the wine bottle.

"I drink so little that I can afford to treat myself," Jan Olav says.

"That's us told, Julie," Kristian says.

It takes a moment, but then Julie gets it, she gives a short and unnaturally loud laugh, seizing the chance to get back at Jan Olav by laughing at Kristian's little dig, that's what she's doing.

"No, no, I didn't mean it like that," Jan Olav chuckles.

Julie raises her glass.

"No, of course not," she says, grinning as she takes a big gulp of her wine.

I see how the smile immediately seems to fade from Jan Olav's face, he looks at Julie for a second, saying nothing, then he carries on clearing the table. I swallow, feel my face grow hot, suddenly I'm blushing again, I look at Julie, try to catch her eye to let her know that this is no way to behave, but she doesn't look at me.

"Well, cheers," Kristian says.

"Cheers," says Julie.

I swallow, try to smile as I pick up my glass.

"Cheers," I mumble.

Two seconds.

"Be-yooteeful bo-kay," Julie says, exaggerating and distorting the vowels, her way of mocking Jan Olav's wine-connoisseur act. She's got over what just happened and now she's having another little dig at him. "But what's the alcohol content?" she asks, still grinning as she picks up the bottle, shuts one eye, and peers at the label on the back. Then: "What—only eleven and a half percent!" She raises her eyebrows, feigning shock, implying that the alcohol content is all that matters to her and she can't believe anyone would buy wine with so little alcohol in it, she's making herself out to be more common and simpleminded than she actually is now, trying to play down her middle-class affiliations and accentuate her working-class roots, that's what she's doing when she carries on like this, she enjoys good food and good wine as much as the rest of us, but now she's trying to make out that all that sort of thing is just a pose, pure snobbery. She feels she made a fool of herself when she didn't get Jan Olav's joke and started talking about her own background, and now she's trying to make up for this by showing how proud she is of that same background. As if this will dispel the sense of having made a fool of herself. It doesn't, though, it just makes the whole situation worse, the whole evening will be ruined if she carries on like this. I try to catch her eye again, but with no luck, she's looking at Kristian with that dopey red-wine grin on her face, and Kristian seems to find it highly amusing, he's laughing at her stupid jokes, I can feel it getting to me, he should be helping me to make Julie see that she's making a fool of herself, instead of encouraging her. But he's not, he hasn't changed, Kristian, he's so insensitive.

Then Kjersti reappears, she smiles at Kristian as she takes his plate.

"Thanks again," Kristian says. "That was lovely."

"Glad you enjoyed it."

"It's just a shame there wasn't any saffron in it," Julie says. She flashes Kjersti an artless little smile before turning back to Kristian, sits there for a moment or two, mouth working, then bursts out laughing, Kjersti tries to smile and ignore her, but her face is a little tight as she picks up Julie's plate and places it on top of Kristian's. "Oh, sorry," Julie gasps. "I can't help it," she adds, putting her hands to her face, shaking her head, and laughing far too hard, she doesn't think it's that funny, in fact she doesn't think it's funny at all, I know she doesn't, laughing like this is just an attempt to convince herself and everyone else that Jan Olav and Kjersti are ridiculous. But no one else is laughing. Not even Kristian is laughing now, only Julie, and she won't let up, it's as if she thinks the more she laughs, the more convinced the rest of us will be that there's something to laugh about, but there isn't, this isn't the least bit funny.

Then Kristian puts a finger to his lips.

"Shh," he says, looking at Julie and nodding toward the kitchen where Kjersti and Jan Olav are.

"Oh dear, oh dear," Julie giggles, trying to make us believe that she can't stop laughing.

Kristian leans across the table slightly, still with his finger to his lips.

"Now we have to behave ourselves," he whispers.

"Okay," Julie whispers back, eyeing Kristian like an ally of sorts, they seem to have hit it off, these two, it's not as though they fancy each other and I have cause to be jealous, that I don't believe, they're far too different from each other for that, no, I think it's more that they've both reached the same level of drunkenness, that they're both in the same place, you might say.

"I'll try to pull myself together," she adds. She sits quietly for a moment, then turns toward the kitchen, blinks slowly, and gazes at Kjersti and Jan Olav. It's a while since I've seen her this drunk, her head seems to be only loosely attached to her neck, it wobbles from side to side. She turns back to Kristian.

"Is she cross, do you think?" she whispers.

"Naaah," Kristian says with a flick of his hand, as if waving away the whole problem.

"But she might be if you carry on like this," I say, speaking softly so Kjersti and Jan Olav won't hear.

Julie looks at me for a moment, getting annoyed now, then turns to Kristian again.

"Did you hear that?" she says.

"What?" Kristian says.

"He can talk!"

A split second, then they burst out laughing again, I feel a twinge of annoyance, I don't like to hear her joking about this, she should be better than that.

"What did he say?" Kristian asks, playing along.

"What did you say, dear?" Julie asks, giggling at me.

I eye her gravely, letting her know that enough is enough.

"I think he's said his piece for today," Julie says, turning back to Kristian.

"Damn shame we didn't catch it, then," Kristian says.

And they laugh again.

I shut my eyes, sigh, and open them again.

"Julie, please," I murmur.

"What, am I embarrassing you?" she says, grinning at me.

"Julie, don't do this."

She turns to Kristian, leans across the table, and lays her hand on his arm.

"He doesn't think I'm . . . how shall I put it . . . *intellectual* enough, you see."

"Nah," Kristian says. "I don't believe that."

"No, it's true. Just after he started at that dender . . . dendo, no . . . den-dro-chro-no-lo-gical laboratory . . . God Almighty, even the name of the place where he works is too hard for me . . . oh, well, never mind! There was this one time, right, just after he started there, when we were on this kind of getting-to-know-you weekend with his colleagues and this one evening we were playing Trivial Pursuit . . . oh, God, I couldn't answer a single question and you should have seen him, he was so mad," she says and she bursts out laughing again. "I didn't care because I know I'm not stupid and I don't give a shit what other people think of me. But *Marius*, oh my *God* . . . when I guessed that the Spanish Civil War took place in the sixteenth century . . . well, I'm telling you, if looks could kill!"

"That's not why I was mad, Julie," I say.

"Oh, no? Okay, so why were you mad?"

"You were nearly as drunk then as you are now, that's why," I say, looking her in the eye, trying to make her see that I'm serious and that she'd better not go any further, but she just grins.

"You were mad long before I got drunk," she says. "You're always in such a bad mood when we're out with other people."

I look at her, I'm really annoyed now, but I don't let it show, nor will I, there's nothing worse than a couple having a stand-up row at a party, bothering other people with their personal problems, big or small, and I don't want us to be that sort of couple, better to leave it until we're alone.

"Yeah, right" is all I say.

"But it's *tru-ue*," Julie goes on. "You hardly ever want to go out anymore, all you want is to stay home with me," she says with a little laugh, neglecting to mention that she's a monophobe and doesn't really like being left alone in the house, making out that it's my own fault I don't get out much. "What you'd really like, though, would be for us to live out in the forest at Namsskogan," she goes on, then she turns to Kristian and smirks, she's going to start making fun of my project at the cottage now, I'll bet, I can tell by her face, she wants Kristian to laugh at my project too, but fortunately she doesn't get that far because Jan Olav and Kjersti emerge from the kitchen.

"Coffee," Jan Olav says, I look at him and smile, look at Kjersti and she looks back at me as she sets out the coffee cups, she twists her lips into a smile meant to reassure me and tell me not to take it to heart and I give her a strained little grin in return, to let her know that I've given up, but that it's okay. I turn and glance across at Jan Olav, over by the drinks cabinet. He opens the door and takes out a bottle of Otard cognac, smiles as he puts the bottle on the table, but then his smile stiffens, there's something about Kjersti, she's standing there with her mouth half-open, frowning at him. It takes a moment, but then it dawns on me, she's annoyed because he means to serve cognac with the coffee. She feels Kristian and Julie have had enough and coffee on its own will do.

"Oh—er," Jan Olav splutters, he hasn't thought this through, I can tell, he stands there looking flummoxed as Kjersti gives a quick shake of her head and walks straight past him and into the kitchen. Jan Olav heaves a little sigh, then he turns, takes brandy glasses from the drinks cabinet, probably doesn't feel he has any choice now that he's put out the bottle.

"Not for me, thanks," I say. "I've had enough for tonight."

"Aw, what's the matter now?" Kristian asks, staring at me and acting stunned.

"I've got an early start in the morning," I say.

"But aren't you on holiday?"

"Yes, but I'm thinking of driving over to Grong," I say, don't know what makes me say that, it's a while since I went to see Torstein and the family and I probably should take a run over there, but I hadn't actually been planning on going there tomorrow.

"Oh, well, for heaven's sake, you don't need to leave all that early, do you?"

"Aw, he's not going to Grong," Julie says. "Marius hates Grong, he only goes there a couple of times a year because he feels he has to, that's just his way of telling me the party's over," she says, looking at Kristian and grinning, she knows she's long since overstepped the mark, but she carries on in the same fashion, doesn't want to lose face, I suppose, that's probably why she's going even further than she's already done, it's a desperate attempt to convince herself and everyone else that she's on a roll and having great fun.

"Ooh," Kristian says. "Sneaky!"

"Here you go," Jan Olav says, placing a glass in front of Kristian. "Would you like a brandy, Julie?"

"Bring it on," says Julie.

Jan Olav sets the glass in front of her, flashing me an apologetic glance, as if to say he's sorry for being so thoughtless, I don't say anything, just smile quietly back at him, letting him know it's okay.

Then Julie leans across the table, looks at Kristian.

"Excuse me, is that all you get?" she whispers, frowning as if to say she's not quite sure what the form is here.

"Yeah, 'fraid so," Kristian whispers back.

"Okay," she says, blinking and straightening up. "I had to ask, you see, because I'm not used to being in such grand company." She smirks, picks up her glass, and knocks back all the brandy in one go, she just keeps pushing it and pushing it, she knows she's being vulgar and rude, but she's frantically trying to convince herself and everyone else that she's actually being funny. I look at her, this has gone far enough, I have to stop her before she does irreparable damage, this is my best man's home, after all.

"I think it's about time we were going, Julie," I say, with a little yawn.

"You see," she says, looking at Kristian and shaking her head. "The minute he sees me having fun, it's time to go home, it never fails," she says and she picks up the empty brandy glass, puts it to her lips, and tilts her head back. She sits like that for a moment or two as if hoping it might not be empty after all, then she starts to laugh,

22

soundlessly to start with, her shoulders quivering, then she puts down the glass, squeezes her eyes shut, and slaps her hand over her mouth as she doubles up and bursts into an exaggerated fit of the giggles.

"What's so funny?" Kristian asks.

"It just struck me . . . ," Julie gasps, but can't get any further.

"What just struck you?" Kristian shouts.

"Marius," Julie giggles. "If I'm coming home . . . if I'm coming home from a night out on my own, he tells me to stuff my jacket up under my dress," she says, howling with laughter, her eyes still closed. She didn't laugh at the time, though, not at all. When I suggested she should stuff her jacket under her dress, she thought it was a good idea, but apparently she's changed her mind, apparently she now thinks it was a stupid idea because she's laughing harder than I've ever seen her laugh, although it's hard to tell, maybe she still thinks it's a good idea but is pretending not to, because she wants to pay me back, because she knows everyone else here will agree that it's a stupid idea and because she wants me to look like a fool in their eyes.

"Stuff your jacket under your dress?"

"Yeah, a rolled-up jacket . . . to make it look like I'm pregnant. He thinks there's less risk of me getting raped if I look like I'm pregnant."

"Really?" Kristian says. "Is that true?" he asks. I see his jaw slowly drop, he looks at Julie, looks at me, looks at Julie again and she shuts her eyes, claps her hand over her mouth, shaking with suppressed laughter. And then Kristian shakes his head and he too starts to laugh, he doesn't say anything, seems to have no words to describe how hilarious he finds this, this is obviously pure comedy hour for him and he laughs and laughs. I look at him, look at Julie, feel myself growing more and more annoyed, I don't usually mind being kidded or teased, but I draw the line at people making fun of me simply to feel better about themselves or to pay me back for something they think I've done, that's where I draw the line.

And that's what Julie and Kristian are doing now. Julie knows she's made a fool of herself, so she's trying to bolster her ego by making me and Jan Olav and Kjersti look stupid, and Kristian is probably just feeling frustrated with his own situation, he still doesn't have a girlfriend and the fact that I brought my girlfriend with me when I moved back to Trondheim makes him feel even more of a failure than he already did. Like: even Marius has a girlfriend— Marius, who no one ever thought would amount to anything, even he has found himself a girl before me, that's what he's thinking, so he vents his frustration by making fun of me in front of my girlfriend, I feel myself growing more and more annoyed, feel myself getting angry now, but I mustn't let it show, so I just look at him and smile as pleasantly as I can, and he looks back at me, not laughing now, simply regarding me with an expectant smile on his lips, and suddenly I notice that Kjersti and Jan Olav are also gazing at me, Julie is the only one not looking at me, she's fiddling with something in the bag slung over the back of her chair, I look at her, then at Kjersti, then Jan Olav, he's standing at my shoulder, smiling agreeably.

"What?" I say.

"Would you like some?" Jan Olav asks.

"Some what?" I say, and at that Kristian bursts out laughing again, slumps across the table, and laughs and laughs. Only then do I notice the French press Jan Olav is holding,

I don't know how long he's been standing there like that, don't know how many times he has asked me if I'd like coffee, but it must have been a few, otherwise Kristian wouldn't have laughed like that, that's why he's roaring with laughter, I suppose, because my mind was somewhere else, because I was lost in thought for a moment. I swallow, feel myself starting to sweat again, feel the sweat break out on the back of my neck and my brow.

"Oh, yes, please," I say quickly, then I give a little laugh, trying to sound rueful, laughing at myself while wiping the sweat from my temples, first one side, then the other.

"Sorry," I say. "I was just thinking about something."

"No, you don't say?" Julie drawls. She removes her lighter and a pack of cigarettes from her bag, pulls out a cigarette and pops it in her mouth. She's not going to smoke in here, surely? She can't be that far gone. I take a sip of coffee, say nothing, she sits there patting her pockets for a few moments before it dawns on her that she's got her lighter out already, she gives a silly little titter, crosses her eyes as she grasps it and goes to light up.

"I'd rather you went out onto the balcony if you're going to smoke," Jan Olav says.

"You'd *rather*?" Julie says, looking at Jan Olav and fluttering her eyelids slightly. Jan Olav raises his eyebrows despairingly, but he keeps smiling. "Relax, Mister Best Man, I'm only joking," Julie goes on, then she gets up, staggers across the room, and out onto the balcony.

Silence.

"Sorry about that," I say, looking at Jan Olav.

"Don't give it a thought," he says, smiling.

"We've all had a bit too much to drink at one point or another," Kjersti says, coming in with a little bowl of chocolates. "But I think maybe we'd better put the brandy back in the cabinet."

"Absolutely," Jan Olav says. He picks up the bottle and crosses to the drinks cabinet.

Kristian raises his eyebrows and opens his mouth, he knows why Jan Olav is putting the brandy back in the cabinet, but he's acting as if he can't believe his eyes.

"I sincerely hope you're not intending to be this boring when we go to the mountains," he says.

"No danger of that," Jan Olav says as he closes the door of the drinks cabinet. "So how's it going with your balance?" he asks, eyeing me as he pulls back his chair and sits down.

"I get the results of the blood tests on Friday, but it's been much better than it was, so I think it was just stress," I say. "It's been pretty hectic at work lately, I had so much to get done before I went on holiday."

"So you are coming to the mountains?"

"Yes, of course," I say.

"Great," he says. "And Kristian has promised to teach us how to fly-fish, haven't you, Kristian?"

"Mm-hmm," Kristian says, shutting his eyes and nodding, he's pretty well on himself now.

Silence.

Then suddenly there's a short, piercing scream, followed by a dull thud on the gravel and I feel my blood run cold: it's Julie, she's fallen off the balcony, she must have been sitting on the railing, smoking, and she's toppled backward.

"What was that," Kristian mumbles.

"Oh, my God," Kjersti cries.

I dash out onto the balcony, Kjersti and Jan Olav right behind me.

"Julie," I call, planting my hands on the railing and leaning over it, peering down at the driveway, first right, then left, there's a shattered window box on the gravel, but I can't see Julie anywhere. Then I hear someone laugh behind me. I whip around and there she is, standing against the wall, she looks at us, points at us and shakes her head, laughing harder and harder.

"You should have seen your faces," she gasps, doubling up and putting her hands on her knees, laughing her head off at the looks on our faces. And we just stand there, don't say anything for a moment. Jan Olav gapes at her and shakes his head in despair, Kjersti snorts and mutters a soft but infuriated "fuck" and after a second they both go back inside, fuming.

"This really isn't funny, Julie," I say.

She looks me in the eye and smiles.

"I didn't think it was particularly funny either, Marius, when you threatened to kill yourself," she says.

I don't say anything for a moment, just stand there staring at her, is that what this is about, was that why she pretended to have fallen from the balcony, was it a way of getting back at me for what I did that time, it rather seems like it, but I don't know, it could just as easily be that she's ashamed of the way she behaved just now and is somehow attempting to link her own shame to an incident for which she was not to blame, so to speak, that it's a way of blaming me for everything. She's propped up against the wall, trying to laugh, but it's no use, she's close to tears now, her smile starting to crumple, she turns, looks away, then turns to me again. "Do you realize how worried I was about you?" she says, swallowing once, twice, then she puts a hand up to her face.

"That was almost a year ago, Julie," I say. "I thought we'd put that incident behind us." I hear Kristian laughing in the living room as the words leave my mouth.

"Was it just a joke?" he cries gleefully, he's loving this, he clearly finds the whole thing hugely entertaining, moron that he is.

"I'm just a little mouse," Julie says through her sobs. Now she's talking about being a little mouse, she's drunk and incoherent and I'm having trouble following her train of thought. I lay a hand on her shoulder and draw her gently to me, feel the warmth of her body. We stand like that for a moment and then her shoulders start to shake.

"Come on, Julie," I say and I lead her back into the house. I raise my eyes and look at the others as we walk into the living room, see their solemn faces, even Kristian is managing to keep a straight face now, he stares at the table and twirls his beard.

"I know that's what I am to all of you, a little mouse," Julie says, still sobbing. "I'm not as interesting as you lot, and I . . . I can't follow your intellectual discussions, I ask stupid questions that confuse things and spoil the conversation and send it off in directions you don't want it to go in . . . and . . . every time I try to start a conversation, you dismiss what I say as boring and irrelevant," she says.

I look at her and swallow, I love her so much and it hurts to hear her say this, it makes me cry inside.

"Oh, Julie, that's not true," I say.

"You think I didn't see the way you all sat there rolling your eyes when I was talking about the wedding?" she says, trying to laugh, laughing and crying at the same time. "You think I didn't see all the knowing looks and smiles you sent one another? I saw it as plainly as you did, Marius, and I know what it means, I'm not stupid, I know everybody in this room thinks I'm shallow and . . . but I'm *not*, I may not have spent ten years at university, but I'm no shallower than any of you," she says, then she turns to Jan Olav, glares at him, the tears streaming down her cheeks. "Just because I make a big deal of my wedding, that doesn't mean I'm shallow, you know. Unlike you, I wasn't being ironic when I talked about my childhood, I . . . I haven't always had it so easy and you know what, Jan Olav, ever since I was a little girl I've looked forward to the day when I would get married. I know you and everybody else here thinks that's ridiculous and pathetic and terribly American, but that's just how it is. Ever since I was a little girl I've dreamed of the day when I would be a princess, the center of attention, and walk up the aisle with everybody watching and thinking how beautiful I was. I played weddings with my dolls, I drew pictures of myself as a bride, and now that I'm grown up and am actually getting married, I want everything to be just right," she says, then she pauses briefly, stands there looking at Jan Olav with the tears streaming down her cheeks, and I'm crying inside, I love Julie so much, I want so much for her to be happy, and it's so hard to listen to this. "That's why I talk so much about the wedding," she continues. "Too much for your liking. But that doesn't mean I'm shallow. It's so easy for people like you to be flippant and say it's shallow, but for someone like me, from my background, it's a bit different, you see; where I come from a wedding means something other than, and more than, simply being able to inherit from one another."

Dear David,

My name is Marius Rosendahl and I want to help you to find out who you are and where you come from so I'll come straight to the point. On the fifth of January, 1970, a mistake was made at Namsos Hospital. A member of staff in the maternity ward got two baby boys mixed up, with the result that I was given to your mother and sent home with her and you were given to my mother and sent home with her. In other words, you and I have been living each other's lives. You should have grown up in the big yellow house in Bangsund, you should have had the room that my pals envied because it was so big and because it had a door onto a little balcony with a fire escape running down from it, making it easy for a teenager to sneak in and out of the house at eleven o'clock at night. Not that I ever did that. I was a very boring teenager, I'm afraid, and long after other boys of my age had started going dancing and playing snooker at the youth club—which we called "the Doctor's" because it had been set up in the old doctor's house—or getting drunk and throwing up at home-alone parties on Saturday nights, I was still holed up in my room, reading *Science Illustrated* and books about great men in history. Charles Darwin. Carl von

Linné. Copernicus. Galileo Galilei. Magellan and Vasco da Gama. Scientists, inventors, and discoverers, in other words. This was my favorite reading and I remember wishing, as a child, that I was shortsighted and had to wear little round glasses like one of the boys next door because I thought that would make me look a bit more like a scientist. Because obviously I was going to be a scientist. Either a botanist or a paleontologist, although I felt the latter seemed a rather childish answer to give when grown-ups asked what I wanted to be when I grew up: a pale-ontologist, which is to say: somebody who studies dinosaurs. Even Roger Dahl in my class could have come up with that reply and he was a real dummy with absolutely no interest in or fas-cination with dinosaurs. With the exception of *Tyrannosaurus rex*, I suppose. No, then it was better to say I wanted to be a botanist. It sounded more grown-up. Besides which, I'd been drying and pressing plants and learning their Latin names since I was eight, so when Mom and Dad had visitors and I announced that I was "considering becoming a botanist," all I had to do was show them my herbarium and nobody could be in any doubt that I really meant it and wasn't just trying to make myself appear interesting. "Exceptionally bright, quite possibly a genius," I imagined visitors thinking and could never resist the temptation to try to prove them right: "You've prob-ably heard of Gregor Mendel," I would say when we came to the pea plant in my herbarium, knowing full well that very few people had heard of Gregor Mendel. "No? Well, he's my big hero, he's regarded as the father of classical genetics," I would say, often then proceeding to subject the listener to a brief lecture on how in 1856 Mendel conducted systematic hybridization experiments with different pea plants in the monastery garden where he worked, and how the sensational results of these ex-periments enabled him to formulate Mendel's laws of heredity.

The thought that this might lead to me being regarded as an irritating and really quite arrogant child never crossed my mind. Personally, I didn't see how anyone could resist a kid who knew as much as I did, and when my invariably polite audience fled to the bathroom or took advantage of a break in my stream of words to turn to the other grown-ups and attempt to take part in their conversation, I would simply hang around, waiting for the chance to pick up where I had left off and share still more of my knowledge with them: "And did you know that Gregor Mendel was born in Austria in 1822? In later life he became abbot of the monastery. You know what an abbot is, right?"

But if I was arrogant, inasmuch as I simply assumed that everyone was bound to be interested in hearing what I had to say, in other ways I was anything but. We weren't as well-to-do back then as we became after Dad started the fish farm and production of fish vaccine, but the proceeds from the furniture factory had made us more than wealthy enough for Dad to consider it necessary to continually remind me and my brother, Rikard, that having money "didn't make us better than ordinary people," as he put it. If either of us was rude about one of our classmates, for example, he would immediately suspect us of looking down on the person concerned and we would be subjected to a minor interrogation, where it was up to us to convince him that this was not the case: "But I never said anything about Pål Nordbakk's clothes being raggedy, I never said a word about his clothes, why would I? He spat on Else's shoes, all right! That's why I said he was disgusting. I should be able to say he's disgusting if he's going around spitting on people's shoes." That sort of thing. And if we didn't have a good explanation and Dad's totally mistaken suspicion that we were getting too big for our boots was confirmed, he wasn't beyond punishing us. I've never seen Dad as angry, for example, as he was the day when Rikard came home with a note to say that he and some other boys had been picking on a new boy in the class because his mother cleaned the school bathrooms. He had never laid a hand on Rikard or me before, but when he read the note in Rikard's orange report book, smoke came out of his nostrils as he laid his pipe in the ashtray and then, without saying a single word, slapped Rikard's face hard. He deeply regretted doing this, I remember, and apologized shortly afterward, but that didn't stop him from ordering Rikard to clean the bathrooms at the furniture factory every day for a week. Not that Rikard minded much. He knew he deserved it for nicknaming the new boy "Crapper Morten" and neither of us was a stranger to work. We learned early on that most people took it for granted that we were, but the truth was that we had to work far more than all the other children we knew. I clearly remember, for instance, how shocked I was when one of my friends told me that he had to tidy his room, make his bed, and take out the trash for his pocket money. As far as I was concerned, that wasn't work at all. That was just what you did, a bit like getting dressed in the morning, and you didn't expect anything for it. Those friends of mine who seemed to do most at home moaned and groaned about having to cut the grass, clear the dinner table, and possibly do the washing-up a certain number of days in the week, but even that didn't impress us. Those were the sorts of chores that Rikard and I raced through before or after our real work, which is to say our work at the furniture factory. I don't know when we started there, but what I do know is that by the time I was fourteen, Rikard and I were helping out there three evenings a week. Only two and a half hours each evening, it's true, but that was as much as we could manage if we were also to have time for our homework and our various extracurricular activities. And that wasn't counting our Saturday jobs at the sawmill, where we collected all the offcuts and put them into sacks for Dad to give to his workers as Christmas presents. "With warm wishes" he used to write on the cards, I remember, and I can still recall the day when it dawned on Mom that this greeting had a double meaning. "The wood doesn't just come with a wish that it will warm their homes, he also hopes the gift of it will warm their hearts," she said one winter day when Rikard and I were loading sacks onto the back of the truck. She looked at us as though she had just presented us with the answer to all the ills of the world or a new, groundbreaking theory on the origins of the universe and for the first time in my young life I dared to admit to myself what I had suspected for some time: that Mom was not as clever as I would have liked. Only later did I realize that she had a way of acting dumber than she actually was.

Anyway: one might think that since Rikard and I worked as much as we did, we would get whatever we asked for, but no, far from it. Compared to the aforementioned Roger Dahl we were spoiled rotten, of course—Roger, who had to use his mother's bike and turned up for the ski carousel with one of his skis broken and nailed back together—but I well remember being envious of the twenty-odd percent of kids in my class who always had the latest toys, games, and sports gear. If Rikard or I asked if we could have whatever they had, we were forced to go through a process whereby it was up to us to convince Dad that the item in question was useful and preferably essential if we were to keep up and make progress in a field in which he deemed it important that we kept up and made progress—e.g., at school, on the sports field, or in the development of a solid work ethic or a good, all-round education. So we could forget about asking for video games or the new little electronic games that our classmates played with in the schoolyard (*Donkey Kong*), because we would promptly be treated to a variation on the lecture we received the time when we hinted that we wouldn't mind having cable TV installed so we could watch MTV and Sky Channel: first, scathing criticism of all the mind-numbing, stultifying entertainment programs that were now rife and ruining the youth of today, followed by a string of well-meant words of wisdom, all making the point that time is money and not, therefore, to be wasted. We did, however, persuade him to buy a VCR. To begin with he was as opposed to the idea as we had expected, but when a cunning Rikard put on his most solemn face and just happened to mention that he would have gone up at least one grade in German if he had been able to tape our favorite German detective series, *Derrick*, and watch it again and again, Dad went from being dead set against it to showing some interest and when Rikard quoted our German teacher's assertion that it was essential to listen to native German speakers if you wanted to gain a proper command of the language, Dad said he would think about it. And sure enough, the following Saturday he came home from Namsos with a VHS video recorder and a carrier bag containing three blank tapes. "But if your German grade hasn't improved by Christmas, I'm selling that machine straightaway," I remember him saying. Not without a wry glint in his eye.

In other words, things had to prove profitable, preferably in some concrete and readily quantifiable fashion. To say that playing computer games was fun or that we thought Levis jeans were better than Wranglers wasn't enough and if we also made the mistake of resorting to the old, rather whiny, childish complaint that "everybody else has one," we risked being given a real tongue-lashing, because that sort of language was a sign of a herd mentality and even though Dad didn't want us to stand out from the crowd by flaunting the fact that we had a lot more money than other kids, there were few things that riled him more than the herd mentality. Maybe because he associated it with socialism in general and the trade unions in particular, I don't know.

This same logic was reflected in an almost morbid compulsion to repair old things time and again before reluctantly having to throw them away and to buy things secondhand rather than new. If I needed a new bike, having outgrown my old one, I had to wait till the autumn when the police auctioned off lost property, including bikes that had been stolen and never claimed by their rightful owners. And then there was the time when Mom asked him for a new Mixmaster and he came home with a five-year-old Husqvarna mixer, having got wind that the old folks' home at Vemundvik was investing in a new kitchen and selling off old equipment cheaply. "The way Kåre reads the For Sale ads in the paper, you'd think it was pornography," Mom said once when they had a dinner party and she'd got a bit tipsy on white wine, and the roars of laughter that greeted this remark were clear proof that their guests could just picture it. Auctions, secondhand stores, house clearances, flea markets, Dad was known to be a great one for such things. He loved to nose around, hunting for bargains, and he loved to haggle. Not just for the fun of it, as many notorious hagglers would maintain, but purely and simply because he enjoyed the feeling of having saved money. Oh, God, how Rikard and I used to cringe when he stood there wrinkling his nose and trying to look as though he was doing the dealer a favor merely by picking up and looking at an article that was already dirt cheap and that he had long since decided to buy. We thought he was the stingiest man in the whole world, and when he then began to reel off all the flaws and faults that made the item in question worth only half the asking price, if that, we would duck down behind shelves, nip behind bookcases, or flee as far back in the shop as we could go, beet red and furious at a father who was worth millions but acted as though saving fifty kroner was a matter of life or death.

Actually, I remember us being just as embarrassed and almost as angry when we were nine and ten, the one time we managed to pester him into taking us to see a film with a PG-13 rating, when he brought along a plastic soup tub full of homemade popcorn rather than buy popcorn at the cinema kiosk, which, according to Dad, was ridiculously overpriced. As far as he was concerned, it would do us no harm that the other kids laughed at us and were still talking about it long afterward. Quite the opposite, we had to learn to do what was right and have the courage of our convictions, even if we were mocked and criticized for it. So from that point of view, he told us later, the incident with the soup tub was a good thing:

"You saved twenty kroner by making popcorn at home, lads."

"Dad. Don't start!"

"So in effect those pals of yours who bought popcorn at the cinema kiosk gave away twenty kroner to the shopkeeper, right?"

"Dad."

"Okay, now let's say, for simplicity's sake, that those same pals go to the cinema and buy popcorn there five times a year. That's a hundred kroner a year, right?"

"Aw, stop it!"

"A hundred kroner's not an awful lot, you might think. But let's say that this popcorn purchase isn't an isolated instance but a sign of a habit they have formed. Let's say that they give away two hundred kroner a year to the bookshop and maybe three hundred to the sports shop and so on and so forth."

"Da-ad. We get it!"

"And then let's say that they carry this habit with them into adult life, when their car and their house and electricity and food all have to be paid for. How much do you think we're talking about then? How many hundreds of thousands, not to say millions, do you think that eventually comes to? Eh, Marius?"

"Dunno."

"Rikard?"

"Dunno."

"No, neither do I. But I can assure you we're talking about sums of money that make it worth putting up with a bit of scoffing in the schoolyard."

Oh, he could drive us crazy when he carried on like that. He was a pain in the neck. A real drag. Not that there wasn't an element of humor and playacting in there too, because there most certainly was. Dad could always laugh at himself and secretly enjoyed being seen as a caricature of himself. He liked pretending to be even more of an eccentric, pigheaded old cheapskate than he actually was and liked to see Rikard and me acting even more frustrated and exasperated by him than we actually were. And Rikard and I enjoyed it too. For both Dad and us it was a way of expressing love, so we actively sought and provoked such discussions and wrangling matches, all three of us. At the same time, though, I knew that he used all the jokes and the laughter to slightly soften his extremely common-sensical and strictly rational way of thinking and acting. Even so, I was always aware that there was a limit to how far you could push him. To put it simply, he could joke and laugh at himself so long as he got his way, but on those rare occasions when Rikard or I stuck to our guns and refused to follow his advice, he would lose his temper and was capable of punishing us in ways that can best be described as childish. Take, for example, the time when Rikard didn't put at least two-thirds of his pay in the bank so he could see how money gathers interest, as we were expected to do, but chose instead to buy a down jacket with leather patches on the shoulders that cost the outrageous sum of 1,000 kroner.

"Oh, by the way, Rikard, a bill arrived for you," Dad said one day when we got home from school. He stood there puffing on his pipe of Capstan and doing his best to sound as though there was absolutely nothing unusual in fourteen-year-old Rikard receiving a bill in the post.

Rikard ripped open the envelope: "Huh," he said, "it's my subscription to *Okej*."

"Oh?" Dad said, acting as though he didn't already know that perfectly well.

Rikard just stared at Dad for a moment.

Dad removed his pipe from his mouth.

"What's the matter?" he said, smiling innocently and trying to look as though he couldn't see how shocked Rikard was to find that he could no longer take for granted that Dad would pay for his subscription to his Swedish teen mag, as he had been doing so far.

"Er, um . . . so do I have to pay it myself now?" Rikard stammered, thereby giving Dad his cue to come out with a remark that he'd made so often before, one which I'm sure he looked forward to uttering every single time.

"Well, of course," he said, totally unable to conceal the childish delight he took in this. "If you can afford to buy a jacket costing one thousand kroner, then you can afford that as well." Then he popped his pipe back in his mouth and strolled off into the living room as casually as he could.

Now that I think of it, it used to embarrass me that he smoked a pipe. Years later, when I was a freshman and willing to do anything to look intellectual, I took to smoking a pipe myself, but as a child and as a teenager it seemed terribly old-fashioned to me. It was bad enough that Dad had gray hair and was ten

or fifteen years older than my friends' parents without him behaving in ways that made him look even more like a retiree. And
it wasn't only the pipe that made him seem like an old man.
The way he still persisted in using the old Danish-Norwegian
forms of certain words rather than their modern equivalents
and, according to Mom, wore suits and shoes that went out of
style along with the top hat had the same effect. "They don't
make them like your dad anymore," Mom told Rikard and me
and she was right. He was like a relic of a bygone era. A fair
but strict and autocratic father at a time when men appeared
to be growing softer and the ideal parent was supposed to
discuss things with their children and treat them like equals.
He was also, not least, a businessman of the old school, a
capitalist who thought and acted in a way I felt I recognized
from novels I read set in the late nineteenth or early twentieth
century. A bit like the merchant Mack in Knut Hamsun's *Pan*.
Always looking for a way to make money, to run things better,
more efficiently, but also so steeped in the traditions of the
social-liberal wing of the Norwegian Conservative Party that
he saw red every time he read or heard of instances of what
we now call turbo-capitalism and the culture of greed. "With
money comes responsibility," he would say and as far as he was
concerned, there was nothing worse than capitalists who were
not mindful of this responsibility, businessmen who awarded
themselves enormous salaries and might well be ruthlessly
exploiting their resources and their workforce into the bargain.
"No wonder people become socialists," he would say as he sat
at his horseshoe-shaped desk, wreathed in tobacco smoke and
reading the business pages.

For his own part he was strongly influenced by the paternalistic management style practiced by our grandad when he
ran the family firm. He liked to see himself as a boss who cared

about and looked after his workers to the best of his ability and as far as the company finances would allow, and who expected people to be conscientious, loyal, and obedient in return. He took it hard when the workers joined a union and his blood would boil if he felt that they were making unreasonable demands. They had no idea how difficult it was to survive in the market, he would growl. Demanding this, demanding that, but what would they say, he wondered, the day he went bankrupt and they were out of a job? And what thanks did he get for giving them firewood for Christmas every year? Not to mention all those Christmas baskets! Well, large cardboard boxes, actually, packed with Dutch Edam and Swedish *gräddost*, pickles and silverskin onions, anchovies, rolled lamb, headcheese, and plenty more, from him to them. And to the boxes for his three semiskilled workers, whom he depended on and was therefore terrified of losing, he even added a half bottle of brandy and a Cuban cigar from M. Sørensen's tobacconist's in Trondheim, the most reasonably priced brands, it's true, but still. How many employers did that for their workers, he would ask, only then to answer himself: None! Absolutely none! And what thanks do I get? Yes, you guessed it, fresh demands. More, more, more.

Some years later, in the early nineties to be exact, when I was a student radical in Trondheim and staying at Bangsund only during the holidays, I criticized, not to say ridiculed, my dad for this paternalistic management style. Like most young men who have had more schooling than their fathers, I took it for granted that I knew more than he and I blush now to think how arrogant I must have seemed, sitting there sipping his whisky and lecturing him on how paternalism was a way of concealing the real balance of power between employer and employee. With a faint sneer on my lips I would remind him and anyone else who happened to be listening of how he had tried to make friends with the workers, citing the affectedly coarse language, the dirty jokes, and all the little mannerisms he adopted when he was with "the guys on the floor": talking and laughing louder than usual, spitting remarkably often, and occasionally putting a finger to his nose, pressing one nostril, and sending a gob of snot shooting out of the other—things he would never have dreamed of doing in the company of his friends from the Masonic lodge, the Namsos Conservative Club, or his fellow businessmen in the local chamber of commerce. And those Christmas presents, what were they if not an attempt to bind people to him by putting them in his debt? I would ask before going on to harangue him on the devious way in which he would punish those employees who failed to show him the gratitude and loyalty that he felt he deserved. "And what about making Kalle Evensen shovel snow and do all sorts of rotten odd jobs just because he raised the problem of the air quality with the union?"

I didn't realize then how familiar and trivial such criticism was to Dad. While it would be an exaggeration to say that reading about paternalism at university was a momentous experience for me, I did recognize and felt I understood more about the way in which my father ran his company and the way the workers behaved toward him and, young and naïve as I was, I thought that he would too, that he would see the light, so to speak. But of course he didn't. Not only had he had to listen to and defend himself against such accusations for years, from the unions, political opponents, and others, he was also far better read and far more knowledgeable than I had imagined; of course he knew all about paternalism and of course he was well aware that forming personal bonds with his employees made it harder for them to shirk their duties or be disloyal. I don't know what infuriated him more, the know-it-all and fairly sarcastic tone of my accusations or the fact that his older son had suddenly gone and become a lefty, but infuriated he was. Particularly when I suggested that the solicitude he felt for his workers was not sincere and the chummy manner he adopted with them was a kind of opium for the masses. What the hell did I mean by that? he asked. Was he supposed to treat his employees worse? For the sake of sincerity or something? Was he supposed to stop being friendly and instead become an arrogant, authoritarian bastard of a boss just so the workers would understand that he was more powerful than them? As if they didn't know that already. And anyway, he went on, surely I hadn't been living away from home so long that I'd forgotten that Bangsund was a small town and the furniture factory was a small firm. Everybody rubbed shoulders with everybody else here whether they liked it or not, so it was in everybody's best interests to tone down conflicts and foster good relations with the people around them, otherwise life would be damned intolerable. "But maybe that's what you want?" he said. "The furniture factory is a good place to work, I think all my workers would vouch for that, but in your eyes, would it be better if it wasn't? Crisis maximization, isn't that what the Marxists call it?"

While Dad was relatively uncomplicated, almost a caricature, in fact, of a typical thrifty inhabitant of Sunnmøre (he had lived in Ålesund until he was six years old), Mom was complex, unpredictable, and a mass of contradictions. When I try to describe her she seems to elude me, not only now, as I write this letter, but at other times too. That's how it's been for as long as I can remember. When Rikard and I used to discuss and analyze our parents, for example, the way teenagers and young people tend to do from time to time, somehow we were never done talking about Mom. If I mentioned one thing about her, I always had the urge to cite some other aspect of her character that would moderate or contradict what I had just said, and unlike our chats about Dad our views of her were often diametrically opposed. "Practical? The woman who managed to paint herself into a corner when she varnished the living room floor," Rikard might say. "Yeah, I know, but she did install that new shower stall without so much as looking at the instructions after Uncle Frederik had been struggling with it for hours and getting nowhere," I said. This last was typical of Mom actually. She would do one thing with aplomb only then to suddenly make some amateurish mistake; she could be all thumbs in one situation only then to prove dazzlingly adept in another. She played little piano pieces by Chopin with exquisite technique and so much feeling that one of the music teachers at Nauma Senior High simply assumed she was a professional musician, but when he spoke to her afterward, he discovered that Mom had no idea what she had been playing or which key she had played it in. It was just something she had learned by heart years ago, she told him, before adding: "A musician, me? Ha-ha, I can't even read music." It was the same story with her general knowledge and level of education. She knew the names of all the main Egyptian pharaohs and when they had lived but thought that the Iron Age came before the Stone Age. She was very much on the offensive in debates on membership of the EU before the referendum in 1994 and showed herself to be impressively well informed, but then it came out that she didn't know the name of the Norwegian foreign minister. Dad thought she was joking, but when he realized she wasn't, he was shocked, then angry. "Damn it all, woman, you must know who the foreign minister of your own country is!"

Uncle Frederik, Mom's older brother, actually put this side of Mom's character down to the fact that she had been an afterthought. She was fifteen years younger than him and seventeen years younger than Aunt Rebekka and, according to him, like most afterthoughts Mom had been spoiled rotten. Grandma and Grandad had done everything for her and this friction-free childhood had quite simply rendered her much too lazy to learn anything properly. She was exceptionally gifted in many areas, Uncle Frederik believed, but everything she turned her hand to was done half-heartedly and everything she started was left half-done. When he saw what the assurance that everything would turn all right in the end had done to Mom, well, he was very glad he had had something to push against when he was young, because this meant that he had learned to work hard and never give up, he said. Or no, he didn't say that. He implied it. Uncle Frederik was a master when it came to insulting people in the nicest possible way and he managed very cunningly to make this theory, let's call it that, sound like a huge compliment to Mom. "If I'd had only half your gifts fifty years from now I'd be in the history books," he used to say.

Aunt Rebekka said much the same. As a girl, with her long, blond curls, blue eyes, and milky-white skin, Mom had been very pretty and popular, she told us. Unfortunately, though, later in her teens her good looks had deserted her. At fifteen there were a lot of girls who were far prettier than her, and by the time she was seventeen, she really wasn't pretty at all, no more than average looking. "The thing was . . . ," Aunt Rebekka said to Mom, then paused for effect, as if to indicate that now she was getting to the nub of the matter. "The thing was that by then you had already managed to acquire a lot of the quirks displayed by girls who know they're prettier than everybody else. You were used to always getting your way. You were used to getting away with being uppity, pert, and conceited," she said, before rounding off with a remark she had made so many times that it had almost become her trademark: "Oh, well, you know me. I believe in calling a spade a spade." As if the fact that she knew she was committing a character assassination was justification enough.

Aunt Rebekka, "the Steamroller," as Dad called her. Not only was she disconcertingly forthright and dauntless, she was also the sort of person who believed everyone was dying to hear what she thought about everything under the sun. She talked nonstop, far too loudly and in far too much detail, she interrupted people when she felt like it, and she could go for an entire evening without ever noticing that hardly anyone else had got a word in edgewise. She was like a landslide or a hurricane, a sort of blind force that swept through the room, leaving in its wake dazed and exhausted souls here and seething, smarting wretches there. She and Uncle Frederik paid us a visit every summer and every single time the same thing happened. It was like a ritual: on the third day our aunt and uncle would start to accuse Mom of having forgotten where she came from and of thinking she was better than them and then, after a somewhat hesitant phase during which Mom endeavored to be polite, she would start to fight back. Not by arguing clearly and calmly that she was not uppity or spoiled or lazy, but by adopting an ironic stance that she would maintain for the remainder of their visit. When Uncle Frederik said that she was more gifted than him but too lazy to do as well as he had (he owned a small car-repair shop in Fredrikstad and was extremely proud of this), she might, for example, smile sweetly and say something to the effect that an idiot will hail anyone who is semi-intelligent as a genius—if only to feel semi-intelligent themselves for a little while. And when Aunt Rebekka construed what Mom said and did as signs of arrogance, Mom didn't say what she always said to Dad, which was that Aunt Rebekka was jealous and had an inferiority complex and that this had given her an insatiable

46

urge to "drag me through the muck." She chose instead to assume and then overplay the part of the snooty rich-man's wife. I had never seen her use a cigarette holder, for example, but one summer when Aunt Rebekka was there, she kept saying that she simply didn't know where she'd put her cigarette holder. She didn't like smoking without a holder, she said, she found it rather common. "Shall we go through to the sitting room?" she said on one occasion. "I feel like having my coffee on the chaise longue." And when Aunt Rebekka said: "The chaise what?" Mom simply smiled indulgently, much the way one would smile at a cute toddler who has asked about something that anyone over the age of four would know. "The sofa, then," she said. That's how she carried on. She'd say, for instance, that she was going up to change for dinner, or that she didn't know how she had managed when we had only one car (this being a dig, of course, at our aunt, who could only dream of being able to afford a car) and more than once I heard her say that she thought we ought to have a gardener to "tend the grounds." As if even in his wildest fantasies Dad would ever have agreed to spend money on something like that.

And she always got her way. Our uncle and aunt would seethe and fume, their sniping would become sharper and sharper, their barbs more and more caustic, and as their annual visit drew to a close, the atmosphere would become so tense and so unpleasant that they didn't even pretend to like each other. Well aware of what would happen, Dad used to flee the house before they arrived. Normally he never took time to pursue his own hobbies, but whenever Uncle Frederik and Aunt Rebekka announced that they were coming to stay (they always came together, partly because Aunt Rebekka wasn't well off and could save money by getting a lift from Uncle Frederik and partly because they felt that all three siblings ought to get together every now and again), he always happened to be going hill walking with his friends from the Rotary club. At the time it never occurred to me that these two things were connected and I didn't realize that my aunt and uncle were being sarcastic when they stood there with their enormous suitcases, looking flabbergasted because their visit had clashed with Dad's trip with the guys yet again. No-oo, surely not, had they missed him again? It became a standing joke, repeated year after year, but until I was well into my teens, I thought they were serious and I clearly remember going out of my way to make excuses for Dad: he was really sorry not to be here, I would say, he'd been so looking forward to seeing them.

Actually, writing this, it strikes me that the ironic stance Mom adopted toward Aunt Rebekka and Uncle Frederik is yet another example of how hard to fathom she could be. The way she turned into a caricature of the person they accused her of being shows how elusive she was. When Uncle Frederik accused her of being lazy and Aunt Rebekka accused her of being arrogant, she simply rendered herself so lazy and arrogant that anybody in their right mind could tell it was an act, thereby taking the sting out of their accusations: it was all so silly, she seemed to be saying. Mom simply could not be pigeonholed, she was always something more, always somehow different, always somewhere else.

She was much the same as a mother in fact. Not that she wasn't nice and kind and loving. She comforted Rikard and me when we needed comfort and helped us when we needed help. She listened and never judged when we told her things we were ashamed of and every single night, until we were well into our teens, she would come into our rooms and tell us that she loved us. But she would also laugh and joke about that side of herself, in such a way that she seemed almost to be making fun of her own mother love. That was how it sometimes felt to me at any rate. I think both Rikard and I knew deep down that she loved us, but when, for instance, she said "I love you and all that" and not just: "I love you," I was left with a sense that the love and the care that she showed us were some sort of compulsory exercise that bored her. And if Rikard or I went to her expecting a pat on the back for something or other, it was much the same story. She would shower us with praise in a way that was quite out of proportion to our achievement, then she would burst out laughing and say: "Oh, listen to me, laying it on too thick again," and this, in turn, left Rikard and me feeling that we really didn't deserve any praise at all. She didn't mean it, she was just pulling my leg, I would find myself thinking. It was exactly the same when Rikard or I was sick or in pain. Again, she would overdo it and act far more worried than the situation called for and then, as soon as she saw herself from the outside and realized this, she would burst out laughing and make fun of the way she had suddenly gone all maternal—which of course made Rikard and me feel that she wasn't actually sorry for us at all. Even though we knew at heart that she was, that was how we felt.

In other words: she also seemed reluctant to wholeheartedly embrace her role as a mother. Here too she felt the need to maintain a certain distance, the need to be exempted. I could get both angry and upset when she sowed doubt, as it were, on her own mother love in this way, but I think it was probably worse for Rikard, who was bullied a lot as a kid and had, therefore, even more need of love and care. He was extremely sensitive to the things Mom said and did, I remember. He was terrified of being rejected and he could become positively distraught with grief and rage if Mom didn't play the part of worried mother, proud mother, loving mother, et cetera, sincerely enough. He would run off to his room in floods of tears, lock the door, and refuse to come out until Mom had stood for minutes on end with her forehead pressed against the door, alternately apologizing and assuring him that he had misunderstood.

In fact it was me, not Rikard, who was the bullies' obvious target. I was tall and skinny and so pale skinned that I was sometimes stopped in the street by elderly ladies who would admonish me to take more iron ("You need to eat beets, son"), while Rikard was slightly shorter but much more robust with a fresh, healthy complexion that—when I picture him now— makes me think of cold milk, whole-wheat bread, and long skiing trips in subzero temperatures. While I was a daydreamer and a scatterbrain and equipped with motor functions so poor that I was forever tripping and knocking over glasses, Rikard was the sort of monkey-like child who could hardly pass a tree without climbing it. While I was hopeless at all sports except the standing long jump, he was strong, lithe, and fast and, as far as I could tell, an excellent winger with the Bangsund under-tens. While I was a shy, quiet bookworm, interested in things that al- most no one else of my age was interested in, Rikard was bright, cheerful, and outgoing. He told jokes, laughed loudly and often, and was a definite optimist who only rarely felt down in the dumps. "What a grand boy," as Aunt Rebekka always said.

And yet it was he, not I, who was given the cold shoulder by the cool kids in class and at school, he was the one who was sneered at and had snide comments hurled after him in the schoolyard, the one who didn't get invited to the class party even though everyone else in his class had been, the one who had both his bike tires slashed when he popped into the gas station to use the bathroom. And so on and so forth. I don't know how many times Mom and Dad had to speak to the school and I don't know how many times the school had to speak to the culprits, but it was a lot. It did no good, though. Things might be better for a month or two, but then it would be back to the same old story. "I don't know what they've got against Rikard," Mom or Dad would say. "There's usually no rhyme or reason to who gets bullied and who doesn't," the headmaster and his class teacher would tell them. But even back then I knew that they were both wrong and that they both knew they were wrong. Mom and Dad and the representatives of the school were all, in fact, very well aware that Rikard was bullied because he was "a little Gandhi," as I recall one girl in ninth grade calling him so aptly. Because as a child Rikard was the most infuriating goody-goody. He never missed an opportunity to wax indignant when he witnessed a bit of perfectly harmless kidding in the schoolyard and he and the two Christian girls in his class were the only ones to be morally outraged and offended when a classmate read out the following self-penned poem in class:

Herpes, AIDS, and gonorrhea
Syphilis and diarrhea
Odd Einar is sick
and so is his dick

While the rest of the class hung over their desks howling with laughter and the teacher was struggling not to do the same, Rikard stuck out his chin, put up his hand, and said: "But what about people who have those diseases? Do you think they would find that funny?" That was him. If anyone vandalized the school or covered its walls in graffiti, he would get upset, then angry, and he was genuinely shocked if someone stole something from the Co-op during break. "I don't see how you can enjoy a stolen chocolate bar," he told the guilty parties and he not only meant it, he made no secret of the fact that he intended to tell the teacher on them before the start of the next class, "for your own good," as he said. And when we were about thirteen or fourteen and some of the kids were starting to experiment with tobacco and alcohol: shocked then too. He just didn't get it. Both were illegal at their age, expensive and addictive and none of the kids who tried them even liked them, he said. On the contrary, he had heard of people who thought they both tasted absolutely horrible but still carried on drinking and smoking. He understood, of course, that they wanted to look older and cooler than they actually were, but surely they knew that nobody thought it was cool to see a fourteen-year-old smoking and drinking, it just looked stupid.

Since then Rikard and I have often laughed about all this and even if the adult Rikard has never exactly defended those who tormented him as a boy, he has taken much of the blame for what happened on his own shoulders. Whether this is an attempt to convince himself that he was in control in a situation in which, in reality, he had no control, and thereby regain some of the self-respect he had lost, I don't know, but as an adult he has certainly said that there was a part of him that liked to provoke the bullying, that even wanted what happened to happen. Which is not to say that he harbored some sort of masochistic urge to subject himself to pain. Far from it. It was more as though the role of bullied victim made him feel even more morally superior than he already did. "I never fought back and that in particular made me feel like a very good person," he has said himself. Putting up with all the taunts and sly remarks, pretending to ignore them, and simply carrying on smiling and being nice to the people who hadn't invited him to the class party, "not sinking to their level," an expression I remember him using when we were in junior high, gave him a wonderful sense of being better than everyone else, a sense of being "a little

Gandhi," as that girl in ninth grade had called him. And that, naturally, was like a red rag to a bull. Dad had, as I've said, done everything he could to ensure that Rikard and I never considered ourselves better than everyone else just because we had a lot of money, but I don't think it ever occurred to him to immunize us against this particular form of arrogance and I believe that this actually antagonized the other kids more than any amount of expensive designer clothes or other signs of wealth might have done. Not that Rikard didn't have some friends, he did, and the bullying he suffered was not of the worst sort, after all. But on the whole he was not well liked, it was as simple as that. Children who were normally open and friendly did their best to avoid him and children whom Dad regarded as well brought up said and did things to Rikard that they would never have said or done to anyone else. Rolf Inge Johnsen, for instance, a nice, kind, polite boy whom I remember crying openly when our teachers showed us a film about poor children in Africa, once punched Rikard when they were having words in the middle of a circle of kids in the schoolyard. Smack in the face and apparently quite unprovoked. Afterward Rolf Inge was tearful and distraught, not merely because of what he had done, but because he didn't know why he had done it. And I think there were many who felt the same way. They didn't realize that it was the way Rikard behaved that made them feel like bad and morally warped individuals when they were around him. Or maybe they did realize it, but as children they weren't able to put it into words.

Trondheim, June 24th, 2006. Plenty of matches there

I press Play, look across at Julie as Daniel Johnston's brittle voice fills the room. She's sitting on the sofa, flicking through a Star Tour brochure with a big yellow sun and a red parasol on the cover, so she must be finished with the place cards, I thought she'd never make up her mind about the color and the font, but it looks like she has finally come to a decision. I pick up my coffee cup and take a sip, I suppose I ought to finish packing, although to be honest I'd rather stay home, I don't really know why, maybe because Jan Olav and Kristian are always so cheerful, so full of life, and because when I'm with them it always reminds me of how miserable I am. It's very tiring, being confronted with your own shortcomings for a whole weekend. Well, there's nothing to be done about it, I can't back out now, I said I'd bring the tent and most of the dried food and I have to leave in less than an hour, I can't let them down at the last minute, can't let down Jan Olav at any rate, not when I've been beating myself up over the thought that we're not as close as a groom and a best man ought to be, and I'd just go on doing that if I stayed at home, these trips to the mountains are proof of a sort that we're good pals, and right now I need that proof, it makes it easier somehow to believe that he was the obvious choice for best man.

I turn and look out of the window, seems like the chain has come off the bike of one of the neighbors' boys, he's got it turned upside down and is standing watching while the old man upstairs from me tries to reattach it, laughing and chatting with the Iranian from across the yard as he works.

"Tenerife, thirteen thousand six hundred kroner," Julie mutters. I turn to look at her. "With a sea view and everything," she says, not taking her eyes off the brochure. Don't tell me she's going to start on about a honeymoon again. I know a honeymoon is part of her idea of the perfect wedding, but it's no good, I can't be bothered getting into that discussion again. "That's cheap," she says, softly, as if to herself, but she's talking to me, this is her way of telling me she still hasn't given up the idea of a holiday in the sun.

"Julie, for heaven's sake."

"What?"

"I thought we'd agreed we couldn't afford a holiday abroad. We can barely afford the wedding as it is."

She puts on a face that is both surprised and hurt.

"But—er . . . I never said we could."

"Okay," I say, smiling at her. "Sorry, I must have misunderstood."

Two seconds.

"God Almighty," she says, eyes on the brochure again, "am I not even allowed to dream now?"

I don't say anything, I know this is just a roundabout way of asking if we couldn't manage a holiday in the sun anyway, but I can't be bothered arguing, there's no point.

Silence.

"Well, I can't face spending the entire holiday at the cottage, just so you know," she snaps.

I sip my coffee.

"So what you're trying to say is that you do actually want a holiday abroad," I say, attempting to smile and show that I'm just joking really, but she doesn't smile back, she gives me the same look as before, that look of surprise and hurt.

"Would you stop being so suspicious of me all the time," she says. "I meant just what I said. I'm not interested in spending the holiday watching you playing at being self-sufficient at the cottage."

"Fine, fine," I say, putting my hands in the air as a sign to her to take it easy, stay like that for a moment, then lower them again, I don't want us to fall out so I smile at her, but she doesn't smile back, she's staring at the brochure again, she's always touchy when she knows she's going to be home alone, but she seems even worse than usual today.

"True love will find you in the end," Daniel Johnston sings. And Julie looks up from the Star Tour brochure again.

"What is it you're actually preparing for up there, anyway?" she asks. She's asked me this same question so many times, but she looks and sounds as though this is the first time, it's a way of showing her contempt, implying that what I do at the cottage is so bizarre, so ridiculous, that no one else could possibly understand it, that's what she's trying to convey. I almost say this to her, but I don't, it'll do no good for me to start accusing her of not saying what she actually means, she'll only fly off the handle: "There, what did I say, you're always so suspicious of me," that's what she'll say. I shouldn't be too hard on her, though, she really is afraid to be alone in the house, so I'll just have to put up with her taking her frustration out on me.

"I'm not preparing for anything in particular, Julie," I say.

"Yeah, right."

"Julie," I say, smiling at her. "I can't just lie around in the sun all day when I'm on holiday, I need to be doing something, preferably something different from what I do every day . . . something more substantial. It helps me to relax."

"Exactly," she says, picking up the holiday brochure again.

"Aw, c'mon, Julie, don't be like that."

"No, no," she says, lowering the brochure and giving me a frosty smile. "Having to can and store tons of meat and fish and vegetables in order to relax is perfectly normal. It's me that's weird, of course it is."

"Julie, it's . . ."

"Oh please, don't start," she says, breaking in. "I've heard it all before."

I just stand there looking at her. It's so tiring when she's in this mood, it's such heavy going. I take a sip of my coffee and turn to look out the window again; if it hadn't been for all the neighbors, I'd have taken my coffee outside, but there's no chance of getting any peace and quiet in the yard, there's always somebody who feels duty bound to be sociable.

Moments pass.

Then: "Could you turn that music down?" Julie says, with a note of irritation in her voice.

I turn around. She has put down the holiday brochure and picked up what looks like the notepad with her wedding to-do list on it, she's scribbling something down.

"Of course! Sorry," I say, turning off the music.

"That's not what I said."

I try to smile.

"I know. But we can just have a bit of quiet, if that's what you want."

"If that's what I want?"

"Hm?" I say, acting as if I didn't catch that last part.

She looks at me, gives a little snort, then she sticks her pen between her teeth, looks down at the notepad again.

I take a slug of coffee.

"I'm not really sure whether I can be bothered going to the mountains after all," I say suddenly, it just comes out, but there's no way I can back out now, so I don't quite know why I say it, maybe because I'm feeling guilty about going off with the guys when she's feeling so scared and when she's so stressed out about the wedding, because I need to hear her say that she'll be fine and that of course I have to go, yeah, that's probably it. "I was just wondering whether I ought to call Jan Olav and tell him I'm not coming," I say, still giving her an opening to say of course I should go, but she doesn't.

"Okay," she says, not taking her eyes off the notepad. She waits for a moment, then looks up at me again. "Why do you always have to start this? We both know you'll end up going."

I don't say anything, try to look as if I don't know what she's talking about, but can't quite manage it.

"Well, we do, don't we?" she goes on. "You're only saying that so I'll think you're not happy about going or something like that."

"Maybe," I say. But I'm not happy about going. "And it doesn't exactly make it easier that you have as much against it as you obviously have."

"So you think I should just act as if I think it's perfectly okay?"

"No, not *act* as if you do. But . . . well, I just think, if you don't dare to be alone, why don't you stay at your mom's . . . and anyway, I think you're making more of a fuss about the wedding arrangements than you need to," I say.

"Mom's going to Sweden with one of her friends this afternoon to pick up cigarettes and bacon. And how do you know I'm making more of a fuss about the wedding than I need to when you've never taken any interest in what has to be done?"

"Julie, I can't be bothered arguing."

Short pause.

"And besides, I don't know how you can bring yourself to go off to the mountains with that snob. I'd end up killing him, I'm sure I would," she says. She's ashamed of how she behaved at dinner the other evening, it's so obvious that that's why she's saying this; she's trying to blame Jan Olav for the little scene she made, as if it was his snobbishness that caused her to do what she did, that's what she's implying. I look at her, am just about to say this, but I don't, and I won't, I need to cut her some slack.

"He's not so bad when you get to know him," I say. I don't think Jan Olav's at all snobbish, but I say it anyway, to help her shed a little of the guilt she's feeling, it's a good way of mollifying her slightly.

She gives another snort.

"Yeah, right."

Two seconds.

"Julie, hey."

"What?"

"How much fun do you think this trip's going to be for me if I leave when we're like this?"

After a moment or two she sighs and I see her shoulders sink a fraction, then she looks at me and blinks.

"I'm sorry, Marius. Of course I want you to have fun. Go, I'll be fine," she says, blinking again. She looks tired and drawn when she does that; this is her way of telling me she doesn't mean what she just said, I suppose: she's telling me to go and enjoy myself, says she'll be fine, but the look on her face and the slump of her shoulders are signaling that she's exhausted and depressed and I really ought to stay home. I'm just about to say this straight out, but I don't.

"Thanks, it means a lot to me to hear you say that," I say, smiling at her, but she doesn't smile back, she doesn't like me taking her at her word like this, it annoys her when her attempts at emotional manipulation don't work, I can tell by her face, which has suddenly taken on a look of indifference, an air of disinterest designed to let me know that she can manage perfectly well without me, thus making me feel less worthy in some way. She doesn't say anything, keeps her eyes fixed on her notepad.

"Oh, by the way, do you have time to run down to the superstore before you go? I thought I'd write the place cards today," she says, knowing full well that it's the middle of the Friday rush hour and I don't have time to drive down to the superstore for her now, that's exactly why she's asking, I'm sure it is, she's asking because she wants me to feel bad when I say no.

"I wish I could," I say. "But I . . ."

"Fine! I'll do it myself," she cuts in, eyes on the notepad again.

"Julie, please. Don't start all that again."

"All what?"

"Julie, hey."

"I just thought you might do me that one small favor. To save me having to go into town today."

"But I don't have time. I'm meeting Kristian and Jan Olav in forty-five minutes. And I haven't finished packing yet."

"Huh," she says, inhaling sharply.

I just stand there looking at her, am about to ask her whether she shouldn't take a break from the wedding arrangements and relax a bit, but I don't, she'd only jump at the chance to tell me how little I'm doing. Well, somebody's got to do it, and since you can't be bothered, it'll have to be me, that's what she'll say, or something of the sort. And then I'll say it's not that I can't be bothered helping, but for one thing I don't see the point in planning everything right down to the smallest detail, and for another it doesn't matter what I do, it's usually wrong anyway—she corrects just about everything I do and whatever she doesn't correct she double-checks to make sure it's been done properly—and if that's the way it's going to be, then I might as well leave most of it to her to start with, that's what I'll say, or something along those lines, and then the argument's off and running. I run my hand through my hair, feel myself growing more and more resentful.

"Marius?"

"Yes."

"You're talking to yourself again," she says and she shakes her head, never taking her eyes off me. I put my coffee cup down on the table next to the stereo, am about to excuse myself by saying I was just thinking about something, but

I don't, I'm getting really pissed off now and I don't feel like apologizing for anything.

"Yeah, right" is all I say, then I walk out of the living room and into the hall. Her phone is lying on top of a pile of magazines on the bureau, I pick it up, check her text messages, I can't help it, she and Kristian were thick as thieves at dinner the other evening—not that I think there was anything like *that* going on between them, but I can't resist a quick peek, to be on the safe side, but no, there's nothing new since last time I looked, so I check her recent calls instead, with a quick glance over my shoulder to make sure she can't see me, she can't, so I turn back to her cell, her mother called, but otherwise there's nothing new there either. I put the phone down and go down the stairs to the basement feeling slightly relieved, only for a moment, though, and then I'm struck by a twinge of guilt: I had made up my mind not to do that anymore, I don't want to be a jealous loser who has to keep tabs on his girlfriend at all times and I never thought I'd be like that when Julie and I got together. I remember being happy to have a girlfriend who wasn't particularly attractive and whom I didn't therefore have to worry about losing to another man, I thought that meant I'd be able to relax a little, but no, I can't stop myself from checking up on her, I don't understand it, I need to pull myself together and stop this nonsense, try to show a little faith in her. I open the door to the storage room and step inside, go over to the workbench. My good mood seems to have deserted me, I feel less and less like going, it's way too late to call off, I know I have to go, but I'm feeling even more unhappy about it than I did a few minutes ago. Not so much because I'm afraid Julie will take it into her head to do something stupid while I'm away, more because I won't be able to enjoy the trip when things between us are the way they are at the moment, my conscience will be pricking me all weekend, I know it will. I pick up my fishing rod, take off the reel, and stick it in the top pocket of my rucksack, feel myself growing more and more resentful. I yank the zip shut, then plant both hands on the bench, shut my eyes, and stand there, breathing through my nose.

"Fuck, why do we always have to do the right thing," I mutter, then I open my eyes and take my hands off the bench. After a moment I hear the beep of a text coming in. I pull my cell from my pocket and check it, it's from Jan Olav. "Have to pop into the Wine Monopoly, running fifteen minutes late" is all it says. I type "OK," press Send, and lay the phone on the bench.

Then: "Marius," Julie calls. "Where are you?"

I don't answer straightaway, don't feel like it, want to be alone awhile longer.

"Marius!"

I turn, step across to the storage room door, close it gently, so it will sound credible if I say I didn't hear her calling me, then go back to the bench. I pull the top section of the rod out of the bottom, hear the little pop as the two pieces part company, I take the blue canvas bag off the bench, slip both sections into it, and tie the strings around it.

Then I hear the faint creak of the door opening.

"So this is where you are."

I turn and look at her, she has a sheet of paper in one hand and the ballpoint pen in the other, she seems to be in a better mood now. She smiles at me.

"Yes?" I say.

"It's this seating plan. I can't figure it out."

I turn away without saying anything, sigh as I pick up the larger tackle box—she's going to start fussing about the fucking seating plan again.

"Oh, I know you think I'm a control freak," she says. "But the seating plan is important, if everyone is to have a good time."

"I'm sure it is," I say.

"Oh, for God's sake, Marius. We're getting married. You could at least pretend to be a *little* bit enthusiastic."

"Yeah, yeah, but—er," I say, my shoulders sagging. I wait a moment, then turn back to her. "Do we really have to go over the seating plan again? I thought we got that sorted out ages ago."

"More or less, yes. But it suddenly struck me that Robert and Heidi should be seated farther apart. They had a bit of a thing before Robert started seeing Vibeke, and since Vibeke is what you might call the jealous type, it might be better to put her and Robert somewhere else. But where, that's the question . . . you see, I thought of putting them at the middle table down the far end, but Vidar's sitting there and you know what he's like when he's had too much to drink, so that's no good, we need to have someone there who won't mind the odd dirty joke. So maybe it would be better to . . ."

"Julie," I say, breaking her off. I stand there, staring at her, it's on the tip of my tongue to say that I'll be leaving in a minute and we'll have to talk about this later, but I don't get the chance because suddenly her cell phone rings, she puts her hand in her pocket, takes it out, and looks at the display.

"It's Mom again," she mutters and puts the phone to her ear. "Hi," she says, then she turns, steps out into the hall, and closes the door behind her: more talk about the wedding dress, no doubt; that or something else I'm not supposed to know anything about. I give a little sigh as I turn and open the big tackle box. That's the second time today her mother's called and it's only three o'clock, I'm so sick of all their fussing, the one's as bad as the other, Julie and her mother, it's great that they're going to so much trouble to ensure that we have the best possible wedding, I want it to be a great wedding too, of course I do, but they go way overboard, talking and acting as if even the tiniest detail is a matter of life or death. One of them freaks out and starts bawling and shouting at the band for having double-booked, the other can't sleep at night for agonizing over the color scheme for the bridal bouquet. The wedding arrangements take up all their time and energy. I thought that sort of thing happened only in rom-coms, but obviously not, it's bordering on madness. I take a couple of spinners and a little box of lead sinkers out of the large tackle box and put them in the small one.

Then I hear the door creak open again.

"Well, that's that settled, at least," Julie says.

I say nothing, I know this is my cue to ask what's been settled, but I can't be bothered, it's a pretty dumb way of letting her know that I've just about had enough, but that's too bad, I don't turn around either, take a little box of hooks from the big box and put it in the small one.

"Oh, I forgot to ask if you'd called the doctor," Julie says.

"Yeah, you did," I mutter.

"Oh, Marius. Don't be like that. It's just that I've got so much on my mind, what with the wedding and all."

"Uh-huh."

I hear her sigh.

"Well, did you call?"

"Yes," I say and leave it at that.

"Okay, so how did it go?" she asks, a little more sharply.

"Not too well," I say, don't know why I say that, the test results were absolutely fine, but here I am telling her they weren't good.

"Oh? What did he say?"

"I've got MS," I say, just like that, it's the sort of joke that Julie can't stand, but it just slips out, I don't know why.

I hear her sigh.

"That's not funny!" she says.

"I never said it was," I say.

Silence.

"I called a minute ago," I add, pointing to my phone on the bench, there's silence for a moment or two and I nearly tell her that I'm only kidding, but I don't.

I keep my back to her, close the small tackle box, lift the top flap of the rucksack, and pop the box into the main section, give no hint that I'm joking. I've just lied and told her I have MS, I don't quite know why, maybe as yet another way of letting her know that the plans for the wedding have got out of hand, maybe as a way of reminding her that whatever she may think there are actually more important things in the world than what font to use for the invitations, an attempt to get her to put things in perspective and calm down a bit. I draw the main section of the rucksack closed, flick the top flap over, then turn and look at her. She's standing there staring at me, stock-still with her arms hanging by her sides, she's speechless, stunned, not only does she think I'm telling the truth, she's almost in shock, I can tell by her face. Oh shit, no, I can't do this to her, I have to tell her I'm only joking or this little white lie will turn into something more spiteful and I don't want that, I have to tell her the truth now: my blood pressure was a little on the high side, the doctor said, but otherwise everything was absolutely fine, and I have to tell Julie this. But I don't, I take a sort of bittersweet pleasure in getting through to her the way I'm doing now, for the first time in ages she actually understands what I mean when I say there are more important things in the world than the color of place cards, and I'm so happy, it's rotten of me, I know, but I can't help it.

"So, you don't have to give any more thought to that seating plan," I say with a tight little smile, then I turn away again, pick up the small bag containing my maps, compass, and pen, and stuff it into the side pocket of the rucksack.

She still says nothing.

"As soon as I get back I'll send out a letter to say the wedding's off," I say, it just comes out, I almost jump when I hear myself say it, oh, but no, I have to stop this, I can't do it, but I am, I am doing it, and this bittersweet feeling just grows and grows inside me, getting stronger and stronger. "But maybe you could call the vicar and let him know," I ask, then I turn and look at her, she has put her hands up to her face, stands there with a hand on each cheek, staring at me, she still doesn't say anything, she's totally flabbergasted, okay, now I really ought to drop it, I can't carry on like this, now I ought to own up and apologize. But I don't, I hate to see Julie like this, but that bitter-sweet feeling just keeps growing and growing inside me, I'm filled with a sort of malicious glee, a terrible, but wonderful, feeling. "And your mom, she needs to be told right away," I say. "It'll save her all that work on the wedding dress. There was still a fair bit to do to it, as far as I know," I add, then I turn my back on her again, pick up the little bag containing matches and firelighters, open it, take out the matchbox, and give it a little shake to check that there are still some matches in it, it gives a faint rattle. "Plenty of matches there," I say, talking now as if nothing has happened, as if everything is perfectly okay. There's silence again for a moment, then I hear Julie sniffle. I've made her cry now, what on earth am I doing, what's got into me, why am I doing this, it's not purely to make her calm down and get the wedding into perspective, that's not why I'm tormenting her like this, although that may be what triggered it, but there's something else behind it now, is it because it makes me feel powerful, because I want to prove to myself and to Julie that I can still change my mind if I want to, is that why I'm lying about having MS and talking about canceling the wedding? To prove to myself that it's still not too late? Yes, maybe it is. And underneath that again, perhaps, lies that old familiar fear of commitment, the fear of losing my freedom, another cliché, I'm as big a cliché as Julie and her mother. A moment, then Julie comes up to me, puts her arms around my waist, and presses herself against me, she doesn't say a word, just stands their holding me and it feels so good, I realize how much I love her, she's the one for me, her and no other. I may have a fear of commitment or at least a fear of taking the huge step that marriage actually is, but my love for Julie is stronger than all that, I may be overcome by fear and doubt now and again, but my love for Julie always drives the fear and doubt away, as it's doing now. I close my eyes and feel her warmth. One second, two, and now I have to come up with a way of getting myself out of this, I can't just say it's not true, not when I've let it go on as long as this, maybe I should say the tests showed that I might have MS, something like that, and that I won't know for sure till Monday or something like that, yeah, I could do that, then I could call her at work and tell her the results were negative, I hate to think of her having to live with the uncertainty till then, but there's no other way. It's better than telling her the truth at any rate.

"I don't know . . . I don't know what to say," she says.

She squeezes me even tighter and it feels so good to have her holding me and comforting me like this, feeling so sorry for me, it feels good, I can't help it, it's rotten of me to make her feel sorry for me when there's no reason to feel sorry for me, but I can't help myself.

"Well anyway, it's a good thing I found out before the wedding. At least this way we'll be able to cancel it," I say, not letting it go, leaving the way open for her to say she loves me and that we're going to go ahead exactly as planned, love conquers all and so on, that's what I'm angling for her to say. But she doesn't say a word. "Don't you think?" I ask. Moments pass, but she still doesn't say anything, just stands there with her arms around me, she's not playing along, not saying what I'm giving her the chance to say. There's total silence and then I feel a ripple of unease, my stomach starts to flutter, does she think we should call off the wedding as well, has she changed her mind about marrying me, now that she thinks I have MS? Is that why she's not playing along, is that why she doesn't say anything when I've just given her a cue to say that she loves me and that we should go ahead with the wedding exactly as planned, does her love run no deeper than that? MS is a terrible disease, of course, both for those

afflicted by it and for their families, and of course Julie
knows a lot about what it means to live with someone in
need of care, having grown up with a paraplegic father,
but still, is that really enough to make her want to call off
the wedding? Apparently so, or she would have said something long before this, she would surely have protested
when I asked her to call the vicar and tell him to cancel
the wedding or when I asked her to call her mother and
tell her to stop work on the wedding dress, but she didn't,
she let everything I said go unchallenged. I stand quite
still, my unease growing, I swallow once, then again, give
it another second or two, then gently prize myself free of
her embrace.

"I've got to finish packing," I say.

"You're not serious?" she says.

"Of course I am."

"You can't go to the mountains now," she says. "We need
to talk."

"What more is there to talk about?" I say, then I pick up
my rucksack, turn around slowly, and look her straight in
the eye, stand there waiting for an answer, but she doesn't
answer, she knows very well what I mean and she has no
answer, she holds my eye for a couple of seconds, saying
nothing, then she swallows hard, looks down, looks up at
me again.

"Bye then," I say.

"Marius, please," she says, placing her hand on my arm,
making a rather half-hearted attempt to hold me back,
but I ease myself out of her grip, walk out of the storage
room, up the basement stairs, into the hall, and over to
the shoe rack, then I sit down on the stool, grab my hiking boots, and start to put them on. I deliberately tie the

laces wrongly, do it quite instinctively, giving her time to follow me and stop me, but she doesn't, she stays in the basement, she doesn't mean to stop me, she means to let me go. I undo the knot, retie it, do exactly the same with the other boot, then I prop my elbows on my knees, sit there staring at the floor as this terrible unease grows and grows. My stomach churns harder and harder, what on earth have I done, what have I started? I close my eyes and put a hand to my brow, rest my head on my hand, I have the urge to go back downstairs, have the urge to put my arms around her and confess everything, tell her I was lying, that it just happened, that I don't know why, but that I want everything to be the way it was. I can't, though. Things can never be the way they were, not knowing what I know now, I wish I'd never discovered it, but I have. And maybe this was what I wanted all along, maybe all this came about because I needed to know whether she really did love me or not, maybe that's why I lied about having MS, maybe I did it to test her, I don't know.

Namsskogan, July 9th–11th, 2006

I know I'm in danger of sounding like some women's magazine agony aunt, dispensing good advice and words of wisdom, but I'm going to say it anyway: happiness depends to a great extent on choosing the right moments at which to consider and comprehend one's life objectively. I've suspected for some time, I suppose, that I haven't always been as good at doing this as I might have been, but it's only now, since I started writing this letter to you, that this has really been brought home to me.

But I'll come back to that.

Anyway: Gjert Rosendahl, Dad's brother, started a fish farm in Flatanger and when he died, single and childless, in 1988, Dad inherited a business that would take the family from being rich in a way that people could imagine to being worth the sort of money that neither we nor anyone else could relate to. Initially, though, the outlook was not nearly as good as one might think. Fish farming in the eighties was, as we know, plagued by furunculosis and other fish diseases and these, along with substandard net pens and the resultant large-scale escape of fish, meant that Uncle Gjert had been running at a considerable and more or less consistent loss during his time as director, so when Dad took over the place in 1988, no one dreamed that it would become as hugely successful as it did in the nineties and aughts, or that he would become known as the Salmon King of Bangsund. Not even Dad himself, I'm sure.

To cut a long story short, its success came about due to Dad—in collaboration with the district council and two other investors—closing the furniture factory in Bangsund and turning the premises into a plant for the development and production of fish vaccine. He then bought an old herring-oil factory and used this as a testing station for the vaccine. The financial investment was enormous, many people were extremely skeptical of the whole project, and his plans would have been impossible to implement had it not been for the support provided by Statoil and the sovereign oil fund, channeled through what was then known as the Norwegian Export Council (now Innovation Norway). In principle these funds were earmarked for a variety of international projects (as part of Statoil's drive to raise its profile and, as such, an attempt, I presume, to present itself as an attractive prospect in the competition for new oil fields) but Dad and the other investors argued that fish farms in other countries would also benefit greatly from the vaccines. After a bit of to-ing and fro-ing, their application was granted and suddenly Dad wasn't only the owner of several disease-free fish farms, he was also the main shareholder in Aqua Central, a company that would eventually dominate the global market for vaccines for salmon and trout.

But the road to that point was long and hard and here I'm not just thinking of the many great business obstacles that had to be overcome: Dad first began to notice that he had a problem in 1986, but he was fifty-five, so he simply took the accumulation of fluid in his legs and the increasingly frequent need to urinate, the fact that he had to get up two or three times a night to pee, as signs that he was getting old. The same went for the change in the color of his urine. If I went to the bathroom after

Dad had been there and forgotten to flush (something he was always doing, much to Mom's annoyance), the bowl was always full of rusty-brown pee that smelled as rank and penetrating as the boys' restrooms at school, where certain ninth graders thought it fun to pee on the floor and the wall. "Old man's piss," Dad would say, "perfectly normal." And the fact that he felt like doing less and less and was tired and out of breath after the sort of physical exertion that he would never even have thought of as such a year earlier was explained away in similar fashion: "Ah, well, I'm not sixteen anymore, you know," he would say when pushed to explain why he no longer felt up to taking a walk up Flakkfjellet or down the Bangdalen valley to pick cloudberries with Rikard and me. "Wait till you get old, then you'll understand."

This was, of course, a way of ignoring the problem. Dad was terrified of doctors, and even though Mom tried everything short of putting a gun to his head, as she put it, to persuade him to have himself checked out, he flatly refused. He got annoyed if we hinted that he ought to make an appointment and would blow his top completely if we said it straight out. "Stop fussing, dammit," he would snap. "I told you, it'll pass." But it didn't pass. It got worse. He had always had the same fresh, ruddy complexion as Rikard, but now he began to look pale and wan. His breath smelled so bad that I balked at getting too close to him when we were talking and no matter how often he brushed his teeth or how scrupulously he flossed, it got no better. But the worst of it was the change in his character. His steadily deteriorating state of health made him anxious, tired, and tense. This in turn meant that he wasn't able to work as well or as much as before, which was probably one reason why the furniture factory wasn't doing as well as it once had, and this made him even more anxious, tired, and tense. And so it went on. All of this resulted in a state of mind that sometimes made Mom wonder whether he was becoming what we now call bipolar, but that at that time was described as manic-depressive. For days on end he would be withdrawn, moody, and irritable and never opened his mouth except to bite someone's head off, as Mom said at one exasperated moment. Take, for example, the time when I was woken by them returning from a dinner party at which, as far as I could gather, Mom had been a little friendlier toward another man than Dad liked.

"I was only trying to be sociable," Mom said. "He's just lost his wife."

"It's just like I'm always saying. He has all the luck, that one."

"And what's that supposed to mean?"

"Work it out for yourself, if you can," Dad said. "So, are you staying up for a while or are you going straight to bed?"

"Oh . . . I don't know, it's nearly midnight, so I was thinking of going to bed."

"Fine. In that case I'll stay up for a bit."

That's what he was like. And not just with Mom. With Rickard and me too. Despite being habitually stubborn, difficult, and endowed with what he himself described as "a Latin temperament," he had been a great father. He had been interested and supportive and always there for us in all sorts of ways, no matter how busy he was with work. But not anymore. He took less and less interest in how we were doing at school, for instance. Previously, he had always made a point of knowing when we had a test coming up, he saw to it that we were well prepped on whatever subject we were being tested on and would ask to see the test papers once we got them back. But now he didn't even check how we had done in our exams, and when we told him, he didn't seem proud and happy, the way I knew he would have been had he been himself. "Okay" was all he said. And if we just stood there, a little confused and probably unable to conceal our hurt at the lack of praise, he would look us straight in the eye and ask whether there was anything else we wanted. No? Well, in that case he would like to be left in peace, if we didn't mind. And unlike before, when his angry outbursts were understandable and could usually be put down to Rikard or me having said or done something we shouldn't have, now they came as a complete surprise. He could explode over the smallest thing and use words and expressions that I associated mainly with Nielsen the butcher's fat son who, according to the butcher himself, had learned to say "crap" before he could say "Papa." Dad simply wasn't the same person at all. And yet there were some signs that our good old dad was still in there somewhere. Like the fact that he clearly felt guilty for the way he was behaving. Not only was he remorseful and apologetic when he had been unreasonable and not only did he assure all of us that whatever had happened was no one's fault but his, he also endeavored to do something about the problem. There were times when he would try so hard to be nice that it became strained and awkward. He would push himself to work much more than he was actually able to and at least as much as when he was fit and well and he was making plans for himself and the furniture factory that were totally unrealistic, considering the state we all knew he was in. This would go on until he grew tired of fighting and succumbed to all his underlying frustration and anger.

But there was no way he was going to the doctor.

All of this was very hard on Mom. Some people actually thought she was talking about herself when she said she wondered whether Dad was suffering from manic depression or possibly just depression. That it was somehow a case of projection. There had never been anything pessimistic or melancholy about her. On the contrary, as I mentioned earlier, she had always had a bright and easygoing nature. Over all her contradictions and her seemingly irreconcilable qualities and idiosyncrasies there had always hung a kind of indifference. Or no, not indifference exactly, more like a particular knack for not brooding over things she couldn't change, an ability to say "oh, well, never mind" and move on. But not anymore. She lost her sparkle, was less quick to laugh, and seemed constantly to be looking for something to worry about, any excuse to look on the black side. If there was a tiny cloud in an otherwise blue sky, it was bound to rain, as Rikard said. And alongside this she had developed a quite extraordinary gift for self-deprecation. She had always seemed so self-possessed, so confident, but now she acted as if she had somehow taken a drastic drop in worth, possibly because Dad didn't show her that he loved her the way he had before he became ill or possibly because Rikard and I were becoming more independent and she no longer played such a large part in our lives. I don't know, it's hard to say, but her self-esteem was certainly at a low ebb. "I know they don't like me," she said, for example, on one occasion when Dad had summoned up the energy to go to dinner at the Schröders' and Mom suddenly decided she didn't want to go after all. "Where on earth did you get that idea?" Dad said. "I just know," Mom said. "But how do you know?" Dad asked. "You can just tell," Mom said, knowing full well that there's no arguing with such feelings and that Dad didn't have a leg to stand on. In the old days she would have laughed at how negative she sounded when she said things like this: "Oops, there I go, doing my Eeyore act again," she would say, or something like that, then she would cheer up and go to dinner anyway. Not now, though. She was convinced that people disliked her and were laughing behind her back, so she was forever looking for excuses to stay home. On her birthday that same self-loathing raised its ugly head again. We had always gone to Tino's for a birthday dinner, but this particular year she told us she didn't want to celebrate her birthday at all, and even though she never said in so many words that she didn't think she was worth celebrating, we all knew she wanted us to understand that that was how she felt and that we were now supposed to jump in and assure her that she was wrong: "Of course you're worth celebrating, Mom, come on, let's go to Tino's." That's the sort of thing she wanted us to say, and when we didn't, when we simply said "okay" and the day itself looked like being no different from any other Tuesday, with gray skies, housework, and fish cakes for dinner—which was what she said she wanted—she didn't merely go into a terrible huff, she was also genuinely upset. At one point I went down to the kitchen for a glass of water and found her crying and banging her head gently against the door of the cabinet above the sink. I thought, therefore, that she would be relieved and happy when it turned out that Dad had gone against her wishes, bought her a present, and organized a little party for her anyway. But no. To our great surprise, not to say shock, she was furious. "Why does no one pay any attention to what I say?" she cried. "I told you I didn't want any presents, that I didn't want to celebrate my birthday, why can't you ever take me seriously?"

As if all of this wasn't enough she was also turning into a hypochondriac. "Something's not right," she kept saying about herself and her body, but this wasn't meant as a way of reminding us that things could go wrong and that disaster lurked around every corner. Or, at least, that may often have been what she was trying to say, because not only had she developed an exceptional ability to fret over the slightest thing, the sudden change in Dad's state of health had shown us all how fragile life could be and perhaps she felt the need to share this insight with others. But still: such announcements were often a way of warning us that she would soon be taking to her bed, suffering from some imagined ailment or other. For example, when, like most middle-aged people, she began to have difficulty reading the newspaper without glasses, she became convinced that she had cataracts. "It often starts with failing sight," she said. For several days after this she lay in bed, feeling all the other symptoms she imagined that she had. "I have such a terrible headache," she said, and "my eyes have been watering an awful lot recently, I can hardly watch TV without the tears streaming down my cheeks, so yes, unfortunately I think it's as I feared." And then, after she'd been to see the doctor and he had told her that she did not have cataracts, she would be right as rain for a little while—until, that is, she again began to suspect that there was something seriously wrong with her. Pancreatic cancer. A congenital heart defect. Marfan syndrome. There was so much to choose from if you read the medical handbook as assiduously as Mom did back then.

I'm not sure what the connection was between the change in Dad and the change in Mom, but I and just about everyone else who knew our family took it more or less for granted that Mom's problem was a reaction of sorts to what Dad was going through. "Klara has never had to struggle, so when Kåre started going downhill, she caved in right away, you don't need to be a rocket scientist to see that," Aunt Rebekka said when she and Uncle Frederik came for their annual visit. She then went on to give a long account of how she, on the other hand, had stayed strong throughout her late cancer-stricken husband's illness. "I had no choice, I couldn't take to my bed, I had a young child to see to," she said. That that same child had been placed in a foster home after her husband's death due to some form of neglect, the nature of which was never disclosed, was apparently not deemed worth mentioning.

Uncle Frederik, for his part, seized the chance to tell a funny little story about how jealous Mom had been when he broke both legs and had to move back in with Grandma and Grandpa to be nursed and cared for. "Remember how you daubed your legs with blue paint and said it was bruises so Mom and Dad would feel sorry for you?" he said, and then he laughed as if to show that this was simply a sweet story, one that he had just happened to remember and definitely not what everyone knew it to be: namely, a sly way of insinuating that Mom was a pampered drama queen who only feigned illness and went around looking woeful to get attention. Oh, Uncle Frederik, he could be so scathing in such a sympathetic fashion that it still makes me mad to think about it, ten years after he was crushed to death in a tragic accident at his repair shop.

Nevertheless, Rikard and I took a slightly more positive view of it all. We had grown more and more different from each other as time went on, but we still had plenty of good chats and during one of these Rikard expressed a thought that had crossed my own mind many times: that it was the fear that Dad was seriously ill and might die that caused Mom to "feign illness and go around looking woeful," as our uncle had put it. In words very different from those I'm using here we agreed that the change in Mom was an unconscious attempt to tell herself and Dad that his problems were neither as uncommon nor as serious as one might think. "I mean, just look at me, I'm not the person I was twenty years ago either, my health is failing as well" was what she was trying to say. Seen in that light, the change in her was a strangely beautiful declaration of love and a desperate, if somewhat warped way of asking Dad to see a doctor and then fight whatever was wrong with him.

In any case: there we were, with both Mom and Dad reduced to mere shadows of themselves, when Aunt Rebekka came steamrolling into our lives in a manner very different from what she had done every summer of our childhood. Aunt Rebekka, always clad in red or purple and wearing lipstick and eyeshadow that she believed matched, but that Mom thought made her look like a madame from the Reeperbahn. Aunt Rebekka, always with a story to tell and her menthol cigarettes, chewing gum, and a gossip mag within reach. Aunt Rebekka, who was always on some diet or other but who ate rum babas or Napoleon's hats every day and consequently had flabby, quivering upper arms as thick as my thighs. Now she sold her flat in Oslo and moved to Bangsund to support and assist Mom. "I couldn't, in all conscience, do anything else," she told people, going on to add that "the real estate agent said I would get a lot more for my apartment if I waited a while before selling, but no, I told him, I can't, I said, my sister needs me now, and if that means I lose a lot of money, well, so be it, I said."

She might well have got a little more for her apartment if she had held off and she might well have felt it was her duty to help Mom, but it should also be said that she had been talking for some years about moving back to Namsos or Bangsund. "There's nothing to keep me in Oslo now," she used to say, I remember. But this additional piece of information would have shown her in a less heroic and self-sacrificing light than she would have wished so she was careful not to mention it.

But whatever her motives, Aunt Rebekka moved into the apartment in the extension at the back of the house and even I, a scientist who cannot abide the misuse of the word *energy*, have to admit that from the day and hour she arrived, the house seemed to be filled with new, well, energy. I had always regarded my aunt as a lazy woman, partly because I usually only ever saw her for a few drowsy summer days each year and partly because she was on disability benefit—and like so many other people I automatically associated fat people on disability benefit with laziness. But I was wrong. Aunt Rebekka was astonishingly efficient and proved to be incredibly hardworking. She could wash down the whole house in roughly the same time it took Mom to explain to Dad why we ought to hire a cleaner, and once she'd done that she would start polishing the silver, cutting the hedge, or making mutton and cabbage stew. She'd been told not to clean Mom and Dad's room or to touch the things on the desk in the office, but she paid no heed. She made their bed and changed the duvet whenever she felt it was necessary and I was forever hearing my dad muttering to himself that he didn't know where some document or letter had got to: "I put it right here, dammit," he would say, only a moment later to roar: "Rebekka! Have you been tidying my papers again? Rebekka!" She was a positive whirlwind. If she was alone in the house for a couple of hours and had nothing else to do, she was quite liable to rehang the pictures on our walls or rearrange the living room furniture. "There now, doesn't that look nice," she would say to Mom and Dad when they came home. And once, when I was lying stark naked on my bed, relaxing after a shower, I suddenly found myself looking straight into the eyes of Aunt Rebekka, who was up a ladder, cleaning my window. "You could at least warn me before you do that," I told her, but it was like water off a duck's back. "Oh, relax, I've seen naked men before and I was no more shocked then than I am now!" she said. As if it was to save her blushes, not mine, that she ought to inform me before she started climbing up and gawping through my bedroom window.

But even though she did sometimes encroach too much on what ought to have been the family's privacy, we were all happy that she had moved in, and not until much later did Mom begin to refer to Rebekka's efforts as "an investment in her own future" and "part of an extortion scheme." Even Dad, who always used to flee the house when our aunt and uncle came to visit, eventually became glad to have her there. Not only because she was a hard worker and took care of all the chores he and Mom were no longer able to do, but also because he liked her as a person. Yes, she talked the ears off him, as he put it, and she had neither the manners nor the tact to refrain from saying things that were hurtful or that infuriated him, but she was also thick-skinned and endowed with enough self-irony and wit to cope with him being equally blunt with her, which meant he could relax and be himself, as he said. Like the time when Aunt Rebekka told Dad off for smoking in the car when Rikard and I were there.

"Passive smoking doubles the risk of contracting lung cancer," she declared.

"Passive chatter is just as harmful," Dad retorted.

And they both burst out laughing.

One might think that Rikard and I—who were both in late adolescence and so sensitive and unsure of ourselves that now, as an adult, it's hard to imagine—were permanently crimson with embarrassment from having to listen to Aunt Rebekka's utterly brazen questions and remarks from morning to night. "I know you've gone without shaving for a while, and I know you call that a moustache, but that doesn't make it one, so shave it off, for heaven's sake, it looks like your father's ear hair," she said to me once, at the top of her voice, when two of my chums could hear. And: "Now, don't forget to use a condom when you have sex," she told Rikard and a girl who had come to see him. But we weren't embarrassed. Aunt Rebekka was Aunt Rebekka and you just had to take her as she was: an entertaining addition to our daily lives, a breath of fresh air. Like Dad, we felt we could relax around her and be ourselves. Indeed, the fact that she didn't appear to hide anything from us made us less concerned about hiding things from her and it got to the stage where we would go to her rather than Mom or Dad if we had questions of a more delicate nature. Or I did, anyway. So when I discovered two brown spots on the underside of my penis and couldn't sleep at night because I thought I had skin cancer and would need to have amputated the one body part that I was most afraid of losing—apart from my head—it was my aunt I eventually turned to. "Pigment change, that's all, nothing to worry about," she said. And again, when I felt there were rather too many stray hairs on my pillow in the morning and started buying tins of brewer's yeast, which I hid in the cupboard and took on the sly to at least delay the hair loss, it was her I consulted. "Bald? You? What a load of rubbish. We shed hair all the time. Sometimes a little, sometimes a lot," she said. And since, as Dad said, she was known for not mincing her words, I trusted her more in such situations than Mom, for example, who I knew had a tendency to gloss over things to make me feel better. I don't know how many times I left Aunt Rebekka's apartment feeling as though a ton of weight really had been lifted from my shoulders.

That said, however: Aunt Rebekka was not, strictly speaking, the person to go to if you had a medical issue of any sort. Or at least, not if her diagnosis of Dad's problem was anything to go by: a brain tumor, that's what it was, she confided to Rikard and me one evening when we came down to the kitchen and found her sitting there all alone, looking very grave. She was sure of it. She had had a colleague at the telegraph office when she was a girl and his personality had changed completely. He had been quiet, polite, and nice as could be in January, but when he returned to work after his summer holiday, he was crazy as a loon, she told us. "Went around yelling at coworkers for all to hear, calling them this, that, and the other, we thought he'd lost his mind, but it turned out that he had a tumor as big as an orange between his ears," our aunt said.

Fortunately, though, she was wrong.

Dad had strenuously resisted going to the doctor for far too long already, but when, on top of everything else, he began to grow breasts, he finally saw sense and agreed to go for a checkup. Chronic kidney failure, the doctor said and gave Dad the choice of a kidney transplant or dialysis every day for the rest of his life. Dad couldn't bring himself to ask any of us to donate a kidney, but he made it pretty clear that there was nothing he would rather have. This was just after he had inherited the fish farm from our uncle, he was in the midst of building up the new business and kept saying that there was no way he could go in to Namsos every day for two hours of dialysis—as he had started doing as soon as his illness was diagnosed—not with all the work he had to do. "We could have done something really great here, but now I suppose we'll just have to abandon the whole project and sell the damn thing, don't you think?" he said, this being our cue to shake our heads and say, no, no, and then suggest that one of us donate a kidney for him. Which was exactly what we did. Rikard, Mom, and I all offered to do the needful and just a few days later we underwent tests to see who would be most suitable as a donor. The test results showed that all three of us were more or less equally suitable, but after a brief discussion Mom decided that she should do it. Rikard and I had our whole lives ahead of us, after all, as she said, and we never knew whether we might have need of that kidney, which, at the moment, we could in principle manage without.

And she got her way.

The doctors said the prognosis was good, so we were all feeling relaxed and cheerful when Mom and Dad packed their tartan suitcases and set off for the University Hospital in Oslo one day in early April. Well, all except Aunt Rebekka, that is. Although none of us quite understood why, she seemed oddly anxious, she wept and was quite distraught; she could hardly open her mouth without talking about the dreadful state of the Norwegian health service: "You'd better be fit as a fiddle if you have to go to the hospital in this country," she said before going on to give us a little lecture on everything from hospital bacteria that could cause serious streptococcal infections to incredible and probably fictitious tales of surgeons amputating the wrong feet and leaving scissors and forceps inside patients' stomachs. "Yeah, but some people do get better after a spell in the hospital, you know," Rikard protested, grinning and endeavoring to bring her back down to earth with a little wry humor, but she was having none of it: "Show a little respect, you idiot," she snapped.

But the operation went well. For a short time afterward it looked as though Dad's body might reject the kidney, but once they changed some of the medication used to suppress the immune system, everything went according to plan. Still, however, all was not well. It was as if Dad's new personality had somehow stuck with him. A couple of months or so after the operation he was physically as strong, fit, and well as he had been before he fell ill, but his mood swings were as bad as ever. Worse, in fact. His fits of rage became more frequent and more violent and at times he was so cranky and contrary and so foulmouthed, particularly toward Mom, that I wasn't the only one who began to wonder whether he might be mentally ill after all. He constantly, and deliberately, misunderstood Mom, crediting her with thoughts and motives that she did not have and calling her "unspeakable things," as I heard her tell a visiting woman friend one time.

"I don't deserve this, Kåre," I heard Mom sob late one evening when they were in the living room and thought no one was listening. I had been woken by the sound of them arguing and Dad calling her a "female psychopath" and was sitting on the stairs to the ground floor, listening.

"I don't deserve this," Mom said again.

"Why, because you've just given me a kidney?"

"Kåre?"

"Do you think I'm stupid, Klara? You think everything can be the way it used to be just because you volunteered to act as a donor, that's the problem."

"Kåre, you're scaring me."

"You keep reminding me of what you just said," Dad said, and then he put on a whiny, woman's voice, supposed to sound like Mom: "I don't deserve this," he mimicked. "You never get what you deserve, woman, this is all about you wanting me to think you don't deserve to be abandoned, right? You want to make it impossible for me to leave you."

I frequently caught myself thinking that he was trying to provoke and punish Mom by pretending to have grown closer to Aunt Rebekka than he actually had. He could be deep in quiet and demonstratively confidential conversation with our aunt, only when Mom walked in to promptly find some excuse to leave the room: "Yes, well, I'd better be getting back to the office," he might say, or: "But we can talk about this again some other time, Rebekka." Then he would get up and leave, smiling and apparently quite unfazed. I had also noticed that he would laugh and work himself up into an artificially good mood when he was with our aunt, but only, I noticed, when he knew that Mom could hear or see them. If Mom was elsewhere, there would be nothing unusual about his behavior. Not as far as I could see, anyway.

There were times, I remember, when I interpreted all of this as the psychological aftereffects of the kidney transplant. I thought of what I had overheard while sitting on the stairs, and from that I formed the notion that Dad felt Mom had some hold over him because she had given him her kidney and that acting like a complete asshole in order to alienate her was part of a subconscious attempt to feel freer and more independent. But I was far from certain, I don't even know if it was ever more than a half-formed thought. Mom and Dad didn't talk to me or Rikard about what was going on, so all in all this was a confusing time for me. I had the feeling that everything around me was falling apart, but I didn't know why or how. Nor did I have anyone to talk to. Aunt Rebekka, who was normally so outspoken, preferred not to discuss the matter, I could tell, because whenever I made some remark that invited her to comment on what was happening in the house, I came up against a brick wall. She would either act as if she didn't know I was fishing for her thoughts on the situation, or find some excuse to leave the room. Rikard was as much in the dark about what was going on as I was, so he was no help. He didn't care anyway, or at least he tried to give that impression. When Dad took a little dig at Mom, for example, and Mom responded by looking even more hurt than she really needed to—possibly to make Dad feel guilty, I don't know—Rikard would laugh and make it very clear that he regarded this as no more than a bracing little interlude.

Of all the family Rikard was the one who changed the most during this time. Although I'm not sure when it started, he slowly but surely changed from a "little Gandhi" to being, if not exactly nasty, then at any rate the rather aggressive and arrogant sort of cynic that often comes to mind when the terms "West Side brat" or "Young Conservative" are mentioned. Or no, come to think of it, maybe he didn't change that much after all. His Gandhi-like manner had, after all, also been a sign of a certain arrogance and aggression, a means of making other people—not least his former tormentors—feel like reprobates and losers; a passive-aggressive psychological weapon, in other words. So maybe Rikard hadn't really changed all that much, maybe it was the climate at business school, which he went to straight after junior high, that encouraged him, as it were, to become a new version of himself, a persona tailored to fit the preppy mentality up there in Tromsø. Actually, when I think about it, I'm sure that's it. And the fact that Dad was busy building up the new company at that time and that he was referred to in the newspapers as an entrepreneur, a captain of industry, and "the Salmon King of Bangsund" may also have been a contributing factor. Maybe this led Rikard to see himself as a future business magnate and maybe this in turn inspired him to give vent to this inherent arrogance and aggression in ways he considered befitting a budding captain of industry. I don't know. In any case, he gradually adopted a style that went perfectly with the copy of the *Wall Street Journal* he always had tucked under his arm. He wore his hair slicked back and used expensive aftershave. He ironed his own shirts as soon as they were washed and while he may not have panicked, he certainly felt very out of sorts if he happened to forget and had to go to school wearing a creased shirt, anybody could see that. Aunt Rebekka called him "our little banker," but "our little yuppie" was more like it. I certainly wasn't the only one to suspect that the famous yuppies whom the papers were so full of in the eighties were his role models and that he had a vague dream of becoming some sort of playboy, with a bottomless bank account, a mobile phone (a real status symbol in those days), and a red convertible with a busty blonde in the passenger seat. Had it stopped at that, my relationship with Rikard might not have been as bad as it actually was at that time, but it didn't. Rikard was as unsure of himself and as intent on discovering who he was and what to do with his life as everyone is at that age, I suppose—and the fact that he overdid it and turned himself into a caricature of a yuppie was in itself, of course, evidence of that. But just like some rockers I knew who tried to define their identities by disdaining people who exercised and ate healthily, so Rikard tried to define himself by disdaining and abhorring everything and everyone that he associated with anti-capitalism and socialism. He had nothing but contempt, for instance, for the friends I had made in high school. With a couple of exceptions, although none of them were avowed socialists, they were all doing social studies and since Rikard believed that the social studies department was a fucking breeding ground for socialists, he couldn't understand why I would want anything to do with them. And the way they looked: some of them had long hair and wore clothes that must have been picked up at flea markets or the secondhand store at Namsos Rock Club. "I mean honestly, do they ever wash? Do they shower after phys ed?" he would ask, trying to look as if he was asking because he really wanted to know, but I knew, of course, that this was his way of telling me that he associated my friends with dirt and squalor. Not literally, but in the sense that they were liable to sully me with their radical ideas and radical tastes if I didn't steer well clear of them. And in that he was, to some extent, right. During my years at high school I became quite the little radical. But that's not the point here. The point is that Rikard strove so hard to live up to his obscure yuppie ideals that he eventually became insufferable. His inherent arrogance and aggression didn't only take new forms, they reached new heights. He saw himself as a king, a world champion, and he acted as if everyone else existed merely to cater to his needs. This was evident, not least, from the way he treated his girlfriends. Take Hilde, for example, whom he started dating soon after he started business school, and who received the following birthday greeting in the *Namdal Workers' Weekly*:

> Hilde, hereby single, will be nineteen on Saturday. Happy birthday and best wishes for the future, from Rikard.

But despite his appallingly cynical behavior, of which this was just one of hundreds of examples, he was very popular with the girls. Or rather, now that I think about it, possibly because of it. His urge to break the rules and go against the norms and his way of not seeming to give a shit about anyone else may have given him an air of strength and self-confidence that girls found attractive. Or maybe every girl who fell for him wanted to prove that she was the exception to the rule, that she was the one irresistible person whom Rikard would love so much he would never dream of treating her the way he had treated previous girlfriends. I don't know. It doesn't really matter anyway. What matters is that Rikard was the same as ever and yet completely different. He was no longer someone I felt I could talk to freely about anything under the sun. Indeed no one in our family was speaking to anyone else at that time. As I said, everything seemed to be falling to pieces. We all seemed to be drifting further and further apart. And then one day, without any warning, Aunt Rebekka moved out. I knew nothing about it until three plump ladies of Latin American appearance turned up on the doorstep, saying that they had come to clean the apartment in the extension and could I please give them the keys.

Børgefjell, June 24th, 2006. The greatest guitarist in the world

I look at my cell phone, but no, still no word from Julie. I left home hours ago, but she still hasn't sent so much as a text, it's unbelievable, how could she do this, canceling the wedding the minute she thinks I've been diagnosed as having MS, failing me when I need her most, so to speak. I never thought she'd do that. I stick my phone in my pocket, lean forward, prop my elbows on my knees, then straighten up again, sit like that for a moment or two, then lean forward again, I can't settle, it's like I've become infected, like my whole body is inflamed. I sigh, sit here gazing at the water. A little gust of wind ruffles the dark surface, Jan Olav's and Kristian's floats bob gently back and forth and behind me I hear the faint, brief buffeting of the tent wall.

"This coffee tastes really odd," I hear Jan Olav say. Strange how well their voices carry up here, they have to be at least a hundred feet away, but they could be sitting right next to me.

"I like it," Kristian says. "Proper campfire coffee."

Jan Olav takes another swallow, blinks, and screws up his face as the coffee hits his mouth, then promptly turns and spits it out onto the rock.

"Aw, Jesus! It tastes fishy, don't tell me you haven't noticed?"

Kristian puts the little wooden cup to his nose, sniffs.

"Yeah, well," he mutters with a little wag of his head. "I did wash the kettle before I left, but I suppose the taste of fish might still cling to it a bit. It's a few years old now, after all."

"Might still cling to it?" Jan Olav repeats. "Don't tell me you boil fish in that kettle?"

Kristian stares at him, trying to look surprised.

"Er . . . well, I'm hardly going to bring a whole *battery* of pots and pans with me," he says, sounding as if only a madman would take two cooking utensils with him on a trip to the mountains, making himself out to be some sort of Bear Grylls character. True outdoorsmen and adventurers take only the bare essentials on their expeditions, obviously, and Kristian is a true outdoorsman and adventurer, that's the impression he's trying to give, I can tell, in fact I'm sure I've seen Bear Grylls cook fish in the same kettle that he uses for his coffee so that's probably where Kristian got the idea.

"If you ever wonder why you're still single, Kristian, that's one reason right there," Jan Olav says.

They look at each other and laugh.

"Asshole," Kristian says.

Jan Olav gives another little laugh, glancing at me as he does so, as if wanting to include me, wanting me to laugh along with them, but I can't find it in me, I don't feel like laughing, so I pretend I haven't noticed. I yawn and turn away as casually as I can, stare blankly at the black lake for a moment or two, then slip my hand into my pocket and take out my cell again, it's ridiculous to check again so soon, but I can't help it. I flip up the cover with my thumb and take a look, but no, no texts and no missed calls, I can't believe this is happening. I snap the lid shut and pop the phone back in my pocket, gaze at the ground, gaze out across the lake, then down at the ground again, I can't relax, it's like I've been infected, I can't settle, it's a bit like the time when I had a slipped disk and tossed and turned in bed, unable to find a single position that didn't hurt.

Silence.

"Hey, have you ever tried Sauternes with Roquefort?" I hear Jan Olav say.

"I've tried it with port, but not Sauternes," Kristian says.

"Well, you'll get the chance later. I've got an eighty-six Château Lafaurie-Peyraguey in my bag."

"*Here?*" Kristian asks.

"What?"

"You lugged cheese and wine all the way up *here?*"

"Yeah," Jan Olav says. "Only the one bottle, though."

Kristian just stands there staring at him for a moment, then he grins and shakes his head.

"Cheese and wine on a fishing trip," he says. "Are you sure you're not gay?"

They eye each other and laugh quietly and I immediately avert my gaze, I know Jan Olav's going to look this way and try to get me to laugh along with them, but I can't, a little later maybe, but not right now. I get up, go over to the little stack of firewood farther up the slope, pick up a pure white branch, snap off the biggest twigs, and put them all on the fire, glancing across at Kristian and Jan Olav as I do so. Kristian has caught another fish, I see, he's got the line in his left hand and is trying to grab the wriggling trout with his right. He struggles for a few seconds before getting a firm grip on it. He prizes the hook out of the trout's mouth, makes a fist, and punches it on the head, once, twice. I almost burst out laughing when I see this, that's another thing he's picked up from those wilderness survival programs, that's exactly how Bear Grylls kills a fish.

"Well, that's dinner organized," he says.

I sit down on a rock, regard them.

"I'll carry on awhile longer," Jan Olav says.

"But we've plenty now," Kristian says.

"Yeah, I know, but I'd like to catch something before I call it a day."

Kristian looks at him, trying to appear both amused and amazed.

"I want to catch something too," he says, smirking. "What are you, seven?"

"Ah, but you see, I fish mainly for the fun of it," Jan Olav says.

"I realize that. But if you do catch a fish now we'll just have to throw it back. And that's kinda stupid, don't you think?"

"Aw, give me a break, man! I'm married with three kids, I get enough hassle at home!" Jan Olav says, laughing, but he means it too, I can hear it in his voice, he's not all that happy about Kristian's antics either: the way he seems to expect us all to play at being team Grylls on expedition, all the little digs he just has to get in, the comments he makes every time we say or do something that doesn't fit with the game, Jan Olav is getting a bit sick of it too, I can tell by his face and his voice. But Kristian doesn't notice, or at least he doesn't appear to, he chuckles happily as he fastens the hook to the eye on the reel.

Silence.

I pick up a twig and poke it into the fire, stir the embers a little. I never thought Julie would fail me like this, that she would let me go just when I need her most. I was sure she would send me a text once she'd had time to think things over, I thought she'd write to say that she'd been in shock and not thinking clearly, that she felt awful and wanted me to come home, that she loved me, that we'd always be together, something along those lines, that's what I had hoped she'd do, what I expected her to do. But I haven't heard from her at all. Not a word. She simply doesn't want me anymore, not now that she thinks I have MS, I can't believe it. I draw the twig carefully out of the fire, the tip has caught light, and a thin, slanting streamer of smoke rises from it. Then I hear Kristian humming, I look up and there he is, coming toward me with his fishing rod in one hand and a string of five trout in the other.

"Nice fish," I say, with an attempt at a smile.

"Gosh, are you here as well?" he says.

"What do you mean am I here?" I ask, acting as if I don't know what he's talking about.

He leans his rod against the front of the tent.

"What's up with you, anyway?" he asks.

I don't answer straightaway, don't know what to say, all I know is that I can't tell him the truth, I can't have it getting out that I lied about having MS, not when it's had the consequences it seems to have had, I couldn't bear that. And I can't lie to them as well and tell *them* that I've got MS, although to some extent it would make sense to tell Kristian and Jan Olav the same story as I've told Julie, there's always a chance that one or the other of them might mention it to her at some point, so it's important that I tell them all the same story, but I just can't face sitting here all evening being showered with sympathy that I don't deserve, I'm not that sentimental. Nor do I have the conscience for it.

"Hey?"

"What?"

"I asked if anything was the matter."

I just sit there looking at him for a moment.

"I'm a bit tired, that's all," I say, trying to give him a tired little smile. He nods, but he doesn't believe me, he knows there's something wrong, I can tell by his face. He holds my eye for a second, then he wanders back down to the water, lays the string of fish on the rock, pulls his knife from its sheath, and starts to clean them.

Then Jan Olav appears, he's called it a day after all. He grins at Kristian.

"I'm only here because I'm dying for a drink, okay?" he says. "Just don't go thinking that I listen to a word you say."

Kristian gives a little laugh and carries on cleaning the fish, Jan Olav looks at me and smiles good-naturedly as he props his rod up next to Kristian's. I shut my eyes, open my mouth, and give a long yawn, I'm not the least bit tired, but I yawn anyway, possibly in an instinctive attempt to make them think I'm worn out and use this as an excuse for being even more distracted and quiet than usual, I don't know, but whatever the case I have to get a grip now, I shouldn't take what's happened between Julie and me out on Jan Olav and Kristian, I have to play along with Jan Olav when he tries to include me, I don't want to be the sort of killjoy who resists all efforts to cheer him up and who slowly but steadily drains everyone else of energy. I know I can be like that sometimes and that that's how I've been so far on this trip, but now I've got to snap out of it, it's not easy, but I've done it before and I have to at least make an effort. I poke the stick into the embers and twirl it around, hear the soft rustle of coals and cinders shifting, the fire's almost dead, I'll have to go and find some more firewood soon. Kristian and Jan Olav have seen to dinner, so I guess I'd better do my bit. I glance across at them as I pull the stick back out of the fire. Sounds like they're talking about music, they've talked a lot about music on this trip, and now they're at it again.

"Hey, have you heard *The Runners Four*?" Jan Olav asks.

"Aw, yeah, holy shit," Kristian says.

"Great, eh?"

"Brilliant."

"Just their use of contrast," Jan Olav says eagerly. "All the changes in tempo and rhythm, the shifts from those full-on, hard-hitting passages to the softer, more pared down sections, not to mention the lead singer, that sweet little-girl voice, the way it offsets the fuzz guitar and the dynamic drumming. All that, all those contrasting elements, they make it so . . . rich."

"I know," Kristian says. "It reminds me a bit of the Pixies, but this is actually even more interesting and effective. I think it has to be one of the most powerful things I've heard in a long time."

Brief pause.

Then Jan Olav turns to me and smiles.

"Have you heard *The Runners Four*?" he asks.

"I've heard one album," I say, it just comes out. I've never heard *The Runners Four*, never heard of the band at all, in fact, but I say it anyway, in an instinctive attempt to join in the conversation. "A while ago," I add. "I can't quite remember what it was called, but I liked it, I remember that much."

"You've heard one album?" Kristian says. "*The Runners Four is* an album, Marius. It's the latest from Deerhoof."

He turns to Jan Olav, grinning, and Jan Olav grins back. I swallow, feel my cheeks start to burn.

"Isn't there a band by that name as well?" I venture, but it's no use, they know I've never heard of a band or an album called *The Runners Four* and they're laughing at this pathetic attempt to act as though I know more than I do, they don't even reply to my question.

"Good old Jethro Tull, are they still where it's at?" Jan Olav says, trying a bit of friendly leg-pulling now.

"*Aqualung*!" Kristian says, smirking. "Is that still their best album, Marius?"

I look at him. I mustn't get upset, it would be stupid to get upset by a little thing like this. It might be okay when you're fifteen and being part of the gang is all that matters, but not when you're thirty-six. I try to chuckle, to show that I can laugh at myself, but it doesn't sound too convincing, I don't want to get upset, but I am, they can tell just by looking at me.

"Oh, well," Jan Olav says, sounding as if he's ready to leave it at that, as if wanting to let me off the hook by changing the subject. But Kristian won't drop it, he's still grinning.

"Okay, so who's the greatest guitarist in the world?" he says, talking now the way we used to do fifteen to twenty years ago, like he's implying that I haven't moved on from there. "Clapton or Hendrix," he goes on, turning to Jan Olav and grinning and Jan Olav sniggers back at him, he's feeling sorry for me and he doesn't want to laugh, but he can't help it. "Or Jimmy Page, maybe?"

"Believe it or not, I have actually listened to other music over the past few decades," I say, unable to conceal the note of irritation in my voice, I look straight at him and try to grin back. "Even if I haven't been listening to the same stuff as you."

"Okay, so what have you been listening to?" Kristian asks. He must have guessed that I don't keep up with what's happening on the music scene anymore and he doesn't mind challenging me on this, he looks straight at me, still grinning, waiting for me to reply. I hold his eye, frantically trying to think of an artist or a band that I like, a name he might not have heard of, but I can't, I feel my irritation growing.

"Oh, this and that" is all I say.

"Like what, for instance?"

"Oh, for Christ's sake, guys," Jan Olav says, staring in astonishment at me, then at Kristian, then he gives a little laugh. "What *is* this?"

Kristian and I hold each other's eyes for another second or two, then we both laugh awkwardly, laugh as if we were only joking, trying to ease the tension and move on by pretending that we weren't really spoiling for a fight.

Silence.

Jan Olav saunters up the slope to the tent, unzips the flap, and ducks inside, I hear him rummaging around in there, then he reappears clutching a bottle of whisky.

"Fancy a drink, anyone?"

"What is it?" Kristian asks.

"Springbank."

Kristian shrugs.

"It's probably way too expensive for me to have heard of it," he says. He sets his knife down on the rock, dips his hands in the water, and rinses off the fish blood. "But I'll have a taste."

"It's not expensive at all," Jan Olav says, unscrewing the top, I hear the faint snap as the seal breaks. "But it's good. Bob Dylan's favorite whisky, actually!"

"Wow, Bob Dylan, eh!" Kristian says. He puts a hand to his face and twirls his beard, looking at me and grinning, says nothing for a moment. He's trying to come up with a joke about how I'm still listening to the same sixties and seventies music as we were listening to twenty years ago, that's what he's doing, I know it is, this should be just the whisky for you, Marius, that's what he's about to say, or something like that, but he doesn't get the chance.

"Yeah, yeah," Jan Olav says. He knows Kristian inside out and he realizes as well as I do what he's thinking.

"What?" Kristian says, pretending to look baffled, as if he has no idea what Jan Olav means. They eye each other for a moment or two, saying nothing, and then they both laugh knowingly. I feel an immediate surge of annoyance, their shared laughter only seems to confirm that they see me as somebody who got left behind twenty years ago and that pisses me off. I give it a second, then I open my mouth and give a long yawn, I just do it, possibly in an unconscious attempt to make them think that I'm bored, that I'm not bothered by what I'm hearing, I simply don't find it funny, that's the impression I'm trying to give, I suppose.

"Honestly, you two," I hear Jan Olav say. I turn to him, slowly and as casually as I can. He laughs softly and shakes his head as if he despairs of us as he pours whisky into Kristian's wooden cup. "You sound like an old married couple, do you realize that?" he says, trying to smooth things over between Kristian and me. Comparing us to an old married couple is a way of reminding us that we used to be the best of friends, that we're really very fond of each other and this is all just a bit of harmless banter. "Well, I for one get enough of marital bickering at home. A weekend away with the guys should be a break from all that," he says. I don't think he really has any serious marital problems, although you never know, of course, but Jan Olav and Kjersti certainly seem like the perfect couple, so he's probably just saying this in order to strengthen the bonds between us guys, lying about having the odd marital spat to show Kristian and me how much our friendship matters, it's like an arena in which we can get away from all the hassle and the nagging and simply be ourselves, and we have to cherish this and not spoil it, that's what he's trying to say.

"Sorry?" he says, raising his eyebrows and looking at me with a smile on his lips.

"Hm?"

"Arena?"

"Arena?" I say.

"You said *arena*," Jan Olav says.

I look at him, saying nothing; *arena*, did I say that, I wasn't aware of it, but if he says I did, then I must have. There's silence for a moment, then Kristian bursts out laughing, looks at the ground, shaking his head and laughing wryly. I swallow, suddenly feeling my cheeks start to burn again, sweat breaks out on my brow and the back of my neck, I raise a hand to wipe it away, try to make it look as though I'm brushing away a speck of grit or something, I'm embarrassed at being embarrassed, so I try to hide it, do it quite instinctively.

"Have a whisky," Jan Olav says, smiling amiably and holding out the bottle.

"No thanks," I say, although I wouldn't mind a whisky, actually, and I regret it as soon as I've said it.

"Sure?"

"Positive," I say. I don't know why I say it, a form of protest perhaps, an act of defiance maybe; declining the offer, not taking a drink on a guys' trip is like refusing to be sociable and maybe that's what I'm trying to do, they made me feel like an outsider, laughing at me like that, so maybe this is an instinctive attempt to prove to them and myself that I'm not particularly interested in being sociable anyway, an attempt to tell them that I don't need them.

"Okay," Jan Olav says, sounding rather disappointed, looking disappointed too, he turns away with a tight, frustrated smile on his lips. I understand his frustration, of course, he's doing all he can to cheer me up, to make me feel included, and I reject every one of his advances. I don't mean to, but I do—I can't help thinking about what went on between Julie and me, it was so awful but still, I can't go on like this, I don't want to be a drag, draining the others of energy, I don't want to be like this, moody and tight-lipped and not entering into the spirit of things. I look at Jan Olav and swallow, I need to snap out of it, do the sociable thing and accept the offer of a whisky after all. Hey, you know what, I should say, maybe I will have a wee dram after all. Either that or say I'd rather have a vodka, but I wouldn't mind trying the whisky afterward, there would be nothing strange about me saying that, it would sound perfectly natural, so I ought to just say it. But I don't, I can't, my mouth won't open, my thoughts seem to congeal in my head, they seem to solidify before they can be put into words and I just sit here, moody and tight-lipped, sinking deeper and deeper into myself. I watch Jan

Olav wander a little farther up the slope. He screws the top on the bottle and sets it down in the heather, then he bends his head and goes back into the tent, I hear him fumbling with something, poor Jan Olav, he's doing every-thing he can to make me feel included, but I'm resisting all his efforts, I hate myself when I'm like this.

Silence.

I straighten one leg, stick my hand in my pocket, and pull out my cell phone again, I just have to check one last time, I wish Julie would get in touch to say that she wasn't thinking clearly and that she wants me, of course she does, even though I have MS, so I can't resist checking. I flip up the cover, look at the screen, but no, still no word from her, I can't believe it, I thought her love went deeper than that, I ache inside just thinking about it. I swallow, raise my eyes, and look at Kristian as I snap my phone shut. He shoots me a slightly exasperated glance, his eyebrows raised higher than usual, looking as if he's about to sigh and mutter "for Christ's sake," but he doesn't. He turns away without a word and carries on gutting the fish, sticking the knife into a trout and slitting the belly open. It takes a moment for it to dawn on me what he's so pissed about: of course, it's my cell, phones are exactly the sort of thing that make it hard for Kristian to lose himself in his son-of-the-wilderness role, that's why he looks so fed up every time I take out my phone, he thinks I should have switched it off and left it in the car, the way he did. I look at him, feel myself growing more and more irritated by this ludicrous pose of his, he's never been the outdoor type and I'd bet anything he'd never last half as long in the wilderness as I would, but now here he is acting like Bear Grylls, it's too ridiculous for words. I wait a moment, then open my phone again. I shouldn't antagonize him more than absolutely necessary, it's childish of me, but I can't help it. I look at him, then down at my cell, then up at him again, wait for him to turn and glance this way, but he doesn't. He sticks his hand into the fish's belly, pulls out the glistening entrails, and slings them off into the undergrowth, he makes no move to turn around, instead he hunkers down, dips the fish into the water, and alternates between rinsing it and scraping the inside. I wait a moment longer, then I go into Settings and activate the function that causes the phone to beep every time I press a key. There, I think, that's sure to make him turn around. I grin to myself as I press some keys at random, the beeps they make are soft enough, but they still sound pretty loud out here, where it's so quiet, and Kristian immediately turns to look at me. I pretend not to notice, put the phone to my ear, and pretend to be waiting for someone to answer.

Silence.

And then, all of a sudden, he starts to sing: "No woman, no cry." I look at him, it's no coincidence that he's singing this, of all songs, that I don't believe, he's made the connection between me constantly checking my phone and the fact that I've been so quiet and distracted, and from that he's made the assumption that something has happened between Julie and me, that must be it. I feel a stab of resentment, I'm starting to get angry, but I can't let it show, because then he'll realize he's right on target, and I'm not going to give him the pleasure. I snap my phone shut and slip it back into my pocket. He's still sitting there singing "No woman, no cry," singing a little louder now.

Two seconds.

"Don't make more of a fool of yourself than you have to,

Kristian," I say. I don't want to rise to the bait, but I can't help it.

"What? Is my singing that bad?"

"Asshole."

He grins, waits.

"Yeah, well, when the cat's away and all that," he says, still grinning, waits a moment more, then turns away again and goes back to cleaning the fish. It takes a second for me to realize what he's getting at. I feel my anger rising, he's trying to suggest that Julie is being unfaithful to me, or, at least, that I'm afraid she will be while I'm here, he's implying that I'm a jealous loser who's obsessed with keeping tabs on his girlfriend, that that's why I'm forever checking my cell, and there is some truth in that, I do have a bit of a jealous streak, but he doesn't know that, or at least I don't think he does.

"Yep, I'm glad I only have myself to think about."

A wry laugh escapes me.

"Yeah, that'll be right."

"Hm?" he says, laying the freshly cleaned trout on the rock.

"D'you think I don't know what you're doing when you talk and act like this, you're trying to convince both me and yourself that being single is a whole lot better than it actually is," I say, sneering at him.

"What are you talking about?"

"Ever since you got your degree and started work, all you've wanted is to have a wife and family and acting as though being single is better than having a girlfriend is just a way of dealing with your frustration, d'you think I don't see that?" I say. "As though it's somehow easier to cope with the sadness of not having a family if you can convince yourself that it's great to be single, right? Plus it's a good way to boost your self-esteem. You feel you're a failure because you'll be forty soon and you still don't have a girlfriend and the only thing you can do to feel better about yourself is to convince yourself and everyone else that the single life is something you've actually chosen, d'you think I don't see that?" I say, getting more and more worked up, talking faster and louder now, never taking my eyes off him. "You've got desperation written all over you, Kristian, it's there in just about everything you say and do. Look at all the changes in style you've gone through over the years. They're all part of the same thing: If the black-clad rocker look doesn't win you a woman, you go to the other extreme and try your luck as a slick-suited politician, stand as a candidate for the Trondheim branch of the Labor Party and all that. And now you've reinvented yourself as Bear Grylls."

"Bear Grylls?"

"Yeah, now you're playing at being the son of the wilderness, that's the image you'll be presenting, for a while at least."

"Oh, really?"

"Don't pretend you don't know what I'm talking about," I sneer indignantly, shutting my eyes and shaking my head.

"But I *don't* know what you're talking about," he says, looking amused. He spreads his hands and smiles broadly, shaking his own head.

"My God," I sneer. "You've thrown yourself into the part of the great adventurer as wholeheartedly as you do every new persona, so nobody can help noticing. Not only have you taken up fly tying and fly-fishing and God knows what all, you've even started acting the way all converts do.

You frown on everything that doesn't fit with this fucking wilderness ideology of yours, or whatever you call it. You hate the fact that Jan Olav brought some cheese and wine with him. And every time you catch sight of my cell phone, you look like you've stepped on a nail. Any reminder of the modern world, of civilization and culture makes it harder for you to see yourself as some sort of wild man of the woods when we're up here, that's why you can't abide the fact that we've brought them with us, right? It ruins your image of yourself as the great adventurer on an expedition into the wilderness," I say, almost shouting now, the words spilling out, my voice almost cracking from spite and fury. I suddenly notice that my chin is wet, I put up a hand and quickly wipe away the spittle from the corner of my mouth, never taking my eyes off Kristian.

He opens his mouth, raises his eyebrows, and shakes his head.

"So this is what's been going through your mind, this is what you've dreamed up while Jan Olav and I have been enjoying ourselves?" he says.

"Really, though, we should be as hairy faced and scruffy as you," I say, simply picking up where I left off, I've hardly said a word for the whole trip, but now it's pouring out of me, I'm so mad. "And obviously we should have subscribed to the same spartan ideals as yourself, and made a game out of traveling as light as possible, right? Calculating how many calories a particular type of food contains compared with how heavy it is to carry, all that sort of thing. A fanatic, that's what you are. No matter what fucking persona you adopt, you always have to take it to the extreme," I snarl, not taking my eyes off him, I glare at him and he just sits there smiling, with his mouth half-open and his eyebrows raised, trying to look both surprised and amused.

"Is that so?" is all he says.

"Marius," says Jan Olav.

"And underneath it all, of course, you're actually so deeply insecure and so disappointed with yourself," I say.

"Marius . . ."

"You're so full of self-loathing, Kristian, you always have been, but your lack of success with women has made you a thousand times worse. You try frantically to find yourself a girlfriend, but it gets you nowhere, and if no girl will have you, you don't want yourself either, so you shed your skin, so to speak, you reinvent yourself," I say. A shudder of triumph runs through me as I hear myself say it, it's well observed and well said and I glare at him, grinning that furious grin. "You do it again and again and again. And always with the same total commitment and desperate enthusiasm. And now you're playing at being a son of the wilderness. Now that's the image you're trying on for size, to see if that will help you to achieve your goal. It's so pathetic words fucking fail me," I say, then I let out a fierce bark of laughter and whip around to face Jan Olav, he's standing outside the tent, eyeing me gravely, looking troubled and sad. I fix my eyes on him, shake my head, and give another bark of laughter, as if laughing like this will convince Jan Olav that I'm right, that Kristian really is pathetic and ridiculous. As if laughing like this will persuade Jan Olav to take that grave, troubled look off his face and laugh at Kristian along with me. It won't, though, I know that, it's such a shrill, unnatural laugh, the sort of manic laugh that no one would ever believe could had been brought on by something funny, even I can hear that, I can hear how demented I sound, but I have to stop now, here I am, laughing this laugh that I don't recognize, it's like some other man is laughing through me. Just a moment more, then I take a deep breath and snap my mouth shut, cutting off the laughter: I really have to get a grip now, I can't go on like this. I shut my eyes, put a hand to my head, dig my fingers into my hair, and pull back sharply, tug my hair so hard that the corners of my closed eyes are slanted upward to my temples and I feel my scalp shift a fraction over my skull. I sit like that for a moment, then I loosen my grip and let my hand drop into my lap.

"Sorry, Kristian," I blurt, doing a complete about-face and apologizing to him. I wait a moment, then I open my eyes and look at Kristian, he's crouched down, staring at his hands and shaking his head helplessly, his face as grave as Jan Olav's now. "I didn't really mean it," I say and a soft little laugh escapes me, a very different laugh from before, but just as unnatural, a laugh that says this is no big deal, an attempt to laugh the whole thing off. But it's no use. This is no laughing matter and Jan Olav and Kristian are both stone-faced. I lower my eyes, my laughter subsiding to a faint, hesitant chuckle, then I just sit there, smiling wanly, staring at the fire, I feel my face flushing, the sweat breaking out on my brow and the back of the neck.

Silence.

"Well, what a great trip this turned out to be," Kristian says, jumping to his feet. "Fuck!"

"Kristian," Jan Olav says, in a voice that's begging him to let it go, not to lose his temper.

"You see, what did I say?" Kristian fumes and I feel my

stomach churn, I look at him and swallow, look at the fire again, they've obviously discussed this beforehand, weighed up the pros and cons of having me along on this trip, I can tell from Kristian's words, neither of them was all that keen on me coming, they were afraid I would put a damper on things, but Jan Olav must have felt they had no choice but to ask me, I suppose he felt obliged to invite me, what with him being my best man and all, I feel my cheeks getting hotter and hotter, feel my brow burning.

"Kristian," Jan Olav says again, in the same beseeching tone as before, and Kristian shakes his head at him, gives it a moment, then snorts. He looks like he's struggling to comply with this plea to keep his temper and let it go, but he can't, he turns to face me again, I swallow and promptly look away, gaze into the fire again.

"You ought to take a bit more part in the conversation, Marius," he says. "If only to give yourself a reality check every now and again."

"Okay" is all I say, my voice suddenly very flat, I feel flat too, flat and empty.

"You seem to want things between us to be the same as they were fifteen or twenty years ago," he says. "You want us to be the same as we were back then and you seem to regard any change in Jan Olav or me as a betrayal of some sort. That's why . . . that's why you're so afraid of change and so fucking wary of it, you see ghosts in broad daylight and you paint a picture of me that . . . well, that I simply don't recognize. The man you've just described, Marius, he doesn't exist anywhere except inside that terrified mind of yours."

"Okay," I say again, staring fixedly at the fire, hot and red-faced. I swallow.

"All right, guys, now let's all calm down, otherwise the whole weekend will be ruined," Jan Olav says.

Silence.

Kristian looks at the ground, snorts again, and gives a little shake of his head, sits a moment, then takes a deep breath and sighs.

"I'll drink to that," he says.

Namsskogan, July 12th, 2006

December 23rd, 1993: I had just got off the local train from Trondheim to Steinkjer and thought I had plenty of time to walk up into the town center and grab a hot dog before the bus left for Namsos. I would have had too, I'm sure, if I weren't so notoriously clumsy. As it was, I managed to sprain my ankle pretty badly in stepping off an unexpectedly high curb and instead had to limp slowly back, moaning and groaning, only to see my bus leave the station and turn out onto the road, much too far away for there to be any point in frantically waving my arms in the air, which of course is exactly what I did. So there was nothing to do but park myself on one of the benches inside the station building and wait for the next bus. And then I saw her: Aunt Rebekka. I hadn't laid eyes on her since she had packed her bags and left Bangsund several years earlier. She looked even fatter, her face even puffier and flabbier, but her step was as firm as ever, her red lipstick as vividly scarlet; she was wearing a big red hat with matching gloves and a dark brown, almost black coat that looked to me like fur but was most likely a cheap fake. She was genuinely happy to see me and even happier when I told her that my bus didn't leave for another two hours and that I had both the time and the inclination to go home with her for a cup of coffee.

It turned out that she lived only a couple of minutes away, in an apartment that her son, the much-talked-of but to me as-yet-unknown son who had been fostered out, had bought for her when he moved to Steinkjer some years earlier. "He's an architect," Aunt Rebekka told me. Not once, not twice, but a whole five times.

I remember thinking, as I sat there eating Christmas cookies, sponge cake, and almond wreath—which she said she was so glad to have help to finish—that she had decorated her surprisingly spacious apartment for Christmas in typical Aunt Rebekka fashion. On every windowsill and table, on every free space on the floor she had arranged homemade Christmas elves and little families of mice dressed in dolls' clothes so rich in detail that they must have taken her years to make. The walls and doors were decked with wreaths, seasonal wall hangings, and bellpulls proclaiming "Merry Christmas." Ornaments, baubles, and tinsel had been hung from curtain rods and festive curtains and the plastic Christmas tree was so heavily adorned it was a wonder the branches could bear the weight. In short, Aunt Rebekka had decorated her home according to the late, lamented Liberace's motto that too much of a good thing is wonderful. And that was my aunt to a T: she was too much of a good thing and she was wonderful. But there was one thing missing, I noticed: there were no presents under the tree. I distinctly recall sitting there staring at the bare Christmas-tree foot and suddenly being filled with a sense of sadness, one that grew and grew. I tried to dismiss this feeling by accusing myself of being too sentimental. She was bound to have lots of women friends; she probably wasn't as lonely as the absence of parcels might suggest, I told myself, but it did no good, and a moment later our eyes met and I could see that she knew what I was thinking. There was silence for a second or two and then, out of the blue, I found myself saying I wished she would come to Bangsund and spend Christmas with Rikard and me and Mom and Dad, nobody should be on their own at Christmas.

Unfortunately that was not possible, she told me, before proceeding to give me an explanation that began with the words: "As I'm sure you realized long ago"—although this could not have been more wrong, since it had never occurred to me that she and Dad "were a little more than just good friends when I was staying with you," as she put it. "We tried to fight it, but we can't always control these things. You're old enough to know that, I'm sure," she went on, and while I sat there, feeling dazed, confused, and more than a little shocked to think that my father—whom I had never imagined as having any more sex drive than was needed to get Mom pregnant twice—had in fact been unfaithful to her, and with her sister at that, she went on at length about how jealous Mom had always been and how livid she was when she walked in on my dad and my aunt in the office one morning. "I left that very evening and I haven't spoken to Klara since. She wanted nothing to do with me and to be perfectly honest I don't think she'd be too happy about you being here now either," Aunt Rebekka said, lighting a menthol cigarette and blowing the smoke out of the corner of her mouth. "You mustn't blame Kåre, though, he really tried to fight his feelings for me, but he couldn't, he was as much in love with me as I was with him and you have to remember that this was just after he had been told that he wasn't your father, so he was convinced that your mother had been unfaithful to him, you know? And he felt he had the right to do the same. It wasn't till much later that they found out you had been mixed up with another baby in the maternity ward and that Klara wasn't your mother, you see."

My face must have been an absolute picture.

"Oh, dear God in heaven. You didn't know? They never told you? After all these years? Not a word?"

That same evening I confronted Mom and Dad with what my aunt had said and they were forced to tearfully admit that it was all true. The blood tests that had been taken to find a suitable kidney donor had revealed that I couldn't possibly be Dad's biological son and it was this news and not his kidney trouble that had been mainly to blame for the manic depression I described earlier. The same went for Mom. She had never slept with anyone else, she told both Dad and the doctors, so I *had* to be his son. But more tests were done, with exactly the same result, and this, together with the fact that she could only look on helplessly as Dad and Aunt Rebekka grew closer and closer with every day that passed, led her to sink into the same darkness as Dad. The day after she kicked our aunt out, she and Dad had agreed it would be best if they got a divorce and I'm sure they would have done, if yet another discussion with the doctors had not revealed that there was no match between her blood group and mine either, so we couldn't possibly be mother and son.

I felt bewildered, stunned, and angry at them for having known about this for five or six years and never saying anything to me about it, but by the next day I had recovered enough to speak and think relatively rationally about what had happened and by the end of that evening, Christmas Eve of all nights, we had all kissed and made up and assured one another that we loved each other every bit as much as before. My biological origins didn't matter, we agreed. They were my parents and I was their son, nothing could change that, and I was no more interested than they were in tracing my real parents and the boy with whom I had been confused.

But only days after this, late in the evening on New Year's Day, something happened that put that love to the test. Because Mom began to wonder how on earth Aunt Rebekka could have known that she was not my real mother.

"I've never told a soul, and certainly not Rebekka, I haven't seen or spoken to her since the day she left this house," she said.

"Must have been a breach of confidence," Dad muttered, suddenly finding it necessary to bend down and hunt for something in the newspaper basket. "What?" he said, when eventually forced to look up and act as if he had just noticed that Mom was still sitting staring at him. She didn't say a word. "Well—er," he said with a shrug. "They happen all the time, don't they— breaches of confidence, or so I've heard, and once word gets out, it spreads fast in a small town like Namsos."

Mamma said nothing for a moment.

Then she said: "And another thing I've been thinking about over the past day or two. That apartment in the center of Steinkjer, how could she afford that, I wonder? I mean, Rebekka's on disability benefit."

Dad shot her a look, as if to say what the hell was she insinuating, but it didn't quite work. The surprised, hurt, angry expression left his face as soon as his eyes met Mom's and he was left looking exposed, frightened, and uncomfortable.

"So, she finally did it," Mom said with a short, sad laugh and a shake of her head. "From the moment I was born, she's been jealous of me, she begrudged me everything I had and anything she couldn't take away from me she would do her best to destroy: I actually thought I had managed to save our marriage, but no. She never gave you up, Kåre, she never gave up you or your money. Well, I have to congratulate her, because it looks like she won in the end."

I had been meaning to leave the next day anyway, but since I couldn't bear to see or speak to Mom and Dad, I got up earlier than planned, left a brief note on the kitchen table, and headed back to Trondheim to continue my studies. At first I tried to do what my parents and I had agreed would be best: pretend that nothing had changed. I had had a happy childhood, I loved my mom and my dad, and I told myself that I didn't need to know anything about my real parents or about you, David. But as time went on I began to see my life from another angle, so to speak, especially my life as it had been in recent years. To cut a long story short, I began to see how differently my parents— and my father in particular—had treated Rikard and me after they learned about the hospital mix-up. Dad had never made any difference between us before, but as soon as he learned that I wasn't his natural son, he started planning for Rikard to take over the business after him. He did this in such subtle and reasonable fashion that I never thought twice about it at the time. It was only once I was back in my studio apartment in the early days of 1994 that it suddenly dawned on me why, for example, he had never interfered in my choice of study but had insisted that Rikard—who had never shown any more aptitude for or interest in economics and business management than I had—should go to business school and then to the Norwegian School of Economics. And not only that, suddenly Dad wanted Rikard to learn how the company worked, he tried to involve him in the day-to-day running of it and was keen to discuss ideas, plans, and business strategies with him. I remember how proud and pleased he was when Rikard graduated from business school with flying colors. My grades in my last year at senior high, which were, quite frankly, even better than Rikard's, did not meet with anything like the same enthusiasm. Nor did he try to involve me in his business affairs in any way. Not that he was dismissive on those rare occasions when I showed an interest and asked about things to do with the company, but he didn't exactly encourage my interest. Quite the reverse, really. He spoke and acted as if he thought it was perfectly okay, and actually quite endearing, when I said something that proved how little I knew about economics and business management. "Ah, well, we're all different," he chuckled when I misunderstood the term *insider trading*, and "It's just as well you're going to be a biologist," he chortled when I confessed to having no idea what stocks and bonds actually were. If Rikard had done the same, Dad would have got annoyed and told him to pull himself together, but he seemed to regard this inadequacy on my part as a welcome confirmation that he had done the right thing in choosing Rikard to take over the business.

The more I thought about it, alone in my studio apartment in Stadsingeniør Dahls gate in Trondheim, the harder it became to convince myself that genetics didn't matter. Since apparently it did, to Dad at any rate. When you got right down to it, I couldn't compete with Rikard, not now, not ever, and nothing could change that, not even the fact that Dad liked me better as a person than he did Rikard. And he did, I was sure of that. Because as time went on, Rikard became harder and harder to like. Dad had hoped and believed that he would shake off his preppy mentality and yuppie ideals as he got older and become more mature, but instead he did the very opposite, becoming more and more extreme, until he had not only turned into what, a few years earlier, Dad would have called a greedy, irresponsible capitalist, he actually became a representative of a social elite given to cynicism and arrogance in all particulars, highfliers who didn't even try to hide the fact that they regarded anyone earning a paltry 200,000 kroner a year as an inferior species. I visited Rikard in Oslo one summer and I'll never forget how surreal it was to meet the people he mixed with. We tend to imagine that all the stereotypes and prejudices we have about people will be confounded once we get to know them a little better and I honestly did not believe that such people actually existed. I was reminded of characters from a costume drama set in a decadent upper-class society in which everyone wore a stiff upper lip, but these people were real, they were living, breathing Norwegians. To the best of my knowledge they had all grown up with the same social-democratic ideals and values as you and I, David, and yet they had espoused a lifestyle and a mode of behavior whereby it was evidently perfectly natural to order champagne costing thousands of kroner per bottle on a night in town and everyone considered it a terrific joke when a young man of their number decided one evening to see how far a poor junkie in a blue-striped tracksuit was willing to go for the thousand kroner, which was apparently the street price for a hit. "Give me twenty push-ups and the same number of sit-ups," Rikard's friend said. "That's it, yeah. Okay, now twenty high knee lifts." That was how he went on, while the others stood around them on the pavement, watching this ritual humiliation and hooting with laughter. Afterward, the party continued at a modernist villa belonging to parents who were on a skiing holiday somewhere in the Alps. I clearly remember the glammed-up party girls with their eye-wateringly expensive handbags constantly vying with one another to see who could be the most bitchy and sarcastic. Seemingly innocent questions proved, in fact, to be snide insinuations, and what sounded like kind words and compliments were more likely to be gross insults. To begin with I could make next to nothing of what was going on. These young women had their own tribal language and I probably would never have caught on to the fact that they were being bitchy had it not been for the reaction when some veiled insult hit home. "You look fabulous in that tent dress, Sonja," one girl remarked to another and not until a few seconds later, when Sonja responded by spilling champagne into the first young lady's lap accidentally on purpose, did I realize that Sonja had just been called fat. Likewise, when a girl who bore a striking resemblance to Agnetha Fältskog of ABBA as she looked in the seventies, explained how she loved to stay at Jenny's after a night in town because she didn't have to shower and put on makeup before she went out to get breakfast. It didn't dawn on me until the next day, when I asked Rikard why Jenny had been in such a bad mood for the rest of the evening, that this was a way of poking fun at her because she lived in a slightly less stylish neighborhood than the other people there.

It was strange to see Rikard moving in circles so far removed from the world in which he had grown up. But there he was. Not only that, but he appeared to be something of a leading light within the group, someone whom the others looked up to and liked to be seen with. It did no harm, of course, that he was also good at his job, that he had made a lot of money out of buying and selling stocks and shares in his spare time, and, not least, that at some point in the not too distant future he looked likely to become the main shareholder in a company that had the potential to make it very big. It seems to me, however, that it must have been just as important for him to suppress and jettison, so to speak, the last traces of the person he had once been. But that he actually managed to do this, and—not least—that he wanted to do so, that was what I found so hard to understand. The mere fact that he had decided to drop his native Trøndelag dialect and switch to speaking the Bokmål of the southeast, for example. I hadn't known anything about this beforehand and when he and his new girlfriend picked me up at the airport and Rikard started talking to me in a perfect Oslo drawl, I simply assumed that either he was joking or that his girlfriend was foreign and still learning Norwegian.

But no, I was wrong on both counts. This was how he spoke now, he told me, without batting an eyelid. It has to be said, though, that later that day, when I met his aforementioned friends, I began to see why he had done this, because not only did they keep asking me to repeat Trøndelag words and phrases they evidently found incredibly funny, and not only did Jenny and Sonja agree that they felt like putting on their national costumes when they heard me talk, but the girl who looked like Agnetha Fältskog expected everyone to believe her when she said she couldn't understand a word I said and suggested that they all speak English when I was there. Nonetheless: I can't imagine many people changing the way they talk simply because they've encountered such ridiculous prejudice. And as if that wasn't enough, Rikard carried on talking like a southerner even when we were alone. I remember how ridiculous I thought that was. We were brothers, we had spent our entire childhood and most of our youth under the same roof, yet there we were, carrying on a conversation in two different languages. Now and then I almost caught myself wondering how this guy could know my mom and dad, he seemed such a stranger.

Dad could not abide this side of Rikard. Mom may occasionally have felt it was a bit much, but she was, nonetheless, far more forbearing. Unlike Dad she could see the funny side of it. Which is not to say that she thought this new Rikard was ridiculous, because I don't think she did. But she realized that there was an element of role-playing to his snobbery, a touch of the tongue-in-cheek; that he knew exactly what he was doing and that he deliberately overdid it—sometimes to tease and provoke anyone who left themselves open to being teased and provoked and sometimes simply because he liked feeling every bit as successful and superior as the role he was playing would have it. The fact that Mom possessed many of the same tendencies—take, for example, the way she used to goad Aunt Rebekka and Uncle Frederik when they were children—probably also made it easier for her to accept the new Rikard than it was for Dad. On this particular point he was more American than British, you might say. He didn't have the same appreciation of irony and subtle wit as Mom. So when, for example, some people came to the door collecting for the annual television charity appeal, Rikard slipped 500 kroner into the collection box with the words "There you go, some crumbs from the rich man's table," Dad's eyes looked as if they were about to pop out of his head, he was so angry. There were many such incidents. Dad did not find Rikard's snobbery any easier to swallow merely because Rikard knew he was being snobbish, and every time Rikard and I came home for a visit, they seemed to me to have grown further apart. Dad and I enjoyed each other's company, we laughed a lot together, but the moment Rikard walked in, the mood would change. Dad became truculent, edgy, ready to pounce on everything Rikard said or did, while Rikard for his part responded to all critical remarks and questions with sarcasm and sneers.

Still, though, I could never compete with Rikard. Not when you got right down to it. Or at least, that's what I convinced myself of as I sat there in my studio apartment, thinking back on the subtle and no doubt carefully planned way in which Dad had prepared for Rikard to take over the business. Rikard was his flesh and blood, and despite all assurances to the contrary, this meant much more to Dad than the fact that on a personal level he got on better with me than with Rikard. I remember how, when I was thinking about all this, I was reminded of a film I had seen once. I don't know what it was called, only that it was set during the Second World War and that in it there was an awful scene on the railway tracks outside a concentration camp, in which a young Jewish woman with two children is taken aside by a German SS officer. The SS officer tells her that one of her children will be allowed to live, that it is up to her to choose which, and that if she doesn't agree to this, they will both be sent straight to the gas chamber. I burned with shame for daring to compare the situation between Dad, Rikard, and me to that of this poor Jewish family. Even though the comparison had been completely involuntary and even though I did my best not to think like that, I still felt ashamed. Nevertheless: I was absolutely certain that in such a situation Dad would have chosen Rikard. And so would Mom.

And no sooner had the idea that one's biological origins really did matter begun to take root in me than it became difficult, of course, to act as though I didn't need to know who my real parents were. Where did they live, what did they do, and what were they like? Did I resemble them in appearance and manner? Did I have siblings? Did I have grandparents still living? For weeks my head buzzed with questions, night and day. I couldn't concentrate and I began to worry that it would affect my studies. So I went back home to Bangsund, to Mom and Dad and told them straight: I totally respected their wish to let bygones be bygones, but I needed to know where I came from.

And so I was told. No sooner said than done, in fact. To the great surprise of both Dad and me, it turned out that Mom already had the answers to most of my questions. She and Dad had agreed not to go digging into my background, but Mom couldn't resist it and not long after they discovered that I was not their natural son, she had managed to get hold of a list of the other women who had given birth at Namsos Hospital on the same night as she. Then it was simply a matter of elimination. Three of the six mothers had had girls, so they could be ruled out straightaway. That left Mom, Berit, and a woman from Malm by the name of Ragnhild Eilertsen. Since Berit lived closest, Mom approached her first and once they had met, there was no need to contact Mrs. Eilertsen.

Berit had learned of the mix-up years before through a close friend who worked at the maternity ward in Namsos, so she was more relieved than shocked when Mom told her why she was there. With the exception of this friend, she had never spoken to a living soul about what had happened and there was so much she wanted to get off her chest, so much she had always wondered about. Not a day had gone by when she hadn't asked herself who her own son was growing up with, how he was, and what sort of person he was, but for your sake, David, she had refused to give in to the urge to trace him, so to finally have her questions answered was a huge relief. Berit and Mom talked for hours. They wanted to know everything about their respective sons and the families in which they had grown up and they arranged to meet again the following week, partly to exchange photos of each other's children and partly to decide how to proceed, now that they had found each other. But only a couple of days before they were due to meet, Berit died, suddenly and most unexpectedly. Mom thought long and hard about getting in touch with you and telling you the whole story, but for the same reason that Berit had refrained from looking for me, she decided not to. Instead she contented herself with becoming a stalker, as she put it. To begin with scarcely a day went by without her driving past the house where you and your girlfriend lived, hoping to catch a glimpse of you. She went to events that, from the way Berit had described you, she thought you might attend, and if she was lucky enough to run into you in town, she would follow you. She sidled up next to you when you were browsing in Karoliussen or Torgersen bookshops or flicking through re-cords and CDs in Øyvind Johansen or LP-Hjørnet and on more than one occasion she sat at the table next to yours when you were in a café with friends. But she never made contact. "I just wanted to make sure he was all right," she said.

Grong, June 29th, 2006. Patties are proper grub

I crouch down and the dog lifts its head off its paws. I reach out my hand, let it lick it, then put my hand behind its ear and scratch gently.

"What's his name?" I ask.

"It's a bitch. Her name's Conny," Torstein says from the kitchen.

"Hello, Conny," I say. I run my hand from the back of her ear to the top of her head, stroke her crown, drawing the hair back and turning her eyes into narrow slits. Then Torstein appears in the doorway, regards me with those ice-blue and rather watery eyes, he seems even thinner than the last time I saw him, the chalk-white skin of his face looks like it's pasted to his cheekbones and his throat is so stripped of flesh that his carotid artery stands out in a way that gives me much the same feeling as I get when I see operations on television. Have to try not to look at that artery, it makes my stomach turn.

"We were really only meant to be looking after her while my brother was in the Philippines," he says. "But what do you know, now we're dog owners."

"So Rune decided to stay down there?" I ask.

"Rune died two days ago."

I feel my jaw drop at this, although I didn't really know Rune. I met him only that one time when Torstein invited the whole family over to meet me and on that occasion he had had to leave early to attend a church service or something, he was very religious, I remember, and that's pretty much all I remember, but still, even though I didn't know him, this news comes as a bit of a shock, not because he was my biological uncle, but because he was so young, he can't have been more than forty-seven or forty-eight.

"Oh, my God," I say, offering him my hand. "I'm so sorry."

"Thanks."

Then Gunn Torhild emerges from the kitchen.

"Gunn Torhild, I'm so sorry to hear about Rune," I say.

"Thanks," she says in her husky smoker's voice.

"He got run over by a bus," Torstein says. "The traffic's absolutely crazy down there."

"So we're in mourning, you could say," Gunn Torhild says.

"Yes, I understand," I say, nodding. "But for heaven's sake, why didn't you say when I called?" I ask.

"Say?" Gunn Torhild asks.

"That it wasn't a good time. I beg your pardon. I'll go again," I say.

"Oh no, don't," Gunn Torhild says.

"No, it's okay," I say. "I'm staying at the cottage at the moment so it's not far to drive. I can come back some other time."

"Not at all," Torstein says. "You're family, aren't you? And besides, we need to think and talk about other things now and again."

"We're glad you're here," Gunn Torhild says, smiling at

me, then she mutters something about the dinner burning, turns, and goes back into the kitchen.

"Well, if nothing else, we've got a dog now," Torstein says with a little laugh, trying to put a brave face on things now, trying to joke around, to show that he's still functioning, I suppose, that he's able to talk about other things, even though he's grieving for his brother. "She's a damn good hunting dog, you know," he says, kneeling down and scratching the dog behind the ear. He tilts his head to one side and tries to look into Conny's eyes, making little crooning sounds. His neck becomes very long and exposed when he does this and I notice how his carotid artery bulges even more. It's so horrible to look at, I can't do it, have to turn my head away.

"You can sit down now," Gunn Torhild says, switching off the range hood midsentence so that the last words seem almost to be shouted out.

"I just need to go to the bathroom," Torstein says.

I stroll into the kitchen, the air is thick with cooking fumes, and Gunn Torhild is leaning across the countertop, fiddling with the catch on the window.

"Oh, to be able to afford a new range hood," she says, waving the fumes away. "This one sounds like a small plane taking off, but it sucks up hardly anything."

I smile at her as I turn on the tap and wash my hands.

"Simen, you go and wash your hands as well," Gunn Torhild says.

"What?" Simen says from the living room.

"Wash your hands before dinner," Gunn Torhild says.

I dry my hands, then turn around. Simen is already sitting at the dining table—it's the weirdest sensation every time I see him, like seeing myself at the same age, he's every bit as long and lanky as I was and he has my face. He looks at Gunn Torhild, snorts, and gives a typical teen-age sneer.

"Would you like me to put on my suit as well?" he mumbles.

I watch him as he gets to his feet. It's obviously not standard procedure to wash your hands before meals in this house, that must be why he's reacting like this. Gunn Torhild probably only asked him to wash his hands because she wants the family to show itself in a better light than it did last time I was here. I watch Simen walking toward me, it's like looking at an earlier version of myself, almost like going back in time, I can't get over how much he resembles me. I almost reach out a hand and offer him my condolences, but I think better of it, he's so sullen faced, doesn't look like he wants to shake hands with me or anyone else.

"Sad to hear about your uncle, Simen" is all I say, careful to say "your uncle" and not "Uncle Rune," I don't know if he still feels as threatened by me as he used to, but it's best to be on the safe side. If he thought I regarded myself as a fully paid-up member of the family, he might well feel threatened and then I would just end up scaring him off, the way I did last time.

"I didn't know Rune any better than you did" is all he says, walking over to the sink and starting to wash his hands.

I watch him for a moment before going back through to the living room and sitting down, I've been given a plate with a crack in it, I see, a thin, dark line cutting across the white china.

"It's only beef patties, I'm afraid," Gunn Torhild says.

She lifts a pile of hunting and car magazines off one end of the dining table. "Would you mind handing me those papers," she says, motioning toward a couple of bills that are lying on the table in front of me, two final reminders it looks like, one from the electricity company and one for cable TV, I pretend not to notice what they are, she might find it embarrassing to have her poor finances laid bare like this, so I'm careful to look straight at Gunn Torhild as I hand her the papers.

"Patties are great," I say and am immediately struck by how strange it feels to say the word *patties*, I don't think I've ever used the word before, I've always called them rissoles.

"Oh, I know," she says, crossing to the big wooden seventies unit with the colored glass door on the middle cupboard, lays the pile of magazines down on it. "But if I'd had a bit more time I could have rustled up some proper grub, a game stew or something," she says. She heads back to the kitchen and I follow her with my eyes, *grub* is another word I've never used, a word that has never been part of my vocabulary, somehow.

"Patties *are* proper grub," I say, using both *patties* and *grub* in the same sentence, possibly in an effort to ingratiate myself with her and the rest of the family, I don't know. It feels odd, though, to talk like this, almost like stepping outside of myself.

Then Simen and Torstein return.

"I don't give a shit whether it's eco-friendly or not," Torstein is saying. "You knew damn well I didn't want an economy shower, so you can just go back to the hardware store and get that shower head changed first thing tomorrow." His eyes stay on Simen as he sits down next to me. "Damned economy showers, takes you fifteen fucking minutes to get wet, so little water comes out of them," he says, lifting his backside off the seat and pulling in his chair. Simen doesn't say anything, nor does he look at his father, he gazes into space and gives a long yawn, trying to show his father just how uninterested he is, I suppose— "See how much I care," that's the message he wants to send to Torstein by sitting there yawning like that. But this little demonstration is lost on Torstein, he flicks his red hair aside and reaches for one of the bottles on the table.

"What the hell," he suddenly exclaims. "You bought *light* beer?"

"Yes," Gunn Torhild says as she comes in carrying a large bowl of steaming corncobs.

"Christ, woman, you should have been in the fucking Gestapo!" he says.

Gunn Torhild laughs hoarsely as she places the corn on the table. Torstein laughs too, a wheezy cackle of the sort made by cartoon villains, as he puts down his bottle of light beer and rolls up the sleeves of his green flannel shirt. I eye his tattoo, the blue lines of a naked lady on his pale, freckled forearm.

"Tormenting a man with light beer!" he mutters, looking at me. "There, you see what I have to put up with?"

I give a little chuckle.

"Oh, I don't know, I think you should be pretty happy with the wife you've got," Gunn Torhild says.

"Where some things are concerned I'm very happy," Torstein says. "But we don't discuss sex at the dinner table, not when we've got company, at any rate."

And they both laugh again, Gunn Torhild emitting a rasping smoker's chuckle and Torstein his hoarse cartoon cackle, looking at me as he does so, and I manage a little laugh as well, although this is a bit near the bone for me, it's a little embarrassing, I feel my cheeks growing hot, but I laugh anyway.

"Damn fool," Gunn Torhild says, shaking her head as she goes back into the kitchen.

Torstein stops laughing, sits there eyeing Simen and grinning, because Simen's not laughing, his face is as sullen as ever.

"And you've won the lottery again, I see," Torstein says, still eyeing Simen and grinning as he plants his hands on the table and gets up. "No, goddammit, if I'm gonna have a beer, it's gonna be the real thing," he says and he follows Gunn Torhild out to the kitchen.

"*If I'm gonna have a beer*," Simen mutters with a faint sneer. I look at him, this is his way of letting me know that Torstein is still drinking as much as he's always done, I can tell.

"So how are you doing, Simen?"

He glares at me.

"Oh, I'm fucking fantastic!"

At first I don't really know what to say to this so I just nod and smile feebly.

Then Torstein reappears, humming to himself and carrying two cans of beer.

"There you go," he says, setting one of the cans in front of me, then he flicks his red hair aside and sits down.

"Thanks," I say, "but I'm driving."

"Aw, one beer won't do you any harm, will it?"

"I'd better not, thanks."

He raises his eyebrows, gives me a look that says he's never heard the like: no one in their right mind says no to a beer, do they, even if they are going to be driving, that's what he's trying to say, or something of the sort.

"Please yourself," he says, opening his own can with a little pop.

"You see," Gunn Torhild says, coming in with a bowl of something white and steaming, "that's why I bought light beer. Because I knew we had a decent guy coming to dinner."

"Oh, well, all the more for me then," Torstein says, laughing a little too loudly, a little too heartily, a laugh designed to make us think he's just joking, that he would never dream of drinking all this beer himself.

"Help yourselves," Gunn Torhild says, placing the bowl on the table.

"What the hell's that?" Torstein asks.

"Couscous," Gunn Torhild says, briskly and a mite too confidently. She obviously hasn't been sure how to serve this and she must have known Torstein would turn up his nose at it, but she took the chance anyway, probably thought it was something I would like.

"Huh?"

"Couscous."

Torstein turns to me.

"Have you heard of it?"

I nod.

"It's really good," I say.

"Yeah, sure," he mutters as he pulls the bowl toward him and inspects the contents, it looks like the kind of couscous that you pour boiling water over and leave for five minutes before serving, a sort of instant couscous.

"Well, it's fun to try something different now and again," says Gunn Torhild. "Or I think so anyway," she adds, looking at me, feeling sure that I'll agree with her, I suppose.

"I'll give you something different," Torstein mutters, pushing the bowl away.

"Oh, go on, Torstein, try it," says Gunn Torhild.

"Not on your life. You can keep your colored food," he says. "Are there any potatoes left from last night?"

"There's a dish in the fridge," Gunn Torhild says.

He gets up and disappears into the kitchen. Gunn Torhild turns to me and raises her eyebrows, as if to say she's tired of Torstein not wanting to try anything new. I doubt if she's much for it herself either, not normally—well, in any case, for some reason she seems to be trying to behave in a way she thinks I'll appreciate.

Then Torstein comes back carrying a dish of cold potatoes.

"And anyway," Gunn Torhild says, "you don't say *colored*, you say *black*."

"Colored food," Torstein sniggers, glancing at me, trying to get me to laugh along with him, but I don't, can't bring myself to, I merely flash him a quick smile, then look down at my plate as if I'm too busy eating.

"You know what I mean," Gunn Torhild says.

"Sometimes."

"I just don't like you talking like that in front of Simen."

Torstein merely gapes at her.

"Well, I *don't*," she says.

"Is it Marius you're trying to impress by acting so fucking refined all of a sudden," Torstein says, smirking at her.

"I'm sorry?" she says, pretending not to understand what he means, although she does of course, I know she does, her cheeks have gone pink and I can see that she feels offended.

"Simen's sixteen," Torstein says. "How do you think he talks when he's with his pals?"

"Oh, for fuck's sake, that's got nothing to do with it," Gunn Torhild retorts. "It's a matter of setting a good example."

"Good ex—" Torstein sneers, shaking his head. "At his age I was working as a stevedore down at Namsos docks, did you know that?"

"Let's just say you have mentioned it once or twice."

"Yeah, well, down there I worked alongside men whose language was so bad it made the seagulls blush."

"That explains a lot."

"And when I joined my first ship two years later it was even worse. Not to mention what it was like when I started on the rigs out in the North Sea," he says, talking through a mouthful of cold potato. "But these days you can scarcely say boo without people rushing in to whisk kids off to safety," he says, grinning and shaking his head as he spears a chunk of patty with his fork. "And see how the kids turn out."

"Don't start moaning about Simen," Gunn Torhild says. "He's sitting right there."

"Did I mention Simen?"

"No, but . . ."

"There, you see!" he breaks in, raising his voice slightly, he's getting worked up now, I fix my eyes on my plate and try to look as though I'm concentrating on eating. It's not pleasant when they start going on like this, I hate it. "I was talking about kids today in general. They're growing up into a generation of sissies, that's what I was saying. And it's not their fault, it's your generation that's bringing them up that way," he says, probably trying to justify his conduct as a father to Simen, sounds like he's trying to convince both himself and us that all young people would be better off if their parents were as strict and as hard on them as he appears to have been on Simen.

"Our generation's fault?" Gunn Torhild says.

"Damn right it is," Torstein says. "It starts in kindergarten. Two boys get into a fight and old women come running from all directions to tell them how bad they are. And the minute they climb onto a bike, some old woman races over and shoves a helmet on their head."

"Ah, so it's the women's fault?"

"Huh?"

"So it's us women's fault that kids are growing up to be sissies, as you call them?"

"I don't know. I can't tell the difference between women and men anymore. I'm talking about *old women*. And there's old women of both sexes out there."

"Oh, dear God, give me patience."

"It's un-fucking-believable, you know. Boys aren't even allowed to play soldiers anymore," he says, still intent on justifying his parenting of Simen, getting more and more worked up, sitting there seething at everyone who might think there was something wrong with his child-rearing skills, that's what he's doing. I try to smile and look unfazed, but I can't quite pull it off, it's hard to keep the corners of my mouth upturned, so it's a hesitant, rather insipid smile. "Or cowboys and Indians," he goes on. "They're not allowed to throw spears or shoot with bows and arrows. So don't talk to me about setting a good example, that's what I was saying. It's a hard world out there and without the examples that were set for me when I was a kid, I would have knuckled under long ago."

"Just as well Simen had such an old man for a dad then. There was no danger of him growing up to be a sissy," Gunn Torhild says.

"Yeah, well, so long as you keep all that Liberal Democrat bellyaching to yourself, everything will be fine, you'll see," Torstein says.

"Liberal Democrat bellyaching?"

"You don't say *colored*, you say *black*," he says, mimicking her.

"When the hell have I ever voted Liberal Democrat?"

"Have you ever voted at all?"

"No."

Nothing for a moment and then they both burst out laughing, eyeing each other and guffawing loudly, and I immediately feel myself relax slightly, I'm not comfortable with the way they talk to each other, but it's slightly easier to cope with when they're not arguing.

"Yeah, well, I can't really blame you for *that*," Torstein says. "The politicians we have now, fucking useless, the lot of them," he says and then he looks at me, nodding slightly as he finishes what he has in his mouth. "You know, I've actually been thinking of going into politics myself. Actually *doing* something, instead of just sitting on my backside and complaining," he says, then he pops another chunk of beef patty into his mouth. I look at him as I swallow my food, is he serious, is he deranged enough to think there could be any place for him in politics?

"Hm," I say, pretending that my mouth is still full to save having to say any more, don't know how to respond to such a pronouncement, so I just sit there chewing on air while I nod and try to look as though the thought of him going into politics is no more remarkable than that of anyone else doing so.

"And if I was elected, the first thing I would do would be to set up a local neighborhood watch," he goes on, picking up his can of beer and taking a big swig. "All the fucking riffraff that's roaming the streets these days, it's just unbelievable. Gypsies and traveling gangs from the Baltic countries and Eastern Europe robbing businesses and private individuals blind. I mean, just in the spring, for instance, there was this bunch of Romanians going around here, knocking on doors and offering to do any odd jobs. They all but pushed their way into the homes of old folk and started sharpening knives and fixing things even when people had said no thanks, you know? Mending gutters and clearing drains and cisterns and all that and then demanding outrageous sums of money for it, right? Wanting five thousand kroner for sharpening a set of knives, I mean, I ask you . . . is that what we want in our country?" he asks, trying I suppose to sound like a politician with the way he delivers this last sentence, probably imagining that this is the sort of question a real politician would ask a gathering. He gives me a stupefied look and shakes his head.

"No, it certainly isn't," I murmur and feel my face flushing, I'm embarrassed for him.

"And the police don't lift a finger, of course, they're too busy arresting folk for driving sixty miles an hour in a fifty-mile zone," he goes on, raising his voice a little, grinning and shaking his head, he appears to be getting himself worked up again. "So we'll just have to do it ourselves," he says, throwing out his arm. "Not so much for people like me. I don't need any neighborhood watch, I can look after myself," he says, picking up his beer can again. "I've got my shotgun ready if anybody should be dumb enough to try and I don't care who knows it," he says. He raises the can to his lips, about to take a drink, then changes his mind and lowers it again. "I've told Simen as well: if anybody tries to break into this house when I'm not here, he has my permission to shoot them down. I'll take full responsibility. Right, Simen?"

Simen looks at him, just for a second, then drops his eyes to his plate again, he doesn't say a word, merely nods, he knows how immature his father seems to other adults, he knows what I'm sitting here thinking about Torstein and he finds it embarrassing, poor kid, I can tell by his face. I glance across at Torstein again, he doesn't appear to have noticed that Simen's embarrassed for him, he sits there clutching his can of beer, stares at Simen for a moment, then raises the can to his lips, takes a big slug, and puts it back on the table. I open my mouth, about to express my opinion on what Torstein has just said, but I stop myself. I should maybe speak up, for Simen's sake, but I'm reluctant to get drawn into a discussion about this, there's no point in telling Torstein what I think anyway. I mean, where on earth would I start? By talking about the key principles of democracy and the rule of law in modern society and explaining how much safer and better Western society has become since these principles were established, give him a brief introduction to history, as it were? But that would just be absurd, not only because he probably has neither the patience nor the energy to listen to or consider such things, least of all now, when he's already pretty plastered, but also because he's probably not interested in the political aspects of this problem at all, he's just using this particular subject as an excuse to give vent to all the anger and frustration that's been building up inside him over decades of failure and humiliation.

"Hm?" he says and I see that he's staring at me. I look back at him, not saying anything, he must have asked me a question, but I didn't catch it.

"Sorry," I say. "I didn't quite catch that, what were you asking?"

He regards me for a moment, as if studying me with those sad, bleary eyes of his.

"I asked if I'd shocked you," he says.

I give him a strained smile.

"No, of course not."

"I'm glad to hear it. We believe in speaking our minds in this house, you see. And I intend to go on doing that when I'm elected to the district council," he says, sounding as though he's already been elected, saying "when" rather than "if," it's unbelievable, he's even worse, God help me, than the last time I was here.

"I've got to go now," Simen says.

"Go?" Gunn Torhild says.

"Yeah, I've got a Nature and Youth meeting."

"And that's another thing," Torstein says. "This Nature and Youth business." He pronounces the organization's name as if it were an STD, but Simen doesn't so much as glance at him, keeps his eyes fixed on Gunn Torhild.

"You've got time to finish your dinner, though," Gunn Torhild says.

"I need to go now if I want to get there on time," Simen says, he's probably desperate to get out of here as soon as possible, it must be hard for him to have to sit there, feeling ashamed of his father, it's embarrassing enough for me so I can't imagine what it must be like for him, being sixteen and all.

"I doubt if the sea level is going to rise that much in the time it takes you to finish your dinner," Torstein says. "Do you?" he adds, smirking at Simen, but Simen doesn't answer, doesn't look at Torstein either, he's trying to act as though his father doesn't exist as far as he is concerned. "Do you?" Torstein says again, a little louder this time, irked by the fact that Simen doesn't answer. But Simen refuses to respond, he completely ignores his father.

"It's just that the meeting starts at seven," he says, looking at Gunn Torhild as he speaks.

"Do you, Simen?" Torstein says for the third time, raising his voice another notch. Most individuals will usually try to shield other people from their personal conflicts and problems, but Torstein doesn't give a hoot whether I'm here or not, he doesn't even seem to notice that I'm finding this very unpleasant.

Silence.

Then Simen blinks slowly, inhales, and lets out a little sigh as he turns to face Torstein.

"No, I don't," he says and turns to face his mother again.

"Look at you, acting big just because we've got company," Torstein says and I feel my face start to burn at this, it's like he's dragging me into their argument by mentioning me in this way, turning me into a pawn in their game, as it were, and I don't want that, I don't like it, this is becoming more and more unpleasant.

"Acting big?"

"Don't think just because Marius is here that I wouldn't dare to put you in your place," Torstein says.

"What have *I* done?" Simen asks.

Torstein grins balefully, waits a second or two, then: "Just you finish your dinner. We'll talk about this later," he says, smiling and holding Simen's eye and Simen looks at him in dismay, there's a veiled threat in these last words, what he's really saying is "Wait till I get you alone," and Simen is both angry and afraid. He breathes rapidly through his nose, eyes flicking back and forth.

"Aw, let him go," Gunn Torhild says. "He really wants to make that meeting."

Torstein stares at her, gives it a second. Then: "Oh, well! In that case," he says.

"Yes, but Torstein, he . . ."

"I said okay, didn't I?" Torstein says, breaking in. He glowers menacingly at Gunn Torhild, holds her gaze until she looks away, then bends his head over his plate and carries on eating. "I obviously don't have any say in this house now anyway," he adds.

Silence.

I stare at my plate, chewing on beef patty and couscous, this is becoming more and more unpleasant, I don't know why I came, you'd think I'd have learned by now, every time I've been here it's ended in shouting and arguing, and yet I come back, I don't get it.

"Are you still here," Torstein cries suddenly, staring at Simen and Simen goes on standing there saying nothing. "Well, on you go then, go to your damn meeting." Simen looks at him and swallows, turns to Gunn Torhild, looking bewildered, he doesn't know what to do, the poor kid.

"Just go, Simen," Gunn Torhild says. "I'd drive you there but that blasted old junk heap out there won't start. God, what I wouldn't give for a new car," she adds, then she turns away and carries on eating.

"I could take you," I say. "I'm on a four-wheeler, but there's room for one passenger." I look at Simen, I'd like to help him, wouldn't mind having some time alone with him too, would like the chance to talk to him without Torstein and Gunn Torhild leaning over our shoulders.

"I'll take my bike," Simen says.

"Are you sure?" I say. "I'd be happy to give you a ride, you know."

"I'll take my bike."

"Oh, well, that's great, you use your bike and we might have the Gulf Stream till over the weekend at least," Torstein chips in, his face splitting in a grin as he tosses a piece of patty to Conny, still making fun of Simen for caring about environmental protection. This obviously runs deep. I suppose it might have something to do with Torstein's past career as a North Sea diver. Yes, that must be it: he put his life and his health on the line so Norway could become the wealthy oil nation it is today only to find himself with a son who joins Nature and Youth and maintains that our great oil adventure was actually a tragedy for us and that the oil has been a curse, not a blessing as Torstein has always believed it to be, that must be what's behind this, but that's really neither here nor there. I realize he might feel hurt, but as a father he has a duty to rise above such things.

Simen goes on standing there staring at him, just for a second or two, then he turns on his heel and walks out.

Silence.

Then Torstein jumps up and goes after him.

"I'm sorry, Simen," I hear Torstein say and I feel myself relax slightly, I thought for a moment he was going to blow his stack completely out there, but now he's done a complete about-face and is apologizing to Simen instead. Sounds as though he means it too, he sounds genuinely remorseful.

"It's okay," Simen says.

"I didn't mean it. It's just that . . . I've had a lot on my plate lately. What with Rune and everything . . ."

"It's okay, I said," Simen says. He doesn't want to talk anymore about it, I can tell by his voice, he sounds ill at ease, flustered.

But Torstein won't let it go.

"I don't mean to be an asshole," he goes on, wanting Simen to assure him that he's not an asshole, I can tell, trying to salve his conscience by coaxing Simen into saying something nice about him. "I . . . I want to be a good father," he says, sounding more and more upset, his voice shaking in a way meant to show how full of remorse he is, and I'm sure he is full of remorse, it's not that, but there's something so mawkish and self-centered about the way he's talking and acting, he's more intent on feeling better about himself than about making things better for Simen.

"I've *got* to go," Simen says.

"But Simen, hey," Torstein says. "I'd like to square things between us before you go, you understand that, don't you?"

"Look, I told you, we're good, okay!" Simen says desperately. He's only sixteen, but he can detect Torstein's mawkishness, his self-centeredness and I can tell by his voice how much it bothers him, he just wants to get away.

"Yeah, but . . ."

"I've really *got* to go now," Simen says. "I'm going to be late."

"I see," Torstein says, in a voice designed to let Simen know how disappointed he is, to make the boy feel bad, make him feel that this is all his own fault, it's unbeliev-able, it really is.

"Bye then."

"Bye."

I hear the front door being opened, then closed, then Gunn Torhild turns to me and smiles.

"Fathers and sons, eh?" is all she says, with a little shake of her head, trying to play down Torstein's be-havior now. She knows as well as I do that it's neither normal nor acceptable for a father to behave like this, but she doesn't want to acknowledge it so she's trying to convince herself and me that what we've just seen and heard was merely a perfectly normal father and son thing: every now and then they'll have a huge row, but it's okay because they love each other and they always end up as friends, that's what she's trying to say, trying to put a good face on it.

I smile vaguely at her, bend over my plate, and pop the last chunk of patty into my mouth.

"Should we have coffee on the veranda?" Gunn Torhild asks. She's finished eating too, she takes a half-eaten patty from the dish and tosses it into the corner where Conny is lying. There's a sharp click as the dog's jaws snap shut.

"Yes, why not," I say. "Thanks for dinner! It was deli-cious," I add. It wasn't delicious at all, but I say it anyway and am about to rave a little more about the couscous, but fortunately I manage to stop myself, I'd better not compliment the food too much or it won't ring true, it would only sound as though it had been so bad that the cook needs a little moral support and some people might take that as an insult.

"I'm glad to hear that somebody likes to try new things,"

Gunn Torhild says as she reaches across the table for a pack of cigarettes down at the far end.

I smile at her as I pick up the dish of corn, put it on top of my empty plate, and lay my cutlery in it. At that moment Torstein comes in carrying a bottle of brandy and two glasses.

"Aw, just leave all that. Gunn Torhild'll see to it later!"

Gunn Torhild stares at him openmouthed.

"Excuse me, what fucking century are you living in?" she exclaims, giving a faint shake of her head and a supposedly shocked laugh, looking first at him, then at me, trying to make me believe that their relationship is more equal than it really is, I can tell. She does most of the housework, but she doesn't want to admit it, not when I'm here, she's act-ing as if it's not simply assumed that she'll clear the table.

"Not *more* Liberal Democrat bellyaching," Torstein asks, looking at her and shaking his head and Gunn Torhild gives her husky laugh as she plucks a cigarette from the pack. "Christ, you'll be going around wearing only one earring next," Torstein adds, and he laughs too as he steps out onto the veranda.

"It's okay, just leave it," Gunn Torhild says, turning to me.

"Well, I can clear away my own plate, at least," I say and I carry it and my cutlery through to the kitchen. Torstein has already made the coffee, I see. I rinse the plate and the cutlery and put them in the dishwasher, then I take three coffee cups from the cabinet, pick up the coffeepot, and go back out onto the veranda.

Silence.

Gunn Torhild is smoking her cigarette and surveying the yellow fields on the other side of the road. Torstein is sip-ping his brandy.

I set the cups on the table and pour the coffee.

"Excuse me, are you working here now?" Torstein says, grinning at me. I look at him, does he think I'm making myself too much at home, bringing things out, pouring the coffee, is that what he's getting at?

"Well, the coffee was ready, so I thought . . ."

"It's okay, it's okay," he says, raising his hand as if to reassure me. "I was only joking."

Silence again.

"You're looking very thoughtful," Torstein says, turning to Gunn Torhild. She's still puffing on her cigarette and gazing at the yellow fields.

"Is it any wonder?"

"No," Torstein says, waits a moment, then: "Not really."

Pause.

"I simply don't know how we're going to manage it," Gunn Torhild says before taking a drag of her cigarette.

"No, I know," Torstein says.

Another pause.

I look at them, is it my turn now, am I supposed to ask why Gunn Torhild was looking so thoughtful, it seems rather like it, it sounds as though they've just been discussing something they want to do but find it hard to tell me about, so they're trying to make me so curious that I'll have to ask.

"And we don't have that much time either," says Gunn Torhild.

"That's for sure."

Silence again. And now I'm going to have to ask what they're talking about, because that's obviously what they want and to not take the hint and not ask would seem rude and standoffish somehow, although it isn't, of course, it's ruder to try to coerce me into joining the conversation, but still, I'll feel like a cold and uninterested guest if I don't ask what they're prompting me to ask.

I wait a moment, swallow.

"Manage what?" I ask.

Gunn Torhild turns to me.

"We need to come up with the money to bring Rune home from the Philippines. One hundred thousand kroner and we only have a few days."

"One hundred thousand?" I exclaim, instinctively raising my eyebrows, it sounds extortionate.

"That's what it costs, or so the embassy says."

"But . . . didn't he have insurance?"

"The Norwegian insurance companies don't cover the transport home if the deceased has lived abroad for more than forty-five days," she says. "And Rune had been there for nearly three months when he died, he had a girlfriend there and everything."

"But still, one hundred thousand?"

Gunn Torhild sighs.

"Well, actually it costs twice that. But Rune had some money in the bank and if we add the little bit that's left after his girlfriend got away with all she could get, it comes to just over a hundred thousand."

A white lumber truck thunders past on the highway and a flurry of sparrows rises from the roadside.

"It would cost a fraction of the price to have him buried down there, of course," she says.

"Forget about it," Torstein says firmly. "My brother will be buried in Namsos. That slanty-eyed bitch wouldn't even visit his grave, she only wanted someone to spend money on her, she couldn't have cared less for Rune when he was alive and she certainly doesn't care about him now," he says, then he raises his brandy glass to his lips and knocks it all back in one go. "Rune is going to lie next to Ma and Pa and that's that!" he says, setting his glass on the table with a thump.

Gunn Torhild shrugs.

"Well, then we'll just *have* to sell the house and find something smaller and cheaper. Because we'll never get a loan."

I look at them and swallow, look at the floor, then up again, do they want me to pay for Rune's coffin to be sent home to Norway, is that what this is about, is that why they're telling me all this, so that I'll feel sorry for them and offer to help? Yes, I bet that's it, they know a hundred thousand is chicken feed to my family and they're hoping that I'll help them with this problem. They don't know that I haven't been in touch with Mom and Dad for God knows how long, they think I have free access to the family fortune, so to speak: a quick phone call and the money would be there in their bank account.

I take a swig of coffee, say nothing, feel a flicker of annoyance. They're desperate, I understand that, of course I do, but still. I mean, if they'd asked me straight out I wouldn't have minded at all, but to go about it like this, well, somehow I feel they're trying to put one over on me, that they're trying to manipulate me by playing on my emotions and my conscience and I don't like that.

"Oh, I don't know, I really don't," Torstein says.

"No," Gunn Torhild sighs. She takes a long pull on her cigarette, then she leans across the garden table and stubs it out in the ashtray. "Well, if we have to, we have to. It'll be with a heavy heart, though, that's for sure," she says, blowing smoke out of her nose. She's not about to give up, she's still trying to wangle money out of me by appealing to my conscience. I say nothing, feeling more and more uncomfortable.

Silence.

Suddenly Simen appears in the doorway and stands there looking at us. He couldn't bring himself to go to that meeting after all, I suppose, Torstein must have succeeded in making him feel guilty and he has turned around and cycled home again. I smile at him and again I'm struck by the resemblance, it's weird, like looking at myself when I was younger.

"Finished saving the world already, are you?" Torstein says, baring his yellow teeth in a big grin. There he goes again, mocking his son's concern for the environment. I don't get it, why can't he curb his frustration and his anger for a moment, if only for his son's sake. A look of sadness and anger comes over Simen's face, he stands there scowling at his father for a second, then he turns and goes back inside.

Silence.

"I know, I'm an asshole," Torstein says, still grinning. It's a slightly different grin now, though, an agonized grin, the grin of a troubled man. He leans across the table and grabs the brandy bottle, fills his glass.

"No, you're not," Gunn Torhild says.

"Yeah, I am," Torstein says.

"Stop it, Torstein."

"But it's true, isn't it, Marius? I'm an asshole, aren't I?" he says, looking at me, still with that pained grin on his lips, and I smile uncertainly back at him, I don't know what to say, don't know what he expects me to say when he asks a question like this, is he trying to get me to do the same as Gunn Torhild and tell him he's not an asshole, is that what he wants, does he want help to play down what just happened and thereby boost his self-esteem?

"Asshole?" I say, acting as if I don't know what he's talking about.

Torstein doesn't reply, he knows full well I'm making myself out to be dumber than I am and he makes no secret of it, smirks as he picks up his brandy glass.

"It's nice of you to take it like that," he says, looking straight at me as he drinks, he makes me feel like a gut-less little loser when he carries on like this, he knows I do think he's an asshole, but he also knows I can't bring myself to say it to his face, so I do seem gutless when he asks if I don't agree that he's an asshole, he's making me look a fool and I'm letting him do it, sitting here grinning sheepishly. I feel my cheeks starting to burn again, I don't want to be the shamefaced loser he's making me out to be, don't want to let him make me squirm like this, but I am, I wish I could say that it was because I feel sorry for him, that I'm putting up with more than I should because I regard him as a victim, someone deserving of a little more understanding, and to some extent I am being more understanding, because he is a victim, Torstein, it's all the stuff he went through during and after his time as a deep-sea diver that's turned him into the tormented character he is today, I know that, but that's not why I'm letting him treat me like this, or, at least, that's not the only reason, it has as much to do with the fact that I'm a coward.

"Okay, now you've lost me," he says.

"Sorry?" I say.

"Deep-sea diver?"

I stare at him, saying nothing.

"You said *deep-sea diver*," he says.

I stare at him for a moment longer. I wasn't aware of having said anything at all, but apparently I did, I feel my cheeks growing even hotter, I need to explain, if nothing else I need to show that there was some thinking behind what I said.

"I think a lot of this has to do with your time as a deep-sea diver," I say quickly.

"What?"

"You sacrificed your health and well-being so Norway could become the wealthy oil nation we are today," I say, then I swallow. "And some of your best friends gave even more, I know, they gave their lives. And when you see Simen getting involved with Nature and Youth, well . . . you don't just feel that he's refusing to acknowledge the gift that you and your buddies sacrificed their health and their lives to bestow on all of us Norwegians, you feel he's blaming you personally for the greatest problem of our age—climate change, that is," I say. "And that . . . I realize that that hurts, I realize it upsets you and makes you angry to hear him talk of our great oil adventure as a tragedy. You have to remember, though, that Simen is only sixteen, he's at that stage where he needs to break away from you and become an independent human being and at that stage it's perfectly normal for kids to declare themselves totally against everything their fathers are in favor of, and in favor of everything their fathers are against. In fact it's not just normal, it's more like a law of nature, it's something young men do without meaning to or being conscious of doing, as it were, and . . . and, well, obviously you have to show a little tolerance and a little patience. Even if it's not always easy," I say. I pause for a moment and suddenly I realize I'm sitting hunched over with my eyes shut, chopping the air with my hands, the way I tend to do when I get carried away by what I'm saying. I feel my face flaming, feel it turning crimson. I open my eyes, try to smile and look relaxed, but all I can manage is a twitch of my lips.

Torstein and Gunn Torhild exchange a glance, look at me again.

Silence.

"That was a bit beyond.me, all that, I'm afraid," Gunn Torhild says.

Torstein takes a swig of his brandy.

"Yeah—fascinating, though, to have your feelings explained to you," he says, gently smacking his lips as he sets down his glass.

Gunn Torhild almost bursts out laughing but stops herself just in time.

Silence.

I'm hot and flushed, there's sweat on my brow and the back of my neck and I want to get away, I can't stay here any longer, but here I am, I don't know what to say, don't know where to look either, because not only have I been sitting here with my eyes shut, waving my hands about like an idiot, I was also rude and totally out of line, well, I mean, how condescending can you be, I come to see them two or three times a year at most and then I carry on as though I know them better than they know themselves, how unbelievably arrogant, and anyway, what right do I have to express an opinion on any of this?

"Well, well," Torstein says.

Silence.

"I need to use the bathroom," I say, I don't need to use the bathroom, I simply need a little time-out, I can't stay here any longer, don't know why I came to see them anyway, why I make this same mistake again and again. Initially, when I looked them up, well, that was understandable: I was curious and badly needed to know where I came from. But that I still keep visiting them, that I come back again and again, long after it's become clear that we really don't want anything to do with one another, and of my own free will at that, I simply don't understand it. I paste on a smile as I plant my hands on the arms of the chair, can't meet their eyes so I keep mine lowered as I get up and turn to go inside. I walk straight past Conny, who's lying on her side, asleep, go through the kitchen and into the bathroom. I lock the door and stand there with my eyes closed for a few moments, stand there as if my feet are frozen to the floor, then I open my eyes, flush the toilet, wash my hands, and go back out. I swallow, have to put this out of my mind, it's not worth worrying about. More often than not things that seem like personal disasters to me turn out to be mere bagatelles to other people, so this is not a problem, it'll be fine, I don't know why I came here, but it doesn't matter, I'll be on my way back to the cottage soon anyway, I'll just finish my coffee, then I'll leave, another five minutes and then I'm out of here. I take a deep breath and let it out again in one long sigh, then I walk into the living room, spot Simen straightaway, he's sitting by the coffee table at the back of the room eating potato chips, drinking cola, and watching something on his laptop, some comedy film it sounds like, at any rate there's some guy in it talking in the sort of voice people put on when they're trying really hard to be funny. I stick my hands in my pockets, wander over to him, but he doesn't look up, just keeps his eyes riveted on the screen.

"What are you watching?"

"*The Nutty Professor*," he says.

I position myself next to him, hear Conny whimper softly in her sleep.

"Is it funny?"

"Hilarious. Got me laughing till I cry."

Silence.

"It'll get better, Simen," I say softly. It just comes out and I start to worry as soon as I've said it: I have to be careful not to act as though we're closer than we are, mustn't behave too much like a brother either, that would only alienate him even more. He looks up at me, he knows I'm referring to the way things are between him and his father, I can tell by his face that he does, he looks me in the eye for a second, then turns back to the screen.

"Yeah, sure," he says.

"I had my own run-ins with my dad when I was sixteen," I say, although I didn't really, I got on really well with my dad when I was that age, but I say it anyway, I have the idea that it might be some comfort to him to know that it's not unusual to have a somewhat strained relationship with one's father at his age. "I lived in a studio apartment for my last two years at high school, I couldn't bear to stay at home," I say. I didn't actually move into an apartment until I was nineteen, but I say it anyway. "I could help you find a place in Trondheim, if you like," I blurt, give a start when I hear myself say it, I'm going too far now, interfering in things that have nothing to do with me and I feel my cheeks start to burn.

He looks at me.

"He's not normally like this, if that's what you think," he says.

I swallow.

"No, of course not," I say, although I'm pretty sure this is exactly how he is, in fact I wouldn't be surprised if he was even worse when they're alone, with no witnesses, but I can't say that. "I know this is a particularly hard time for him, what with having just lost his brother," I say. "And to have these money worries on top of that . . . the cost of bringing Rune home to Norway, no wonder he's at the end of his tether."

His eyes go back to the screen.

"Cremate the guy and that'll be one problem out of the way, at least."

"Okay . . . ?"

"The guy Mom spoke to said it would cost ten thousand kroner to cremate the body and send the ashes home and two hundred thousand to fly Rune home in his coffin. And it makes no difference to the dead person whether they're cremated or not. Well, that's what I think anyway."

I don't say anything, just stand there watching *The Nutty Professor*, feel the back of my head turn cold—it can be no accident that Torstein and Gunn Torhild omitted to mention that, how could they, they're trying to rip me off, that's what they're doing, first they try to trick me into giving them 100,000 kroner, which they say will be spent on having Rune's coffin sent home, then they'll opt for the cremation, pay 10,000 for that, and pocket the rest, they've been planning this ever since I called to say I was going to come over, they must have been, or am I being paranoid again, I don't know, and it doesn't really matter anyway, I neither will nor can give them so much as a single krone. In any case, I'm leaving now, I can't stay here any longer, as soon as I've had my coffee, I'll say bye-bye and head back to the cottage. I breathe in and let out a little sigh, pull myself away from *The Nutty Professor*, and go back out onto the veranda.

"Lovely sunset," Torstein says, acting as if he's forgotten all about my little outburst, smiling and nodding at the red sun that seems to be drifting across the blue mountain on the horizon.

I nod and sit down.

"You didn't say anything to Simen, did you?" Gunn Torhild says. "About us selling the house, I mean?"

I shake my head.

"Good," she says. "He'd only get upset and I'd like us to do absolutely everything we can to come up with the money some other way before we have to talk to him about moving. It's his childhood home, you know, so it's a big thing," she adds, trying to play on my emotions again, that's what she's doing, I'm sure, she knows how keen I've been for Simen to accept me as his brother so she's trying to blackmail me into giving them money by telling me how upset the boy will be if they have to sell the house and move somewhere else, that must be what she's trying to do, or am I just being paranoid again, I know I do tend to become obsessed with exposing people who I think are out to get me, and maybe that's what's happening here, I don't know. I look at Gunn Torhild and swallow.

"Ah, we'll get through this as well, Torstein, you'll see," she's saying, smiling at him, doing her stiff-upper-lip act, she knows very well that it's easier to like and take pity on a valiant victim than on one who whines and complains, so this is just another ploy to gain my sympathy, I'm sure it is.

"I suppose we will, one way or another."

"What doesn't kill you makes you strong, isn't that what they say?" Gunn Torhild says, not about to give up, she's doing everything she can to swindle me out of money for them to spend on drink and debauchery. God, the cold, calculating cheek of it, it's unbelievable, just look at the way they keep reminding me how broke they are, they've been doing it ever since I got here, I was barely in the door before Gunn Torhild started moaning about the range hood, how useless it is and how expensive to fix.

"Beg pardon?" Gunn Torhild says.

I regard her mutely, she raises her brows and eyes me enquiringly.

"What do you mean by that?"

"By what?"

"Expensive to fix," she says.

I stare at her, frowning slightly, I must have done it again, spoken out loud without being aware of it, and now she's alleging that I said "expensive to fix."

"That range hood you have is useless, but you can't afford to get it fixed," I say, trying to sound as though I was well aware of saying what I apparently just said. I look at her and swallow and she gazes at me wide-eyed, clearly not following me. "And the car's a junk heap, but you can't afford to take it in for repair," I continue, I might as well tell the truth, there's no point in concealing the fact that I've seen through them, I know what they're up to, so I look at Gunn Torhild, shaking my head and laughing in a way that says the game is up and none of us needs to pretend any longer, a sort of "it was fun while it lasted" laugh, but she still won't quit, she sits there trying to look as though she doesn't know what I'm talking about.

"And all those props. My cracked plate and the two final-demand letters that just 'happened' to be lying on the table where I couldn't help but see them," I go on, closing my eyes and making air quotes around the word *happened*. "They were all props in your little charade. It took a while for it to dawn on me, but I see it now. And . . . and all your efforts to act proper. You've done everything you could to convince me that you've shaped up since the last time I was here. Simen is told to wash his hands before dinner, even though he obviously isn't used to doing so, and you, Gunn Torhild, you suddenly get the idea to serve light beer with dinner and refuse to have anything stronger, so I won't worry that you'll spend all the money on booze, right? Very clever, I have to hand it to you, very well done," I say, nodding quickly several times. "And . . . and . . . and when you still can't control yourself, Torstein, I'm obviously meant to put this down to the recent loss of your brother. You're also a reformed character, that's what I'm supposed to think, but right now you're grief stricken and you need a drink to help you to switch off for a while." A moment passes and then I realize that I'm hunched over with my eyes closed, chopping the air with my hands, exactly the way I was doing only minutes ago. I open my eyes and straighten up sharply. They both stare at me for a second, then they look at each other, turn to me again, arch their eyebrows, and do their utmost to look dumbfounded, they want me to believe they've no idea what I'm talking about, I can tell, they're not going to admit anything.

"Thanks for coffee" is all I say, then I rise and go into

the living room. And there's Simen, watching *The Nutty Professor*, I feel so sorry for him, he doesn't deserve this.

"Give me a call and I'll help you find a place to stay," I say. "I might even be able to help you with a job," I add, looking back at him as I walk out of the living room and into the kitchen. He looks so like me it's not true, I can't get over it, it's like seeing myself at sixteen, and maybe it's because I see myself in Simen that I keep coming back here. When I see Simen and, not least, when I see Simen as he is with his father, I feel I have some idea of what it would have been like to grow up with Torstein, and maybe that's exactly what I'm looking for when I come here. I stop short halfway across the kitchen, shut my eyes, and stand there nodding to myself. Yes, and when I feel sorry for Simen and want to save him by getting him away from Torstein, maybe it's really myself I want to save. I suffered a trauma when I was robbed of a life with my biological parents and lifting my brother out of the life he has now could be a way of reenacting and thereby controlling that traumatic experience, yes, that has to be it, forcing myself to visit the biological father whom I cannot stand is, quite simply, a way of making sense of what happened in that maternity ward. I've been coming here because I needed to prove to myself not only that I can live with what happened back then, but that it was the best thing that could have happened. And this has become even more important since I cut all ties with Mom and Dad and Rikard. I've always known in my bones that it was a mistake to break with them and continuing to visit Torstein, even though I hate it here, is my body's way of telling me that I have to get back in touch with them. I have actually sought out these strangers in order to remind myself of where I truly belong, that's what all this is about, or is it, am I getting lost inside my own head again, are my thoughts running away with me and concocting theories again. My brain is overheating, or that's how it feels.

"Marius."

I open my eyes and look straight at Torstein.

"Yes," I say. I realize I'm standing with my hands on my head and promptly lower them.

"Are you okay?" he asks.

"Yes, of course," I say.

Bangsund, July 14th, 2006

It's so strange to sit here gazing out of the window of my old room at home. When I see the fjord from this particular angle; when I see the blue mountains in which I used to look for faces as a child; when I see the avenue lined with the tall, leafy poplar trees, which are apparently riddled with rot and which Mom has, therefore, been nagging us to cut down for the past twenty years; when I see the gray stream where Rikard and I used to build dams in the autumn, the dog rose bushes where we used to pick the hips, to split them open and get at the seeds, which we then sprinkled on the backs of the necks of the girls next door ("itching powder" we called it); when I see all this, I can't help thinking and feeling that here everything is just as it's always been. But it isn't, of course. It never has been, to paraphrase the old saying that history's not what it used to be. Obviously it's only my own nostalgia that tricks me into imagining that everything is still the same here in Bangsund, my own yearning for a time I recall as happy and carefree—that and my own craving for security and stability perhaps, I don't know.

But I can fool myself for only so long. Take this morning, for example, when I was sitting here with the window wide open, drinking coffee and listening to the chirping and twittering of the birds, the sound I used to wake up to as a boy. Suddenly the birdsong was drowned out by a deep and rapidly growing roar and when I got up from my chair and looked out of the window, I saw a helicopter coming in low over the hill. It circled the roof of the vaccination plant (which is still known as "the Furniture Factory," by the way) before landing on the round tarmacked platform they've built where we used to store stuff in the seventies and eighties, and then, while the rotor was still spinning, the door opened and two Asian-looking men in suits stepped out, clearly afraid of being late for what I later discovered was a meeting concerning one of Rikard's subsidiary companies, which had invested heavily in scampi farming somewhere in Southeast Asia—Thailand or Vietnam I think it was. There was nothing particularly unusual about that, not at all. But five minutes later, when I sat down again, I found myself viewing the scene outside my old room in a slightly different light; I noticed other things, not just those that had always been there and had scarcely changed since the seventies: at the quayside, where Dad's thirteen-foot Rana used to lie, I saw the huge cabin cruiser that Rikard had bought, but that, according to his wife, he never had time to sail. Over by the white picket fence I saw Rikard's gardener, caretaker, and odd-job man climb onto one of those tractor-style lawnmowers and proceed to cut the same grass that, twenty years ago, Rikard and I had taken turns at cutting with a rusty and heavy (to put it mildly) manual mower, and on the red paved square outside the window of the production plant stood the sculpture for which the company paid over 200,000 kroner last year and that annoys the blue blazes out of Dad: "What the hell is that supposed to be? Give me a hundred kroner and I'll make you something a lot nicer than that." The sight of the employees on their way to work wasn't the same as it had been twenty or thirty years earlier either. From my window back then what I saw was a stream of roll-up-smoking men in flannel shirts and jeans coming over the hill, all carrying their lunch boxes and thermos flasks in Co-op tote bags. They showed up on heavy-pedaled Diamant and DBS bikes with chains that emitted a grating screech-screech as they rubbed against dented chain guards. Either that or they drove to work in ten-year-old Datsuns and Opels, which often refused to start on winter days when it was time to go home. This morning, on the other hand, what I saw were well-paid lab technicians of both sexes. Many arrived in gleaming new SUVs with four-wheel drive and engines far more powerful than they would ever need. But most of them, more in fact than twenty years ago, were cycling to work. Not on old boneshakers without any gears, of course, but on carbon-fiber bikes costing as much as 30,000 kroner and weighing next to nothing—no effort involved in lifting one of these into a bike rack—and not in flannel shirts and jeans with the wind in their hair, obviously, but in skin-tight cycling gear with helmets on their heads.

This is 2006, this is Rikard's time.

Dad still owns the company, but since around 2000 he has been taking more and more of a back seat to the point where he has now resigned all his posts and has, it seems, dedicated his life almost exclusively to catching up on all the things he previously had to forgo because he was working so much and so hard. Several evenings a week he can be found down by the River Namsen, fishing for salmon, he has set up his own fly-tying bench in the basement, he and Mom have visited four European cities already this year and he can hardly wait to pick up Rikard's children from kindergarten and take them to the beach, to a café in town, to the Namsskogan Family Park or simply to spend time with them here at home. I had expected, and I know Rikard had feared, that Dad would don the mantle of patriarch when he "took up his new position as Grandpa," as he put it, but Mom says that hasn't happened. According to her, during Dad's first years in charge of the furniture factory, our own grandfather couldn't resist interfering and Dad decided way back then that he would not make the same mistake when he retired. Besides which, he and Rikard have such very different ideas of how to run a business that Dad knew it would only end badly if he tried to shove his oar in, she says. He did so anyway, though, I know. Just before I severed all ties with the family, it came out that one of Rikard's subsidiaries had sold eggs and fry carrying the highly infectious ISA virus and that the fish-farming industry in the importing country (somewhere in Latin America) had collapsed completely. This, in turn, led to mass layoffs and huge social problems in several areas along the coast. But what really made Dad's blood boil was the fact that Rikard and the company denied all responsibility and refused to help clear up the mess they had made. And not only that: from what I can recall of Dad's tirades in the living room, they tried to hush up the matter and conducted something approaching a witch-hunt against anyone who attempted to document what had happened and call attention to it. "Where there is no shame, there are no limits," I remember Dad roaring.

But that was then, not now. It may be that Mom tends to paint a rosy picture of things and that Dad plays the patriarch and does still interfere, I honestly don't know, I've only just returned home after a fairly lengthy absence, but retirement certainly appears to agree with the Salmon King of Bangsund, in fact he seems to be very happy, not to say positively thriving in his old age, which is good to see. It's also good, not least, to see that he and Mom have found each other again. It makes me so glad to see them sitting on the veranda in the evening, drinking red wine and surveying all they have built over a long life together; to see Mom fretting when Dad defies his seventy-five years and insists on climbing the local crag that we call "Klompen," or to get up in the morning and find him preparing breakfast in bed for Mom. And the way they speak to each other, the warmth in their voices. The ease. And, not least, the humor. To listen, for example, to Mom pretending to be much more exasperated by Dad's penny-pinching ways than she really is and the childish delight Dad takes in the opportunity this presents for him to parody himself: "Hey, go easy on that washing-up liquid," he told Mom only yesterday, when she was washing a saucepan. "You use far too much when you squeeze the bottle like that. Just turn the bottle upside down and give it a little shake—a couple of drops is plenty for one little pan." "Oh, thank goodness you pointed that out to me," Mom said. "Now we'll be able to pay the electricity bill this month as well!"

That's how they carried on. That's how they carry on all the time and always while trying hard not to laugh.

But you'll soon be able to see all this for yourself, David, when you come to Bangsund. As I'm assuming, and hoping, you will. I wasn't quite sure whether I should reply to that newspaper ad and tell you everything I've told you in this letter, but although I may not have lost my memory, I have experienced something of what you're going through now, I have also lived with uncertainty, I have also felt driven to learn more about who I am and where I come from, so I do understand what it's like and I understand how important it is for you to know the truth. Which is why it didn't take me long to decide that replying to the ad was the only right thing to do. This may sound very high-minded, it may even sound like I'm boasting. But I would like to add that it has done me a lot of good to write this letter, I've learned a lot about myself in the process, become wiser. Not only that, but for some time I've had the idea that you're the only person who can identify with how I really feel, so from that point of view this letter also serves as an aid to self-help, or at least it will if it brings us together. We've been living each other's lives and even though I've never met you, this is something we share, something that makes you the only person to whom I can ever hope to truly relate, it's as simple as that.

But to close by donning my Dear Abby hat again: I only hope that you will choose the right angle from which to view and understand your life, even after you've read this letter. And, not least, after you have met and got to know your new family in Bangsund.

SUSANNE

Trondheim, June 24th, 2006. Fake Rolex

A loud cheer goes up in the living room as someone puts on the Buena Vista Social Club. I tilt my head to one side, lift my hands to my right ear, and slip in an earring, looking at myself in the mirror on the wardrobe door as I do so, try to smile, not very successfully, I'm not exactly in the mood for a party, all I really want is for it to be over, but that's not going to happen anytime soon, it's only quarter past twelve, I can't ask people to leave now, I have to be a good hostess, have to try to pull myself together. I could have a bit more to drink, of course, but I'm not sure I want to, there's been enough drinking recently and I don't feel like getting plastered again tonight, I'd be better off trying to dance myself into a good mood, it's the right music for it anyway, real feel-good music. I look at myself in the mirror and stretch my lips into an even wider smile, try to look much the way I do when I'm in a good mood and ready to party, try to trick myself into feeling good, it's helping too, I can tell, feel my spirits lifting. I give it a second, then turn, bend over the bed, and burrow my face in the hollow of Rex's throat.

"Who's a lovely dog then, hm, who's a lovely dog?" I coo, nuzzling his warm coat, stay like that for a moment, then straighten up again. Rex raises his head sharply and eyes me expectantly, he thinks he can come out now, I know. "No, no, you have to stay here," I say, stand there smiling and looking at him for a second or two, then turn and leave the bedroom.

"Susanne," I hear someone say behind me. I turn around and see Tone over by the kitchen door with Antony and the tall Cuban guy from the Latin American Group. I wander over to them. "Aren't we going into town?" Tone asks. She smiles at me and I smile back, I'm not really in the party mood and it would suit me fine if people gradually took themselves off, but I can't bring myself to say so, not when it's Tone who's asking at any rate, it's like there's some part of me that wants to humor her. I tend to feel like that when I'm with people as fabulous looking as her. I don't want to be this way, it reminds me a bit of when I was a little girl, doing all I could to please the most popular girl in the class, even though I knew she wouldn't like me any better for it.

"Everyone seems to be enjoying themselves, though, don't you think?" I ask. Everyone is obviously enjoying themselves, but I ask anyway, part of me wants Tone to agree and say what a great party it is and how much everyone is enjoying themselves.

"Oh, absolutely. We're having a great time. Aren't we?" she says, tucking her long blond hair behind one ear and turning to Antony and the Cuban guy, but they don't catch it, they're too busy inspecting Antony's wristwatch.

"Of course it's genuine," Antony cries, eyes wide, as if he's never heard the like.

"No fucking way is that a genuine Rolex," the Cuban says laughing. "You picked that up for a few cedi on the street back home in Ghana."

Antony manages to look indignant for a few seconds longer, then he gives up and laughs as well.

"Yeah, okay," he says. "But nobody can tell."

"I could tell," the Cuban guy says.

"Yeah, but—aw . . . Christ, what a fucking nitpicker," Antony mutters to Tone, shaking his head and making his dreadlocks sway gently back and forth, then he laughs again. And the Cuban guy laughs too, clearly happy to be called a nitpicker.

"Cheers, here's to a great party," Tone says, raising a bottle of Sol.

"Cheers," say Antony and the Cuban guy.

"I'm just going to mix myself a drink," I say with a smile and stroll off into the kitchen. The two women from International Socialists are sitting at the table, eating empanadas off red paper plates and listening to Nina going on about African dance, it sounds like she's trying to recruit them. I find it hard not to laugh, these two are the last people I could ever imagine shaking their butts to African drums, they seem so touchy and uptight, I can't see them being able to let themselves go in any way, not when sober at any rate. But Nina is like most converts, she's never done a day's exercise in her life, as far as I know, but now she's taken up African dance and she's on at everybody and their grandmother to try it too. I cross to the kitchen counter, make myself a gin and tonic, and go back to Tone, Antony, and the Cuban guy, flash them a smile as I take a sip. Then I realize that that damned earring is about to fall out again, there must be something wrong with the catch. I set my glass down on the bureau, put my head on one side, and take out the earring to check it, but I drop it and it lands on the floor. I turn away and bend down to pick it up, but it's so small I can't get hold of it, it slips between my finger and thumb, once, then again.

"Mmm, I like that position," I hear Antony say.

At first I don't understand what he's talking about, but then it dawns on me that I'm bent over with my backside in the air, wiggling it about just in front of his crotch. I turn my head and look up at him without straightening up, he makes some little thrusting movements with his hips and grins, his eyes flicking between my rear end and the other two. What the fuck does he think he's doing, what the fuck does he mean by it, standing there pretending to take me from behind, is he insinuating that I'm flaunting myself at him? I grope about a bit more and finally manage to pick up the earring, then I straighten up, cheeks flaming, and turn around, seething inside, but he's no longer there, he's heading down the hall, making for the bathroom it looks like, he glances back at us, grinning, as he puts his hand on the door handle, his white teeth gleaming in his dark brown face. He opens the door and disappears into the bathroom. I don't say anything, just look at Tone and swallow as I pick up my glass and take a sip of my drink. She thinks it's funny, but she can see I'm angry so she presses her lips together to stop herself from laughing. The Cuban guy, on the other hand, doesn't try to hide that he thinks it was funny, he gives a low chuckle, eyes on his rum and cola. Silence for a moment or two, then Tone giggles as well, she can't help it. But I'm not laughing, although I probably should, if I'd laughed right away the whole thing would have been forgotten by now. What Antony said and did wasn't particularly funny, it's the fact that I let it get to me, that's why they're laughing, the fact that I've allowed myself to be forced into playing the humorless, pompous feminist.

"Aw, c'mon, Susanne," Tone says. "You should take it as a compliment."

"A compliment?"

"He wouldn't have said it if he didn't find you attractive."

"Has he ever said anything like that to you, Tone?" I say, I need to control my temper now, need to try to stay cool. I look at her, try to smile.

"No. Not really."

"And why is that, do you think?"

She looks at me and shrugs.

"Well, maybe he doesn't find me particularly attractive," she says, taking a swig of her beer.

I don't answer right away, put my head on one side, and give her a look that says what a stupid remark that was; she looks so good she could have anyone she wanted and she knows it too. A moment and then she smiles, a smile that seems to say yes, she knows it was a stupid thing to say, admitting that she knows how good she looks. And maybe that's what she was after when she suggested that Antony might not find her attractive, she knew I would dismiss such an idea as ridiculous, thus confirming for her how much better looking she is than the rest of us. I almost say this to her, but I don't, I wouldn't give her the satisfaction.

"He doesn't say things like that to you, because you've got a boyfriend, Tone," I say. I'm burning with rage, but I keep smiling, speaking as calmly as I can. "As far as Antony is concerned, you belong to another man and he doesn't say things like that to you because it would be like insulting your boyfriend. You're another man's property and that he respects. But when he treats me the way he does, there's no man to insult. I'm single and I'm no one's property, so he thinks he can say and do pretty much whatever he likes to me—as long as he doesn't break any rules, of course. And that, Tone, is what gets to me."

She smiles at me indulgently.

"You shouldn't . . . you shouldn't take everything so seriously, Susanne."

"So seriously? We're talking about the right to be treated as an individual who's worth something in their own right . . . regardless of whether she happens to be living with a man or not. Are you saying I shouldn't take that seriously?" I say, incandescent with rage, but still smiling, doing everything I can to make this sound like a perfectly normal discussion and not an argument. I take a sip of my gin and tonic, feel an ice cube bump gently against my front teeth.

"No, of course not. What I mean is that you read too much into what he says. For God's sake, Susanne, it was just a joke," she says. "You don't have to be so . . . you're so . . . so *outraged*."

"So I'm an outraged feminist, is that it?" I say, letting out a little laugh. "Outraged, resentful, and bitter, needs a good lay and all that."

"Oh, come on, Susanne. Now you're doing the same to me as you did to Antony."

"Doing what?"

"You're twisting my words."

"No, I'm not, Tone," I say. "I'm just trying to show you the effect your words can have."

"What's that supposed to mean?"

"Well, it seems to me you don't totally disagree that what Antony just said and did is unacceptable. You simply think I should take it a little less to heart. That I should put up with it. That I shouldn't get so outraged, as you put it. But don't you see that that's exactly the sort of remark that makes it even more difficult to protest when we women are subjected to harassment? I mean, who wants to be thought of as resentful and bitter and humorless? Better to give the impression of always being perfectly happy and contented and let the harassment continue, right?" I say, finding it harder and harder not to show how angered I am by her, I still have a smile on my face, but it's gradually turning into a sneer.

She stands there looking at me for a moment, not saying a word, then she raises her eyebrows, heaves a little sigh, and gives a faint shake of her head.

"I can't help it," she says. "I did actually think it was quite funny." She sends me a rather apologetic smile. "Okay, so maybe I'm a little naïve, but . . ."

The smile I give her is a little too sweet.

"But . . . ?" I say.

Suddenly she looks confused.

"What? Do you want me to tell you you're not naïve, is that it?" I ask, feeling a stab of remorse as soon as I hear myself say it, I can't talk to her like this, I can't be so spiteful and rude, especially not when I'm the host-ess and it's up to me to make sure that people have a good time. This isn't right. I look at Tone and swallow, I'll have to apologize now. I believe and I stand by everything I've said, except for that last part, not only was it a mean thing to say, it was also untrue and I ought to say something to that effect, but I don't get the chance. Tone's mouth falls open and she glares at me as if to say "Oh, well, *excuse* me." She stays like that for a moment, then arches her eyebrows, turns her back on me with a teen-like sniff, and stalks off into the kitchen. I turn and watch her go, then make to follow her only to be stopped by Nina.

"The bathroom, where is it?" she asks.

"Down the hall, second door on the left, the one with the Sandino poster on it," I say. I'm about to tell her there's someone in there when Antony comes swanning over, he looks at me and smiles, totally unfazed by what just happened, there's nothing in his face to indicate that he thinks he's done anything wrong, he truly believes he has the right to treat a single woman like that, it's so offensive, the fact that he simply assumes we'll put up with being treated this way, it offends the hell out of me. I look at him, seething inside, but with an artless, almost sweet smile on my face.

"Cool watch," I say as he walks past me and into the kitchen. He stops and wheels around, dreadlocks swaying gently as he does so.

"Thanks," he says, sounding almost pleased.

"What do you call that, ghetto chic?" I blurt. Hear myself say it, can't believe I said it, but I did.

The kitchen goes very quiet, as if all the babble and chatter around the table has been swallowed up by what I just said. One of the International Socialist women stops munching and stares at me openmouthed, I can see the food in her mouth glistening in the glow of the candles.

"What did you say?" Antony says. He looks as though he can't quite believe his ears. His eyes narrow and he stands there kind of squinting at me.

"I said that fake Rolex is real ghetto chic," I say, but this is so out of line, I can't say things like that, I'll have to try to make a joke of it, either that or excuse myself by saying it was just a bad joke, but I don't, I won't put up with being treated the way he just treated me and I can't contain my anger. I look straight at him and give him that sweet smile again. "You seem so well integrated in other ways," I go on. "Not that there's anything wrong with that. But all it takes is a bit of cheap bling and suddenly you look . . . how can I put it . . . you start to look like a real black dude. And I mean that as a compliment," I say, then I take a sip of gin and tonic, oh, but this really is so out of line, I'm not just being a bad hostess now, I'm going to ruin my own party, this is absolutely outrageous, I have to get a grip now.

Antony simply stares at me. He draws breath, about to say something, but nothing comes out, probably because he doesn't know what to say, he's utterly speechless. He looks around at the others, as if to check whether they heard it too, then he turns back to me. I just stand there, leaning against the doorpost, giving him that sweet smile, I should maybe apologize, but I don't, I try to look as if everything is absolutely fine, try to do the same to him as he just did to me: try to act as if I've every right to talk to him like that. It's not something I planned, but that's what I'm doing, I feel more cheerful as soon as this thought strikes me, feel relieved as soon as I realize that I'm perfectly entitled to do what I'm doing.

"You may think that's funny, Susanne," he says, "but I'm not laughing."

"I didn't laugh either when you implied that I was coming on to you just a few minutes ago," I say, still smiling sweetly. "Even though I'm sure you'd say that *that* was just a joke," I add, trying to keep my voice as light and ingenuous as I can. I pause, take another sip of gin and tonic. Then: "Mmm, really good gin and tonic," I say. I don't know where that came from, it just slipped out, but it accentuates the airy tone I'm trying to strike, this rather ingenuous tone designed to let him know that I have a perfect right to speak to him the way I'm doing. "Much better with lime than with lemon," I add, still smiling and running my eye around the others in the kitchen, I can see how disconcerted they are, they've no idea what's going on here and I get a little kick out of that. Then Nina returns from the bathroom, she smiles as she walks past me and over to the counter again, she doesn't seem to notice how quiet it is, doesn't notice how bewildered, how stunned everyone is, she simply sits down, takes a sip from a half-full plastic glass of red wine, and carries on where she left off, apparently responding to a question on African dance that she hadn't got around to answering before she went to the bathroom. And then the talk starts up again, softly and hesitantly to begin with but gradually growing louder and more animated. I don't say a word, simply stand there, leaning against the doorpost, drinking my gin and tonic. Every now and again someone shoots a little glance at me and I feel my cheeks start to burn, they all find my remarks incomprehensible and offensive, I can see it in their eyes and suddenly I feel a surge of embarrassment, I feel embarrassed and ashamed, but I don't want to feel like that, I refuse to, what I said and did was no worse than what Antony said and did, and if he has no reason to feel embarrassed, then neither do I.

"You should come along too, Susanne," Nina says out of the blue, she has dipped the tip of her finger in the little pool of molten wax that's gathered around the wick of the candle and is now picking it off. She smiles at me, she probably thinks I'm looking a little lost and alone and wants to include me in the conversation, she hasn't registered anything of what's been going on, so there's nothing to stop her from doing that. "To African dance," she adds.

"No, I don't think so, Nina," I say.

"Why not?" she goes on, as positive and enthusiastic as ever, and now I'm going to have to pull myself together and be equally positive in return. She looks at me, smiles as she brushes the congealed flakes of wax off the edge of the table and into the palm of her left hand and I try to smile back, not too successfully. I'm feeling hurt and angry and ashamed, so it's more of a pained grin than a smile. "You love to dance. It's great fun, the company's good, and, not least, it's an excellent way to lose a few pounds," Nina says, giving me a knowing little smile, a smile that says this last was meant as a word from one fatty to another. As if either of us was fat. Okay, we may not be exactly sylphlike, but we're not fat either, we both look perfectly normal, and yet she's talking as though it goes without saying that we both need to lose weight, it's such a typical female thing, this self-loathing, all these demands we make on ourselves and are always trying to impose on other women, there's nothing worse.

"Oh, so you think I need to lose weight?" I say, I really

shouldn't call her on this right now, not when I'm already so close to exploding, it'll only make matters worse if I get into an argument about this as well. I regard her, try to smile and look as if I was just being facetious, but it doesn't quite work this time either, it comes out as a wry smirk.

"I didn't mean it like that," she says, smiling uncertainly at me as she drops the flakes of wax onto the tea tray under the candle.

"Oh, yes you did, Nina," I say.

The kitchen falls silent again. I don't say a word, I can't carry on like this, it's totally out of line, I can't invite people to a party and then go around picking fights with them, one after another, but that's what I'm doing, I look straight at Nina, still with that wry smirk on my face, she gazes at me in bewilderment for a moment, then glances to one side, then the other, she knows something is wrong, but she clearly doesn't know exactly what.

"Susanne, are you all right?" she asks.

"Yes, thanks. And you, Nina?"

Silence.

"Susanne, what *is* it?" Tone asks, staring at me.

"I'm angry," I say, speaking calmly, almost cheerfully. "As a woman, everywhere I go I'm forever being confronted with people who say and do things that *ought* to be regarded as grossly offensive. In the last five minutes alone I've been subjected to things that are every bit as disrespectful and degrading as what I said to Antony, but these are things we women are so used to hearing and experiencing that we actually tolerate them. In fact, not only do we tolerate them, we actually believe that this is as it should be. We don't recognize humiliating behavior when we see it and hear it, and even if we did, if we do feel hurt or angry or resentful, we automatically think there must be something wrong with *us*. We start to blame ourselves, we feel guilty, and we . . . we . . . we think we're so fucking liberated and equal," I cry, flinging out a hand. "People in our field in particular . . . we look down on women in the countries we work with, although we'd never admit it. We say we admire them and that the women are the driving force in third world societies, but in actual fact we look down on them because they put up with being as oppressed by men as they are. But we're actually just as oppressed," I say, getting it all off my chest now, saying exactly what I think. "We struggle with low self-esteem, with eating disorders, depression and anxiety and we don't realize that most of this springs from different forms of oppression. We think there's something wrong with *us*. Always!"

"Susanne?" Tone says, a note of concern in her voice now, she looks concerned too, she thinks I don't mean what I'm saying, she thinks this is something I'm saying to hide the fact that I'm having a hard time of it at the moment or something like that, that's why she looks so concerned, I know it is.

"She's drunk," Antony says under his breath so I won't hear, but I do hear, I look at him, he half closes his eyes, gives a faint shake of his head, and sends the International Socialists a look, as if to say: pay no attention to her.

"Since a lot of what I'm saying touches you and the other men here, Antony, I can see why you would want to belittle my comments and dismiss them as drunken ramblings," I say. "But I've had two gin and tonics and believe it or not even a mere woman can handle that."

"Susanne," Nina says, concern in her voice too now. She comes over to me quietly, places a hand on my arm, and eyes me sympathetically. "I know this is a difficult time for you, what with your niece being in the hospital and everything," she says softly. I gaze at her in bewilderment, she clearly thinks my outburst has something to do with Agnes's accident, she simply cannot believe that anyone could actually mean the things I've just said, not really, although she's said much the same thing herself in discussions and conversations, as have Tone and all the other women here, but it doesn't run very deep, not with any of them, and as soon as they meet someone who takes equal rights seriously, they assume there has to be an ulterior motive. There's no ulterior motive here, though, I mean what I say, mean it with all my heart, it's not the drink talking, and it certainly has nothing to do with Agnes. I look Nina straight in the eye, feel my temper rising, it's so infuriating to have people belittling my opinions, putting my outburst down to problems in my personal life. God, I hate it when people do that.

"Come on, Susanne," Nina says, giving me a gentle, kindly nudge backward, obviously wanting us to go somewhere where we can be alone and I can get all the stuff about Agnes off my chest or something. I allow myself to be pushed back a step or two, then I close my eyes and lift her hand off my arm, open my eyes, and meet her sad, solicitous gaze, feel an instant stab of anger in the pit of my stomach and am just about to say that's it, the party's over, all set to tell the whole lot of them to get the hell out of here, but fortunately I manage to stop myself, I meant everything I said and I have a right to be angry, but I can't kick people out after I've invited them, I have to get a grip, have to swallow my anger and be the perfect hostess for the rest of the evening.

"No, Nina," I say, smiling as brightly as I can and shaking my head gently, making it quite clear that I've no intention of going to the bathroom or the bedroom to get anything off my chest.

Dear David,

"(. . .) oxytocin is commonly referred to as the love hormone or mothering hormone. Immediately prior to and during birth the female brain releases large amounts of oxytocin, which, as well as stimulating the organs involved during childbirth—synthetic oxytocin is often administered to ease a difficult labor—stimulates the flow of milk to the breasts. More interesting in this context, however, is the fact that such large amounts of oxytocin greatly heighten the mother's sense of smell and the scent of the infant is thus associated with the feeling of well-being, which the hormone gives her. This in turn strengthens the social bond between her and the child. It is quite simply the mother's oxytocin level that determines the depth of her mother love. Experiments carried out on rats and sheep have shown that blockage of the oxytocin receptors causes the mother to reject her offspring and, conversely, if the animal is given a dose of synthetic oxytocin, it will exhibit maternal feelings and happily adopt strange young."

The last time I saw you was just before Christmas last year. The restaurants and cafés had just stopped serving and my friends and I had gone into Burger King to grab a bite to eat before we went home when I suddenly heard that old, familiar voice of yours drawling on about some half-finished novel you were writing, which, according to you, dealt with "the secure but deadly boring middle-class existence in oil-rich Norway." I didn't say anything, I didn't even turn to look at you, I simply picked up my cola and my burger, got up, and walked out into the chilly, star-frosted Trondheim night, leaving my friends wondering what was going on. Only then did I turn around to look at the table where you were sitting; you had a stylish woman in her early twenties on your knee and you looked fitter, not to say younger, than you did all those years ago, something that didn't just surprise me, it annoyed me and made me even angrier than I already was, I remember. I simply didn't feel you deserved to look so good.

That was the last time.

The first time I met you was in the cafeteria at Dragvoll in 1996. I was sitting with a few of my fellow students, I remember, leafing through the orange student handbook and discussing which subjects we would take once we had completed the General Education course in history of philosophy and history of science, and some of the others admitted that they weren't only not sure, but utterly daunted by the range of options available to them. I wasn't the slightest bit daunted, though. Not because I felt I had plenty of time and could afford to try and fail, as some of us did, but because I had already made up my mind to go into environmental protection when I left university so I had my course of study pretty well worked out: I had already done a foundation course in political science and biology; after completing my GEs, I would take a foundation course in social anthropology, followed by political science at intermediate level, and then—if I got in, as I used to say, well aware that anybody who knew me would laugh and say of course I would get in, I was so clever—the plan was to persuade my boyfriend at the time, Torkild, to move with me to Oslo where I would write my political science thesis, either on the opening of the Barents Sea to drilling and exploration in 1989 or the role of climate policy in Norwegian oil production. "It's so easy for you, you've found your calling in life," I remember Kjersti Håpnes saying, and even though I eventually did something quite different from what I had envisaged back then, she was to some extent right. At least I didn't lie sleepless at night fretting about making the wrong choice as she appeared to do.

Anyway, it was almost lunchtime. The lecture halls, seminar rooms, and reading rooms began to empty and the cafeteria was starting to fill up. A few of us had already found ourselves a table and were sitting there talking and eating the hot dish of the day when you and two or three of your pals came over, each balancing a tray, and asked if you could join us. I had noticed you before, not because you had "eyes that made me go weak at the knees," as Kjersti Håpnes would say later, but because you had a weird thrift-shop way of dressing and used to ride around on an ancient black DBS bike with an old army rucksack strapped to the baggage rack—all of which marked you out as an adherent of the left-wing of Norwegian politics, as was I. I don't know, but I'm pretty certain that it was the vague sense of fellow feeling kindled by this that emboldened me to ask, with a slightly mocking smile, whether you had really meant it when you told your friends that you had just read Erlend Loe's latest novel and thought it was brilliant.

I had read *Naïve. Super* as soon as it was published and I can't remember now what I thought of it when I finally put it down. I may have enjoyed it, but if I did, I soon forgot that, because my boyfriend, Torkild, didn't, and at that time I took all of his opinions for my own, the way young insecure women with older and more experienced boyfriends often do, unfortunately. Oh, I'm almost embarrassed to think how much I admired Torkild back then. Not that I don't still admire him just as much, or more in fact, but in a completely different way. In those days I was dazzled mainly by all the things he knew and, not least, by the panache and aplomb with which he expressed himself when he "climbed down off his high horse and shared some of his wisdom with us ordinary mortals," as I remember one disgruntled opponent saying after Torkild had stepped up to the lectern at the union and wiped the floor with him in a debate on civil disobedience. When I met him, he had a BA in the unusual combination of chemistry, philosophy, and political science, he had been among the best in his year in all three subjects, and yet he did not see himself pursuing an academic career, nor did he have any plans to do a master's, never mind a PhD. No way was he going to spend his life writing articles that no one outside of academia would ever read or understand, he would say, before going on to describe graduate and doctoral theses so narrow in scope that it bordered on the absurd: "There are actually people who spend three, four, or even five years of their lives writing about the use of the dative case in the Verdal dialect— even though they know no one is ever going to read it," he would say, and then he would throw out his arms and shake his head to show how flabbergasted he was. He, on the other hand, meant to make a difference in the world, to use his own words, he meant to do something that really mattered, and what really mattered, what was in fact the greatest and most pressing issue of the day, was of course environmental protection. When we met, he had almost finished his stint of civilian national service, working with Friends of the Earth (Norway), and had been asked to stay on with them, an invitation he had accepted, despite having been offered a job with a consultancy firm by three old friends from university—a job for which he would have been paid almost double what he was getting with Friends of the Earth—and even though Friends of the Earth really couldn't afford to hire him at all and the job with them was, therefore, very insecure. When I told him that I admired him for staying true to his convictions and not thinking only about the money, he tried to look as though he didn't know what I meant, but he kept bringing the conversation around to it again, so it wasn't hard to see that he was pretty pleased with himself as well. In fact we were very pleased with ourselves altogether in those days, as I recall, pleased to the point of smugness and arrogance. When I see young radicals on the street in Trondheim today, I often find myself smiling and thinking how sweet they seem, but back in the nineties it would never have occurred to me that anyone over thirty-five might think the same of me and my friends. Never. I was quite certain that we won respect and recognition wherever we went. Granted we did have the odd sarcastic remark hurled at us, usually something stupid, such as "Get your hair cut and get a job," and granted we were frequently told that we were naïve idealists who would soon swap our bikes for cars once we came up against the realities of everyday life, but I automatically interpreted such comments as lame excuses from people who weren't selfless or strong enough to do what they knew, deep down, was the right thing. In other words: even they respected and admired people like me. Or so I thought. And who could fail to look up to us as we came striding across Elgeseter Bridge, on our way to yet another Saturday meeting at the union, Torkild in his Icelandic sweater and faded jeans, me in an old, battered combat jacket with a badge on the collar ("Hands off my buddy") and a Palestinian kaffiyeh around my neck and both of us wearing big black Doc

Martens boots, an essential part of any would-be radical's uniform in the nineties? We had commitment, responsibility, and altruism written all over us. We were the advance guard of a generation that was going to change the world, we were the nineties' answer to the WACs and resistance fighters of WWII, who could help but look up to us?

But to get back to *Naïve. Super*. Torkild had slaughtered this book. Not in the scathing way in which he would blast an academic work or article with which he violently disagreed, but more in the manner of a father reading an essay by a son or daughter who has no talent for writing; he assumed the air of a long-suffering reader, one who was not happy with what he was reading but was doing his best to find something good to say about it. It wasn't that it was exactly bad, he explained to me, it was fairly enjoyable and had actually made him laugh a few times. But it was not, of course, serious literature, it was a bit of fluff, a harmless piece of entertainment.

It wasn't till later, long after we split up, that I realized this was how he spoke and acted when he was unsure whether what he was saying was correct, or rather: not just unsure, it was how he often spoke when he was saying something he didn't actually mean. So I wouldn't rule out the possibility that he had actually enjoyed *Naïve. Super*. It could well be that this book struck a chord with him as it did with many members of his generation, but he couldn't bring himself to admit this to himself or to me. Maybe it was hard for him to accept that a book as seemingly apolitical as *Naïve. Super* could speak to someone as politically aware as himself, I don't know. But his verdict was at any rate clear: here one had yet another sign that the younger generation of Norwegian writers were egocentric, nostalgia ridden, and passive. These young writers did not involve themselves in and come to grips with the most vital questions of their day, as writers such as Solstad and Fløgstad (Torkild's favorites) had done and still did. Instead they covered page after page with descriptions of their own childhoods and youths, of banana- or licorice-flavored bubblegum and Apache bikes with speedometers and pennants flying from the back, of BRIO pounding benches, beloved *Children's Hour* characters and down jackets with leather patches on the shoulders. Charming enough in parts, of course, but deeply unsatisfying.

When I adopted Torkild's thoughts and opinions, I usually adjusted them slightly here and there to make it easier to convince others, but mainly, perhaps, to convince myself that I was an independent-thinking individual. And that was exactly what I did when I got into a discussion with you about *Naïve. Super* in the cafeteria at Dragvoll. Which is to say, the opinions I expressed and the points I made were essentially Torkild's, but I didn't present them in the forbearing and rather condescending tone that he had used. Like most insecure young people I was more Catholic than the pope, taking everything a bit further and making myself out to be more extreme than my role model. I gave the impression that I couldn't stand *Naïve. Super*, that I positively hated it in fact. Where Torkild had said that Loe's book was self-indulgent and self-absorbed, I maintained that it epitomized the rampant individualism and egoism we saw all around us in smug, oil-sated Norway, and where Torkild had confined himself to calling the book dull and inconsequential, I declared that it served to draw attention away from books that addressed the key issues of our time and was, therefore, damaging and dangerous. "And you've actually recommended people to spend time on something like that?" I asked.

Your reply threw me completely, I remember. You hadn't meant to overhear, you said, but hadn't we just been looking through the student handbook and talking about how bewildered we were by the range of options available to us, and how we even lay awake at night worrying about choosing the wrong subjects?

Er, yes.

But that was exactly what *Naïve. Super* was about, you said—kids like us. It was neither self-obsessed nor nostalgic, it wasn't an example of a passive form of literature that cultivated the subjective and the personal and shied away from the big, important social questions. Far from it. *Naïve. Super* endeavored to depict and analyze how our generation related to an age and a society characterized by rapid change, fragmentation, and a vast stream of information, by globalization and the breakdown of traditions, by the discrediting of old truths and ideologies. It wasn't exactly easy to be a small individual trying to find one's way, to get one's bearings, to put things into perspective and see the bigger picture in such a society and in such an age. These days young people like us had no idea what to choose, we were so afraid of making the wrong decision and thereby wasting the little time we had on this planet that we often tried to avoid having to choose. We might let other people make the decisions for us by following the crowd or some authority figure, for instance; we might put off making a decision till later or we might react as the central character in *Naïve. Super* does: by regressing, by retreating and escaping into an earlier or imaginary world where we feel safe, confident, and in command. So Loe's book was not passive, you said, it was about a passive generation and how and why this generation was passive, and you simply could not understand why I, who was clearly a politically radical and socially conscious young woman, did not embrace a book like this instead of dismissing it out of hand.

All of this, which for simplicity's sake I have presented here as a sort of monologue from you—banal, but all too typical of the times—actually came out in the course of a long, involved conversation during which I kept asking questions and making comments on what you were saying. I crossed my arms and cocked one eyebrow to make myself look as critical and on the ball as I could and every now and again I would frown and give my head a little shake to make it clear that, we-ell, I wasn't sure I agreed with you there. Generally speaking, I did my best to resemble the image I had of a student and an intellectual, an image possibly inspired by an old but well-known black-and-white photograph of Jean-Paul Sartre, Simone de Beauvoir, and other intellectual leading lights deep in discussion around a table in a café in Paris. Or by an old photo of the student radicals behind the Norwegian literary magazine *Profil*, or maybe a combination of the two, I don't know. But no matter how critical I tried to seem, I made no attempt to hide that you had made me change my mind about this book. There would have been no point anyway because everyone present knew that the objections I raised were nothing but hairsplitting and quibbling and that nothing I said could shake your central argument. As I've said, at that time I was a fairly cocky and strong-minded young woman and I may well have felt humiliated by this, but I honestly don't believe I did. At any rate I can recall many other similar situations in which I managed to put a positive spin on what felt like a defeat. Having the courage to yield to a better argument is the mark of a true intellectual, I would tell myself, thus giving my dented ego a welcome boost.

Contrary to what I may have thought, however, you showed absolutely no respect for the fact that I bowed to your arguments and conceded that you had made me look at *Naïve. Super* with fresh eyes. You didn't understand people like me, you said, shaking your head and laughing. "First you loathe the book and advise everyone not to read it, but as soon as I put it into a social context and come up with a simple, off-the-cuff interpretation involving some sort of political message, you change your mind. For Christ's sake, woman, you're what— twenty-two? twenty-three?—but you act like a cranky, uptight old Maoist. Everything in that book has to add up somehow, and not only add up, it has to add up in such a way that it can be used to some 'socially useful' end" (here, I remember, you raised your hands and made quotation marks with your fingers). "You don't seem to think a book is any good until you've reduced it to a trite battle cry."

Not until long after this did I realize what an impact your words actually had on me. I don't recall how I reacted at the time, but I don't think anything dramatic happened. The discussion probably just petered out as such discussions tend to do, one of us may have got up and said he was going to get more coffee, did anybody else want some? Somebody may have looked at his watch and been surprised to see how late it was, his next lecture started in a couple of minutes, he had to run. Or maybe a third person asked who was up for going to Café 3B that evening, it was Tuesday, after all, cheap wine night. I don't know.

But your words stayed with me and in the months that followed I found myself thinking about them—not every day, possibly not even every week, but now and again they would cross my mind and almost always due to something Torkild had said or done that annoyed me. When I was listening to music, for example, and he simply had to let me know how awful he thought it was. Not that he ever said it straight out, not normally, anyway, he liked to come across as an open-minded, easygoing sort of a guy who respected the fact that my taste in music was different from his, so the slaughter was usually conducted in subtle and benign fashion. "Is someone torturing that man?" he would joke when Kurt Cobain's voice rose to a distorted wail at the end of "Where Did You Sleep Last Night," and "Not exactly Bob Dylan," he might remark when he felt moved to point out the stupidity or banality of some song lyric. And it wasn't uncommon for him to then play a record that he declared to be a pioneering number within the same genre as the Norwegian band I had been listening to. "Listen to this instead," he would say, putting on one of Neil Young's earliest records. "The deLillos do their best, but they can never match their hero, and that's putting it mildly." I would then be treated to a long lecture on the unique qualities of Neil Young's music.

As is so often the way with men, Torkild was, you see, intent on shaping me in his own image. Not that he ever said as much, of course, but he aimed to teach me. Train me. Make me his disciple. And he was well on the way to succeeding too. It became rarer and rarer for me to play music I knew he didn't like, not just when he wasn't home, but also when I was on my own in the flat. And if I did, I always had a vague feeling of guilt and shame. It was the same with books, films, television, and even food and wine. My conscience would prick me if I listened to bright, poppy Radio P3 rather than the more cerebral P2, if I bought a frozen pizza for myself instead of making dinner from scratch, if I read one of the tabloids, *VG* or *Dagbladet*, instead of a serious newspaper like *Morgenbladet* or *Klassekampen* or, worse still, yielded to the temptation to watch what you would later dub "a folk tale for our times," but which Torkild naturally regarded as trashy light entertainment—namely, *Hotel Caesar* on TV2. As a teenager living at home with Mom, I had been hooked on a number of soaps, but by this time I was only ever watching the occasional episode, always in deepest secrecy, and it's no exaggeration to say that I felt dirty afterward. In fact, however ridiculous it may sound now, more than once I tried—albeit unconsciously—to make up for this by picking up a particularly weighty novel shortly after switching off the TV.

For a long time, when forced to explain why I tried so hard to embrace high culture and reject its popular counterpart, I blamed forces beyond my control. "I was so much in love, I would have done anything to be the way I thought Torkild wanted me to be," I would say. "I was plagued by guilt every time I watched a romantic comedy or listened to some light, bubbly pop music because I felt I was letting him down," I would go on before describing—a mite ruefully—how I would force myself to read books I was in no way equipped to understand, and how I therefore became a sort of female equivalent of that guy in *A Fish Called Wanda*, you know, the one who quotes Nietzsche without understanding a word of it. On other occasions again I've spoken of intellectual snobbery when describing myself at that time in my life. I've talked of my own so-called class journey, of how I was brought up by a single mother who had to do two jobs in order to feed me and my two sisters and spent most of her free time watching American talk shows, and of how she and I became more and more estranged after I went to university, of how she accused me of showing off by using fancy foreign words and extolling all the things that ordinary people knew nothing about, and how this in turn increased my dislike of the popular culture that she represented.

There was some truth in all of this.

Today, though, I can see that ideology and mental attitude were even more important keys to understanding why I was so ridiculously eager to cultivate my inner connoisseur. Because this too, of course, came down to the most important issue of our age: environmental protection. I had been a member of Nature and Youth for several years before I met Torkild, so the idea that we in the West needed to reduce our consumption

dramatically to prevent a future climate crisis was not something I got from him. Not at all. The concept of reduced consumption was already deeply ingrained in me, a mantra I repeated in
discussion after discussion. It was an indisputable truth as far
as I was concerned, and before moving into my first sublet I
actually persuaded the landlord to install an economy shower
and weather-strip the leaky window. I cycled, walked, or took the
bus everywhere, I was heavily into recycling and bought most
of my clothes from goodwill shops or flea markets—none of it
particularly heroic, perhaps, since I was living on a student loan
and had to watch my money anyway. But still, when I met and
eventually moved in with Torkild, something changed. Slowly
but surely the battle zone expanded, to use Houellebecq's
words. Torkild was even more obsessed with restricting one's
consumption and leading an environmentally sound life than
I was, he was more consistent and thorough, more extreme, if
you like. But that's not really the point here. The point is that
the philosophy behind this commitment to environmental
issues colored every aspect of his life. To someone who takes
environmental preservation seriously and actually has decided
to reduce his own personal consumption, it is of course important that what he does consume should be of the best. And this
was what made Torkild a connoisseur. This was why he would
rather we share a bottle of amarone costing 250 kroner than
get plastered on five bottles of cheap plonk, why he abhorred
processed foods and insisted on serving microscopic gourmet
dishes prepared by him in our very sparsely equipped student
kitchen, and why he was always on the lookout for the real and
the authentic in art and culture, for things that were original
and innovative, classic, things that were indisputably good
and that he could therefore justify spending time, effort, and
money on. The idea of rationing, which was all part of being a

true environmentalist, imbued everything he said and did, in fact it strikes me as I write this that it may even have influenced the way he spoke and acted. It was as if the need to be prudent, to exercise moderation and self-restraint applied here as well. He detested small talk and idle chatter, for example. As far as he was concerned, if you didn't have anything sensible to say, you should simply shut up and read a good book. He had only a handful of close friends and he told me straight out that he had no great need to get to know my university pals, he simply didn't have time for any more friends.

And Torkild was gradually instilling all of this, this attitude to life, so to speak, in me. Or at least, *instilling* is possibly the wrong word. I was, as I said, already resolved to keep my consumption low and environmentally friendly before I met him, so it's perhaps more correct to say that he was in the process of polishing me. When I met him I was a sort of rough diamond and now he was going to make me shine. And not only to shine in his eyes, mark you, because even though I harbored feelings of shame and guilt and a fair bit of resentment at being corrected and schooled, I was pleased with the progress I was making. I was convinced, you see, that suppressing my own bad taste and my simple and occasionally vulgar needs was all part of my personal maturation process. If I was to grow as a human being, I couldn't just fritter away my time and energy—by sitting slumped in front of the television for example—and every time I resisted the temptation to do exactly that I proved to myself, if you like, that I was on the right track, something that was, in itself, deeply satisfying. But there were lots of positive sides as well: most importantly perhaps all the great discussions we had, all the interesting articles and books I was introduced to, all the wonderful music, all the delicious and exciting dishes, the walks in Rondane National Park, skiing expeditions in the

Dovre and Børgefjell mountains. Because it wasn't, of course, as though I actually disliked or didn't understand everything that Torkild introduced me to. Much of it gave me a lot of pleasure.

But still, something wasn't quite right. There was something fundamentally wrong with my life. To begin with it made itself felt in relatively lengthy spells of depression that I couldn't quite explain. I would feel sluggish, listless, and unable to go to lectures. I had no motivation, no interest in going anywhere or seeing anyone. I couldn't face answering the phone or opening the door if someone rang the bell and I would stay in bed till noon. I could be irritable and out of sorts for days at a time, and when Torkild asked what was wrong I would often make up some excuse: I had my period, I was worried about my exams, and so on. Just as the need to present a cogent and coherent account may lead me to caricature Torkild slightly in this letter, so it is also quite possible that this same need has led me to give you more credit than you strictly speaking deserve. But let me say it anyway: it was what you said in the cafeteria at Dragvoll that made me see what was wrong with me. "For Christ's sake, woman, you're twenty-two, but you act like an old Maoist," you said. And there it was, that was my problem. Not only was I becoming extremely earnest and sensible, not only was I becoming rigid, orthodox, and ruthlessly dismissive of anything that could not be justified according to the philosophy I have just outlined. I was a student in her early twenties with the mindset of a middle-aged woman. Whether biology had anything to do with this I don't know, but to me at least it seemed as though I had skipped a stage in life, a stage we are all actually supposed to go through.

For where was the wildness of youth? Where was that don't-give-a-fuck mentality, that madcap spirit, not to mention the carefree, fun-loving, commitment-free life of student days?

All gone. Or no, not gone, it was all still there, but stifled by a philosophy that imposed on me the virtues of moderation and pragmatism. There was a scatterbrained teenager inside me, but I was forcing myself to live the way one ought to live at the age I am now and maybe not even then. And it was you who put this into words for me. When I turned down an invitation to go to Café 3B with the girls in my class because Torkild had bought scallops from Hitra or a locally produced blue cheese and a bottle of good Tokay for us to enjoy that evening, I would find myself thinking about what you had said. When Torkild sneered at those same fellow students for choosing to go and see an action movie at the local cinema instead of coming to the Trøndelag Theater with us to see a modern production of An Enemy of the People (which, according to Torkild, was actually all about environmental protection), your words came into my head again. When I scoffed at Mom for liking James Dean and then found myself arguing that the United States had colonized Norway with the aid of inane light entertainment and that she was, in fact, an American, the same thing happened. But the feeling of being "like an old Maoist" was never stronger than when I was with my sisters, May Lene and Mette, even though they were both quite a bit older than me.

Mette and May Lene were alike both in looks and in personality, but as Mom once said: "I've never met anyone who would have guessed that Susanne was related to either of you, and certainly not that she was your sister." While Mette and May Lene looked like Dad and were tall and blond with almost fashion-model good looks, I took after Mom and was small, dark, and very ordinary looking. While my nights out were spent at Café 3B (usually in "Africa," the darkest, smokiest corner in the place, right behind the toilets), Mette and May Lene went dancing at clubs such as Frakken or Bajazzo. While I spent ten minutes in the bathroom before going out and always wore some variation on the aforementioned student radical uni- form, Mette and May Lene could spend two hours putting on their makeup and getting dressed and when they eventually emerged, they would have looked perfectly at home on the most exclusive of red carpets. They loved getting all dolled up, and unlike me—who preferred to look as natural as possible and felt embarrassed to admit that I did actually use a little makeup now and again—they made no secret of the fact that it was important to them to look good. They used creams and lotions that cost as much as I spent on clothes and shoes in a year and had no qualms about it. In fact they seemed to be annoyingly unburdened by any feelings of guilt or shame. They were bright, forthright, and outgoing. When they got drunk, they could become loud and boisterous, dance on tables and get a sing-along going, but they could also be extremely sexy and sultry, not to say vulgar. They seduced and allowed them- selves to be seduced, they had one-night stands at the drop of a hat, and when we met for coffee at Erichsen's the next day (we always had coffee at Erichsen's on Saturday), they would regale the rest of us with stories of their Friday night exploits. "He was like a rabbit in bed," May Lene said once, laughing. "I felt like an acrobat at the circus," Mette said on another occasion. "He kept wanting to change position, first he had me on my stom- ach, then on my back, then on my knees, and then he decided he wanted me to sit on top of him. My head was spinning by the end, I kid you not, no exaggeration." That's how they went on. They were living proof, to me at least, that Marilyn Monroe was right when she said: "Blondes have more fun" (it was she who said that, wasn't it?). I tried to tell myself that they were less intelligent than me and more naïve, I tried to pigeonhole them as dumb blondes, but I knew that wasn't true, or not the whole truth anyway. My sisters might not have read as many books as I had and they couldn't quote Arne Næss or Sigmund Kvaløy Setreng and talk about deep ecology, but they were no less deep than me. And certainly no less intelligent. Although I hate to admit it, to myself or anyone else, Mette was smarter than me. Not only was she better with numbers than I was and far better than me when it came to mental arithmetic—which was only to be expected, I suppose, of someone who had gone to business school in Bergen—but more than once I've also known her to comprehend and grasp the essence of a complex text or conversation much more quickly than I could—and that was a far greater blow to my ego, that really hurt. Well, I would tell myself, at least I lead a much fuller life than they do. While I endeavored to grow a little more as a human being each day, their lives were marked by "the unbearable lightness of being," they squandered their time and energy and talents on things that would, in the long run, prove worthless and one day they would look in the mirror and discover that their once lovely features had been replaced by the wrinkled faces of elderly ladies, and come that day, the day when boys and men no longer turned to look at them on the street, they would be filled with regret, then they would realize that they had wasted their lives on fun and games and frivolity. This is what I tried to tell myself. In slightly less dramatic terms, it's true, but this was what I told myself. Mere excuses all of it, of course. There was absolutely nothing to suggest that the things they filled their lives with were a substitute for something more profound and more meaningful that they couldn't be bothered striving to achieve, there was nothing to suggest that the makeup, the expensive clothes, and the casual sex were a way of escaping from the realities of life. They simply did more of whatever they felt like doing, they were more honest with themselves than I was, they took their own needs seriously, and not only their intellectual needs, all their needs. That was why they were happier than I was.

All of this I figured out during the first months after you told me I was "like an old Maoist" and slowly but surely I was filled with a deep, quiet anger. I was no longer depressed, I was furious. Mainly with myself for not being strong enough to be present in my own life, but also, naturally, with Torkild, who had taught me to be the person I had become.

I look at Mom, she still seems a bit shocked, standing there openmouthed, staring at Rex.

"But where's he to be when you're out gadding about, Susanne?"

"Here, I suppose," I say.

"Alone?"

I wait a moment before answering, tilt my head to one side, and smile at her.

"Oh, Mom, it's only a dog, not a baby," I say.

A flicker of disappointment and resentment crosses her face.

"You don't need to tell me that," she mutters, glancing sidelong at the floor and giving a little sniff.

I immediately feel myself bristle, here she goes again, she never misses a chance to remind me of how disappointed she is that I've chosen to live the way I do, no matter how many times I've asked her to stop criticizing me for rejecting a traditional family life, she still harps on about it. I stare at her, but she won't meet my eye. I'm about to ask her to just leave it, but I don't, there's no need, she knows she's gone too far. She stands there, eyes lowered, takes a deep breath, then lets it out, as if pulling herself together, then she looks up at me again, a strained half smile on her lips.

"Would you like some coffee?" I ask.

She doesn't answer straightaway, glances past me and into the kitchen.

"No thanks," she says.

I swivel around and look into the kitchen, but I can't see anything unusual, don't know what she could have seen in there. I turn to her again. She still has that smile on her face, a long-suffering sort of smile.

"What?" I say.

"Susanne . . . there is such a thing as coffee-machine cleaner, you know."

I glance behind me at the coffee machine. The inside of the pot is coated with a brownish film and the water container is maybe not as clean as it could be either, but it's not that dirty. She's only saying this to make a point, she may not even realize it herself, but the underlying message here is that I ought to spend my time on the kinds of things that she spends her time on, I know it is. I turn to face her again. She stands there for a moment longer, looking at me with that long-suffering smile on her face, then she gives a little laugh, a laugh intended to somehow make light of the fact that she's criticizing me. Either that or to make it harder for me to be annoyed at her, I mean it's not easy to answer back when she cloaks her criticism and accusations in smiles and laughter. I stare at her, smile thinly.

"Next time I'll be sure to clean the place before you come," I say.

That wipes the smile off her face. She tries to look surprised, as if she can't think why I'm annoyed at her.

"Oh, really, Susanne."

"I mean it. At the moment it looks as though somebody actually lives here and we can't have that, can we?"

She opens her mouth, about to say something, but obviously thinks better of it. She shuts her eyes and puts a hand to her brow, stays perfectly still for a moment or two, then lowers her hand, looks at me, and sighs.

"All right, now, let's stop this, both of us," she says.

"Both of us?" I laugh.

"Susanne, please."

"Fine," I say, still smiling thinly. There's a half-full glass of water on the table with a dead mosquito floating in it. I pick it up and carry it into the kitchen, pour out the water, and put the glass in the dishwasher. I open the overhead cabinet and go to take out the French press but stop halfway. "How about a glass of wine then?" I ask as my eye lands on the white-wine glasses, I can't resist it, I know what Mom thinks of drinking in the middle of the week, never mind the middle of the day, but I ask anyway because there's a part of me that feels like reminding her of how old-fashioned, how parochial and provincial she is. At least I think that's why I'm doing it.

"*Now?*" Mom asks, looking flabbergasted, reacting exactly as I knew she would.

"Yes, why not?" I ask, acting as if I'm not quite sure what she means, feeling both gleeful and guilty, because I'm showing her that I don't care about all the rules she has always tried, and is still trying, to impose on me. There's something a little adolescent about her carrying on like this, though. Not that I see anything wrong with having a midweek glass of wine, but it does seem a mite immature to make such a thing of it.

"Er . . . well, I'm not really in the habit of tippling wine on a Wednesday forenoon," she says.

"Me neither, I usually don't have any more than a glass or two. Are you sure you don't want some?"

"But—er," she stammers. I detect a note of irritation in her voice now. "*No*, I *don't* want any wine, all right!"

"Okay," I say, taking out a glass for myself, I don't really feel like white wine, but I can't not take a glass, not after what I've just said, it's stupid and childish of me, I know, but I open the fridge and take out the bottle of white wine, unscrew the top, fill the glass, cross to the door, and stand there. But now I really have to stop it, I have to drop this stupid Contrary Mary act.

"Well, can I get you something else?" I ask, smiling as naturally as I can.

She doesn't answer straightaway, stands there frowning and staring at my wine glass, she can't resist letting me see how much she disapproves of drinking wine on a Wednesday forenoon. I shouldn't let it bother me but it does.

"What?" I ask with a little lift of my eyebrows, feigning innocence, just the way she did after that dig about the coffee machine.

She shakes her head in despair.

"Oh, nothing," she says.

"Are you sure? You gave me such a funny look."

She raises one hand as if to say "Stop right there."

"It's nothing, Susanne."

"Okay," I say. "Well, is there anything else you would like?"

"No thanks. I got to the hospital during visiting hours and I had coffee and cake there, so I've had all I need," she says. She pauses, then looks down and slips her hand into her purse. "I really only popped in to give you this. You left it at the hospital." She pulls out my wallet, holds it up, and looks at me as if to say how careless could I be, a look that says she's shocked and she expects me to look shocked too, expects me to look as though I despair of myself, but I refuse to do that, even though to some extent I do despair of myself. I'm not going to let her know that, though, I won't give her the satisfaction, not when she's being so self-righteous.

"Oops," I say brightly, smile as I go over to her, put out my hand, and take the wallet from her.

"Oops, indeed," she says. "One of the nurses found it in a bathroom along the corridor. With almost a thousand kroner in cash in it, plus your Visa card, driver's license, and God knows what else."

"Oh, good," I say, keeping my voice bright and chirpy. There's no way I'm going to agree with her and be appalled by my own forgetfulness.

"Good?"

"That she found it."

"Well, yes," she says, shaking her head in bewilderment. "Of course it's *good*. But really, Susanne . . . how could you be so careless, I mean . . . anyone could have found it."

"I know, I know, but most people are pretty honest, Mom," I say. I drink some of my wine, set the glass down next to the wooden elephant that stops the books from sliding off the shelf, open my wallet, and check inside. "Oh, but the condoms are gone," I say, purely on impulse. I didn't have any condoms in my wallet, but I say it anyway, she's got it into her head that I have much more casual sex than I actually do, and I know how much she disapproves, which is probably why I'm pretending that I always have a stash of condoms in my wallet. I shut the wallet, look up, and smile at Mom as brightly and artlessly as I can.

"Oh, for heaven's sake, Susanne," she says. She stares at me openmouthed and moves her head from side to side.

I give her a look of faint surprise.

"What? Aren't you glad I use condoms?"

She shuts her eyes, opens her mouth, and gives a quick shake of her head, raises her hand slightly as if in warning.

"I don't want to get into that, that's not why I said 'for heaven's sake,'" she snaps. She breathes, then opens her eyes and looks at me again, shaking her head helplessly.

"It's just that . . . you don't . . . you don't seem to care."

"But I do care. I said it was good that she found my wallet, didn't I?"

"I know, but—er . . ."

"Well, what do you want me to say? Don't I seem grateful enough to you for returning it to me?" I say. "Is that it?"

"Oh, Susanne, now you're being unfair. All I meant was that you . . . well, your mind always seems to be somewhere else. First you manage to leave your wallet at the hospital and then, when you get it back, it's like . . ." She pauses, looks at me, and shrugs. "Like . . . well, of course!" she goes on, with a flick of her hand. "It doesn't seem to bother you, you take it for granted that things will work out all right one way or the other."

"Well, things do have a way of working out all right," I say, maintaining this "don't worry, be happy" attitude, doing all I can to defy her self-righteousness, I ought to be above this sort of thing, I ought to stop being so willful and perverse, but I can't. "I mean look, it did all work out all right, didn't it?"

"Yes, but it might not have. You could have lost a wallet

full of money and important documents, your bank account could have been drained, and . . . and . . ."

"So what you're trying to say is that I should wake up and start worrying a bit more about everything under the sun the way you do?" I say, picking up my wine glass and taking a sip as I lay my wallet in its place.

"Oh, really. Don't twist my words, Susanne."

"I'm not. I'm simply trying to make you see that there's a veiled criticism in almost everything you say to me. Almost everything you say is somehow meant to remind me that I have to stop being me and be more like you instead."

"Oh, Susanne, don't start all that again, please, you have to be able to take . . . it's just that I get a bit tired of you being so scatterbrained. Don't make it out to be more than it is."

"Yes, but that's my whole point, Mom. So much of what you say to me, including this, is more than it seems."

She puts a hand to her brow, gazes at the floor, and gently shakes her head.

"Oh, Susanne, don't tell me we're back to that again," she says, then she raises her eyes to me, a mournful look on her face. "You're thirty-five, we've been having this same conversation since you were eighteen, nineteen. What's happening to us . . . I . . . I would have thought we had enough trouble in this family without you and me slipping back to where we were fifteen years ago."

I regard her, about to say that if we are regressing, then it's her fault, not mine, but I don't, because it wouldn't be true, it's just as much my fault. For some reason she's started criticizing me the way she used to do fifteen years ago, but only because I give her cause, I'm not sure why, but I do, and I ought to be mature enough to admit it. I look at Mom, smile at her, and breathe a little sigh.

"Sorry, Mom," I say.

She smiles sadly back at me.

"It's just as much my fault, Susanne," she says, putting her hand to her brow again. I look at her hands, notice the thick blue veins crisscrossing the back of her hand, I'll never have hands like that, hands marked by a long life of hard work, I suddenly feel something akin to tenderness for her. Dear, sweet Mom, I love her so much, I've had it up to here with her nagging and all the sly little digs she's always making at me, but at the same time I know it's only because she really loves me that she says and does the things she does. I swallow, feel an even stronger rush of tenderness as my eye falls on the red lipstick she's wearing, I'm not sure why, but there's something almost beautiful about a working-class woman from the provinces sprucing herself up a bit for her rare trips to town, something rather dignified.

Silence.

"Are you sure you won't have something?" I say. "I could make some coffee in the French press instead."

She dismisses the suggestion with a wave of her hand, that sad little smile still on her face as she lifts a pile of newspapers and magazines off the armchair, places it on the table with my cactuses, and sits down.

"Oh, for heaven's sake, Susanne, filter coffee's fine. It was just . . . ah, I don't know what it was, I don't know what made me say that about the machine."

I smile at her, happy to hear her say this.

"So would you like some?"

"Yes, please. Preferably just ordinary coffee, though."

"I only have fair-trade coffee, Mom, I don't buy anything else," I say. I look at her, about to add that she knows that only too well, but fortunately I manage to stop myself, it might sound like an accusation, so I shouldn't do that, I have to drop the Contrary Mary act and have a proper conversation with her now.

"But isn't that the stuff with the earthy taste to it?"

I look at her, not quite with her for a moment, but then it comes to me: once when she was here, I gave her some Nica's Coffee that I'd bought from the LAG guys and she didn't like it, that's what she's thinking of.

"No, no," I say, smiling through clenched teeth, then I go back into the kitchen. I put my glass down on the counter, take the coffee pot and give it a good rinse, fill it, and pour the water into the reservoir.

"How were things at the hospital?" I ask.

"Oh, no change."

"How about May Lene, how was she?"

"No change there either."

"She's still refusing to leave the room?" I ask.

"Yes."

I spoon coffee into the filter paper, close the lid, and switch on the machine. I almost say something about how May Lene would have to try to come to terms with it, but I don't, it sounds so cold, it would sound as if I was making light of the whole situation and I would never do that, there's nothing worse than losing your own child, so that's the last thing I want to do. Besides which, I don't know whether Mom has progressed any further than May Lene in the grieving process, she says she has accepted that it can only go one way and that in all likelihood Agnes won't come out of the coma, but I'm not so sure. I pick up my wine glass again, I don't really feel like wine right now, I'd rather just pour the whole thing down the sink, I don't know why I don't. If Mom can be big enough to change her mind and accept the offer of coffee after all, I ought to be big enough to pour out the wine. But I don't, I take a little sip and go back into the living room, look at Mom, she's sitting with my calabash and my bombilla in her hands, eyeing me quizzically.

"What's this?" she asks, motioning to the bombilla and sounding a little anxious.

"It's for drinking maté," I say. "It's a kind of tea."

"Oh, thank God," she exclaims. "I thought it was something you used for smoking drugs," she says with a little laugh as she puts it down next to the pile of newspapers and magazines.

I smile at her as I set my wine glass on the table and flop down onto the sofa.

"So, how are things otherwise?" Mom asks.

"Good," I say. "Busy, busy. I've just finished a long piece on Rigoberta Menchú. On what life has been like for the indigenous people of Guatemala since she won the Nobel Peace Prize in 1992."

She looks at me and nods, says nothing for a moment. Then: "But no sign of anything more permanent?" she asks.

I don't answer straightaway, simply sit there staring at her. I don't know how many times I've told her I prefer to work freelance, but she still manages to make it sound as if I'm just hanging around waiting for a "proper" job to turn up. I did actually consider taking a full-time post not that long ago. I almost said yes to a job with *Adresseavisen*, but Mom doesn't know anything about that, she thinks I'm still as determined to work freelance as I've always professed to be and this supposedly casual question is just another way of trying to get me to do what she believes to be the right thing, I know it is, she thinks it will be harder for me to stick to my guns if she simply acts as if she takes it for granted that everyone actually wants to have a full-time job; she thinks this will make me feel weird and out of step and that this, in turn, will make me change my mind. I lean forward, pick up my glass, and take a sip of my wine, feel my earlier annoyance returning, because it's true what I said to her a moment ago, almost everything she says to me is somehow meant to remind me that I ought to stop being myself and be more like her instead and that really pisses me off. I ought to rise above it, but I can't. I look at her, I'm so close to telling her straight out to stop it, but I don't and I won't, I need to try to keep it civil now. And besides, I'm not even sure she knows she's doing it, not all the time anyway, I rather suspect she doesn't, I think it's just become the way she talks and thinks when she's with me.

"No, I'm much happier working freelance," I say, setting the glass back down on the table.

"But it's so insecure, you never know if you're going to make enough to pay next month's rent, or your electricity and food bills, you don't have the same rights as other people if you fall ill or are disabled or . . . oh, I don't know how you can live like that . . . that you'd *want* to. I mean . . . you're not twenty anymore," she says, as if for the first time, even though she's said it a hundred times before, it's the same old refrain, I'm so sick of it.

"I don't want to write about the terrible summer weather and all the other first world problems that the Norwegian papers are so obsessed with, Mom. I want to write about things I feel are important, and working freelance gives me the chance to do that. Besides, I enjoy the freedom that comes with working like this, how many times do I have to tell you?" I say, unable to conceal the fact that I'm starting to lose my temper.

"Yes, well . . . er . . . of course, I mean, I was going to say it's good that you care about . . . about what's happening to black people in Africa. But what if something happens to *you*? I mean . . . Agnes's accident has shown us how short life can actually be. What if you fell down the stairs tomorrow and lost the use of your limbs, who would look after you?"

"What? Are you afraid you'd have to look after me?" I say.

She doesn't answer right away, just sits there looking at me and I feel a sudden ripple of unease, I realize I'm worried that she's going to say yes, she is, not that I expect her to look after me if such a thing were to happen, because I don't, I think I'm more afraid that the love she feels for me isn't actually infinite, maybe it's the little girl in me who's afraid, I don't know.

"Oh, Susanne, don't be silly," she says.

I smile quickly, relieved by her answer. I feel almost pleased by the way she brushes aside my question, it may be a mite pathetic, infantile even, to take pleasure in something like that but I can't help it.

"I'm only asking," I say.

"I just don't understand how your mind works. It . . . well, you don't seem to be able to look any more than one day ahead," she says. "I don't know where you get it from. Your dad wasn't like that, I'm not like that and neither are Mette or May Lene, it's . . . I don't understand it," she says, her voice suddenly rising. She looks me straight in the eye for a second or two, shaking her head, then she shuts her eyes, takes a deep breath, and lets it out in one great sigh, as if collecting herself. "I'm sorry, Susanne, I didn't mean to . . . I'm sorry."

"Well, at least you care," I say, smiling at her. "And that's a good thing."

"Oh, God, you and your sisters must be so tired of me," she says with a little laugh, putting her hands to her head.

"Rubbish." I pick up my wine glass, knock back the last few drops, and stand up, there's a dried-up peach pit lying on the back page of *The War of the End of the World*, I scoop it up as I get to my feet, feel its little ridges tickle my skin as I roll it back and forth in my hand. "Coffee's ready," I say. I go into the kitchen, put my wine glass on the counter, open the door of the cabinet under the sink, and drop the peach pit into the trash can, then I take down two of the blue-and-green Book Club mugs, pour the coffee, and go back through to Mom. "Oh, by the way, I'm meeting up with Mette at Bare Blåbær tomorrow evening for a glass of wine, why don't you join us?" I say, although I'm not sure why I say it, I see Mette so seldom and it would be good to be able to chat with her without Mom butting in all the time, fussing and fretting, I had been looking forward to talking about something apart from Agnes for a little while, but there will be no chance of that if Mom's there, she's almost incapable of thinking or talking about anything else now. And besides, I know what happens when we're all together, even though we try to avoid it, we all seem to fall back into the roles we played in the family when we were growing up, it's bound to happen.

I set her coffee in front of her and sit down on the sofa, hunch forward with my hands wrapped around my mug, and blow lightly on the piping-hot coffee.

"Oh, no, you don't want your old mother tagging along when you finally have the chance to get together," she says, smiling at me. I glance across at her, raise my eyebrows, let out a little "ha-ha," and try to look as though she's just said something ridiculous and completely untrue.

"Of course we do," I say and take a little swig of my coffee. "Eight o'clock at Bare Blåbær."

"Well, I have a few things to do after I've been to the hospital tomorrow, but we'll see."

I look at her and nod. Then Rex comes waddling over to me, sounds like I'll have to cut his nails soon, I can hear them click-clacking across the parquet floor. I turn to him and give him a big smile, he wags his tail, clearly happy. I bend down and let him lick my face.

"Who's a lovely dog then," I murmur, feel his rough, wet tongue brushing my chin and my cheek. "Yes, you are. The loveliest dog in the whole world." I lay my hand on his neck and ruffle the thick fur before sitting back again, sit there scratching Rex behind the ear and regarding Mom, but what's the matter with her, she looks as though she's about to cry, she's swallowing hard and there are tears in her eyes.

"Mom, what's wrong?" I ask. She doesn't answer right away.

"Mom?"

"Oh, I can't help it, Susanne. It's just that . . . you're so sweet and so kind, you have so much to give. I don't understand," she says, then she puts a hand to her face and wipes away a tear.

I had been planning to take the introductory course in social anthropology, that was what I really wanted to do, but when the time came to complete my application form and send it in, I did what I had promised myself I wouldn't do: I let Torkild talk me into signing up for an intermediate course in political science instead. I had tried for ages to convince myself that social anthropology would give me the opportunity to study "primitive" societies where people were not ruled by the tyranny of Western consumerism, and that this in turn would provide me with insight and knowledge that would prove useful in the fight to save the environment, but after being subjected by Torkild to numerous long lectures in which he dismissed this argument as naïve hippie bullshit, it no longer seemed such a great idea. So political science it would be, that and organizational theory.

In the weeks after I posted my application, I was moody and irritable. Torkild was probably right in saying that political science was more relevant than social anthropology for someone intending to pursue a career in environmental protection. Nevertheless, my heart was still set on the latter. Even though Torkild said, and to some extent managed to persuade me, that social anthropology was a soft, female subject and one of those trendy courses that did nothing but qualify people for unemployment, that was still what I really wanted to do and the fact that, even so, I ended up putting my name down for political science made me really angry. I was angry because Torkild kept trying to force me to be someone I didn't want to be and because he always succeeded. Eventually, though, I began to pay him back by doing things I knew would irritate him: I would pop into McDonald's and buy a burger on the way home from a night out (or "eat the rain forest," as Torkild put it), I would insist on seeing the comedy sketch show *Lille Lørdag* on Wednesday evening (puerile undergraduate humor and a pale imitation of *Monty Python*, in Torkild's opinion), I bought and played a "Best of Elvis" CD (according to Torkild, Elvis wasn't just ridiculously kitsch, he had also been one of America's key weapons in the colonization of Norway, more important than the Marshall Plan), I would neglect to turn down the heating at night, left lights burning in the apartment when I went out, and burned plastic waste in the little wood-burning stove in the living room. I quite simply rebelled. It was a feeble, childish rebellion, but a rebellion nonetheless, an attempt to take back my life and possibly also to show Torkild that we weren't right for each other and it would be better for both of us if we simply called it a day. Which we did, but not until much later because around Christmas 1996 I found out that I was five months pregnant. In April 1997, Malin was born and suddenly everything changed.

We were so happy. Of course we were. Not as happy as society expects new parents to be, I grant you, a fact that made me feel guilty and led me to wonder whether there was something wrong with me, I remember. But we were happy, and during those first weeks, when Malin was still sleeping through the night—inexperienced parents that we were—we would get up five times a night to check that she was breathing and then just sit there together, gazing at her, unable to believe that we could have made something so beautiful. So naturally we were determined to give it another chance, it wasn't even something we discussed, Malin deserved the best and the best obviously meant growing up in a two-parent family. And to begin with everything was fine. All new parents tend to say that having a baby won't change their lives, that they won't crash in front of the TV every evening, that they'll still go to concerts or out for drinks or to a movie with friends, that they'll still read big, fat novels and stay as well informed and involved in the things they used to do in their old lives. They all say it and two or three months later most of them are shaking their heads and laughing: "We had no idea what we were talking about," they say. But not Torkild and me. We actually did manage to hold on to much of our old life. Obviously we didn't go out so much in the evenings as we had done before and obviously the daily routine revolved mainly around Malin, but Torkild's parents were always happy to babysit for us, so we spent less time at home than most couples in our situation, and even though our lives had been given a new focus, we weren't the sort of new-fledged parents who can scarcely talk about anything other than sleepless nights and mastitis, the first tooth, the first step, and how strong their baby's neck is. Not at all. We became even better at inviting people over than we'd been before we had Malin and since none of our friends had kids, the main topic of conversation tended, quite naturally, to be the same as it had always been—which is to say, politics in its broadest sense.

Our old problem hadn't gone away, however, although to begin with I actually thought it had. Or no, I didn't. Torkild still corrected me and told me off as he had always done and I don't suppose I ever expected him to stop doing that, it simply bothered me less and less now that I had Malin to think about and worry about.

What I'm trying to say is that to begin with I thought Torkild seemed more willing to compromise and a little more easygoing when it came to what sort of parents we should be. But no. It soon became clear that he had merely been feeling a little unsure of his new role as a father and all this entailed, and this in turn had made him slightly more hesitant and slightly more inclined to listen to my thoughts and opinions. But as soon as he began to feel more confident of his own parenting skills, he started trying to educate me on that front as well. He insisted that we use cloth diapers, he refused to allow me to drink so much as half a glass of wine as long as I was breastfeeding, and when I stopped breastfeeding and Malin switched to solid food, everything had to be made from scratch and preferably from organic, locally produced ingredients. The idea of buying jars of baby food for her was completely out of the question. It didn't stop there, though. Friends and relatives were told not to buy Christmas and birthday presents for Malin because, according to Torkild, she lived in the wealthiest country in the world and already had all she needed. And if they insisted on getting her something anyway, he would inform them that for 150 kroner they could purchase a goat from Christian Aid or, to be more precise, for 150 kroner they could purchase a certificate stating that their donation would go toward buying a goat for a poor family in Tanzania. It was enough to drive anyone crazy. He felt I washed Malin's clothes too often, he believed I was hindering her language development by saying *bow-wow* instead of *dog* and if I put on a record when Malin was awake, he would smile softly and inform me that I really ought to play something else, preferably Mozart or Bach, since research had shown that listening to Mozart and Bach had a soothing effect on children. The same went for whale song, he said before going on to subject me to a brief lecture based on an American study that had shown that whale song had a beneficial effect on the language development of young children. He was planning to buy a CD of whale song.

I was starting to lose my temper with him again.

It didn't help that Torkild's mother called in every single day and never stopped telling me how spoiled I was. I was sick and tired of hearing her say "When I was young and the children were small" without a grain of irony or any thought for my feelings. "Ah, but you had an epidural, didn't you," she said when we were talking about the difficult labor I had had, "but when I was young, there was no such thing as an epidural or any other pain relief for that matter, so you can imagine what we had to suffer." "You don't know how lucky you are to have Torkild," she said. "When I was young, men didn't normally help with the kids or the housework, but look at him, he changes diapers, he feeds her, takes her out in the baby carriage, and I don't know what all. Oh, you'd better watch out, Susanne, or you'll be out of a job," she said, and then she gave a little laugh, as if to say she was only joking. I felt like pushing her down the stairs.

I tried to talk to Torkild about how I was feeling, but even though he tried hard to understand, he couldn't, not totally at any rate. Torkild believed that all problems could be solved by making even more effort to follow the unwritten rules contained within his philosophy. It would never have occurred to him to bend or break these rules. So no matter how exhausted and how close to tears I might be, I still had to go on hanging cloth diapers on the small drying rack that we could just manage to squeeze in between the desk and the crib, because there could be no thought of switching to disposables. And if we were going somewhere, we had to run ourselves ragged beforehand, making fish stew from scratch so there would be food for Malin when we got there, because popping into the local supermarket and picking up some jars of baby food was not an option. We just had to organize things differently, plan our day a bit better, work a little harder and it would all go much more smoothly, according to Torkild. He was utterly intransigent, utterly incapable of breaking with his own principles. That, more than anything, was what wore me down. It wasn't things like hanging up cloth diapers or making meals from scratch, not as such. It was the fact that there was never any letup, that we always had to be striving for excellence, striving for perfection. That was what I couldn't stand. No matter how hard I tried, I felt I was never good enough. I'd had a serious inferiority complex before Malin was born, but once I became a mother, I felt more inadequate than ever. And the fact that Torkild was so good, so self-sacrificing and hardworking only made me feel even more useless. People commented on it. Mette and May Lene remarked on how much time he spent "on the floor with the baby," as Mette said, and Mom told everybody who would listen how Torkild doted on his little girl: "He's a serious young man, you know, a bit on the strict side maybe, but the minute he sees Malin, it's like there's this totally different person looking out of his eyes, he positively melts," she said. At the risk of sounding like a five-year-old: everybody sang Torkild's praises, no one had a word of praise for me. I'm pretty sure I pulled my weight, but Torkild did a lot more than was expected of a man and a father. I simply did what was expected of a woman and a mother and this made me think even less of myself than I had reason to.

I would sometimes find myself thinking that Torkild's mother was right. After all, what were my problems compared to the problems that so many women and mothers have had and still have to contend with? Mere trifles of course. Compared to them I *was* spoiled. I had had it too easy and like so many others in my situation as soon as things didn't quite go my way

I knuckled under. That's how I tend to see the person I was back then. Especially if I'm having a bad day. And it may be true. But I also know that I gradually began to find my life almost intolerable. When I was curled up on the sofa with Malin at 4:30 in the morning, waiting for *Teletubbies* to come on, and heard other students coming down the street shouting and singing, on their way home from a party, I was filled with a desperate longing to be with them, a powerful urge to go back to the carefree student life I had only just begun to enjoy.

That was the situation when I ran into you again.

It happened on one of my very rare evenings out. Kjersti Håpnes and I had been to Dalí and we'd been thinking of having a last beer at Café 3B, but the line at the bar was so long and moving so slowly that we soon gave up that idea, and then, just as we turned to leave, there you were, with two of your pals. We recognized one another, nodded and smiled, but if Kjersti hadn't known one of your pals and gone up to him to ask whether he knew of a party somewhere, I doubt if any of what happened would have happened. We wouldn't have gone back to your place and got even drunker on awful homemade red wine from the big green glass demijohn on your rickety kitchen table, we wouldn't have played Elvis's "Suspicious Minds" so loud that the music student in the apartment above came down to complain so often that he eventually gave up and joined the party, we wouldn't have debated whether *Pulp Fiction* was as brilliant as you said it was and we wouldn't have ended up having sex in a single bed with a rock-hard mattress and a sheet and duvet cover that probably hadn't been washed for months. But we did.

I had been unfaithful to Torkild once before. Shortly after we started seeing each other, I had sucked off a guy in a restroom at the student union and I remember being almost consumed by guilt afterward. I was a total mess, in actual physical pain. I had made up my mind not to tell Torkild, I remember, but even though I knew how hurt he would be and even though I knew he would never have found out for himself, I couldn't help telling him. I felt so guilty and it hurt so much that I simply had to own up to what I had done and hope that he would forgive me. And he did—albeit after a couple of unbearable weeks. Not this time, however. Although Torkild and I now had a daughter and were, therefore, more deeply committed to each other than we had been the last time I had cheated on him, I didn't feel the slightest bit guilty, not when I was lying there with you panting on top of me, nor afterward. I was amazed at myself, I was surprised that I had done what I had done, that I had actually dared to do it. But I felt no guilt. On the contrary, I felt I deserved it. I felt I had the right to have an affair, that I had the right to get drunk and kick up my heels, to go a bit crazy and have casual, no-strings sex. I honestly felt that I was taking back what Torkild had stolen from me, that I was reclaiming my life.

So I saw nothing strange or awkward about calling you to ask if we should see each other again. My heart was in my mouth as I leafed through the phone book, looking for your number, not surprisingly, but only because this was such a new and unfamiliar situation for me and because there was a pretty good chance that you would say no. You had enjoyed yourself as much as I had, before, during, and after we had had sex, it wasn't that, but I had been totally honest with you about the fact that I was living with someone and had a baby daughter and I knew if it had been the other way around, if I had been single and you were the one with a partner and a child, I would at least have thought twice about agreeing to see you again. But you didn't. "I'm working from home tomorrow, why don't you come over," you said.

To begin with our relationship was purely sexual. Every Tuesday and Thursday when Malin was having her morning nap, I would push the baby carriage over to your apartment in Lademoen and park it outside your bedroom window. Then I would walk into the crooked old wooden building, knock on your door, and wait for you to let me in. The first few times not much was said, we exchanged no more than a few pleasantries. I might have made some comment about the weather, you might have apologized for the mess, and then, after a few shy smiles and tentative kisses, we would strip off and fall into bed. In other words we got right down to it, that was what was so wonderful about those encounters. It was just what I needed. Torkild was always so conscientious when it came to sex. He had a strong, wiry body honed by countless hours of rock and wall climbing, a body that turned me on and to which I could hardly believe that I, small and slightly chubby as I was, had more or less free access. But he was far too considerate in bed, so exasperatingly polite. He always asked me how I wanted it, what I would like. He kept asking if this or that was okay and whispering that he loved me more than anything in the world. He didn't seem to realize that I wanted to be desired, he didn't seem to realize that I wanted to feel like a woman who was so gorgeous that he couldn't control himself. He thought I wanted love and romance and he didn't understand why I didn't come when he was so gentle and tender and loving and the whole situation was like something straight out of *The Joy of Sex*. He felt bad for coming when I didn't, it left him feeling frustrated and dejected. He borrowed a book by a famous American sex therapist that he wanted us to read together and maybe pick up some tips, but that only made things worse, of course, since this sort of didactic approach to sex was part of the problem. It sounds as though I'm pinning all the blame for our less than perfect sex life on him, but that really isn't my intention. It was just as much my fault that it wasn't working—I had as little idea of what I wanted and needed as he did. Or no, that's not entirely true. I think I did know what I wanted. The problem was probably more that I couldn't admit what I wanted, to myself or to him. I secretly longed to do the things they did in the porn movies that I professed to abhor, I frequently fantasized about being ravished by a man who was more interested in his own desires than what he thought I would like, but I always felt dirty afterward. It was a bit like the feeling I had when I yielded to the temptation to watch my favorite soap opera. I felt as though I had betrayed the ideals Torkild and I had tacitly agreed we would always strive to attain.

But after I got to know you, much of this disappeared. I lost my inhibitions, all my feelings of guilt and shame, my shyness and the stiff, tense, awkward way I behaved before, during, and after sex. With you I didn't have to prove anything. We had sex for its own sake, not to show how much we loved each other, and this meant I could relax. It meant I could give myself up to the moment in a way I never could with Torkild. He would probably have described what we did as "coupling." I remember him using that expression once down at the Edgar Kafé during a discussion of porn before a film club screening of *Deep Throat*. He didn't need to see people coupling, he said. Which was both untrue and hypocritical, of course, because whenever we were at a newsstand, his eye would always stray, with studied casualness, to the girlie mags and once, when we were staying at a hotel in Stavanger, he "accidentally" put on a soft-porn movie. He was still watching it when I came out of the shower fifteen minutes later and he didn't exactly look as though he was averse to what he was seeing, if you know what I mean. Torkild was like me. He found it hard to acknowledge needs and desires that most people under retirement age had no great difficulty in admitting to, that was the problem. It appeared to be beneath his dignity to get turned on by something for which he felt no deeper emotional attachment. You, on the other hand, seemed to be blessedly unburdened by any such reservations. Although I think you were exaggerating slightly when you quoted Terence, saying "nothing human is alien to me," you were certainly extremely broad-minded and not at all judgmental where your own and other people's sexual desires, needs, and predilections were concerned. You were always keen to experiment and try new things. If you liked what we did, great, if you didn't, no harm done. You would simply shrug and say: "Oh, well, now we know," or even have a fit of the giggles, as you did when we decided to try a bit of role-playing and you dressed up as a workman but managed to cut yourself and draw blood before you got beyond the bedroom door. With Torkild, laughter and sex were mutually exclusive.

God, how I looked forward to those midmorning visits to your place. In order to cope with my disappointing sex life with Torkild I had tried to convince myself that it was what was on the inside that mattered and that the physical side wasn't really that important. Now, though, I had no difficulty in admitting to myself that being screwed by you was one of the real high points of my week. To see your shining, avid eyes when you stood at the foot of the bed, gazing down on my naked body. To spread my legs and say "give it to me" or "I'm so horny" instead of whispering "slip it inside me" as I did when I was with Torkild. To be taken roughly from behind without being asked if I was okay made me feel hornier than ever before. And afterward I just felt happy and satisfied. Not even the thought of Malin sleeping outside the bedroom window could make me feel guilty. Quite the opposite to be honest. It only made the whole thing seem even more forbidden, even more thrilling, it enhanced the sense of being wild and crazy, of rebelling, it enhanced the schadenfreude I felt at cheating on Torkild. Because infidelity was obviously a way of punishing my own personal jailer. Okay, so I still didn't say anything when Torkild rebuked and corrected and lectured me, but I would smile to myself and think, "Oh, if you only knew, I need another man to satisfy me, so you're not as perfect as you think."

As time went on, however, it wasn't just the sex I looked forward to on my visits to you. I also looked forward to simply being with you, to lying in your bed, with my hair all disheveled, feeling decadent, listening to Beck, Tortoise, or Farmers Market and laughing at all the funny things you said and did; to sitting freshly showered at the kitchen table, drinking coffee and listening to you talk about your thesis and the little you would reveal about the novel you were working on alongside this; to telling you things about my own life and indeed to airing my innermost thoughts and feelings in a way I had never done before. For a long time I thought it was because we shared a secret that I found it so easy to confide in you. We were both terrified that our affair would be discovered and that Torkild would freak out, and this created a bond between us, trusting as we did that neither of us dared or had any interest in telling anyone else. I thought this was what emboldened me to tell you my most embarrassing secrets, such as how, when I masturbated, I sometimes fantasized that I was a cheap hooker, how I felt bad about not being as fond of my mom as I felt I should be, and how I had always been very jealous of May Lene and Mette because they were so much better looking than me. After a while, though, I began to see that it was because you were so easygoing that I felt able to open up to you. The way you never appeared to judge yourself or me or anyone else put to rest to all my fears and inhibitions. I was never afraid of making a fool of myself when I was with you, I didn't try to seem more intelligent or knowledgeable than I was. You were an avowed eclectic, much enamored of the nineties' fusion of high art and pop culture and since you believed that every genre had something to offer, I didn't have to hide the fact that I sometimes liked to relax by listening to pop music, reading crime novels, or watching American soaps (again, as you used to say: "Soap operas are the folktales of our time."). When we had wine, I didn't have to make a big show of rolling it around my tongue as if I'd be able to tell which grape it was made from; I didn't try to fool you into thinking I was familiar with books or records I'd never heard of—not even when they were books and records I suspected I ought to have heard of—and when we discussed something—politics, for example—I gradually became better at saying what I thought rather than what I imagined I ought to think.

This last was possibly the most important. Strange as it may sound, considering that Torkild was so much the dominant partner in our relationship, I regarded myself as a woman who stood up for her rights and was never afraid to speak her mind. Years of involvement with student organizations and the experience gained from all of the attendant discussions and confrontations had possibly helped to foster this image of myself. But after I met you, I became increasingly aware that this was not a true picture, or not entirely so at any rate. Not only did I have a tendency to adopt and embellish Torkild's opinions, I was also apt to argue on autopilot, so to speak. I had a definite idea of the kind of person I was and a definite idea of what such a person would think in this or that situation, so I simply presented these views—without giving any real thought to the opinions I was forever spouting. I was so politically correct. I had been accused of this countless times, but I had always responded by thanking my critics for the compliment. Being politically correct means not being afraid to say what one thinks even when lots of other people think exactly the same thing, I used to assert, it means you would rather be honest than make yourself seem interesting by acting controversial.

After I met you, however, I realized that I was wrong and that I was actually shockingly unliberated. Thanks to the lack of inhibition I felt when I was with you, I would suddenly find myself voicing ideas and opinions I didn't even know I had and that I would surely have disagreed with if they had come from anyone else. I would, for example, catch myself expressing a view held by no one in the Norwegian political landscape except members of the Progress Party. Me, the student radical with the "Hands off my buddy" badge on her jacket, suddenly advocating a tougher immigration policy and stricter rules for people coming to our country. Me, the feminist who had taken part in a feminist assertiveness course and had just written an essay on Mary Wollstonecraft, suddenly not sure I was so convinced that prostitutes were, per definition, victims. All of this would have been inconceivable before I met you. Not because these were things I believed but would never have dared to actually say in front of my radical friends, but because, as I've said, I simply wasn't aware that I had any leanings in that direction—the radical in me censored such lines of thought before I could think them through to their conclusion. I may occasionally have had a vague sense that I didn't always entirely agree with all the views I expressed, I had done ever since I came home from my first Students' Union meeting, but despite this I had never taken the trouble to reassess my ideas. I did now, though. Not to the extent that I changed my fundamental political convictions, of course, I called myself—and still call myself—a socialist and a feminist, I think I've been on every single May Day march since I was fifteen. But after I met you I became less predictable, more true to myself and less true to my political ideals, if you like.

But it wasn't only your easygoing nature that inspired this change in me. Just as important was your way of gently deflating me: you thought it was hilarious to expose and send up my somewhat stilted rhetoric. When I used political jargon and spoke in long, involved sentences peppered with words and phrases that sounded extremely profound but were really nothing but platitudes, you called me Gro, after the Labor prime minister, and when I got all fired up and started spouting assertions all of which ultimately blamed "turbo-capitalism" and "the free market" for everything from the climate crisis and poverty to eating disorders among young people today, you would suddenly change the subject and turn to talking about the student uprisings of the 1970s. You did it so smoothly and so subtly, I remember, and it always took a while for me to realize that you were poking fun at me by playing devil's advocate, which was incredibly annoying. "Shit, why do I never learn?" I would say and then burst out laughing.

All in all I laughed a lot when I was with you, often at things I wouldn't have dared laugh at before and was still loath to laugh at when I was with other people. One day I told you, for example, about someone I knew who had prevented a rape when he was on his way home from a party. You listened gravely as I described the incident in detail and then told me that you had also prevented a rape once. "Oh?" I said and waited expectantly for you to go on. "Yes, I restrained myself," you said with a totally straight face and then, after a brief pause while I tried to figure out what you had actually just said, we both fell about laughing.

Previously I would have jumped at this chance to wax indignant. Not because I thought it was so terribly offensive or provocative in itself, but in order to show what a dim view I took of violence against women; because I wanted to show everyone around me that I was a feminist and proud of it. I was exactly the same when it came to homophobia or racism. When I heard a joke about gay or black people I always overreacted. For me such situations were simply a chance to parade the values and norms that I held dear. "No, you know what, that's not fucking funny," I would say, even when I did actually think that whatever had been said was funny. In some cases this was both right and brave of me, but just as often, in fact more often than not, it was the self-centered and oh-so-smug Susanne who was talking. "Look at me, look what a decent, righteous, upright individual I am"—that was usually what I was trying to say when I reacted this way. But I couldn't see it myself. Not until I met you.

You made jokes about women, gay people, and black people, but it never crossed my mind that you might be a male chauvinist, a homophobe, or a racist. Not at all. The way you joked about them proved that you regarded women, gay people, and black people as your equals. So when the music student upstairs from you moved out and an African guy moved in, you shook your new neighbor's hand and said: "Hey, just what we needed—a token black man!" I could hardly believe my ears, I was sure he was going to headbutt you, but no, he shook with laughter. Not everyone would have reacted like that, so you were possibly rather lucky. Not only that, though. By making a joke like this as if it were the most natural thing in the world, you also came across as an open and inclusive individual. It showed that you didn't regard this guy as essentially a victim. Instead you took it for granted that he was a grown man, secure enough in himself to cope with hearing something like that. There was also an ironic aspect to the way you spoke and behaved in such situations. It was as if you were playing a part in which you hammed it up just enough for most intelligent individuals to grasp that if anyone was being sent up here it was those who said such things and actually meant them.

Even back then this brand of humor raised eyebrows, and to someone as politically correct as I was, meeting you came as a shock. Or no, *shock* is the wrong word. It makes meeting you sound like something negative, and it wasn't of course, far from it. Meeting you was, first and foremost, a liberating experience, liberating in all manner of ways: sexually, politically, culturally, personally. After I got to know you, I realized how uptight I was when I was with Torkild, constantly on tenterhooks, waiting for some sort of judgment to be pronounced, so to speak. I was quite simply a bag of nerves, but all that tension evaporated the moment I walked into your apartment. I know it's a cliché, but I immediately felt physically lighter, it was like slipping off a heavy coat.

Is it any wonder that I looked forward to visiting you? Is it any wonder that I dreaded going home again or that I overstepped the mark and broke the rules I had set for myself? Because I did. To begin with I had, for instance, a rule that said Malin was never to enter your apartment. She was Torkild's daughter, he loved her more than anything in the world, and bringing her inside with me would have been like taking her away from him, it would have been like giving her a second father and a second home. Not in practice, of course, but that was how I felt. As far as I was concerned, that would have been tantamount to driving a wedge between father and daughter and that was the last thing I wanted to do. So if Malin woke from her nap and wouldn't go back to sleep, I always went home. Even if I had been with you for only five minutes and even though I ached to go back to you. But my boundaries did shift. At first

I told myself it didn't matter if Malin sat on the floor and played with pots and pans and wooden spoons while we had coffee, she didn't understand a word of what we were saying anyway. Then I told myself it didn't matter if you dandled her on your knee or got down on the floor to play with her while I went to the bathroom or took a shower to wash off your semen and your smell before going home. Malin was fine, and you made her laugh. And so it went on. Not only with Malin, but also in other ways. I came to see you more often than I had told myself I would, I stayed longer and became more and more careless. If I happened to see someone I knew near the house where you lived, I no longer took another turn around the block to save arousing their suspicion and when I wheeled the baby carriage around to the backyard, I no longer made sure to park it where it wouldn't be seen from the street. But when your landlord stopped me and asked if I would like him to hang a gate across the entrance so that, come the summer, there would be no danger of Malin running out into the road and getting knocked down, I knew I had gone too far. He had simply assumed that you and I were a couple and that Malin and I had moved in, and this made me see that I not only had two men in my life, I had two lives. This couldn't go on, I was going to have to leave Torkild and the sooner the better.

When I told him it was over, Torkild was shocked and upset, I knew him inside out so I could tell, but it was beneath his dignity to let it show, so he tried to look bored, as if I had come to him with a piece of old news. All he said was "Well, there are some practical matters to be sorted out, how are we going to play this?" and when I asked him if he didn't want to sit down and talk about how it had come to this before we started discussing custody of Malin or who was to have what and so on, he asked what good that would do. "I'm more interested in looking forward than in looking back," he added and immediately turned to talking about the practicalities: the studio apartment in his parents' basement was currently empty, so he could move in there and I could stay here, oh, and we'd have to remember to cancel our planned trip to Iceland. He all but yawned when he said it.

And that was how he behaved from then on. He showed a demonstrative lack of interest in me and how things were with me. We met only to hand over Malin when she was moving from my place to his and vice versa, which is to say once a week, and on those occasions he never asked a single question that didn't concern her, not one. And if I began, all unbidden, to tell him about what I'd be doing, if only to be civil, he would immediately cut me off and say sorry but he was in a hurry. He simply did not want us to be on close and friendly terms, he wanted to have roughly the same relationship with me as he had with the checkout lady at the local supermarket.

I understood of course that he was bitter and angry and that he wanted to punish me by making out that I was no great loss. But if this strategy worked and I felt disappointed and upset by his behavior, it didn't last long. The time that followed marked one long upswing for me. The weeks when I had Malin were much the same as they are for all parents of young children, but when Malin was with Torkild, I lived a life largely devoted to making up for lost time.

I loved going to parties with you and your friends. Things were always so unpredictable, anything could happen. In the middle of a deeply serious discussion of different forms of postmodern theory—a frequent topic of conversation among your crowd at that time—you were quite liable to break into an impromptu piece of performance art. Like the time in Café in 3B when some people came in and sat down at the table next to ours and you suddenly let your mouth hang open and pretended to be mentally disabled. You drooled and spoke in a slow, deep growl and became, all in all, alarmingly reminiscent of Leonardo DiCaprio in *What's Eating Gilbert Grape*. I didn't know what was going on at first, but your best pal and drinking buddy, Terje, immediately recognized his cue to take on the part of your social worker. When you said you didn't want to be there anymore and that it was really mean of him to spend all your money on beer, he turned to the people at the next table and grinned as shiftily as he could, well aware that they would interpret this as a sinner's attempt to absolve himself. And so the charade continued: you didn't like him forcing you to drink beer either, you said, you thought it tasted horrible and it made you feel dizzy. And, you went on, you certainly didn't like all the things he did to you after you'd both had a few beers. At this Terje grabbed your wrist, hauled you out of your seat, and dragged you toward the door, snarling that he'd warned you what would happen if you mentioned that in front of other people, well, now you'd gone and done it and you'd be sorry. When I joined the two of you outside moments later, you were staggering about, howling with laughter. "Did you see their faces? Huh? Did you see them?" you both gasped.

And then there was the time when Terje left his jacket in a local pub, Den Gode Nabo. We were headed for a party somewhere up Singsaker way and had just jumped out of a pirate cab when he discovered the loss.

"Shall I go back with you?" you asked.

"Nah, it's okay, I'll pick it up on Monday."

"Okay, but in that case I'll give my jacket to that guy over there," you said, pointing to a man walking along hand in hand with his girlfriend on the other side of the street. "Then we'll be starting even!"

"Starting even? For what?"

You didn't reply, simply marched off across the road, pulling off your jacket as you went. You handed it to the somewhat baffled man and said: "Here, I'd like you to have this, it's a great jacket, real leather and everything." That done, you strode back across to us. Right, so where was this party again, you wanted to know. As if what had just happened wasn't worth commenting on, far less explaining.

Not long afterward I learned that this incident was in fact an impromptu reenactment of a scene from a short story by F. Scott Fitzgerald. I had been impressed by the inventiveness and originality that had to lie behind such a whimsical gesture, so I remember being slightly disappointed by this discovery, but when I told you this, you laughed and called me a hopeless romantic. Nothing comes from nothing, you said, and being original had never meant anything but putting old things together in new ways. You then proceeded to give a long and impassioned lecture inspired by Saussure's reflections on how we are born into a preexisting language system and concluded with a wholehearted tribute to Aphex Twin and his use of sampling, Tarantino and his use of 1970s B movies, and Lars von Trier and his take on the soap opera genre in what you hailed as the best television series in the world, *The Kingdom*. There's nothing new under the sun, you said, not even the words I've just said.

Romantic was, in other words, a dirty word as far as you were concerned. I'm sorry to say that you had the same mistaken notion of Romanticism as so many self-confessed postmodernists in the nineties. To you, Romantics were soppy, genius-worshiping idiots with no sense of history or tradition, who believed that art and literature were the result of divine inspiration. You used to say that there was nothing more boring than all those intense and supposedly agonized budding authors, lounging around half-drunk in Café 3B, smoking and explaining that they wrote because they "had to." Pompous Romantics the lot of them, so full of themselves and so unintentionally funny, you said. I never saw you laugh, though. Anything but, actually. Whenever we did get talking to such characters—which, as regulars of 3B, we were forever doing—you would become so infuriated, I mean so over the top, that it became hard for you to maintain the wry tone you always adopted when you wanted to put down someone you felt the need to put down.

This fury surprised me, I remember. Not least because your own lifestyle inevitably called to mind the romantic myth of the bohemian artist that you were always so keen to mock. The first time I visited your place, for example, I couldn't help thinking of Dostoyevsky's description of Raskolnikov's living conditions. Or, as Terje said: "You almost expect to meet some guy suffering from consumption when you walk into your place, David! Are you sure there's no blood on your hankie?"

Your tiny apartment lay on the first floor of a lopsided old workers' cottage next to the railway line with a swaybacked roof and a hallway that stank of dampness and mold. Despite the fact that together the two rooms measured no more than 150 to 200 square feet, it was nigh on impossible to keep it warm on the coldest winter days. Even with the oil-fired radiator working full blast around the clock, ice still formed on the inside of the windows and the windowsill, you could see your breath in the morning when you woke, and often when I came to see you, especially in the forenoons, I would find you sitting eating in the kitchen, wrapped in your winter coat. And as if that weren't enough: apart from two Chilean immigrants living in Møllenberg you were the only person I knew who still had an outhouse. An outhouse! In the late nineties! I thought you were joking when you told me this, but you weren't. In the backyard was a long, low bathroom containing three stalls and a shower, which you shared with the other tenants.

Not that your place didn't have its charm, though. It gave one the feeling of having stepped into a jam-packed secondhand bookstore or antiques store. Full use had been made of every square inch and one almost had the urge to spend an hour simply browsing around. There were huge stacks of CDs, newspapers, and magazines everywhere and the walls were covered in old maps, film club posters (*The Testament of Dr. Mabuse*, *Fitzcarraldo*, and *Pulp Fiction*), and pictures of your favorite writers and artists. On the windowsill, the desk, and the decidedly dusty shelves lay hash pipes, boxing gloves, fossils, cactuses, a plaster bust of Beethoven, and a mojo you had bought from an American blues musician on tour in Norway. And then, of course, there were all the books: books you introduced me to, quoted from, and read aloud from, books we never tired of discussing. By Duun, Flaubert, Hamsun, Fosse, Mann, Munro, Askildsen, Ulven, Céline, and many, many others.

But for all its charm, not many people would have been willing to rent that place, not even someone as hard up or more so than you. I may be prejudiced, but I find it difficult to picture a science and technology student, say, taking over your apartment, unless the person concerned actually wanted to be an artist and was only doing science and technology in order to have something to fall back on if all else failed. Because, as I've already intimated, it was the perfect place for an artist, and that, of course, was one of the main reasons why you and other students of literature, music, film, and drama had gravitated to that area. True, they wouldn't have been living there if it hadn't been cheap and close to the city center, but all students want to live cheaply and close to the center so if it had been purely a matter of cost and location, this corner of Lademoen would have been crawling with students of every hue. But it wasn't, and I believe this had something to do with the neighborhood's down-at-heel air, which fitted so well with the way you saw yourselves and the way you wanted other people to see you. These were houses that gave the impression of being home to real artists and bohemians, houses that made them feel that they were the true heirs to the writers and artists who had given rise to all those struggling-artist myths.

Oh, I can see you now, in that poky, drafty apartment, working on the novel you'd been writing for over two years but wouldn't let anyone read so much as a paragraph of. I can see that one eyebrow that was always cocked when you were concentrating, the thin face you would bury in your hands every now and again, particularly when you were stuck for words. When that happened, you could sit with your face in your hands for minutes at a time, as if you didn't want anyone to see how frustrated you were. I can see you, see your rumpled hair, the oversized white linen shirt you used to wear, so big it was more like a tunic and always left unbuttoned to midchest, I see all of the yellow notes on which you had scribbled a sentence or two and then stuck to your computer and the wall behind it. The ashtray, your pipe, the specially imported tobacco you used to buy from the tobacconist's in Dronningens gate and, of course, to the right of your keyboard the obligatory glass of red wine, which you carried out to the kitchen every now and again, held under the siphon on the demijohn, and refilled before going back to your writing.

A living, breathing cliché.

But why, when you were normally so easygoing, were you so infuriated by all of the other living, breathing clichés around us, that was what I asked myself. Why, when we fell into conversation with people who seemed so much like you, were you so filled with contempt for them? For a long time I thought it had to do with how important, nay sacred, writing was to you. Because it really was. No one spends two to three hours every single day for years writing a novel if it doesn't mean a great deal to them, especially when the chances of making money from it or of winning fame and acclaim are as slim as they are. When writing is so important to a person, I told myself, when you work so hard on a book, in addition to what is and should be your proper work, when a person devotes so much time and energy to this, then one can hardly blame them for being offended by dilettantes masquerading as "real" writers, amateurs who are more interested in looking like writers than in actually writing. Not until much later did I see that this anger was mainly attributable to what Terje described as a conflict between the sophist and the Platonist in you.

Trondheim, June 29th, 2006. A good burger

"So where was this job?" Mette asks.

I look at her and smile. We've been talking about poor Agnes for over an hour and it feels good to change the subject, good to talk about something more cheerful.

"*Adresseavisen*," I say, taking a sip of my wine. I eye Mette as I put my glass down again, she's wearing incredibly well, she'll be forty-five in September, but she looks younger than me.

"But why turn it down then? If you really wanted it?"

"I don't know," I say with a faint shrug. "Maybe I don't want to admit that I'm almost middle-aged," I add with a little laugh, don't know why I say that, possibly as an extension of the thought that Mette looks younger than I do.

"What's that supposed to mean?" she asks. She props her elbow on the table, rests her chin on her hand, and smiles at me.

"I don't know, but . . . saying no to a steady job that I would really like, well . . . maybe it's because I don't want to accept that I am in fact getting older and my needs have changed. I'd like more security in my life, but I don't dare admit it to myself because that would be tantamount to admitting that I'm not as young as I used to be." I've no idea where all this is coming from, but it sounds pretty reasonable, I'm really quite pleased with myself for coming up with such a good reply to something I've been wondering about myself. "That could be part of it, I suppose. Deep down," I add.

"I understand what you're saying, but I think you're wrong," Mette says. "Turning down your dream job, giving in to a whim, in other words, that's so like you, Susanne. You've always been the same, you haven't changed a bit, that's the problem."

"As hopeless as ever?" I say.

"Well, certainly as hard to figure out," she says.

"Yeah, for a control freak like you, anyway," I say.

We look at each other and laugh as we pick up our glasses. It's so nice just to sit here with her, drinking wine. It strikes me that I've missed her. I mean it's not as though I think about her every day but when I see her again I realize that I've missed her, we really ought to get together more often, it's hard to believe we live in the same city, we see so little of each other. I set down my glass but leave my fingers curled around the stem, tap it gently with my index finger, trying to follow the beat of the music drifting softly from the loudspeakers hanging around the café, I can't remember the name of the song, but it's by a Swedish band, Bo Kaspers Orkester.

"So what did Mom say?" Mette asks as she sticks her hand into the purse hanging over the back of her chair and takes out a tube of lip balm.

"You don't think I've told Mom, do you?" I say. "Are you crazy?"

She lets out a little laugh as she removes the top from the lip balm and gives the revolving base a quick twist to push up the stick slightly.

"Yeah, well, it's maybe better to spare her that. I spoke to her on the phone the day before yesterday and she was worried enough about you as it was," she says. She closes her mouth, runs the lip balm back and forth across her lips, then presses them together as she drops the tube back into her purse.

"Oh?"

"She thinks you don't look after yourself properly."

I smile at Mette and give a little wag of my head, say nothing for a moment, I don't really mind Mom saying I don't look after myself properly, not at all, because it could just as easily mean that she thinks I'm very hardworking, or self-sacrificing, caring more about poor children in the third world than I do about myself, and from that point of view it's more of a compliment, albeit the sort of compliment I don't much care for, the sort you occasionally come across in obituaries: "She put the needs of others before her own" or words to that effect. Such tributes always get my back up, I don't think I've ever seen anything like that said about a man, the deceased is invariably a woman and I've always regarded this as proof of an attitude that says that women *ought* to disregard their own needs, that it's laudable of them to be self-effacing and self-sacrificing. And yet here I am, feeling more pleased than annoyed that my mother says the same about me, I'm not sure why, maybe it's because I know she means well, and because I appreciate the love that lies behind it.

"I don't look after myself properly?" I repeat. "That's just Mom's way of saying that I don't lead the kind of life she would like me to lead. You know what she's like," I say, glancing at my watch. It's already past nine so Mom probably won't be coming after all, which is fine really, it's good to have some time alone with Mette.

"Oh, I know," Mette says, nodding at me. But she obviously has her own thoughts on this subject, there's a more serious light in her eyes, which says she's not sure I do take proper care of myself, she almost looks as if she's a little worried about me and there's a part of me that likes the thought of her being worried on my behalf. I have the urge to say something to make her think she's right—just a hint, but enough to convince her that I'm not really okay so I can bask in her concern, have the urge to use this as an excuse to get even closer to her, I've missed her and it's good to feel close to her. But I don't and I won't, I'm absolutely fine, I'm leading the life I've chosen to lead and there's no need to get too sentimental.

"I'll just nip to the bathroom before the food gets here," Mette says. She grins at me as she gets up and I grin and nod back, watch her as she walks off toward the restroom. It's amazing how well she's wearing, she's forty-five but she has the body of a twenty-year-old. I take a sip of my wine, put the glass down again, hear the soft clunk as the foot hits the table a little harder than expected. The next second there comes an unusually loud burst of talk and laughter from over by the bar. I turn to look, some middle-aged rocker types have just walked in—a bunch of guys, all pushing fifty, with long hair, skinny legs, and sagging bellies. They look like they must be, or have been, in a band. They sit down at a window table directly opposite the bar, peel off their jackets, and start shouting for service. It's so typical—men of that age, it doesn't matter where they go, they always act as though they own the place, it beggars belief, the sheer arrogance of it. I feel a flicker of annoyance, turn away. There are some grains of salt on the table, bright against the dark brown surface, I lean forward and blow them over the edge.

Then I hear a voice say, politely but firmly: "Just a moment." I look around and see the waiter heading toward me with what seems to be our order, he glances at the rockers and smiles as he passes their table, then turns to me. He's so cute. With his long blue-black hair, tanned face, and clean-cut features he's the spitting image of the comic-book hero Silver Arrow. Which reminds me: I had a terrible crush on Silver Arrow when I was young, or so Mom says.

"One Greek salad and one hamburger," the waiter says, flashing me a smile, a smile that makes me melt.

"The hamburger's for me and the salad there," I say, smiling back at him and motioning toward Mette's place.

"Here you are," he says and I catch a faint whiff of aftershave as he bends down and sets the food on the table. "Enjoy."

"Oh, and another one of these, please," I say, pointing to the wine bottle. There's a good couple of glasses left in it, but still. Mette would probably say no if I ask whether we should order another bottle so I might as well do it while she's at the bathroom. The waiter looks at me and smiles, says nothing, merely nods and walks away and I follow him with my eyes. One of the rockers raises a hand and calls out to him. "Six beers," he says as the waiter passes their table, but Silver Arrow pays the guy no more attention than the job requires him to do. "With you in a minute," he says coolly and walks on by. Mmm, I wouldn't kick him out of bed, that's for sure, he's *so* cute. I drain my glass, pick up the wine bottle, and refill it.

Minutes later he's back with a second bottle.

"One bottle of white wine," he says, giving me that smile again. Oh, that smile, it blows me away.

"Thanks," I say. I try to meet and hold his gaze, just for a second or two, then I have to drop my eyes. It's almost like being a teenager again.

He puts the bottle on the table and walks off. Then Mette appears.

"Another bottle?" she says, exactly as I expected her to. I glance up at her, smile, and try to look a little surprised.

"Yes, well, I thought . . . or didn't you want any more?" I ask, stealing a peek at the waiter's retreating back, then turning to Mette again.

"Oh, I suppose I could have a little more," she says. "But I have to be a bit sensible. Tomorrow's another day, and all that."

"Well, you know, sometimes it's sensible *not* to be sensible."

She doesn't say anything, just smiles at me. I turn to look at the waiter again, he has just finished taking an order from the aging rockers, I manage to catch a glimpse of him before he leaves their table and disappears around the corner.

"What are you looking at?" Mette asks. I turn to her, she looks me straight in the eye and smiles slyly as if to say she knows very well what I was looking at. I lean across the table, raise my eyebrows, and give her a big grin.

"He's just so . . . he's just so cute," I say.

"D'you think so?"

"Yes, don't you?"

"Uh, he's a little too . . . how can I put it . . . ethnic for me," Mette says. "And I have this thing about men with long hair so . . . nope! Not my type."

"Well, I think he's gorgeous. Maybe we should move through to the bar once we're done here."

We look at each other and laugh, then Mette bends her head over her plate and starts to pick at her food. I pull the little condiments basket toward me, take out the ketchup bottle, squirt a small puddle of red sauce onto my plate, and dig in as well.

"I simply don't get it, why do they insist on drowning the salad in dressing?" Mette pipes up suddenly. She turns up her nose as she takes her fork and scrapes the dressing out to the side of her plate. I inspect her food, there isn't too much dressing on her salad, not for my taste anyway, more like the opposite in fact. "They ruin the food when they do that," she goes on. "It makes it so greasy . . . yuck."

I consider her while I finish what's in my mouth, am I supposed to compliment her on being so fit and healthy, is that why she's overdoing it, acting slightly more dismayed by the amount of salad dressing than she probably is. I know how much effort she puts into living healthily, I don't know anyone who works out as much or is as conscious of eating right as Mette, and now she seems to be angling for me to say something that will make her feel virtuous, yeah, I'm sure that's it, she's always been the same, Mette. I look at her as I swallow the last chunk of burger. I'm about to say that someone as slim as she is certainly doesn't need to worry about counting calories, but I don't get the chance.

"The portions are big enough, though, I'll give them that," she says, laughing at the supposedly enormous portion she's been served. I glance at her plate again. It's not that big a portion, pretty average, I'd say, but she giggles as she shows me how much food she feels she's been given, as if trying to tell me that she's always careful not to eat more than necessary, I know that's what she's doing.

"And you've got enough there for two, at least," she says, nodding at my plate and giggling again. I glance down at my own food, that too a perfectly normal portion, then look up at Mette again. She used to go on like this all the time in the days when we had more to do with each other and it used to make me so mad, it's starting to get to me now too, but I smile and don't let on, don't want to start a fight now, not when we're getting along so well. I hope she's not going to carry on with this crap, though, I hate it, she must know that I feel pressured into eating less than I might want to eat when she talks like that. If I clean my plate now, I'll feel like a proper glutton, which is what she wants, of course, even though she may not realize it herself, she wants to punish me, I know how much effort she puts into living healthily and how much she denies herself, and when she sees me digging into a juicy hamburger, which I'm sure she'd love to have but can't in all conscience allow herself to indulge in, she feels an unconscious need to punish me, that's why she's carrying on like this.

"How's your burger—good?" she asks.

"Delicious," I say. Actually it's no more than okay, but I tell her it's delicious anyway, to show her that I can eat a juicy burger without feeling guilty, to show her I don't care about all the health and fitness rules she lives by and tries to impose on everyone else, although I do actually care about these rules, I mean I am a member of this society and this culture and I care just as much about these rules as every other woman does, I wish I didn't but I can't help it. My hamburger doesn't even taste as good now that Mette has succeeded in reminding me of how unhealthy

I am. I know I should have followed her lead and ordered a salad instead of a burger, I know that would be better for me, but I can't resist the temptation, I'm not as strong willed as she is. I'm not going to let her see that, though, not as long as she's using me to make her feel better about herself. Because that's what she's doing when she goes on like this, the more unhealthy she makes me feel, the healthier she feels and the guiltier she makes me feel, the more virtuous she feels.

"You should order one of these next time we come here," I say, nodding at my burger.

"I'm not that keen on burgers," Mette says.

"Oh, I love a good burger," I say.

"We eat hardly any meat at all now," she says. "Not red meat anyway."

"Really? But don't you run the risk of not getting enough protein?" I ask.

"No, there are plenty of other healthy sources of protein," she says. "Beans, for example. And lentils."

"Yeah, but beans and lentils, they're no good," I say.

She stares at me for a moment, then she bursts out laughing.

"Oh, Susanne, really," she says, as if she's talking to a little kid, and she gives another, rather condescending, laugh. This is her way of pooh-poohing this last remark of mine, I know it is, that little laugh and that "Oh, Susanne, really" are an attempt to dismiss my words as charming, but childish, the sort of thing that only I could say. I look at her and smile, but I'm growing more and more annoyed, I don't want to get annoyed, but I am.

"No, I mean it," I continue. "I love meat and I'd never dream of replacing it with beans or lentils or soy or any of the other healthy alternatives," I say, knowing full well that this isn't what she wants to hear, she makes a lot of sacrifices in order to live as healthily as possible and works so hard at it, so for me to say straight out that I'd rather eat unhealthy food I enjoy than healthy food I don't enjoy is like saying I have no respect for her ideals, and that in turn makes her feel less virtuous than she would like, I know. And not only that: it reminds her of everything she's missing by forcing herself to live the way she does. I smile at her as I pick up my burger and take another bite.

"No, well," she says, sipping her wine. "You only have yourself to think of, so you can afford to be less careful about what you eat."

"Just because I eat meat every now and again doesn't mean I'm not careful about what I eat," I say, still smiling and speaking as pleasantly as I can, but I'm getting more and more annoyed. Okay, so maybe I don't give as much thought to what I eat as I should, but it's not so much a matter of how much red meat I eat, it has more to do with the fact that I tend to eat too many TV dinners and don't eat as regularly as I should. Mette doesn't know that, though, and anyway TV dinners aren't as bad for you as people say, not the ones I usually buy anyway.

"No, but you know what I mean," she says, smiling as she pushes a lettuce leaf and half a cherry tomato onto her fork. "You have to take your diet more seriously when you have two young children to consider."

I send her a look, point to my mouth to show that I have to finish eating before I can answer. I feel like saying that I think she and Göran's kids might have been better off if she had given a little less thought to all the rules for health and fitness she wants them to live by, it can't be particularly healthy to keep denying yourself all the things you'd like to have. I can't think of a better way to make yourself miserable. I feel like saying this too, but I won't, I have to try to get a grip on myself before the mood turns sour. I finish chewing, swallow.

"Oh, of course, I realize that," I say and leave it at that. I grit my teeth and smile as I pick up my glass. "Cheers," I say.

"Cheers."

I take one drink, then another, concentrate on my food for a little while without saying anything, keep my eyes fixed on my plate, on the white bread of the bun, the glistening meat between the two halves, the french fries and the tiny beads of grease dotted around the china and suddenly I feel a twinge of disgust, that sneaking sense of being unclean, of being dirty. I look up at Mette again. Mette, sitting there picking at her salad—tomato, cucumber, and red pepper, olives, and lettuce. She's achieved her objective, she's managed to make me feel every bit as fat and unhealthy as she always does, I don't want to feel like this, but I do, suddenly here I am feeling dirty. I did consider having a salad when I saw Mette ordering one, but my body wanted a hamburger and french fries and I couldn't fight it. I'm too weak to resist temptation and I'm too weak to defend my weakness. This last, that I find it impossible to resist when Mette tries to make me live by the same rules as she forces herself to live by, that I find it impossible to eat and drink whatever I like without suffering pangs of remorse and inadequacy, that I don't stand up for myself and say what I think, that's almost the worst of it. I get so angry with myself for not doing so. I hate myself for being so spineless that I simply put up with it, no matter what I do I always end up feeling like such a wimp. I finish chewing and swallow, go to spear a french fry with my fork, but stop myself and nudge it to the side of my plate instead.

"You're right," I say, "that was a big portion." Don't want to say it, but I do.

"Mm," Mette says, regarding me as she eats.

"I'm full," I say. I'm not completely full, but I say it anyway, pick up my napkin, and dab my lips, eye the half-eaten burger and the rest of the french fries. I'd like to have some more, and I don't, I'm not full, but I've had enough, the more I eat the dirtier I feel, I can't help it, that's just how I am. I despise myself for being like this, I feel like stuffing the rest of the burger into my mouth just to prove to myself and to Mette that I'm capable of eating with relish and not feeling guilty, but I can't do it. I drop my napkin onto my plate to indicate that dinner is over as far as I'm concerned. I'm allowing myself to be browbeaten by the women-bashing tyranny of a fitness and diet culture that I cannot abide and I hate myself for doing it, I'm such a wimp, I like to see myself as a strong, independent, liberated woman, but the truth is I'm weak.

"Yes, me too," Mette says, pushing her plate aside. Just then one of the rockers yells for chili nuts, drowning out Bo Kaspers Orkester and the chatter of the other café guests. I turn to look at him, a pale guy in a Def Leppard T-shirt with long, straggly hair falling from a receding hairline. Why can't he summon the waiter a little more discreetly, the way anyone else would do? And if that didn't work, he could always get off his ass, go over to the bar, and give his order there. Arrogant prick, how rude can you be? Only a man of his age would ever behave like that.

"Oh, by the way," Mette says. "I'm getting married." Just like that, out of the blue. I turn and look at her. She raises her glass to her lips, beaming so broadly it's all she can do to drink from it. I stare at her, I have to share her joy, I have to be happy for her, but I can't, my good mood from before has evaporated and I'm not as happy as I ought to be, I'm not happy at all, but I open my mouth and try to look surprised and delighted.

"Really?"

"Mm," she says. "Göran proposed three weeks ago."

"Oh, my God, Mette. Congratulations. I mean . . . wow, that's wonderful," I say, trying to sound as thrilled as I can.

"I know, some good news for once. But please, don't tell Mom. It doesn't seem right to make an announcement like this to the rest of the family at the moment, not with Agnes in a coma and all that. Okay . . . I know I've just told you, I don't really know why I did that, I wasn't planning to, but . . . well, anyway, just don't tell Mom, please, I'd rather wait with that," she says.

It takes a moment but then it dawns on me why she's telling me that she's getting married even though she hasn't said anything to Mom. She says she doesn't know why she told me, and that may be so, it may have been an unconscious impulse, but there's no doubt it sprang from her need to show that she's so much more successful than me. She had made up her mind not to tell me or anyone else in the family her news just now when everyone is so devastated about Agnes, but she simply can't help herself, she has to advertise the fact that she's done so much better than I have.

"No, of course not, I won't say a word," I say, struggling to keep my smile in place.

"Oh, it was so romantic, you've no idea. He'd been planning it for ages, he'd bought the ring and flowers and champagne, and he went down on one knee and everything."

"Oh, wow," I say.

"Yeah, I know," she says. "I felt so . . . oh . . . so loved! Can I say that?" she asks, and then she gives a happy, rippling laugh. I don't say anything, just look at her with a big smile on my face and slowly shake my head as if it's just too wonderful for words. "He'd even organized a babysitter and booked a table at Credo for later," she goes on. "And we had dinner there, just the two of us."

"God, talk about the perfect man," I say.

"Oh, he *is*," she trills. "He *really* is the perfect man."

"Well, here's to you and Göran," I say, picking up my wine glass, still with that artificial smile on my face.

"Here's to us," she says.

I drain my glass in one gulp and put it down, am on the verge of asking her about the wedding, but I don't, I know I should, but I simply can't bring myself to do it.

"Well," I say, "I fancy a cigarette." I don't know what makes me say this, I haven't smoked in ages but all of a sudden here I am announcing that I fancy a cigarette, even though I don't, I don't fancy a cigarette, not at all, but I say it anyway, as if it's the most natural thing in the world.

"Oh . . . have you started smoking again?" Mette asks.

I give a little laugh.

"I never really stopped," I say, lying in her face. I don't know why I say that, maybe as a sort of protest against her for being so pure and healthy and perfect, I could never be like Mette and so I need to tell her and myself that I have no ambition to be like her either. Is that what I'm doing when I say I feel like having a smoke, am I trying to say that I want something different from life, that I want to enjoy life without my conscience always pricking me? I place my hands on the arms of my chair, smile at her as

I push it back. "You don't feel like coming out for a quick puff?" I ask, this too just slipping out. Mette would never dream of smoking a cigarette, I don't think she's ever smoked, apart from the odd cigarette at parties when she was a twenty-year-old student, but I ask her anyway, take some delight in doing so, asking her if she wants to have a smoke makes her seem not quite so perfect, it makes her think that I see her as a potential smoker, and she doesn't like that, she doesn't like anyone seeing her as less perfect than she wishes to appear and I get a little kick out of that, it's petty and mean of me, I know, but I can't help it. She doesn't answer straightaway, stares at me in confusion for a moment, then gives a surprised little laugh, a laugh meant to underscore the inconceivability of her ever smoking a cigarette.

"No-ho!" she says. It comes out as a burbling chuckle.

"Okay," I say, smiling as naturally as I can as I get up. "Be right back," I say and away I go, past the loudmouthed rockers and up to the bar. I haven't bought a pack of cigarettes in God knows how long, but I do now. I ask for ten Prince Mild and a box of matches, get them, pay for them, and go outside. The pavement cafés along the harborside are starting to fill up and the buzz of talk and laughter mingles with the din of the traffic on Innherredsveien. I open the cigarette pack, pull out a cigarette, and light it, stand there outside Bare Blåbær smoking and gazing across to Blomsterbrua. This is so childish of me, I'm behaving pretty much the way I did when I was sixteen and took up smoking because it made me feel grown-up and independent. It's hard to believe, but here I am, doing exactly the same as I did yesterday when Mom came to see me, then too I tried to revert to the person I was fifteen or twenty years ago.

"Excuse me, do you have a light?" It's a woman who asks, she comes up to me, smiles at me.

"Yes, of course," I say. I push open the little drawer of the matchbox, take out a match, and light it, study the woman as she puts her cigarette between her lips and leans in to me, she can't be much more than forty, but she has an exceptionally wrinkled face. Her upper lip is a mass of fine vertical lines, it looks rather like a bar code. She sticks the cigarette into the little flame, takes a long drag, cheeks hollowing as she draws the nicotine deep into her lungs.

"Thanks," she says, then she tilts her head back and blows the smoke straight up into the air.

I don't say anything, just look at her and smile and suddenly I feel dirty again because ever since I gave up smoking I've regarded people like this woman as losers. I don't want to see her and other smokers as losers, I've actually tried hard not to think like that, but with no great success. Every time I pass a bar or a restaurant or a public building, especially if it's raining or snowing or freezing cold, and see the smokers huddled, chittering outside, the word that comes into my head is *losers*. And now I'm one of them, a loser myself. Here I am, smoking again, I didn't even want a cigarette, it's so stupid, I only bought the cigarettes as an instinctive protest against the way Mette goes on, but instead I feel like a loser, which is exactly what she wants. I tuck my left arm under my boobs and prop my right elbow on the back of my left hand, stand like this with the smoldering tip level with my face, I part my lips, about to take another drag, but stop myself, turn around, and chuck the cigarette into the big sand-filled ashtray. It felt surprisingly good to have a smoke and I had almost half of it left, but I'm damned if I'm going to be pressured into playing the loser, I refuse to be that childish. I make my way back to the door, suddenly burning with anger, but still smiling, now I just have to go back inside, sit down, and ask Mette about her wedding plans, I have to sound interested and look as though I'm happy for her, and I *am* happy for her, of course I am, but not as happy as I would like to be.

"Would you mind turning off that easy-listening shit," I hear one of the rocker guys say as I open the door and step inside, it's the one in the Def Leppard T-shirt. He's looking at one of the waitresses and screwing up his face to emphasize how dire he finds their choice of music.

"I'll see what I can do," she says with a hesitant, almost fearful smile, she can't be any more than nineteen or twenty and she probably doesn't dare not to do as this guy says. I stare at him, it would do him good to be taken down a peg or two, him and the rest of his brash, loudmouthed crew. It's so typical, men in their fifties, they simply expect the rest of the world to bow to their will and their needs, it really pisses me off, I feel like speaking up and saying I think Bo Kaspers Orkester are great and I don't want the staff to turn them off, but I don't, I'd better not cause any ruckus. I walk back across to our table, need to calm down, need to compose myself, I don't like it when Mette carries on the way she was doing just now, but I need to try to overlook that, mustn't allow myself to be forced into becoming someone I really don't like to be, so to speak, because that's what happens when I find it impossible to turn a blind eye to her antics, I get angrier and more resentful and more negative than I would wish, I don't want to be that way, I like Mette, I love her and I want to be a good sister and a good friend to her, so now I have to be big enough and gracious enough to pull myself together. I have to show her that I'm happy for her, that I'm delighted she's getting married, I have to try to focus on the fact that this is, after all, good news at what is in other ways a difficult time for our family. I look at her and smile as I weave my way around chairs and tables, but what's going on, it looks like she's got the bill, we have nearly a full bottle of wine left, but she has already called the waiter over and he's standing by our table pressing the buttons on the credit card terminal in his hand.

"I'll get it," Mette says, smiling at me, "and you can give me the cash afterward. Is that okay?"

"Er, yeah—fine," I say, looking slightly disconcerted, letting her know that I really hadn't expected to be leaving so soon.

"Here you are," the waiter says, smiling as he places the terminal in front of Mette. She smiles back and removes a card from a very smart white pocketbook with a gold clasp and sticks it in the machine. I look at her, does she want to make sure that I don't order yet another bottle of wine after this one, is that why she took the opportunity to get the bill while I was out for a smoke? Who knows, it wouldn't surprise me, though.

"Er . . . nothing's happening," she murmurs, glancing up at the waiter.

He takes a step closer, peers at the credit card terminal for a moment, then turns on a smile.

"Oh, sorry, we only take Visa," he says.

"Huh?" Mette says, gazing up at him in surprise. He looks at her, bites his lip as he grins and nods at her card. And then Mette looks down at it too and so do I, but the card in the machine isn't a Visa card, it's a card for the 3T gym.

"Oops," she says with an affected little laugh, lifting

her eyes to the waiter again, and he looks down at her and laughs back, looks straight into her eyes, doing exactly what Mette meant him to do, because no one can tell me she did that by accident, she took out that gym membership card instead of her Visa card because she wanted the waiter to know she works out, this is just another way of letting everyone know how fit and healthy and successful she is, another way of making herself seem desirable, I know it is, and it's working too, I can see. They hold each other's gaze, just for a second or two, eyes glowing with mutual attraction.

"Oh, God," Mette says, slips the gym card back into her pocketbook and takes out her Visa card, slides it into the terminal, and keys in her PIN. "I can't even blame it on the wine, I don't think I've had more than a couple of glasses," she says, shaking her head, still painting a picture of herself as superfit and successful, making it quite clear to the waiter that she hasn't had any more to drink than a woman ought to have, letting him know that I've drunk most of the wine we've ordered this evening, which is true enough, but she's saying it only because she wants to impress the waiter. As soon as I told her I thought he was cute, she made up her mind to impress him. She said he wasn't her type, and yet she's sitting there flirting with him, doing it purely to outshine me, I know, doing it simply to prove to herself and me that she's more successful than me. I watch her as she removes her card from the machine, feel my anger returning, I don't want to be angry, but I am, I can't help it.

"There," she says, smiling and flashing her eyes at the waiter again and he meets her glance and smiles back.

"Thank you," he says just as Bo Kaspers Orkester are

turned off and his voice rings out louder than intended in the sudden silence. "Oh!" he says with a little laugh, glancing at the loudspeakers and raising his eyebrows. Then he turns to Mette again. "Come back soon," he says, looking into her eyes, holding her gaze slightly longer than normal to show that in her case this is not merely the standard line he gives to all the café's guests, to show Mette that she is special, and she reacts exactly as he expects her to react.

"Thank you," she says, returning his gaze. "We might just take you up on that."

"Well, I hope you do," he says, and by that *you* he obviously means her and not us, he's flirting blatantly with her now and she's encouraging him, keeping her eyes locked on his and smiling that crooked smile of hers, doing all she can to put me in the shade.

"Well, I'm not going and leaving a full bottle of wine," I say to Mette. "But don't mind me, I mean I know you won't want to be late home, not if it's your turn to get up with the kids in the morning." I say this last for the waiter's benefit, to let him know that Mette is in a relationship and has children, attempting to scupper her little flirtation by betraying that she's spoken for. I rather relish doing this, but I smile at Mette as innocently as I can. She regards me, she knows the waiter sees her differently now he's aware that she has a partner and kids waiting for her at home, she knows I've put paid to her little flirtation, but not that I did it on purpose, it doesn't seem like it anyway, because she smiles brightly back at me. She opens her mouth, about to say something, but doesn't get that far.

"Bye, then," the waiter says.

Mette turns to look at him.

"Bye," she says, smiling, waits till he's gone, then turns

263

to me again. "Oh, well," she says, "I suppose I could keep you company for a while longer." I stare at her: *I suppose I could keep you company for a while longer*, who does she think she is—my social worker? It certainly sounds as if she thinks she's doing me a favor by staying, as if she thinks I'm lonely and will be upset if she goes, or something like that. Yet another sneaky ploy to make me feel like a loser, I suppose, trying to make out that I'm lonely just because I'm single now.

"No, it's okay, just go," I say, boiling inside, but still with a smile on my lips.

"No, really, it's not that late," she says.

"You're absolutely right," I reply, in a voice that says it's not late at all and that to be honest I was surprised to hear her talking about going home so soon. I slip my hand into my purse, take out my wallet, and extract a 500-kroner note and a 200. "Here," I say, slapping the money on the table in front of her. "Before I forget."

"Oh, but . . . no, that's way too much. Five hundred's more than enough."

"Well, you said yourself I had more wine than you," I say.

"Yes, I know but—er, I didn't mean it that way," she says.

"I know what you meant," I say. I lift the Tabasco bottle out of the little condiments basket, unscrew the red cap, and pour a few drops onto the palm of my hand.

"What are you doing?" she asks.

I look straight at her as I toss the little pool of Tabasco into my mouth, I don't really know why I do it, I just do. Then I screw the cap on, pop the bottle back into the basket, and look at Mette again, about to explain myself, but before I can do so, Mom appears. I didn't think she would be coming, not this late in the evening, but here she is. She has already spotted us and is making a beeline for our table. But there's something about her, something's happened, something good, she doesn't take her eyes off us and her face is beaming fit to burst. She doesn't say anything right away, doesn't even say hello, she simply plops herself down on a chair and gazes at us, first one, then the other. She seems to be enjoying this situation, enjoying keeping us in suspense.

"What is it? Is it Agnes?" Mette asks.

"She's come out of the coma," Mom says. "And it looks like everything's going to be okay. She'll live," she adds and then she starts to cry. "It's . . . it's just amazing. Even the doctors are saying it's a miracle."

At some point during the spring term of 1999 you shelved your thesis on Rabelais and stopped seeing your guidance counselor altogether. You'd had it up to here with the whole subject, you said, tucking your hand under your chin. You had chosen this course because you thought it would provide you with a good introduction to international literature and that this in turn would be of help in your own writing, but over the years since you had taken the foundation course in literature your writing had, in fact, deteriorated. That, for you, was the worst part, much worse than having wasted almost two years on a thesis you were unlikely ever to finish. You had lost the knack of playing and experimenting with your writing, you said. The pieces you had written before you started studying literature might have been rough and unfinished, but the tone had been fresher, livelier, and far more personal than your current, technically perfect, but slick and relentlessly pedestrian style. You blamed all that literary theory, it had made you too self-conscious. It was always there at the back of your mind when you were writing. You would find yourself applying the principles of diverse literary movements to your own work and this led you to impose various dos and don'ts on yourself as a writer. Both consciously and unconsciously you endeavored to fulfill the demands you imagined different literary theorists would place on a good piece of prose and no great literature ever came of that. "What's in there," you said, giving your computer a little kick, "has as much in common with literature as practicing scales has with music, it's stone dead." You had known this for some time, you had simply tried not to think about it, but now, having sat up all night reading the manuscript of your novel, you could no longer kid yourself.

In other words, not only was your thesis to be shelved, your novel too would have to be scrapped. I assumed it must be hard to have to acknowledge that years of hard work had, to all intents and purposes, been for nothing and I wanted to console you and sympathize with you, but it appeared that that wasn't what you needed. You were relieved, you said, no, in fact you were happy, you felt better than you had in a long time, because you knew you had made the right decision. "I'm looking forward to making a fresh start," you said. But then you surprised me by telling me that making a fresh start didn't only mean embarking on a new novel, it also involved going abroad. You had been thinking about it for a while, but now you had made up your mind, the time was right. The way of writing and thinking you had adopted in recent years was inextricably bound up with all the things with which you surrounded yourself, you believed, and if you were ever to be able to think and write differently you would have to get away from your tiny apartment, away from the Dragvoll campus, away from Café 3B, away from Trondheim and Norway. For a moment I was afraid you were going to say that you would have to get away from me as well, but fortunately you didn't. On the contrary, you asked if I would like to come with you. I didn't have to start on my thesis till the following term so I could simply take the main set texts with me and study in the evenings when you were writing, you said. And it wouldn't necessarily be all that expensive either. In Central America we could live pretty comfortably on our student loans (strictly speaking you were still a student and, like me, had recently received the latest installment of your loan). You realized, of course, that it would be hard for me to go off and leave Malin. You had become quite close to her so it would be hard for you too, but you weren't planning on being away for any more than two or three months and that really wasn't all that long, was it? Lots of people were away from their children for much longer than that.

I didn't need any time to think it over, I immediately said yes, stifling all objections. Apart from one cycling tour of Denmark with Torkild and a few holidays in Sweden with Mom, Mette, and May Lene, I had never been outside of Norway and I remember feeling that I had missed out there, in fact I was embarrassed not to have traveled more than I had. I don't know what it's like today, but in the nineties going backpacking was pretty much an obligatory rite of passage for young middle-class Norwegians, including many of my friends—the social anthropology students among them never tired of repeating the false mantra of how they had learned more from this trip or that than they had learned in all their years at university. But what, above all else, made me agree without a second thought was that I was a little bit in love with the new me. I so enjoyed being the free-spirited, spontaneous young woman I had become since I met you. If I hadn't let you sweep me away with you, I would somehow have been undermining this image of myself and that would simply have been too hard for me to do. Back then I was always looking for proof that I was as young and wild and independent as I wanted to be and tagging along on a journey to distant lands constituted just such proof. I was also convinced that being strong, free, and independent enough to put my own needs first and embark on such a journey made me a good role model for Malin, that if I showed myself to be a liberated woman and acted accordingly, she would, from an early age, automatically think of herself as an independent individual and the equal of anyone.

That said, though, if it hadn't been for the fact that Torkild had become much more accommodating over the past year, there would have been no trip to Central America for me. The fact was that he was no longer bitter, he had met someone else and long since got over me and where, for the first year after we broke up, his insistence on sticking to the agreed schedule and flat refusal to allow any leeway—as, for example, if I asked him to swap one or two of his days with Malin with me—were all part of his way of punishing me, he could now be quite flexible. Admittedly he did have his reservations about me being away for as long as three months, but Malin was now two and life as a parent was far easier than it had been only six months earlier, when she had hardly slept at all at night. So it would be fine, he said. And besides, he had his parents just upstairs and they were always ready to help.

So it was all arranged. Four days after you had abandoned both your thesis and your novel and asked me to go traveling with you, we went down to the Kilroy Travel Agency, the back-packing experts, and bought our tickets, and two weeks later we touched down at Aeropuerto Internacional La Aurora on the outskirts of Guatemala City. I'll never forget that first day on Central American soil: the staggering, positively sauna-like heat that hit us as we stepped out of the plane, the humid, oppressive air, the reek of cigarette smoke inside the terminal building—a familiar enough smell in itself, of course, but strange and exotic to us, coming from Norway, where smoking had been banned on public transport and in all public buildings since 1988. And then, of course, there was the tremendous air of freedom, the feeling of cutting loose that filled us as we plucked our rucksacks off the black conveyor belt and headed out, all set for adventure, all set to discover a foreign culture and in so doing discover more about ourselves as I—inspired by my social anthropology friends—used to say, and this was to some extent true, of course, it was just that the discoveries we were about to make would bear no resemblance to what we had expected to learn and much of this knowledge would not sink in until we were back in Norway and could get some perspective on the trip. Well, while we were there we were too busy coping with the utter foreignness of the place and taking in all the sights and sounds and smells. I had expected to view everything with an anthropologist's eyes, but before we had even got as far as the bus station, I think I had realized there was no chance of that. Or at least, not in the way I had imagined. I simply wasn't capable of digesting all these new sensations, the whole thing was so overwhelming.

As genuine backpackers it was important for us to be spontaneous and take things as they came, so we hadn't planned too much in advance. The only thing we knew for sure was that we would start by visiting the Mayan ruins at Tikal, near Flores, and go from there to Antigua, which we would use as our base for the rest of our stay. One of my social anthropology friends had told us not to waste our time on Guatemala City, and the *Lonely Planet* guide, the backpackers' bible, said the same. So we took a taxi straight to the bus station in Zona 1 and boarded the bus to Flores. Then, true Norwegians that we were, we immediately started wondering whether the bus wouldn't be leaving soon. The sign said it was supposed to leave at five o'clock, but it was already ten minutes past and we were still almost the only people on the bus. Were we on the wrong bus? No, no, we were assured by one of the ragged young orange sellers roaming barefoot around the bus station shouting "naranja, naranja" in remarkably stentorian tones, we weren't. The bus would be leaving in ten minutes, he said. Not that he knew the first thing about it, of course, he merely wanted to give us an answer. What we didn't know then was that there was absolutely no way of telling for sure when the buses ran. The plush-looking, expensive long-distance buses, with their air-conditioning and bathrooms, ran to a fixed schedule but, as we were to learn, the buses taken by most people simply didn't leave until the driver decided the bus was full enough. And if our yellow-and-black 1950s American school bus wasn't full when we boarded it, it most certainly was by the time we drove off an hour later. Three or four adults were squashed into seats designed for two, people were sitting on each others' laps and crammed shoulder to shoulder down the aisle. And not only people: next to me sat an old lady with a piglet on her lap and on the seat behind us was a farmer in a cowboy hat with a gun at his belt and a cage containing three chickens on his knee. It was a far cry, you said, from the Dragvoll to Lademoen bus. This was a Magical Mystery Tour. It was crazy and it was about to become even more so. No sooner had the bus set off than the driver started playing ranchero music full blast, only then to turn it off again to allow a local fire-and-brimstone preacher in a suit several sizes too small for him to rise from the front seat and take the floor. Neither of us could speak much Spanish at that time, but we didn't need to, we had no trouble understanding the terrible fate that awaited us if we did not take Jesus into our hearts. The preacher gesticulated wildly while declaiming about *el diablo* with a conviction and a fervor as alien to the average Norwegian circa 1999 as the fanaticism seen in the hellfire sermons of Ole Hallesby, Norway's answer to Billy Graham, in the fifties. We were both mesmerized and utterly fascinated, but not as mesmerized and fascinated as we were to become, because shortly afterward the bus stopped and on came a man peddling pills, and we're not talking aspirin here. According to a Dutch backpacker who translated for us, this guy had pills to cure everything from cancer, AIDS, and alcoholism to alopecia and edema. The more garishly colored the pills, the more miraculous their effects, apparently. The worst of it was that people were actually buying them. Men and women who, as I would later learn, were dirt-poor peasants who could neither read nor write and who therefore knew nothing of all of the things that we in the West take for granted were giving their last few centavos for a sugar pill they hoped might help a sick child, a mother, a spouse, or possibly themselves. We simply sat there openmouthed. Didn't they realize they were being hoodwinked? Did they not have the slightest suspicion? No, there was no sign that they did and, tragic though it was, we couldn't help laughing. It was like being in a novel by Knut Hamsun. Indeed, this pill pusher could easily have been August in Hamsun's *August* trilogy. Still, though, it was the bus driver who made the biggest impression on us. On the inside of the windshield he had placed a sign saying "God be with us," and well he might, you said, because neither of us had ever experienced driving like it. The bus seemed to have no brakes to speak of, but that didn't appear to worry the driver much. The time he lost on the steep climbs, where it was impossible to push the bus beyond walking pace, he tried to make up on the downhill stretches, and while ranchero music blared from the loudspeakers and the chickens squawked, we hurtled down the plunging mountainsides so fast that we instinctively reached for each other's hands and held them tight. On just about every bend little wooden crosses marked the spots where people had been killed in traffic accidents and roughly halfway along every downward slope a little exit ramp ran up the mountainside at a tangent, obviously meant to act as a last resort if your brakes failed—an eventuality far from uncommon in a country where every vehicle on the road looked ripe for replacement, to put it mildly. It was sheer lunacy, or certainly seemed so to us, coming as we did from a country where kids weren't even allowed to ride their bikes without a helmet.

Those first weeks in Guatemala were amazing. Although I admit that now, when I look at the photographs we took while we were there—at Tikal, for instance—I can't help laughing. The area was crawling with sweaty, sunburned backpackers with cameras slung around their necks, the *Lonely Planet* guide in one hand and a flask of water in the other, but from the photos it looks as though we have the ruins all to ourselves. We had been very careful not to get anyone else in shot. But crowds or no crowds, the ruined Mayan city lies deep in the jungle and I knew, within five minutes of arriving there, that I would remember this for the rest of my life. We wandered along damp, earthy-smelling paths above which we could see howler monkeys swinging from tree to tree and hear the chatter and screech of gaily colored parrots and other birds whose names we didn't know. Hairy spiders, big as a man's hand, sat motion- less on the tree trunks that our shoulders brushed against as we passed and every now and again a red, blue, and probably deadly poisonous frog hopped across the path, reminding us of the advice given to us by the plump, cheery lady who ran the hostel where we were staying: stamp your feet as you walk along the jungle paths to scare away the snakes. And the sense of being in an *Indiana Jones* movie was only reinforced when the path led us out into enormous clearings where thousand- year-old pyramids and temples stood revealed. We were amazed. Awestruck. Indeed, once we had hauled ourselves to the top of a 150-foot pyramid and sat there in the ruddy glow of the low afternoon sun, gazing over the Mayan city and the endless green jungle surrounding it, listening to the chorus of the tree frogs down below and pointing and saying: look, there's the spot where the notorious human sacrifices were carried out and there, that's where some of the astronomical observations that formed the basis for the famous Mayan calendar were made— well, by then we were nigh on ecstatic, or I was at any rate.

After Tikal we had been planning to go to Antigua, but after hearing a dreadlocked Italian backpacker raving about Belize and Caye Caulker, we decided to go there instead. Oh, the sheer joy of abandoning our original plan and feeling every bit as free as we longed to be, that alone was incentive enough to follow his advice. And after Belize, Cancún and Palenque in Mexico awaited us, then Antigua, Lago de Atitlán, and Quetzaltenango in Guatemala and then Copán and Parque Nacional Cusuco in Honduras. We wanted to take in all the sights worth seeing, but the time went too quickly, of course, and with only three weeks left of our adventure we both began to panic. We didn't want to go home, not yet, and after checking and double-checking our budget, we agreed that we could postpone our departure and carry on backpacking for another two months—if, that is, we lived even more cheaply. So we got in touch with the airline and booked new flights home, two and a half months later.

Later we would both agree that that was a little too long, because after a while signs of fatigue began to appear, in you in particular. I was no longer as eager to see everything "worth seeing" either, I set greater and greater store by simply taking it easy and more and more often I chose to lie in a hammock, reading and writing and drinking beer, rather than spend the day climbing to the top of a volcano, going on an ocean safari to see manatees and dolphins, or visiting markets, museums, and parts of the city renowned for their colonial architecture. But I never really got sick of traveling, as you did. After three months of bumming around you were positively grouchy, you had gone off the whole idea of backpacking and on particularly bad days you were never done telling me how ridiculous it actually was to travel around the way we had been doing. All backpackers loved to see themselves as being footloose and fancy-free, you said. What mattered to them was planning the trip itself, what mattered was to be spontaneous, to take things as they came and be prepared to change course along the way; they scoffed at the herd mentality of package tourists who let travel agencies plan their holidays for them, right down to the smallest detail. In fact they didn't just scoff: some of the backpackers we met were so anxious to dissociate themselves from people who went on package holidays that they refused to call themselves tourists. "We're not tourists, we're travelers," as two American girls informed us. But was the difference really as great as the backpackers would have it, you wondered. We might not have had a travel agency to arrange every minute of our trip for us, but our noses were constantly stuck in the *Lonely Planet* guide and if it said that the Thursday market in Chichicastenango was a "must" and that no one should leave Guatemala without visiting Lago de Atitlán, then, like every other backpacker, that is where we went. The way you saw it, we were no less prone to the herd mentality than people who went to Gran Canaria for their holidays. We all traipsed to the same spots and, like holidaymakers on Gran Canaria, we had much more contact with other tourists than we did with the local people. If our Spanish had been better, it might have been different, you said, but to be honest you weren't even too sure about that. We would have had to get a little farther off the beaten track for that because where we were staying there were as many Germans, Americans, and Scandinavians as Latin Americans, and while the Latin Americans we met there were not exactly westernized, they were certainly so used to people from the West that they weren't particularly interested in getting to know us. Or at least, not unless they thought they could make money out of it, as you said. Backpackers were always saying that they traveled in order to learn about other cultures, but in your opinion any knowledge we gained was of the most superficial nature. Yes, we visited Mayan ruins and museums where we saw helmets worn by the conquistadores and weapons they had used, and yes, we had seen exhibitions of pictures by famous Latin American artists and roamed the streets remarking to each other on how interesting the architecture was in this or that part of the city. The problem was, however, that nothing we saw meant anything to us. If we had had Latin American blood in our veins or had been especially interested in the history of Latin America, say, or if we had at least done a bit of background reading before setting out, it would have been a very different story. Then a visit to one of the countless cathedrals, for example, would have triggered a whole string of associations and reflections: Ah, so this is where the remains of Bernal Díaz del Castillo are interred, we would have said as we entered the Catedral de Santiago in Antigua and it would have meant something to us. The name of Bernal Díaz del Castillo and the sight of the crypt where he lay might have reminded us of major events in Guatemalan history and we could have taken all the information we read on the small signs displayed around the church and hooked it up, as it were, to the knowledge we had just had refreshed, thus learning something new. But Bernal Díaz del Castilla was a name we had come across in the *Lonely Planet* guide only five minutes before we walked through the door and by the next day we'd have forgotten all about him and that damn cathedral, you said. No, you went on, you couldn't take one more majestic cathedral full of weeping Madonnas, candles, and creaking wooden pews. Every time we visited a cathedral, all you could think of was how soon we could leave again and find a spot in the shade to have an ice-cold Gallo. You'd lost count of the number of cathedrals we'd seen and you couldn't remember the name of a single one of them. They all blurred into one. The same went for almost all the other sights recommended by *Lonely Planet* or other backpackers. Spectacular buildings, ancient ruins, beautiful beaches, cities, the whole country, in fact, was just a blur. We backpackers mocked package tourists for flocking to synthetic towns and cities—so-called tourist traps—totally devoid of character. "It makes no difference where you go, whether it's Mallorca, Cyprus, or the Canary Islands, because they all look exactly the same. When you look back on holidays like that, they're totally indistinguishable from one another," you had said at the airport back home in Norway when we saw a group boarding a plane to Tenerife. Now, though, you felt that we backpackers were no different. "I mean, take those two Swedes we met in Quetzaltenango or Huehuetenango or wherever it was," you said. "They described Tikal as a real high point of their trip, but when we got talking about Tikal, it turned out that one of them thought it was the Incas who had lived there, not the Mayans. And when we corrected her and explained that the Incas had reigned in South America, she pretended that it had just been a slip of the tongue, and after some laughter and a few flippant and supposedly rueful comments she assured us that of course she knew it was the Aztecs who had built Tikal. Mayans, Incas, Aztecs—whatever! This was obviously an extreme example, you said, but still: there was far less difference between back-packer and package tourist than we liked to think. In fact sometimes when we bumped into other backpackers, you almost felt like pretending to be a package tourist, you declared. You felt like saying that you'd come to Central America for the sun, the cheap booze, and all those willing girl backpackers and that you weren't particularly interested in learning more about the local culture. You actually had the urge to disown all the values and norms backpackers are so intent on evincing. This urge was particularly strong on those occasions when we fell into conversation with the most extreme representatives of the backpacker culture. You had, for instance, been irritated beyond measure by the far too worldly-wise guy from Bergen with whom we'd had a few rum and colas in Santiago Atitlán. He acted as though he had personally discovered the whole fucking continent, you fumed. Christ, just the way he described his nine-month-long trip had had you picturing a kind of Bergensian Dr. Livingstone armed with a machete, risking his life to hack his way through a dense, impenetrable jungle to eventually discover an idyllic little village, far off the beaten track and totally untouched by other backpackers. This was the aim of all backpackers, up there alongside checking off everything on the *Lonely Planet* "must see" list, but as far as you were concerned, this guy from Bergen was a travesty of the adventuring ideal. "The very fact that he called his journey through Amazonia an 'expedition,'" you sniggered.

You had completely gone off the whole backpacking scene, you couldn't take it anymore. You wanted to get out of Guatemala as soon as possible. We had heard that Nicaragua was relatively free of backpackers and you were wondering whether that was what we should do, go to Nicaragua and spend the rest of our stay there. You could, of course, see the paradox in the fact that one minute you were railing against backpackers who dreamed of visiting places where no other backpackers had been, only the next minute to ask if I would like to come with you to just such a place, but so be it. You wanted to get away from the hordes of young middle-class Westerners, you said, you wanted to find a little town in Nicaragua boasting nothing spectacular enough to attract the tourists, some dull, sleepy spot where you could concentrate on your writing and I could concentrate on my reading.

So off we went to Nicaragua, the poorest, most primitive, most devastated country in the region, on the mainland at any rate. We received our first hint of what lay in store as soon as we crossed the border from Honduras. Suddenly there were hardly any cars on the road, in fact I'm tempted to say that there were hardly any roads. It was the middle of the rainy season and we could be driving along as normal one moment, only the next to discover that the road was gone. In one place it had been swept away by a landslide the week before, in another it had been flooded when a river had burst its banks, and in yet another a bridge had collapsed for the third or fourth time in a year—and no one seemed to be making the slightest effort to fix any of it. We took detour after detour, each one longer than the one before, we had to wait for a tree to be moved off the road and for the bus driver to change some belt on the ancient engine that had snapped, and every so often the male passengers would be ordered to get off and push the bus out of an eight-inch layer of mud. The Nicas on the bus were obviously used to this and took it with amazing stoicism, but we were so tired, hungry, grumpy, and strung out that we could barely speak to each other, because if we did we knew we would only end up arguing. And then, to make matters worse, we learned that the surrounding countryside was swarming with bandits, so it was very important that we reached the nearest town before nightfall. "Oh, if only I'd had the sense to bring a bottle of whisky," I remember you saying, "because this is an absolute nightmare."

But we got there without being robbed. Well, I say "there": the bus was actually meant to be going to Estelí, but for some reason that no one bothered to explain to us we wound up in Matagalpa, a little farther south. We looked at each other and shook our heads when we realized where we were, but we were too exhausted to ask what had happened, and it didn't really matter that much. We didn't know anything about either town anyway.

I don't know how many times we had been in this same situation, I don't know how many times we had found ourselves standing in a strange square, hungry and thirsty and flicking through the *Lonely Planet* guide, looking for a cheap place to spend the night. And yet this time it was all so different. Now that I know more about Nicaragua, I understand that my first impressions of Matagalpa were colored by the grueling bus journey and the tension that had grown between us since you had become tired of traveling, but still: the first thing I thought of as we stepped off the bus was *Apocalypse Now*, that and *Heart of Darkness*. According to the *Lonely Planet* guide the air in the mountain town of Matagalpa was cool and refreshing, but late in the day though it was we were met by a wall of steamy, blistering heat. We were drenched in sweat, our T-shirts and the straps of our homemade fanny packs plastered to our skin. Neither of us said a word, we simply stood there ankle deep in mud, gazing around about. There was not a backpacker to be seen, only Nicaraguans and almost all of them men. Some wore baseball caps and tattered T-shirts, but most sported cowboy hats and battered boots with spurs. They rode or sauntered past us. Several of them carried guns and a few yards away from us four men were sitting in the back of a red pickup truck passing around a bottle of rum while comparing two pistols and clearly disagreeing on which was better. Behind us we heard sounds of laughter from where two small boys were amusing themselves by throwing stones at a dog with an injured paw that was having difficulty getting away from them and on the other side of what was in fact a road, but looked more like a river of mud, stood a row of rickety market stalls. Most of these were closed or in the process of closing for the day, but a few were still open and hanging from the roofs of these, in the blazing sun, were huge red glistening joints of meat, which had presumably been there all day. The air was black with flies, but apart from waving the remnants of an old T-shirt or some other rag around a bit whenever a customer approached, the stallholders did nothing to prevent the insects from landing on the meat. My stomach turned at the sight and I didn't feel any better when my nostrils were assaulted by the sickly-sweet smell of tainted meat and rotting fruit and vegetables mingling with the acrid reek of the countless piles of garbage that lay round about, stewing and fermenting in the heat. "I'm not that hungry after all," I said as we started to make our way toward the guesthouse we had decided on. Some guesthouse. We were the only people staying there and the tiny woman behind the desk didn't seem unduly interested in having any guests—she did not look at all pleased when we walked in and she was forced to leave the soap opera she had been watching on a portable black-and-white set powered by a car battery. She muttered a price in Spanish and when we didn't quite catch what she had said, she didn't deign to repeat it. She heaved a big sigh, snatched the two córdoba notes you had produced, put them into a drawer, and gave you back a few coins. "Number four," she grunted, slapping the key down on the desk and turning on her heel almost in the same action. Our room was on the second floor, at the very end of a dark corridor with cockroaches scuttling around the floor. From the shared bathroom down the hall emanated the stench of the sewers, the shower was a makeshift DIY job with the wiring totally exposed to the water, and had it not been for the fact that we were the only people staying there and that there was a huge common terrace overlooking the river and the jungle where you could write and drink undisturbed, we would probably have checked out again pretty soon. But it was peaceful and quiet, so we stayed.

Matagalpa had merited no more than a couple of paragraphs in the *Lonely Planet* guide and I managed to take in the few sights mentioned on one of the many mornings when you were sleeping off a hangover. From then on my days were mainly spent lying in the hammock on the terrace, writing in my diary, or reading novels (I had brought two of my set texts with me, but as far as I can remember I never got around to reading so much as a page of them), usually with a cold Victoria or Toña within reach. During our first week there I did feel duty bound to take a little walk every day, to get to know the town and the surrounding area. I could read and write at home, after all, and to lie in a hammock reading for hours on end, well, it rather rendered the whole trip pointless, I felt. But eventually I dropped my daily walk. For one thing there was little or nothing to do or see in Matagalpa—for someone like me, who couldn't speak the language, that is. My Spanish was good enough for ordering food and asking directions, but I couldn't hold a proper conversation in it, so I was cut off, so to speak, from any social contact. Previously on the trip not a day had gone by without me exchanging at least a few words with other English-speaking backpackers: Germans, Swedes, Argentinians. We met them on buses, in hostels and guesthouses, we went sightseeing with them during the day and drank beer with them in the evening, talking all the time. But there were no other backpackers in Matagalpa, only Nicas, and none of them spoke English. So for the first time on our travels, when I walked around Matagalpa I felt like a stranger. I felt as though I was in a bubble, locked inside myself. Not only that but being outdoors was not at all comfortable. One moment it was baking hot and so humid and oppressive that it was hard to breathe, the next the heavens would open and a torrential downpour would engulf the town, a massive deluge that went on and on, raindrops the size of pennies hammering down, roads dissolving into rivers of ocherous sludge in which it was almost impossible to stay upright, and puddles of mud reaching almost to my knees. I didn't feel safe, either. Crime figures were lower here than in Guatemala, but they were on the increase, and as a lone, pink-cheeked Western woman, not only did I stand out like a sore thumb, I was also easy prey for anyone whose intentions were less than honorable.

So after a while I only really went out to eat and this made for long, uneventful, and pretty boring days. Then one evening: we had eaten a dinner of beans, rice, tortillas, and bone-dry steak, drunk two or three beers, and ordered a half bottle of rum and two bottles of cola in what we had taken to be an ordinary *comedor*, only to discover that it was in fact a brothel. Suddenly a brawny, bare-chested guy appeared and started moving the furniture about. He pushed all of the unoccupied tables together to form a sort of catwalk running from the bar to the middle of the room, then placed a chair at the end nearest the bar. Whatever was about to happen was clearly a regular event, one held more or less at a set time, because within minutes the premises, which had been almost empty, were jam-packed. Every seat was taken. By men: young men, middle-aged men, old men, some of them so drunk they could barely stand, others looking perfectly sober and all of them trying to secure a place with as good a view as possible of the catwalk. And then the whores emerged from the back room. One by one they stepped up onto the chair next to the bar and from there onto the first table. And while the men whooped and cheered and shouted out comments, either at the whores or to one another, the girls proceeded to walk toward the middle of the room. I had seen similar scenes in western movies or in films depicting the life of Paris's Montmartre and Pigalle districts in the early 1900s, and no doubt in other films too. But the prostitutes in those had looked very different, they had been bawdy and sexy in a charming, femme-fatale way, lusty and generally buxom women who winked confidently and ran their tongues over scarlet lips as they bared a little bit more flesh, and if some horny old goat who couldn't keep his hands to himself tried to grope any of them, she wouldn't hesitate to give the person concerned a well-aimed kick in the face, safe in the knowledge that her minders would protect her if the culprit made any move to retaliate.

But these whores were different. They had obviously been instructed to look and act like the prostitutes in the movies, they wiggled and tried to look sexy, but they weren't convincing. Their movements were awkward, their eyes flicked uncertainly from side to side, and they looked scared, they looked as though they had been driven out of the back room, and unlike the women I had seen on the silver screen, they could never have made anyone believe they were doing this of their own free will. These were ordinary Nicaraguan girls. I had heard of the land wars in this region. I knew that farmers in these parts were being coerced into selling their land to wealthy landowners who had returned to the country from Miami, where they had been living since the revolution. I knew that the farmers were faced with the choice of living as farm laborers (which effectively meant working as slaves on the estates) or of moving into the cities, where unemployment could be as high as an incredible 90 percent and crime and prostitution were almost the only options open to them if they were to feed themselves and their families. All this I knew and I wasn't stupid, I knew that these girls, these terrified, half-grown teenagers parading only a few yards away from me, doing their utmost to look sexy, were the young women I had read about, but here they were in the flesh, every one of them looking like the girl next door. In fact the only difference between them and me or the girls I knew back home in Norway was that these girls were poor and slightly darker skinned and as soon as this thought struck me I became another person, I would put it as strongly as that: I became the person I am today. It happened when my eyes met those of a pretty girl with skinny wrists wearing a white T-shirt with the phrase "I ♥ New York" on the front. Apart from her and the other prostitutes I was the only woman in the place and when she looked my way I could almost see the shame in her eyes. It hit me like a physical blow, I longed to tell her that she had nothing to be ashamed of, but I also understood her reaction. In her place I would have reacted in exactly the same way and for some reason I think it was this, together with the perfectly ordinary appearance of these girls, that led me to identify with them as I had not done with other unfortunates I had come across on our travels. We had seen a lot of misery and wretchedness along the way: grubby street children sitting or lying on the pavements, having sniffed themselves into apathy; families of ten or twelve living in tumbledown shacks that the sand and dust blew straight through; crippled beggars gazing at us with mournful dog eyes and pleading for a few coins for food. The scale of the poverty was massive and manifested itself in the most grotesque ways, but this was the first time I had felt that it had anything to do with me. The young woman whose eyes I had met was a sister. She and the other uncomfortable and terrified girls wiggling along that improvised catwalk were my sisters and it's hard for me to describe the compassion and love I felt for them at that moment. As hard to describe as the fury, nay hatred, I felt for all the men who sat there gawping, eyes brimming with liquor and lust, ready to buy a village girl with money they ought to have been spending on food and clothing for their families. I had been describing myself as a feminist since I was a teenager and an active member of the Norwegian Union of Students, and over the previous year alone I had read masses of feminist literature as part of my course. Nonetheless, I would say that not until that moment, in a dirty little brothel in Nicaragua, was the feminist in me born. It was as if the sight of those poor girls surrounded by hordes of men brought to life all the works of feminist literature I had absorbed. I don't really know how to explain it, but it reminded me of something my dad had said when he was told that he had cancer and no more than a month to live: he had known from the age of five that he was going to die one day, he said, but only now did he realize what it meant. In much the same way only then did I realize what all the feminist literature and all the knowledge I possessed on women's liberation and equal rights meant, only then did I understand that all the theory and all the information I had gleaned from books was actually based on real life.

For a little while I simply sat there very quietly, observing this grotesque scene, then suddenly I was overcome by a fit of un-controllable weeping. Without a word I jumped up, stormed out, and took to my heels. You followed me out and I heard you calling my name again and again as you ran after me down the bemired streets of Matagalpa, but I didn't stop, I ran all the way back to the guesthouse and when you walked in I was lying on the bed sobbing with the sleeping bag over my head. You knew how I felt, you said, but you didn't. I believed then and I still believe today that you have to be a woman to fully understand how I was feeling at that moment and I said as much to you, or no, I didn't say it, I bawled it at you. I was beside myself with grief and fury, you didn't understand a thing, I screamed, you just wanted me to calm down, so you could have peace to work on a fucking novel that was never going to come to anything, certainly not as long as you carried on drinking the way you were doing.

I apologized later for what I had said and we made up over a bottle of rum. But as I say, I had changed and only days later I was seized by another fit of rage. This time it happened after five Norwegians from an LAG solidarity brigade based in a village outside of Matagalpa moved into our guesthouse. The members of these brigades stayed with poor farming families and shared their daily lives, and these volunteers had come to town to write articles and reports on their stay, which they would send home to Norway before returning to their village. It was months since they had seen any other Norwegians, or any other Westerners for that matter, and they were surprised and delighted to meet us. You weren't as happy to meet them, though, and that's putting it mildly. You were nice enough to them for the first couple of days, if a little reserved, but then the shit hit the fan. Partly because they completely took over the terrace in the evening, making it impossible for you to write, but mainly because going on a solidarity brigade mission was an indication of a mindset that really rankled with the ironic observer in you. These people didn't just think they could get under the skin of the Nicaraguan culture and way of life and understand it, you told me. They took the backpacker's search for the authentic to the extreme by endeavoring to become Latin American themselves. It was too ridiculous for words, you said before going on to remind me of what had happened when we arranged to meet them at the Comedor San Ramón for a beer or two: the first guy turned up an hour later than we had agreed and when we smiled politely and said well, better late than never, he first pretended not to understand what we meant and then, when we explained that we had said we'd meet at seven o'clock, not eight o'clock, he laughed at us for being so Norwegian, implying that after a few months in Nicaragua he had forgotten the Norwegian love of punctuality that had ruled his life for twenty-odd years. He and the other LAG volunteers were, it seemed, on "Latin American time." God, you hated that, you said, it was so fucking pretentious. And did I hear what that horse-faced girl had said later on that evening, when you asked whether we should order a bottle of Flor de Caña instead of Ron Plata: "Oh, I'll stick with Ron Plata," she said, "that's what the farmers drink." Had I ever heard the like? Flor de Caña was the only rum to rival the Cuban rums, but she would rather buy Ron Plata, which was absolutely disgusting, simply because that was the only rum the poor farmers could afford. Unbelievable. The one cost about twenty kroner more than the other, a lot for an impoverished Nicaraguan farmer, but nothing to Norwegians like us. It was all well and good to identify with and endeavor to understand what life was like for the poor and the oppressed, you said, but these LAG volunteers were trying to convince themselves and everyone else that they were poor too. "Just look at the way they were dressed," you went on. "For fuck's sake, they looked like they were auditioning for *Oliver Twist* or *Les Misérables*—with holes in the knees of their jeans and shirts so washed out there was no telling what color they had originally been. "Christ," you said, "how much does a new T-shirt cost in this country? Two kroner? Five kroner? Ten?" You didn't know, but you knew it was so little that these guys could have bought every single T-shirt in the whole town if they wanted to and the only reason they didn't do so was that they wanted to dress like poverty-stricken peasants!

All of this came pouring out in an outburst that was, for you, unusually virulent and impassioned. But later that evening, when you were nearing the bottom of the rum bottle and simply couldn't resist telling the LAG volunteers what you thought of them, you presented this same criticism in a more Wildean manner. Or tried to at any rate: "Ah, now you disappoint me," you said when the girl with the horsey face removed her fanny pack and proceeded to count out the dollar bills she was going to change at the bank the next day. "And there was me thinking you really were dirt-poor." And: "Oh, so you can read?" you asked a guy called Edvard, whom you had, of course, dubbed Eduardo. "The Sandinistas must have managed to reduce the illiteracy figures slightly while they were in power then."

That was how you went on. No matter what the LAG volunteers said and no matter what they did, out you would come with some caustic remark designed to remind them that they weren't as Latin American as they tried to make out. But your sarcasm did not have the desired effect. In your head these volunteers were a bunch of excessively earnest individuals desperately seeking authenticity and since you were of the opinion that nothing rattled such people more than sarcasm, you were both surprised and disappointed when they proved to be neither annoyed nor angry, but were actually able to laugh at themselves and at what you said. You kept up your Oscar Wilde act for a while longer, but then you gave up and took to criticizing them as openly as you had when you and I were alone. You repeated what you had said to me more or less word for word and almost as heatedly and concluded with an almost bitter tirade in which you declared that joining a solidarity brigade was the nineties' equivalent of self-proletarization. The Marxists of the seventies were a crowd of middle-class kids who had decided to fight for the workers, the solidarity volunteers were a crowd of middle-class kids who had decided to fight for the poor and the oppressed of the third world. The Marxists dropped out of university and resigned their academic posts to work in the factories, the solidarity volunteers took a break from their studies and left safe, wealthy Norway to live like impoverished farmers in the third world, and both parties identified so strongly with the people they had taken it into their heads to liberate that they did their utmost to erase their own identities and backgrounds and become exactly like them. "How pathetic can you be?" you sneered indignantly. "And who do you think you're fooling with your stupid little slumming exercise. The workers laughed at the Marxists when they showed up with their pen-pusher hands, all set to get stuck in, and they roared their heads off when the Marxists started talking about revolution and the dictatorship of the proletariat. What makes you think those poor Nicaraguan villagers don't do the same thing the minute your backs are turned? Do you really think they're fooled by your peasant getups? Do you think they don't know you've got your Visa cards in your fanny packs? Don't you realize that it's only thanks to those Visa cards that you're allowed to be up there at all? Don't you realize it's your money they're after? You're so fucking naïve and so gullible it's unbelievable," you said, before going on to ask what on earth had possessed them to do something as stupid as joining a solidarity brigade. Did they feel a need to be part of a project that was bigger than themselves? Was this Generation X searching for something meaningful and important in which to invest their energy, was that what we were witnessing here? Or was it the eternal guilt and self-loathing of the middle classes, was that what drove them? As young middle-class Norwegians born after the advent of the country's oil boom they had never known hardship, they had never gone hungry, never been oppressed, they had never really had to fight and struggle to survive. Could it be that this, the knowledge that they were so incredibly privileged, filled them with so much guilt and such self-loathing that they actually felt the need to erase their Norwegian identity and become poor Latin American farmers for a while?

While you sat there on that terrace, pouring all this vitriol on the somewhat taken-aback volunteers, I was growing more and more incensed. Eventually I could stand it no longer. You accused these young people of being ridden with guilt because they were affluent Norwegians, I remember saying. You said that slumming it with the solidarity brigade was a way of doing penance for this, but you'd got it all back to front. You had also grown up in a society where everything had been mapped out for you, with the result that you weren't used to getting involved. You weren't used to taking action, you saw yourself as individualistic and independent, but in fact the opposite was the case. You were just another sheep, I cried, just another member of the whole fucking postmodern flock that had taken over Norwegian universities today. If you had ever stopped to consider what was the right thing to do and acted accordingly, you would probably have done exactly what these young people were doing. You would have got involved, you would have tried to make a difference. And as for self-loathing, I went on, getting more and more steamed up, there was no one here as full of self-loathing as you, you, a backpacker who hated backpackers, a young middle-class man who hated the middle class, a romantic who hated romance. It was yourself you were talking about when you sat there lambasting the LAG volunteers, I yelled. It was your own shame and self-loathing, your own need for meaning and a sense of belonging you were talking about, didn't you see that?

At the time I didn't know where my anger came from. Not till I was back in Norway did I realize that I had changed and that this change had occurred when my eyes met those of a prostitute in a brothel in Matagalpa. Until that incident in the brothel I had, as I've said, been going around in a kind of bubble, I had been closed in on myself and more or less cut off from the everyday realities for people living in this country. Indeed, during our first weeks in Nicaragua I believe I actually came to agree more and more with your criticism of the backpacker culture. Granted, I thought you were exaggerating, but the way we merely seemed to skim the surface, our inability to delve deeper into the culture of the countries we visited became increasingly clear to me as I wandered around Matagalpa alone. But when I saw that girl with the skinny wrists in her "I ♥ New York" T-shirt, it was as if the thin film separating me from my surroundings dissolved. All at once I saw myself as part of a world that, till then, I had observed and approached as a tourist, and from that moment on it was impossible for me to accept your detached and sardonic attitude to traveling. Viewed in that light it is possibly easier to understand why I saw red when you criticized and ridiculed those young volunteers.

Only a few days after this we were back on Norwegian soil and very glad to be there. Simply being able to walk past a newsstand or a shop and recognize all the advertising signs and all the newspapers on the racks, simply being able to walk down the street and catch words and snippets of conversation in one's own tongue, the pure relief of not always having to struggle to understand and be understood, it made me feel more Norwegian than ever before—this was where I belonged, it was as simple as that.

But the joy was short-lived.

Torkild had had his contract with Friends of the Earth renewed several times during the nineties and because he was so brilliant at what he did, the organization wanted to renew it again, but they simply didn't have the money. So his position was scrapped and Torkild suddenly found himself unemployed. But then he was offered a job with an environmental project on Svalbard run by the Norwegian Polar Institute, his partner applied for and got a research post at the university up there, they said yes to both, and moved to Longyearbyen with Malin. Torkild had done everything he could to let me know, he told me, but with no luck. Which was not so surprising. I mean, we had been completely cut off from the outside world for long spells of time. Neither of us had a mobile phone back then and except for a couple of times very early on in the trip we had never tried to find a pay phone and call home. When we were in Guatemala, we had occasionally visited internet cafés to check and send e-mails, but we hadn't seen a single internet café in Nicaragua so I hadn't read the e-mails he had sent me. If Torkild had known where we were, he would have got in touch with the Norwegian embassy and got them to pass on the message, he said, but he didn't even know which country we would be in at any given time. Yes, he had the postcards I had sent to Malin to go by, but they took so long to reach them and we were moving around so much that they weren't really much help. In short, I had been impossible to get hold of and he was very sorry about the whole situation. He knew this must be a terrible blow to me, he said, but I had to remember that they wouldn't be living on Svalbard forever, it was only a one-year project. He and his partner would definitely be moving back to Trondheim after that. And of course I was very welcome to come to Svalbard anytime, I could live with them and stay for as long as I liked.

Trondheim, June 29th, 2006. The dog needs water

"I don't think I've ever been so happy," Mom sighs.

"I know, me neither," Mette says.

I part my lips, sit openmouthed for a moment as if about to say something, then close them again and shake my head, trying to look as though I can't describe how happy I am, and I am happy, of course I am, just not as happy as I'd thought I would be if Agnes regained consciousness, I don't know why, maybe because my anger from before hasn't quite left me, that must be it. I was so stung by the way Mette was talking and acting and I still haven't got that out of my system. I curl my fingers around the stem of my glass, tilt it slightly so that the few drops of white wine left in it run almost all the way up to the glistening imprint of my lipstick. I look at Mom and smile again, hear one of the aging rockers let out a loud *yesss* as another number comes on, sounds like the Rolling Stones, that has to be Mick Jagger singing, anyway.

"Know what, I feel like buying us a bottle of champagne," Mom says, beaming at us as she puts her hand into her purse and pulls out her wallet. "Weekday or no. What do you say?"

"Yes!" Mette says with a big smile, straightening her back

and clapping her hands lightly, as if applauding the fact that we're going to celebrate with champagne. "This is definitely the evening for champagne."

I try to smile even broader, I wish I could be as happy as my smile would have it, but it's no use, I'm in a bad mood because of what happened earlier and it doesn't help that Mom and Mette are so overjoyed, it simply reminds me that I'm not as happy as I should be, and that in turn makes me feel even more depressed. And there's worse to come, I know, because pretty soon Mette is going to tell Mom that she and Göran are getting married, there's nothing stopping her from doing that, not now that Agnes has woken up, and then there will be no containing them. The very thought makes my heart sink even further, because then I'll turn back into the ugly, huffy little sister I used to be. I'll allow myself to be forced into the role I'm always forced into when I'm with the rest of the family and I'll end up saying and doing things guaranteed to wreck their happiness, I'll drag them down with me so I don't have to wallow in the dumps alone. But I don't want to do that, I find it hard to be as happy as I would like to be, but I don't begrudge them this chance to celebrate and be glad.

"Well, have fun, you two," I say abruptly, keeping the smile on my face and rapping the table lightly with my hands to indicate that I'm going to call it a night, because I have to go home now, I have to get out of here before I turn into the horrible little sister.

They stare at me in bewilderment.

"You're not leaving, are you?" Mom says.

"I'm afraid I have to. I just remembered that I forgot to put out water for Rex before I left," I say. I could hardly have come up with a worse excuse and I feel my cheeks start to burn as soon as I hear myself say it.

"Rex?" Mette says.

"I got myself a dog," I say, smiling quickly as I turn to the side, unhook my purse from the back of the chair, lay it on my lap, and turn to face Mom and Mette again. They gaze at me, they know I'm just saying this, and I feel my cheeks grow even hotter. "I know it sounds stupid," I say, it may seem more credible if I admit that it's stupid, no one would willingly make a stupid excuse, not if it wasn't genuine. "But I haven't been home since this morning and it's been a scorcher of a day, he must be absolutely parched, poor boy. I'd love to stay here and celebrate with you, of course, but that would be nothing short of animal cruelty." I can tell that saying this makes my excuse sound even more credible. I feel the heat recede from my face and I smile a little more confidently. They still say nothing, Mom nods and gives a rather disappointed smile, but Mette gives me a look that says I can't possibly be serious, the kind of look she used to give me when we were younger, when she would roll her eyes at everything I said. I feel an instant surge of annoyance. I'm about to ask her what she's gawping at, but instead I just keep on smiling, pop my hand into my purse and rummage around a bit, I've got a pack of gum in here somewhere.

"For God's sake," Mette says. "All this time you've been going on as if you wanted to spend the whole evening here, you just said you had no intention of going and leaving a full bottle of wine, but when we actually have a good reason to stay, you suddenly have to go home."

"Mette, didn't you hear what I said?" I say as I push my keys to one side with my finger, find the pack of gum, and lift it out of my purse. "I only just remembered that I hadn't put out any water for Rex, if I'd thought of it earlier obviously I would have gone home then," I say, growing more and more annoyed, but still smiling. "I might pop back afterward, though, once I've seen to him." I won't, of course, but my real reason for leaving will be obscured still further if I say I might be back—like I couldn't possibly be leaving to avoid being with them.

"I'm sure it won't kill the dog for you to stay and have a glass of champagne with Mom and me," Mette says, tucking her hair behind her ear.

"No, I don't suppose it would," I say, flipping the top stick of gum out of the pack with my thumb and into the palm of my hand. "But he'll feel pretty shitty," I add as I drop the pack back into my purse. Just then there comes a brief explosion of laughter from the old rockers, it sounds rather like the volume on the stereo being turned up full, then hastily turned down again. I go to put the gum into my mouth, but Mom lays her hand on my arm and squeezes it gently a couple of times.

"I know things aren't easy for you at the moment," she says softly, giving me a sudden, sad little smile, and I see threadlike cracks appear in her red lipstick as her lips widen. "I know this isn't about the dog, it's about Malin." I gaze down at her hand for a moment, this hand with the gnarled veins that run from her wrist to her fingers, this hand that she lays lightly on my arm as if to say that she knows everything and I don't have to pretend anymore. I look at her and raise my eyebrows, I mean, what is it she thinks she knows? What the hell is she blathering on about? I do still think about Malin from time to time, but not as often as I used to and I certainly wasn't thinking about her just now. I realize, of course, that Mom believes that's why I got Rex, to have something on which to lavish all my maternal affection, all the love I can't give to Malin, and I'm sure there's some truth in that, but still, my desire to go home now has nothing whatsoever to do with her.

"Malin?" Mette mutters.

Mom turns to her, closes her eyes, and nods slowly, then turns to me again.

"Agnes's accident has taken its toll on all the family," Mom says, replying to Mette, but looking at me and smiling her sad smile, still with her hand on my arm. "It's been worst for May Lene, obviously. But we mustn't forget how hard this has been for Susanne. Not only did she almost lose a dearly loved niece, she has also had to relive the loss of Malin. Almost losing Agnes like that took her back to the time when she lost Malin, and all the grief, all the guilt she must have felt then, but which I think she refuses to admit to, has come flooding back," she says. She speaks slowly, with sympathy in her voice, never taking her eyes off me, and I just sit there gazing at her wide-eyed. What the hell is she saying, it's quite a while since I last thought about Malin, and anyway, what the hell does Mom know about what I think or don't think, going on as though she knows me better than I know myself. "It's no coincidence that Susanne got herself a dog just after Agnes landed in the hospital," she says, still speaking to Mette but looking at me. "And no wonder she's terrified of neglecting her dog, no wonder she would rather go home and give him some water than sit here drinking champagne with us. It's Malin she wants to look after, she abandoned Malin to go off and enjoy herself, and refusing to have more wine, insisting on going home now, it's . . . oh, I don't know . . . a way of trying to make up for that, if you like. Right, Susanne?"

I don't answer straightaway, I just look at her. I can hardly believe my ears, she sits at home day after day, drinking her cheap supermarket coffee and watching those awful American talk shows in which stupid pop psychology is used to resolve personal traumas that their guests claim to have suffered. She doesn't understand that it's all utter fiction, pure entertainment, she thinks that having watched a few seasons of Oprah somehow qualifies her to practice as a psychologist, she thinks it gives her some special insight into what I'm thinking and feeling, and now she's got it into her head that nigh on everything I say and do relates to Malin, it drives me mad, but I'm not going to get mad, I'm going to stay cool, because if I don't, Mom will only take this as a sign that she's hit a nerve and then she'll only be even more convinced that she's right. I give a little chuckle and shake my head as I pull my hand away. Again I go to pop the piece of gum into my mouth, but then I stop and drop it into my purse instead. I don't feel like gum now.

"Oh, Mom, I think you've been watching too much Oprah," I say, in much the way an adult would talk to a child: patronizing, benign, and teasing all at once. But she believes absolutely in what she's just said, I can tell by that quiet, confident smile, a smile that says she knows she's right, it's so annoying, the fact that she thinks she knows more about me than I do, but I keep smiling. "Sometimes a cigar is just a cigar, you know," I add, raising one hand and scratching the left side of my nose, it's not itchy, but I do it anyway.

Mom closes her eyes and opens them again, looks me straight in the face.

"When I came to see you yesterday . . . ," she says, then she pauses and gives me that sad smile, just as Mick Jagger goes into the chorus of "Wild Horses." "You weren't yourself, Susanne. You were behaving the way you did as a rebellious teenager. When I walked into your apartment, I felt as though I was stepping back into the eighties and nineties. Everything you said and did seemed to be an attempt to dissociate yourself from the straight, conventional life that you so despised when you were younger. Drinking wine in the middle of the day, in the middle of the week, and so . . . so nonchalant. The nonchalance of someone desperate to show that she's an independent woman, a free spirit who doesn't care about bourgeois things like cleaning or tidying the apartment or rinsing the coffee machine or . . . I mean, you scarcely turned a hair when I handed you that wallet you left at the hospital. There was a thousand kroner in it, but you behaved exactly the way you used to do when you were eighteen or nineteen and an avowed anti-materialist. The money didn't seem to matter to you, and . . . and—"

"What exactly are you getting at," I ask, breaking in. I put my hand up to scratch my nose again and try to keep smiling, but I can't. I narrow my eyes a little as I shake my head, look straight at her.

Mom gives my arm a little squeeze.

"What I'm trying to say is that I see all of this as a way of rejecting me and the straight, conventional life that I lead and have always led," she says. "A way of rejecting the role of a responsible, grown-up mother and all that this entails . . . and that, in turn, I see as an attempt to defend the choice you made when you gave up Malin. I think you've been haunted by the terrible mistake you made when you gave her up, Susanne. And I think you've had—and still have—a great need to justify your decision, to yourself and to others. A need I believe grew even greater when Agnes was run over. As I say, I think Agnes's accident forced you to relive the loss of Malin and filled you with a tremendous need to justify letting her go the way you did. And this . . . what can I call it . . . this exaggeratedly rose-colored view of the single life, of being fancy-free and apparently against me and everything that smacks of conventionality is, I believe, a way of satisfying this need. To be honest I think it's a way of fooling yourself into believing that being single and childless and fancy-free, that's the life for you. And then there's this whole Rex thing. Only days after Agnes's accident you get yourself a dog, something to which you can give all the love and care you would normally have given to Malin, it's all so . . . so *obvious*," she says.

I look her straight in the eye, I'm so angry, I feel hot all over. I twist my face into a sneer.

"You know what, Mom, you might not be aware of it yourself, but all that . . . pop-psychology jargon they use on your talk shows has become a part of your everyday language. You've been infected by it, did you know that, it's become a part of the way you think and talk, and now here you are, going on as if you know more about me than I do. It's so insulting, do you realize that?" I say, my voice rising, I can't help it, suddenly I'm almost shouting and the people at the next table look around at me for a moment, then turn to face one another again, eyebrows raised.

"Susanne, please," Mom says, lowering her voice to let me know that I'm talking too loud. "Let's not fight, not today of all days. We should be celebrating, we should be happy."

I look at her and swallow, breathe, I'm so angry, I'm burning up, but I have to pull myself together now, I have to calm down, but I can't, I prop my elbows on the table and lean toward her.

"I'm very, very happy for Agnes and May Lene, Mom," I say. I don't raise my voice, but it's shaking, quivering with fury. "Every bit as happy as you are. But it's so damn hard to sit here and look happy with you and Mette carrying on the way you are," I say, looking her in the eye. I pause, then I feel my purse start to slip off my lap, I straighten up, place my hands on it. "Tell me, are you enjoying this, Mom? Reminding me of what I did to Malin . . . does that make you feel like a better mother yourself, is that why you're doing it?"

"Susanne, please."

"Or are you still mad at me for robbing you of your grandchild? Is that why you're carrying on like this?"

"Oh really, Susanne."

"Yeah, maybe that's it," I continue, glaring at her and giving another wrathful sneer. "Maybe it's not me but *you* who's reliving the whole business with Malin, maybe Agnes's accident forced *you* to relive the loss of your other grandchild. And knowing there was a possibility, in fact more than a possibility, that Agnes would die, well, that brought it home to you that we could soon be a family with no children in it, right? And as far as you're concerned, that would, of course, be my fault. Poor May Lene looked like losing her daughter due to an accident and Mette can't have kids and has to content herself with being what she calls a second Mom. But me, I willingly gave my child away. I let the whole family down, our family was in danger of ending with May Lene and Mette and me, and it was all my fault. That's why you're so angry," I say, twisting the strap of my purse around my hand and pulling it so tight it hurts.

"Susanne, that . . . even you don't believe that," Mom says.

I look her straight in the eye, wait.

Then: "D'you know what, Mom, you're absolutely right," I say, my voice quivering with rage and triumph. "I don't. I'm simply trying to show you how ridiculous this whole Oprah-inspired psychobabble of yours is. It's *entertainment*, Mom."

"Well, I think Mom's right in a lot of what she says," Mette says.

I turn to her, she leans back a little in her chair and sits there with her arms crossed, looking at me. I work my hand free of my purse strap and lay it on the table.

"Oh, so you agree with her, do you?" I say with a baleful grin. "What else is new?"

Mette blinks slowly, as if to say she's above such sarcasm.

"Well, for one thing, you've just turned down a steady job, a job you actually wanted," she says, leaning forward again, putting her elbows on the table and propping herself on them. "You couldn't say why," she says, "but you did wonder whether it might have been a sign of a midlife crisis, whether you chose to carry on working freelance because it made it easier for you to see yourself as young and dynamic and free. And that fits with what Mom just said. You're doing everything you can to live like some young thing, not because you're scared of getting old, as you suggested yourself, but because living like that makes it easier to live with the fact that you gave up Malin. You . . . you're out there drinking and partying and living it up for all your worth, you're trying to be the girl you were fifteen or twenty years ago, you're trying to be . . . how can I put it . . . *irresponsible*! You adopt an irresponsible persona and then you use this as an excuse, use it to justify to yourself your decision to give up Malin. It was the right thing to do because you and the life you're condemned to lead are simply not compatible with parenthood."

"Oh, honestly!" I say, positively incandescent by now, my insides seeming to melt and swim around in my stomach. I look at Mette and swallow, then I glance down at my hands, see the red and white welts on one of them from where my purse strap has dug in. I pause, eye Mette again. "Words fail me."

"The way I see it, there's also a self-destructive element to all of this," she goes on. "I think you despise yourself the way you do because you gave up Malin, I think you feel the need to punish yourself, and I think this . . . I think this pushes you to even greater excess. You drink too much, you don't exercise, you're so unfit, and . . . and now you've started smoking again."

I breathe quickly through my nose, feel my nostrils contract and expand as I stare at Mette.

"For the last time," I say, speaking quietly now, speaking in a soft, tremulous voice, which makes it clear that I've had enough and that they'd better not go any further. "I do think about Malin every now and again, of course I do, but since I never see her, it tends to happen less and less often and to claim that nigh on everything I've thought and said and done over the past few years has actually been about *her*, well, that's downright crazy," I say. I pause, then: "Would you like to know why I wanted to go home now, Mette? It had nothing to do with Rex, that was just a poor excuse. So there went that argument, Mom," I say, glancing at her and grinning. "So much for your neat little parallel between Rex and Malin," I add, then I turn to Mette again. "You've been getting on my nerves for most of the evening, Mette. And then, when Mom turned up with the good news about Agnes, well . . . naturally I was as delighted as you two. But I found it hard to show it because I was still so pissed off . . . and I was afraid of ruining your happiness, *that's* why I wanted to go home. It didn't seem right to sit here feeling angry and resentful when I'd just been told that Agnes had regained consciousness. But I was angry, Mette, and I still am. Because . . . you're such a phony. You've been making little digs at me all evening, you make them all sound like perfectly ordinary remarks from one sister to another, but every one of them is intended to make you look like a winner and me like a total loser."

"*What?*" Mette gasps. She stares at me openmouthed, acting as though she doesn't understand a word I've said.

"Aw, don't tell me you don't know what I'm talking about, because I know you do," I say with an indignant little toss of my head. "But the truth is that as a woman you're every bit as oppressed as I am," I continue, bringing feminism into it now—there's every reason to do so, after all, but I'll have to tread carefully because I know how Mom and Mette react when I start to talk about politics or feminism, they roll their eyes despairingly at the mere mention of women's liberation and if I broach the subject of feminism now they'll only see it as a desperate attempt to avoid the home truths with which they're confronting me. "You have such low self-esteem, Mette, and you never miss an opportunity to boost it," I go on. "Like most women you make unreasonable demands on yourself, you try to be perfect in every way, and when you don't achieve perfection—because you can't, of course—the demands made on women today cannot possibly be fulfilled, even by *you* . . . when you fall short, you feel like a failure. You're ridden with guilt and shame because you feel you're not good enough, so you shore up your self-esteem by reminding yourself and everyone else that, if nothing else, at least the people around you are even *less* perfect than you." I notice the glances Mom and Mette exchange at this: helpless, rather sorrowful looks that say: Ah, now Susanne's feeling cornered. I feel an immediate rush of anger, they're not listening to me, they're not even prepared to consider what I'm saying, they automatically construe it as an attempt to derail the conversation, to avoid having to face up to psychological traumas I've never suffered, but that they maintain I've experienced and that makes me so mad, the fact that they never believe I actually mean what I say, that all of my political opinions or observations are interpreted as evidence of personal problems and traumas, that's what drives me wild, but I will not back down. "You're suffering from good-girl syndrome," I say. "And you vent all the frustration with which that fills you on me and everyone else close to you, you've always been the same, but this evening you outdid yourself. That's why I had to get away. I was so angry, you've no idea. From the moment you parked your pert little butt on that chair you've been coming out with all this . . . *humblebragging*," I say, talking way too loud now and glaring at Mette as I raise one hand and point a finger at her, and she just sits there openmouthed, pretending to be shocked.

"Susanne," says Mom. "Let's calm down a bit now."

I don't even look at her, keep my eyes fixed on Mette.

"And the more successful you seem, the less successful I feel," I say. "As a feminist I should be above this sort of thing, of course, I know I should, but I'm a member of this society too, I'm just as influenced by ideals of feminine perfection as you are, so I'm not, I'm not strong enough."

"Susanne," Mom whispers, "lower your voice a little, please. People are looking at us."

"I don't give a shit," I shout. I cross my arms, stare at Mom for a moment, then glance around the café. One or two people are looking over at us, but they turn away as soon as my eyes meet theirs, all except the pasty, paunchy old rockers, they go on staring at us, grinning as they knock back pint number two or three or whatever. I stare back at them for a second or two, making it quite clear that they don't impress me at all, then I turn to Mom again.

"But, Susanne," Mom says, then she pauses, shuts her eyes, obviously considering what to say, then opens them again. "Don't you see . . . don't you see that all the things you're saying, all this feminist talk . . . don't you see that that's also connected to your grief and hurt over Malin. We've talked about this so often, Mette and May Lene and I, and we all agree that feminism is really only something you use as an excuse and an explanation for your decision to give up Malin."

"Something I . . . ," I stammer, dropping my jaw and shaking my head, I don't believe my fucking ears.

"Since time immemorial men have been deserting their wives and children and you've used your obsession with equality and women's rights as justification for doing the same, isn't that so? Well, I mean, if the men can do it, why shouldn't you, a woman, be able to do it. So you see, I think you became a women's libber out of sheer necessity,

Susanne. If it hadn't been for the women's libber in you, you would have gone to the dogs long ago. Every time the pain of losing Malin has become almost more than you can bear, feminism has helped you to believe that you didn't do anything wrong. That's why you see red every time someone teases you about being a feminist and a women's libber, that's why you freak out every time you're witness to anything that . . . well, that so much as *smacks* of male chauvinism," she says.

I simply sit there staring at her. I don't fucking believe this, she even manages to make this fit with her stupid theory: my political views, feminism, and, no doubt, my involvement in poverty and third world issues, all of this is apparently proof of private and personal problems I may have or have had. I glance at Mette, then turn to Mom again, they're both gazing at me sad eyed. I still miss Malin, of course I do, but I've learned to live with that and there's no reason whatsoever to feel sorry for me, and yet they do, and it's so fucking infuriating, my heart's beating faster and faster and I feel like jumping up and spitting in their faces, I hate being belittled like this, to have them stripping me of the ability to think for myself and making me out to be a passive, emotionally driven creature, the way they always trivialize, neutralize, and depoliticize everything that's said or done, thereby diverting attention from the things we really ought to be discussing, it's a social disease and I hate it. I'm just about to get up and leave, but I don't, nor will I, this is far too serious for me to simply run away, no fucking way am I going to back down. I'll swallow my anger and try again to talk to them.

Trondheim, August 13th–17th, 2006

Before we left for Central America you rented out your apartment to a friend and when we got back he moved out and we moved in. It was far too small for two, but since we were out a lot in the evenings and I was at university all day we thought we would be fine there for a while. But we were wrong, it didn't work out. Not because of the apartment, though—because of you. You thought you were still living the bohemian life we had led prior to the trip, but you weren't. I don't know exactly when it dawned on me that you weren't the same person you had been before Central America, but I think it was during one of our many boozy evenings at Café 3B. At 3B it was by no means unusual for cash-strapped students to finish off any beer left in abandoned glasses—we did it ourselves, especially toward the end of term when our student loans were running out. And one evening you and Terje came up with a way of exploiting this custom. You sneaked into the men's room with your empty beer glasses and peed into them, then you took them back out and surreptitiously placed them on empty tables or windowsills, preferably slightly hidden, tucked halfway behind a curtain, for example, so that it would take a little while for someone to find them—the reasoning, according to you, being that "the longer they sit there, the less chance there is of identifying the culprits." You and Terje thought it was hilarious to sit in a corner on the other side of the café and watch the facial contortions of some poor unfortunate who had just taken a great gulp of piss, but those of us who were in on your game found it disgusting, crass, and childish, none of us laughed. On the contrary, we made it quite clear that we thought it was a despicable trick and eventually threatened to tell the staff if you didn't stop it. But you didn't stop, you carried on playing this and other, similar pranks. Time was when I would have been dazzled by all the crazy things you and Terje got up to, but more and more often I now found myself getting angry or feeling uncomfortable and embarrassed for you both. As, for example, when you escorted an almost senseless young student to the railway station and put him on the night train to Bodø, or the time at an after-party when you found a can of red paint and painted the host's dachshund.

It took a while, but gradually I began to see why the pair of you did such things. Your efforts to outdo yourselves and others with your antics were in fact a ploy to convince everyone that you were really fun guys and not just a couple of common drunks. You wouldn't admit that you were turning into the two sad, pathetic thirtysomethings whom you were becoming in everyone else's eyes, so you tried frantically to present it all as youthful high jinks. But this only made you seem even sadder and more pathetic, of course. Most of those who had started university at the same time as you and Terje had long since completed their education. They had jobs and families, they rarely went out for a drink and then only on weekends. And there were you and Terje, hanging out in student cafés and pissing in beer glasses. Not just a couple of times a month, but three nights a week. Always equally drunk and tiresome and always on the hunt for an impromptu after-party in some student sublet. Me, I hopped off the carousel long before the end of term. I sometimes joined you for drinks at the start of one of your nights out, but it was all so predictable and I knew exactly what would happen once you were drunk and out on the town, so more often than not, when you guys were getting ready to go down to Café 3B or Fru Lundgreen, I would pop over to Kjersti Håpnes's place for a glass of wine. I could not be bothered sitting there watching you making a fool of yourself, I could not be bothered having to rescue you from awkward situations or drag you away from people you had upset, I simply could not be bothered babysitting you. Better to lie alone in bed, waiting for you to come stumbling through the door in the early hours.

From time to time I did try to talk to you about this problem. I was perfectly honest with you, I said that you drank too much and that your behavior had changed so much that I didn't like to be around you when you were drunk. I was worried about you, I said. I had expected you to react the way most people with an alcohol problem would when accused of drinking too much, but you didn't. You weren't at all angry. You weren't even annoyed, and you gave no indication that you found it difficult to talk about. At the time I took this as a sign that I was making a mountain out of a molehill and that you were telling the truth when you said you were in full control, but now I know that that was exactly what you wanted me to think. The calm, rational demeanor, the slight air of perplexity were a ploy to save you having to answer any more awkward questions. In fact you were probably every bit as angry as I had expected you to be when I sat down to talk to you. Because by then you were quite obviously losing control. And it showed. Your face was pale, with an unhealthy yellow cast to it, and there were dark circles under your almost chronically bleary eyes. You were putting on weight too. Your cheeks were fuller and flabbier than before, you had a belly and a spare tire that hung a good inch or so over the waist of your pants and quivered when you walked.

I don't know whether you drank because you couldn't write, or couldn't write because you drank, but things being as they were, I began to fear that nothing would ever come of this second novel either. I began to fear that you actually were the lazy, good-for-nothing dreamer who, right from the start, my mom and my sisters had tried to make me see that you were. Oh, how they hated you, Mom most of all. In her mind you had stolen me away from Torkild and Malin and she simply could not forgive you for that, since this also meant that you were to blame for her almost losing touch with the grandchild she adored. I tried to persuade her that it wasn't like that, but I might as well have saved my breath. She didn't really argue, but no matter how many times I told her that Torkild wasn't as perfect as she thought and that it had been I who had pursued you and not the other way around, she still spoke and acted as if she knew better. "Well, well, we'll say no more about it," she would murmur with a deceptively sweet smile, then briskly change the subject. "Now where did you put the egg separator?" she would say, or some other such non sequitur, acting as if it was up to her to save me from having to continue with a conversation in which I would feel compelled to lie. And then, after a brief pause, she would usually proceed to ask questions designed to remind me of how hopeless you were. "No sign of a job yet?" she might ask, knowing full well that you wanted to write and weren't looking for a job at all, or: "How does he manage when he's not earning anything?" even though she was well aware that you were living partly on money from me and partly on social security—apart, that is, from a short spell when you managed to hold down a job as a receptionist in a guesthouse in the center of the city. The fact that you were fired from the receptionist job was regarded by her as yet another opportunity to humiliate us both. "So good to hear that you've got a job,

David," she told you, even though she knew you'd already been fired for repeatedly turning up for work stinking of booze. "How are you getting on, are you enjoying it?" she went on, with a guileless smile that barely concealed how much she was looking forward to seeing us squirm with embarrassment when we had to confess this fresh failure to the rest of the family.

At the time I hated Mom for all of this. As far as I was concerned, she was a real pain, manipulative and spiteful. I see things differently now. Not only do I understand why, as a mother, she behaved the way she did, I wish she had been even more of a pain, more manipulative and spiteful, because then I might have broken up with you sooner, by which I mean before the family gathering at Mom's between Christmas and New Year's when you made a spectacle of yourself by getting blind drunk and climbing into Mette's bed. The rest of us were woken by Mette's outraged yells and rushed to her room to find you curled up on the floor trying to protect yourself, with her standing over you, screaming bloody murder and raining blows and expletives down on your head. When we eventually managed to pull her away and she had stopped screaming, you tried to excuse yourself by saying it was an honest mistake, you thought it was our room.

"But . . . but . . . I thought you were Susanne," you said. We all knew what had really happened, though, and since you knew that we knew, you made only this one feeble attempt at an explanation before, with a sly grin, retreating to our room to sleep it off—alone, of course, because right then and there I made up my mind never to sleep in the same bed as you again.

When I got up the next morning you were gone. One might think that this came as a relief to me, but it didn't. I don't think I've ever been so angry and by packing your rucksack and taking off you deprived me of the chance to have one last, almighty showdown with you for everyone to hear. It deprived me of the chance to vent my wrath on the one person who deserved it, so to speak, and instead I was left with a huge and almost unbearable sense of shame. It was as if, since I couldn't direct it at you, I had turned all of my wrath inward, on myself, so it was with flaming cheeks that I sat down at the breakfast table with the others. Now they could all see that Mom had been right. You were a drunken loser, a selfish bastard, and I was a naïve fool for imagining that you were some sort of misunderstood literary genius. I had looked up to and sacrificed myself for a good-for-nothing slob who had never done anything with his life and probably never would. It had been obvious to everyone but me, I didn't know where to look, I was mortified. But the most humiliating thing of all was that you had climbed into bed with my sister and had said that you'd always fancied her. It was nearly two years before I could even face Mette again after that.

And then it turned out that you were a writer after all.

You made your literary debut in the fall of 2002 and when I picked up your book in the Ark bookshop on Nordre gate and read the blurb on the back of what had been described as an autobiographical novel, I couldn't help laughing. It said that you had had a hard, itinerant life, a life of poverty, casual labor, crime, drink, and drugs and a constant, burning desire to write.

I know, of course, that this was just a pure marketing pitch, an attempt to present you as a writer in the classic male literary genius mold. But it was stretching it a bit, surely, to state that you had led an itinerant life when you had only ever lived in three places in your entire life (Otterøya, Namsos, and Trondheim) and our five-month trip around to Central America was the only time when you were actually on the road, as it were. And wasn't it a bit much to say that your life had been marked by crime just because you'd been involved in stealing a few mopeds and boat engines when you were a teenager? And why mention the few invariably fleeting spells of casual labor you had had in your twenties, but not all those years at university?

With such a skewed, not to say fallacious, jacket note it goes without saying that I was somewhat skeptical as to the veracity of this autobiographical novel. I was, however, positively surprised. Or rather, to begin with I was. The descriptions of the hard-drinking budding author were both painful and honest and even if the central character's increasingly frustrated and exasperated girlfriend was depicted as being a slightly more forceful, aggressive, and humorless feminist than I remember being at that time, I had no trouble recognizing myself and I won't deny that I cried when I read of how much you had admired me and how much you had loved me. This was beautifully and movingly written, and when you also presented a fine and fitting portrait of Mom—whom I had always assumed you hated—I was all set to call you and tell you how impressed I was.

But then came the lines I quoted at the beginning of this letter, taken from the beginning of a long passage in which I'm portrayed as a young mother completely lacking in oxytocin who has, therefore, no qualms about abandoning her daughter to go off and live it up with her artist boyfriend. If this image of me had been presented purely as your personal view and your personal reflections, I might have been able to live with it, but in the novel you have me admitting that I don't feel particularly attached to her, which is much worse. As I remember it, we were in a hostel in Campeche on the Yucatán Peninsula, we were drinking mescal, and, biology student that I was, I had been wondering out loud whether I might be lacking in oxytocin, I don't mind admitting that. But what was not made clear in your novel was that I asked this only because I wanted you to console me. This was one of many times when I missed Malin so much I could hardly bear it and I only mooted the idea that I might have some biological flaw that prevented me from feeling as strong a bond with Malin as most mothers have with their children to get you to reassure me by saying that I hadn't done anything wrong in deciding to come with you to Central America. I was angling for you to tell me that I was a good enough mother, that was all. I wanted you to tell me to stop talking rubbish and then reel off the many ways in which I had proved that I loved Malin more than anything in the world; to remind me of all the sleepless nights, all the hours spent on the swings at the playground, all the kisses and hugs I had given her.

Whether you understood this I don't know, and it really doesn't matter. What does matter is what it says in your book and in that you make it sound as if I was serious. You describe me as a young woman who has no scruples about going off and leaving her child and who wonders whether this might be because her brain doesn't produce enough oxytocin. This image of me as a cold and indifferent mother seems even more credible when viewed in the context of how I'm described elsewhere in the book: as a feminist, that is. That the depiction of me as a feminist accorded so well with the facts meant, for one thing, that people who knew me took it for granted that the portrayal of me as a bad mother was authentic. After all, why should they doubt this particular aspect when everything else rang so true? And for another, I'm fairly certain that the description of me as a feminist triggers a number of preconceived notions in the reader, preconceived notions that help to reinforce the image of me as a bad mother. You know the sort of thing: a women's libber isn't like other women, she's strict, tough, and uncompromising and lacks the warmth, tenderness, and love most women and mothers are so full of, and these preconceived notions—which many people harbor, I know—are borne out, so to speak, when one reads of how I decry my own maternal feelings. The pieces fall into place, as it were, it all fits—and this in itself gives the whole thing a semblance of credibility.

At first, after I finished the book, I was only angry and upset, but as the full gravity of what you had written sank in, I gradually went to pieces. Since most people more or less assume that when a couple split up, any children will live with the mother, quite a few had already questioned why Malin was living with Torkild, and now they would think they had the answer: I was simply not all that attached to Malin, I didn't love her as much as Torkild did. That was why I had chosen to live it up with a lazy, drunken ne'er-do-well of an artist rather than do my duty as a mother. Relatives, friends, and acquaintances, neighbors and coworkers, that's what they would all think. They wouldn't let on, of course, not to me, they would deny thinking any such thing, but still, that's what they would think, and that's what they would say about me when I wasn't there. And as this began to dawn on me, I was filled with a deep sense of shame and embarrassment. For some time I was afraid to answer the phone, afraid to open the door to anyone or to go and see anyone, afraid to go out at all. No matter where I went, I felt people were staring at me, I imagined them sticking their heads together and whispering: there goes that coldhearted feminist bitch, the one who gave up custody of her child. In the supermarket, at parties, or in cafés it was always the same. Not to mention at university. Luckily your book wasn't a great commercial success, but as is often the case with novels about academics or artists it became popular in student circles and something of a talking point, so when I walked into the cafeteria or the reading room at Dragvoll, I always had the feeling that everybody was turning to look at me, the way they would eye an insect they would like to step on. I had broken one of the few surviving taboos in our society, I was a mother who had given my child away because I didn't care about her and as such I deserved all the contempt that came my way. That's what they were thinking, I was sure. I tried to tell myself I was becoming paranoid, that people were far less interested in me than I imagined, but it was no use. No matter how rational I strove to be, the fear and the awful thoughts would not go away. Not only that, but I continually found myself in situations that suggested my worries were not unfounded. Because people were actually talking about me. When I was introduced to someone I'd never met before, for example, it was often pretty obvious that they knew who I was, and not infrequently I was faced with drunk individuals who, with little or no prompting, would launch into a whole spiel about how they didn't see anything strange in fathers having custody of their children rather than the mothers—well meant, of course, but as far as I was concerned merely even more proof that the picture of me you had painted in your novel had stuck in people's minds.

Just after you and I broke up, I tried to get Malin back. I had allowed Torkild to take her to Svalbard on the condition that they would be there for only a year, but at the end of that year when he suddenly announced that they had been offered the chance to stay on for another two years and intended to say yes to this, I no longer felt so amenable. I was furious. Dismayed. Frustrated. Torkild said he knew how I felt but that I had to consider what was best for Malin. She loved their life in Longyearbyen, she had settled in nicely and was doing well at home and in kindergarten and it would be a terrible shame if she had to move now, she needed peace and stability and she should certainly not be moved before she started school. If I were selfish enough to try to bring her back to the mainland, he would do everything he could to stop me. "And you don't need me to tell you what would happen if we went to court," he went on. "Not only did I take charge of Malin when you decided to go off to Central

America to find yourself, but you're a single freelance journalist living in a tiny studio apartment in Møllenberg while I'm in a stable relationship, I have a job, a large house, and a healthy bank balance. That being the case, do you really think a jury would grant you custody?" he asked and I could hear the gleeful burble in his voice as he said it. He was loving this and he didn't try to hide it. This was his way of paying me back and it made me furious and even more determined to get Malin back.

So I contacted a lawyer.

Initially he was as certain as Torkild that he would be granted custody, but when I informed him of our verbal agreement that they would move back to Trondheim after a year on Svalbard and then found out that Torkild had been offered the job on Svalbard before I left for Central America, he began to think that we might have a chance. The second point in particular could work in our favor. The fact that Torkild had assumed responsibility for Malin while I was away but neglected to tell me that he was planning to move to Svalbard in my absence put things in a totally different light, because obviously if I had been informed about his plans to move, I would never have left and we wouldn't have been where we are today. In that case Malin would probably have been living with me. "It won't be easy to win, but it doesn't look nearly as hopeless as it did a little while ago," the lawyer said.

But then came your book. Then came the depiction of the coldhearted feminist who didn't appear to care much about her child. Then came the rumors. The mudslinging. The shame. You might think that all of this would have made me even more determined to win Malin back—surely fighting to regain custody of her would in itself be proof that I loved her—and since it was so important for me to show everyone that the picture you had painted of me in your book was wrong, you might think that the novel and everything it brought in its wake would have given me fresh incentive to pursue a child-custody lawsuit.

In fact it had the opposite effect. Even though I loved Malin with all my heart, I began to see myself as others saw me: I didn't love Malin as much as other mothers loved their children, so I didn't deserve her, I was more interested in realizing myself than in looking after my own child, and from that point of view I was a perfect example of a generation that was incapable of looking after anyone but themselves. That was how I thought. And this last, the well-known notion that people of our generation refused to become responsible, grown-up individuals, became something of a mantra for me. It was something I did my best to believe because it shifted some of the blame off me, so to speak, and onto the times and the generation to which I belonged. Thus, abandoning Malin, leaving Torkild with full responsibility for her, wasn't really evidence of a flaw in my character, it was more a sign of the times I was living in, times Erlend Loe had described so well in *Naïve. Super*. After a while this is what I tried to tell myself.

So, things being as they were, when I began to doubt my maternal instincts and my capacity for caring and nurturing, it was hard to summon up the energy and confidence to pursue a lawsuit that would have been difficult enough to start with. So I gave up the fight before it had even begun.

I wish I could say that everything turned out all right in the end and that Malin and I have a good relationship today. But I can't. I'm guessing that, young as she is, she hasn't yet read your novel, but knowing her father as well as I do, I'm pretty sure she'll have heard what you've said in it and may even have read the passages in which I'm denounced as a bad mother. Whether this is the only reason why she refuses to have any contact with me now, I don't know, but I'm certain that it has a lot to do with it.

And for that I hate you, David.

Only days before Torkild e-mailed me to say that Malin didn't want to see me anymore and that they would like me to cancel a planned visit to Svalbard, I had been writing an article about Rigoberta Menchú and the indigenous Guatemalans and while working on this I came across a little story that would later give me an idea of what to do with all the hate I felt for you. Or no, that's wrong—I'm making it sound much more planned and rational than it actually was. Well, anyway: the story told of how Alfred Nobel came to establish the Nobel Prize. I don't know whether it's true, and it really doesn't matter here. In any case, according to the story it had been rumored, wrongly, that Alfred Nobel had died while on a lengthy trip abroad. The newspapers in his homeland printed this news. They then received and published a number of obituaries, which Nobel naturally read on his return—and was not well pleased with what he read, to put it mildly. Because the picture his obituarists had painted of him was not exactly flattering. As a chemist at his father's arms factory, developer of the explosive nitroglycerin, and in-ventor of dynamite, he had to suffer seeing himself described as a man who had promoted the spread of death, suffering, and destruction during his lifetime. The story goes that he was so upset at being saddled with such a posthumous reputation that he made up his mind to be a better man and to devote the rest of his life to serving humanity. As part of this undertaking he bequeathed the vast fortune he had made from arms sales and the like to a foundation, the income from its assets to be used to award five prizes, a Peace Prize and four others.

You can see where this is going, can't you?

At first the thought of putting an ad in the newspaper to say that you had lost your memory and thus trick people who had known you well into writing about your life was just an idea, something I toyed with at idle moments, a daydream, mere musings. But I couldn't shake it off, it was too good, and as time went on I began to feel that it would be a shame if it was never acted upon. Nonetheless, I don't think I would have yielded to the temptation to put my plan into practice if I hadn't gone to Kjersti Håpnes's place for drinks one evening, got rather merry and very talkative and told her the whole story. Not only did she love the idea and get very excited about it, she also managed to convince me that it was the only right thing to do. "Let the bastard have what's coming to him, he's a rapist and all rapists deserve to know what it feels like to be raped," I remember her saying, and as someone who had always found it offensive to hear people compare the experience of being exposed to public ridicule to rape (misusing and thereby devaluing one of the worst crimes I could ever imagine, I used to say), I realized that I agreed with every word she said. Because in precisely the same way as a victim of physical rape I had been used as a device in your novel. You transformed me from a person into an object with which to satisfy your literary needs. Without giving me any chance to re- spond or defend myself, you defined me in the eyes of the world, and since the way I am regarded determines how I am treated and hence how I regard myself and the world around me, it also determines how I interact with the world. In other words, it's all about power. Just as a rapist exerts power and control over his victim, so you exerted power and control over me.

When the book was first published, I was very surprised to think that you could have betrayed me by committing such a rape, if I can call it that, but looking back on it now it seems per- fectly natural. That was just how you were. What I described, earlier in this letter, as open-mindedness, I could just as easily have described as indifference and cynicism. As I've said, you made me feel secure and encouraged me to talk freely about things I would never have dared to talk to Mom, Torkild, or any of my friends about, but the impartiality that made you seem that way to me was not primarily the mark of a humane and compassionate spirit as I imagined back then. It was a sign that you weren't particularly interested in how I or anyone else was faring. In fact you didn't seem to be interested in the world as such at all. I don't quite know how to put this, but it was as if you viewed the world purely as a story and were interested in it only in that way. Everything you experienced, everything you saw, heard, smelled, or felt, every situation in which you found yourself and everyone you met, everything, absolutely everything was a story to you, a story you adapted, put your own stamp on, and then retold in your writing. That was all you were interested in. You didn't care about—no, more: I don't think you were even capable of envisaging the impact your stories had on the world at large. When you see everything as a story, you eventually lose sight of the world to which the stories relate, and obviously once that happens you cannot see the consequences of the tales you tell either. The same went, of course, for the honesty, outspokenness, and fearlessness I attributed to you earlier. Take the way you laid yourself bare in your novel, for example, the way you put yourself down and described yourself as an asshole and a common drunk, liked by no one. Well, once one knows that you were totally blind to the consequences, it's not hard to understand that you could be capable of this. Contrary to what it says in the blurb on your book, this does not mean that you were brave. It means that you had immersed yourself in your writing and cut yourself off, so to speak, from the outside world. The potential consequences of what you wrote simply did not exist as far as you were concerned. Naturally you were capable of imagining that there would be a reaction and that people would look at you differently once

the book came out, and naturally you were capable of comprehending that I and others would be hurt and upset by what you
had written, but you were not capable of absorbing this, you
understood it, but you didn't really feel it.

Whether you do now, after having read all those letters about
yourself and could, therefore, be said to know a little more about
how it feels to be raped, I can't say. And to be honest I no longer
care. I may have placed that ad in the paper out of anger and a
desire for revenge but over time, and especially since I started
this letter, the self-preservation aspect has become ever more
important. Not that vengeance isn't a form of self-preservation
in itself, of course. But writing down and comprehending what
happened, presenting my own version of our time together and
of what you wrote in your novel, that has proved to be a much
more effective form of self-preservation. Not least because I now
know what to tell Malin when she eventually confronts me with
what I did to her. In fact this letter has been written more for
her than for you. Before I started writing it, I had no clear answer
to how she and I came to lose each other. I've always known, of
course, that it had nothing to do with a lack of mother love on
my part, but only now do I realize what a large part my own
need to be free played in events, and the knowledge that someday Malin will learn this, that someday she will understand and,
I hope, forgive me for the choices I made, that is a great comfort
to me. As for you, David, like I say, I don't care about you. Or at
least, that's not altogether true. To be perfectly honest, after
having read all those letters, I care more than I really want to. I
don't think I will ever forgive you for what you wrote about me
in your novel and part of me hates you with a passion, but the
more I think about them, the more of an impression the letters
make on me and another part of me simply can't help hoping
that all will be well with the person they speak of.

DAVID

Trondheim, June 25th, 2006. Well, use the green pen

I lower the bottle of formula into the pan of warm water and turn to Ingrid, trying to look mildly surprised.

"Is Sara still in the shower?" I ask, even though I know full well she's still in the shower, I can hear her, so I don't really need to ask, but I do anyway, as a gentle hint to Ingrid that I think she's been in there far too long, I thought we'd pretty much agreed that I should talk to Sara as if she were my own daughter, but Ingrid always gets upset if I criticize the girl, she tries hard not to, but she can't help it and I can't face getting into all that right now, I hardly slept a wink last night.

Ingrid kisses Henrik on the forehead, turns to me, and smiles.

"Yes," she says and carries on tickling and fondling Henrik, she doesn't say anything else, doesn't seem the slightest bit bothered that Sara's using up all the hot water.

Silence.

I pick up the coffeepot, pour myself a cup, take a sip, and stand there staring at the bathroom door. God knows how many times I've told Sara not to spend too long in the shower, but she couldn't care less, she stays in there for ages and ages, I don't get it, why can't she be more considerate. I look at Ingrid again, but she has eyes and ears only for Henrik. She lifts him into the air and brings his face close to hers. "Hello, hello," she coos in the babyish voice she always uses when talking to him. She closes her eyes and rubs her nose against his, murmuring "hello, hello" again as she does so, then she sets him back on her lap and goes on cuddling and petting him. I'm just about to ask if she doesn't think it's time Sara turned off that shower, but I don't, I can't face her getting annoyed on Sara's behalf, I'd better wait a little while longer at least.

"When will your mom and dad be here?" I ask.

"This evening sometime."

"I thought I might make osso buco for them," I say.

"Okay," she says, just "okay," doesn't even look at me when she says it, makes it sound as if osso buco would be fine, but no more than that. I didn't expect clapping and cheering, but she could at least thank me by showing a little more enthusiasm, she could have said "Osso buco would be lovely," or "Oh, great," or something like that.

I look out of the kitchen window, a truck from the DIY warehouse goes by, and the chandelier in the living room tinkles faintly as it trundles over the speed bump.

Silence again.

And Sara goes on showering and showering, she must have been in there for at least ten minutes, it's unbelievable, I don't get it, why can't she be a bit more considerate. Well, that's it, enough is enough. I set my coffee cup down on the countertop, stroll down the hallway to the bathroom door as casually as I can, and switch off the bathroom light. I don't think switching the light off while she's in there is particularly funny, but I laugh anyway—an instinctive attempt to conceal my irritation, I suppose, the fact that she spends too long in the shower isn't really that big a deal, not worth getting upset about, so I automatically try to hide my irritation by laughing and making a little joke of it.

"Hey! Turn the light on!" Sara yells.

"You turn off the shower and I'll turn on the light," I say.

"Turn the light on!"

"No."

"Arrgh!"

Then Ingrid wanders up with Henrik on her hip. She smiles, puts her head on one side, and eyes me imploringly, she too treating this as a funny little incident but also wanting me to stop while the going is good, that's what that look on her face is telling me, I know.

"David, come on," she says.

"She's used more hot water in the past ten minutes than I use in seven or eight showers, Ingrid," I say, making myself smile as well.

"I know, I know. But you hardly stay under long enough to get wet," she says.

"I only take a quick shower because I know there are other people in the house who're going to need hot water. And besides, I know how much it costs."

"We're not poor, David."

"That's *no* reason to waste water," I say.

"No," she says, still smiling. "But turn on the light. She's nearly finished."

I look at her, I don't want to turn the light on, but I do as she says, feel my mood sour still further as I do so, it's both cowardly and wrong to let Sara win this battle and it annoys the hell out of me to do it.

"I'm going to buy one of those meters they have on campsites, where you have to put in ten kroner to have a shower," I say, trying to keep smiling. "I'm going to go online and order one this very evening."

"Yeah, yeah," says Ingrid, wagging her head. She sets Henrik down on the floor, crosses to the stove, and takes the bottle of formula out of the pan. "She's fifteen, David," she goes on and I think I detect a hint of irritation in her voice, but she's still smiling, possibly trying to mask the fact that she's annoyed now as well, I don't know.

"So? Last time I checked, hot water cost as much for a fifteen-year-old as for a thirty-six-year-old," I say. She doesn't answer, merely raises her eyebrows and shakes her head despairingly, then she tips the baby bottle upside down and shakes a few drops of formula onto the inside of her wrist, on the pulse point, to check the temperature of the milk. "And did you know that the lifetime of a Norwegian bathroom has been shortened dramatically over the past twenty years?" I say, keeping my smile in place.

"No, David, I didn't know that," she says as she lifts Henrik onto her lap and eases the bottle nipple into his mouth.

"And that despite the fact that the general standard of said bathroom has improved considerably," I continue.

"David!"

"Well, it's true. Time was when people only used to take a shower once or twice a week, but now they shower at least once, sometimes twice, a day and if you're not careful that can lead to problems with condensation and mildew."

"Yeah, yeah, okay!"

"Yeah, yeah? Do you realize that the bathroom is the most expensive room in a house, Ingrid? One hundred and fifty thousand kroner, that's what it costs for a new bathroom, did you know that? And as if that weren't enough, dermatologists say it's not good for us to shower so often, it dries out the skin and makes us more susceptible to skin diseases," I say, then pause. "But hey, what the hell, one hundred and fifty thousand kroner for a skin disease— peanuts, right?"

"Oh, my *God!*" Ingrid sighs, no longer able to conceal her annoyance, she tries to introduce a laugh into that last word, but it sounds more cross than cheerful, that laugh.

"I'm just trying to be sensible, Ingrid," I say.

"Well, stop it, please."

"That wouldn't be very sensible," I say.

"Oh, somebody help me, I'm stuck in here with a tight-fisted northerner," she cries, glancing around the room with a look of desperation on her face, making one last attempt to make a joke of the situation, offering us the chance to treat all of this as a little farce in which I play the role of the oddball, the country bumpkin, and she the exasperated city girl so to speak. I feel myself growing even more annoyed. By making me out to be an oddball, she turns everything I say into silly nonsense and that pisses me off. Because it isn't just silly nonsense. Okay, so I'm exaggerating slightly, which makes it easy, of course, for her to cast me as the crazy guy from the sticks, but I do honestly believe that Sara spends far too long in the shower, I honestly believe she's spoiled, and I honestly believe it's time she woke up and started listening to what we say. After a moment Ingrid turns to me and smiles blithely and with apparent sincerity, inviting me to smile back and thus acknowledge this as an amusing little interlude that is now over, I know that's what she's doing. I look at her, if I smile back I'm as good as admitting that I was wrong and that it's perfectly okay for Sara to carry on the way she's doing, and I really don't want to do that, but I do it anyway, I manage a little grin as I pick up my coffee cup.

"Have you finished the shopping list?" she asks, changing the subject, as if to show that we're totally done with this.

"Yep," I say.

"Right, well, I'll go and do the shopping as soon as Henrik has gone to sleep. Maybe you could wash the hall and bathroom floors while I'm away?"

"Okay, so should I borrow some hot water from next door, or what?" I say, I ought to let it go, but I can't.

"What?" she says, not quite with me, but then the penny drops, she closes her eyes, sighs: "Oh, David, really."

"I'm only asking," I say. I drink the last of my coffee and put the cup in the sink, give her a little smile as I take a couple of slices of crispbread out of the pack and place them on the chopping board.

"Well, ask her to turn off the shower if it means that much to you," she says.

"I just did that."

"Yes, but try speaking properly to her," she says.

"Ah, so I don't speak properly to her?"

"Not always, no," she says.

I look at her, give it a moment.

"Oh?" I say, sounding offended, and I realize that I am rather offended, it's not always easy being stepfather to a fifteen-year-old girl and, all things considered, I think I'm doing pretty well. I never imagined I could be as patient and self-sacrificing as I've proved to be since I became Sara's stepfather and Henrik's father and I don't like to be told that I'm not good enough.

"David," she smiles, putting her head on one side and giving me the look of someone about to explain something that ought to be obvious to anyone.

"You turned off the light and started shouting about condensation and the damage she was doing to her skin and the bathroom with all her showering. That's hardly speaking properly to her, is it."

"Ingrid, I was only trying to make a little joke of it. If I 'speak properly to her,' as you put it, she'll only tell me not to try to act like I'm her father."

"Oh, now you're exaggerating, David."

"Am I?"

She doesn't say anything, just looks at me, opens her mouth slightly, and tries to act surprised.

"Well . . . if it's that bad, we need to talk to her about it," she says.

"Yes, we do," I say, even though she's quite right, I am exaggerating slightly, we have some pretty lively arguments, Sara and I, but we're always friends again afterward. I turn away, take the lid off the cheese dish, pick up the cheese slicer, cut a couple of slices, and lay them on the crispbread, all I can hear are the gurgling sounds from Henrik's almost empty bottle.

There's silence for a few moments.

Then Ingrid says: "Are we okay?"

I turn to her, feel annoyance still grumbling inside me, but try to smile at her anyway.

"Of course," I say.

"Sure?"

"Why shouldn't we be okay?"

She holds my eye for a moment, then smiles and shakes her head.

"I don't really know why I asked that," she says, still smiling as she gently winkles the empty bottle out of Henrik's mouth and puts it on the kitchen table. "But the hall and the bathroom floors?" she says, getting up very carefully, looking at me as she holds Henrik to her chest and stands there rocking him gently, I don't answer straightaway, I hardly slept a wink last night and I honestly can't be bothered washing the hall or the bathroom floors, and anyway, it's not necessary, she only wants them washed because her parents are coming, she always has to clean and tidy and dust when she's expecting a visit from them, even though the house is perfectly clean and tidy already, she still feels she has to do it, I don't get it.

"I'm a bit tired after last night, and I'll have to work for a while today as well," I say, taking a bite of crispbread. "And I've the dinner to make."

"Fine, I'll do it myself," she says.

I eye her as I finish chewing and swallow.

"*Yourself?*"

"Huh?"

"You make it sound as though it's always you who washes the floors," I say. "You make it sound like you were asking me to do you a favor, the way you might ask Sara to do something for you."

"You're awfully touchy today," she says, trying again to

pass it off with a surprised little laugh, but she knows I've hit the nail on the head. I normally do at least as much of the housework as she does and this is just a feeble attempt to make me feel lazy and apathetic.

"Am I?" I say, taking another bite of crispbread.

"Is something the matter?" she asks.

"Don't ask me if something's the matter, Ingrid," I say.

"Huh?"

I blink slowly.

"Ingrid," I say, "you could cut the air in here with a knife and you ask me if something's the matter—like you're automatically blaming me for that. Like you're implying that I've got something on my mind, something that's upset me or put me in a bad mood and *that's* why things are so tense around here. As if it's got nothing to do with you."

She arches her eyebrows.

"I didn't even know things were so tense around here," she says. "I thought we were okay."

"We are, but—er . . ."

"But . . . ?"

I close my eyes and sigh, put a hand to my forehead.

"God Almighty," I say, open my eyes and look at her. She's sitting there staring at me, she looks serious now, annoyed almost, but then she gives a little laugh. She's annoyed and yet she wants us to laugh it all off and start again, I can tell. I shake my head and give a little chuckle as well, trying to do my part to lighten the mood.

"I'll just put Henrik down," she says, giving me a little smile as she goes out into the hallway.

I get the orange juice out of the fridge and pour myself a glass, hear the distant drone of a lawnmower as she opens the front door and goes out to put Henrik in his baby carriage.

Nothing for a minute or two.

Then Sara wanders in, wearing Ingrid's bathrobe and with her head swathed in a blue towel. Without a word she makes a beeline for the kitchen cabinet and takes out a bowl, doesn't even look at me, she's mad at me and she's making sure I know it, as if she has any reason to be mad, if anyone should be mad it's me, it pisses me off to see her going around with that sulky teenage pout on her face.

"Sure you're clean enough now?" I ask, I shouldn't rattle her cage any more than I already have, but I can't help myself.

"Moron!"

I smile to myself.

"David," I hear Ingrid say. She strolls back into the kitchen, smiling and looking me straight in the eye, as if to show that we're okay, but would I please leave Sara alone now.

"Did you at least remember to open the bathroom window?" I ask, eyeing Sara as I bite into the crispbread. She picks up the box of cereal, stares at me like it's the first she's heard that she's supposed to open the bathroom window after she's had a shower.

"Huh?"

I just stand there looking at her for a moment, I don't believe it, is she just doing this to mess with me or is her head so much in the clouds that she still hasn't grasped this?

"For Christ's sake, Sara, how many times do I have to tell you, you have to air the bathroom out aft—"

"Da-viiid," Ingrid breaks in, almost singing my name.

"Right, well—er, go and open that bathroom window, Sara," I say.

"I'll do it later," she says, pouring cereal into a bowl.

"Do it now, please," I say, not backing down, and I'm not going to back down either, I backed down earlier and I won't do it again. "It's all steamed up in there," I add.

"Oh, my God!" she cries, tossing her head and banging the cereal box down on the countertop, she sits with her face turned to the ceiling for a second, but then she actually does as she's told, I hadn't expected it, but she actually gets up and walks off to open the bathroom window—well, I say *walks*, but *stomps* is more like it.

Ingrid smiles and raises her eyebrows slightly. She looks at me as if to say was that really necessary?

"What?" I say.

"Nothing," she says, smiling and shaking her head.

Then Sara comes back, she opens the fridge door, takes out the milk, and pours some into the bowl of cereal.

"Oh, by the way, I need mascara," she says.

"Well, I'm off to do the shopping in a minute. Just put it on the list now," Ingrid says. She smiles at Sara as she draws a white hair tie out of her shirtsleeve, unwinds it from her wrist, and pulls her hair up into a ponytail.

"So where's the shopping list?" Sara asks.

"I don't know, David wrote it."

"It's up there," I say, nodding toward the fridge. "Use the green pen."

Ingrid stares at me, her jaw slowly dropping, she knows I always color-code a long shopping list and yet here she is, looking at me as if she's never heard the like, attempting to lighten the mood by turning this into another little farce in which I play the oddball from the north, I know that's what she's doing. I look at her, I don't want to be the oddball she wants me to be right now, that would be tantamount to admitting that color-coding shopping lists is weird and stupid and I won't have that, it's not stupid at all, on the contrary it's practical and it saves time.

"Don't tell me you've color-coded the shopping list again?" she says.

"Yes, I have."

"You're unbelievable, so you are."

"It takes half the time to do the shopping if the list is color-coded," I say quite seriously, to show that I'm not going to take part in her little farce. "If I write everything that comes under the category of personal hygiene in green, for example, I can simply pick up all the things written in green when I'm in that aisle, right? Then I don't end up wandering round and round and back and forth."

"And you a writer," she says with another little laugh.

"What on earth does that have to do with it?"

"Well, it's just that . . . you tend to think of artists as being a little more, how shall I put it . . . spontaneous!"

"Oh, you and your artistic stereotypes," I say.

Ingrid shakes her head and gives another little chuckle, then she turns to Sara.

"Put *VG* and *Dagbladet* on that list, would you please."

"Yeah, but in what color?" Sara asks, treating me to the sort of scornful look I remember from teenage girls when I was a teenager myself, a look designed to tell me just how ridiculous I am.

"Brown!" I retort as if taking it for granted that she really does want to know—nothing annoys her more than me ignoring her power games—then I look her straight in the face and grin.

"Yeah, use brown, for God's sake, otherwise I'll be wandering up and down the wrong aisle until you come and rescue me!" Ingrid giggles, she obviously hasn't realized that I'm not playing along so she's still treating this whole situation as a comic interlude.

Sara reaches across the countertop, smiles at me as she plucks a blue ballpoint from the basket propped against the side of the fridge, as if to show how little heed she pays to what I say by deliberately using a different color from the one dictated by my color code. I ought to rise above it, but I can't, I feel my annoyance growing, but I keep smiling, I won't give her the satisfaction of seeing me riled, so I give a little yawn to show just how little I care, do it quite spontaneously, watch her as she adds the two tabloids to the list and hands it to Ingrid.

"Right, see you later then," Ingrid says, smiling at me. I give her a rather cool, cursory smile in return and take a little sip of my juice, glance up and look at her again as she turns and leaves the kitchen. I put down my glass and glance across at Sara, but she's careful not to meet my eye as she picks up her bowl of cereal and carries it through to the living room. She's probably going to sit in front of the TV and watch one of those inane and unbelievably grating teen channels while she has her breakfast, they drive me crazy, those asinine American sitcoms she watches, even taking into account the age of their target audience, those programs are depressingly stupid.

"David, where did you put the car keys?" Ingrid calls.

"Where they're supposed to be," I call back.

"I can't see them."

"Well, you're not looking where they're supposed to be," I say.

I hear her muttering "Jesus Christ," she doesn't find this

way of talking and carrying on funny anymore, she's starting to get annoyed again too, I can tell by her voice. I grin
through clenched teeth, delighted to hear that she's getting
annoyed.

"And where might that be?" she asks.

"You mean you still don't know?"

"Dammit, David! I don't have time for this!"

I chuckle softly and go out into the hallway.

"Aren't I funny?" I say.

"Yeah, yeah, you're hilarious," she says, trying to look
as though we're still playing out our little farce, but it's no
use, she's seriously pissed off now and it shows, she knows
it too, I can tell. "It's just a little too much sometimes,"
she adds.

I don't say anything, simply fish the car keys out of the
little cup on the bureau and hold them out to Ingrid, she
lifts her hand to take them, but just as she goes to close her
hand, I pull the key away.

"David, stop it, it's not funny anymore," she says, trying to smile, but I can tell by her face that she means it, I
can tell that she's getting really angry now. I hold the key
out to her, she reaches for it again, and again I snatch my
hand away. "Stop it, for fuck's sake!" she shouts, unable
to contain herself any longer.

I stare at her, slowly open my mouth, and give her a blank,
uncomprehending look.

"What . . . you're not mad, are you?" I ask, acting as
though I've been kidding and fooling about all along and
that I thought she knew this, making her seem like a
spoilsport. She shuts her eyes and sighs, trying to compose herself.

"Give me that key!" she says, shutting her eyes again

and putting out her hand. She stands like that for a moment, then looks at me once more, tries to smile and act
as though she has calmed down. I lay the key in her hand,
try to look as though I'm sorry, hurt almost. "You can be a
pain in the neck sometimes, do you know that?" she says,
doing her best to sound more jocular than angry but not
quite succeeding.

Therapy session

Time: October 2nd, 2006
Place: Fjordgata 69d, Trondheim
Present: Dr. Maria Hjuul Wendelboe, psychotherapist;
David Forberg, patient

MARIA: Are you hungover?

DAVID: No. What makes you think that?

MARIA: Your eyes look a bit glazed.

DAVID: It was May-Britt's birthday yesterday and we went out for a drink. But I'm not hungover.

MARIA: You had a drink, though?

DAVID: I took it very easy.

MARIA: I know I've already explained patient-therapist confidentiality to you many times, David. But since you've told me this, I'm bound to remind you of its limits: what you've done, that stays between you and me. But if it looks to me as if you're likely to commit another serious crime, I am obliged to contact the police.

DAVID: I know. But, I told you, there was no drunken killing. I'd had hardly anything to drink . . . just a few beers and some wine.

342

MARIA: But the risk of you resorting to violence is greater when you drink, isn't it?

DAVID: I *am* careful, Maria.

MARIA: [*pause*] Does May-Britt know about your temper?

DAVID: She has never seen me become violent, no. If that's what you mean.

MARIA: But does she know what you've done?

DAVID: No.

MARIA: Are you going to tell her?

DAVID: I don't see what good that would do.

MARIA: You don't think she has a right to know who she's involved with?

DAVID: I've learned my lesson, Maria. I'm not the man I was before the killing, I'll never hurt another human being, I'm absolutely certain of that. And anyway we're not "involved."

MARIA: Oh?

DAVID: Or at least . . . I don't know. [*laughs hesitantly*] It just sounds so serious.

MARIA: So why are you laughing?

DAVID: She's twenty-two, for Christ's sake . . . it's pathetic. I'm a walking cliché.

MARIA: I sometimes have the impression that you use laughter as a way of playing down your own problems . . . to make them seem so insignificant that you can simply laugh them off.

DAVID: On one level maybe. But I also feel that a man in a midlife crisis is such a tragicomic figure.

MARIA: Why is that?

DAVID: Maybe because he's a kind of . . . because he's fighting a battle that everybody knows he's bound to lose . . . and the harder he fights, the more ridiculous he looks, so to speak . . . something like that. [*pause*] That said, though, I don't think that—a midlife crisis—is the explanation for my relationship with May-Britt. Or not the whole explanation anyway.

MARIA: Oh?

DAVID: [*long pause*] In our first or second session I told you about the time when Ingrid hired a cleaner against my wishes. About how angry I was. Remember?

MARIA: Yes.

DAVID: But what I didn't tell you was that . . . after a while I began to let Ingrid think that I liked the cleaner rather more than I actually did . . . a few lingering glances and the odd compliment that Ingrid was supposedly not meant to hear, you know? And that was all it took for Ingrid to discover that we didn't need a cleaner after all. [*laughs*]

MARIA: You conned Ingrid into firing the cleaner?

DAVID: Absolutely. And it's only recently that I've begun to understand why I did that. At the time I didn't know why I got so worked up about something that was, after all, such a small thing, I mean . . . Ingrid was actually right in a lot of what she said. We were both very busy with work. And the house we were living in was so big that we could never keep it as clean as we would have liked. Besides which, we could easily afford to pay for a cleaner, you know? But recently I've realized that the cleaner was not, in herself, the issue. Her significance was purely symbolic.

MARIA: Really?

DAVID: You see, Ingrid's father was a pioneer in the field of plastic surgery in Norway, a real trailblazer . . . and when he sold his clinics five years ago, just after the terrorist attacks of 9/11, in fact . . . Ingrid's brother was killed in the attack on the Twin Towers and this plunged Alfred into a crisis that resulted in him deciding to devote the rest of his life to something more worthwhile and socially useful than improving the appearance of rich men's wives . . .

MARIA: Really?

DAVID: Yes, but that's another story . . . I don't know what he got for them. According to Ingrid he got a lot less than I might think, but still, it was a lot . . . so we're talking about a wealthy family here, right. They've always been wealthy and that has left its mark on Ingrid. I mean, when she got into ESMOD, Alfred felt she'd done so well that she deserved a new car. And when she got the chance to show some pieces from her small collection at Paris Fashion Week, he sponsored her to the tune of God knows how many thousands of kroner for product development, the setting up of a production system, and so on . . . he rented a shop for her on a prime site in the center of Trondheim and all that—with a promise that he would buy it for her if she fulfilled a number of requirements he'd made regarding profitability. Do you see where I'm going with this?

MARIA: Not entirely.

DAVID: Ingrid is used to being rewarded for her efforts and this has left her with the idea that we always get what we deserve, so to speak. The logical consequence of this being that, basically, she believes a rich man is rich because he's smart and hardworking and a poor man is poor because he's stupid and lazy.

MARIA: I still don't see what this has to do with your cleaner?

DAVID: What I'm trying to say is that Ingrid disdains every-thing and everyone not associated with the upper and upper-middle classes. Or the middle class at least. In other words, she disdains everything to do with the world I come from and this angered and upset me, right, so I responded by refusing to countenance this one element of middle-class life. No fucking way was I going to hire a cleaner, right?

MARIA: Have you and Ingrid ever talked about this? Honestly, I mean.

DAVID: No.

MARIA: This disdain of hers, as you call it, how did this manifest itself?

DAVID: Usually in ways she wasn't aware of, I was about to say . . . you see, she thinks she's the most tolerant and liberal person in the world and she would be furious if she heard me saying she's full of contempt for the section of the population I come from . . . but, well, to take one example . . . earlier this summer we went to a barbecue at the home of one of Ingrid's friends. There were a number of people there whom we didn't know and when Ingrid asked one guy what he did for a living, he told her he was a bus driver, right? And do you know what Ingrid said? "Yes, but what do you *really* do?" Now do you see what I'm getting at? I mean, she automatically implied that there was no place for a bus driver in the circles we moved in, and if there did happen to be one in the company, she simply assumed that the person concerned was only driving buses while writing his doctoral thesis or waiting for a novel to be snapped up by a publisher or a painting to be sold or something of the sort . . .

in her world simply being a bus driver wasn't good enough . . .

MARIA: So she made you feel you weren't good enough?

DAVID: I think it would be truer to say she didn't accept me completely. Anything that smacked of the working class was somehow vulgar in her eyes. And this is the point I was trying to make when I said it wasn't a classic midlife crisis that drove me to have an affair with May-Britt. It was as much a matter of . . . how can I put it . . . a longing for that part of me also to be understood and accepted. Because May-Britt comes, of course, from the same social class as me, right? She's a hairdresser, her mother's an auxiliary nurse, and her father's a bricklayer, and she . . . she reminds me of the girls I grew up with, the girls from my neighborhood who didn't go off to university or college but stayed on in Namsos, "ordinary people" . . . as the working class are called these days. [pause] But at the same time . . . well, I mean, it's pretty complicated, not to say paradoxical, because to some extent it was because of my background that Ingrid fell for me.

MARIA: Okay.

DAVID: I'm not sure, but I think that in some way she saw her father in me.

MARIA: So did he come from a similar background?

DAVID: No, no. Far from it. Alfred was practicing as a plastic surgeon in New York when he met Rita and he moved to Norway with her sometime in the eighties. But as I say, he was a trailblazer. So is Ingrid, of course, but unlike Alfred she didn't exactly start with nothing. Because, well . . . Alfred was a self-made man, right? As am I, in a way . . . I mean I've succeeded in becoming a published author, despite coming from a working-class home with not a book in the house. And I think this is more relevant than it may sound, because you see . . . where Ingrid comes from, being a self-made man trumps everything else. A self-made man is living proof that, ideologically speaking, there's nothing to beat capitalism, right? To succeed against all the odds is proof that capitalism works, it's as simple as that, which is why the capitalist admires anyone who has started out with nothing. . . . So for Ingrid, and indeed for Alfred and Rita, my life story was like a version of the American Dream, right? [*pause, laughter*] Oh, it's so ridiculous.

MARIA: What's ridiculous?

DAVID: That Ingrid fell in love with me because I reminded her of her father.

MARIA: Why is that ridiculous?

DAVID: I don't know. But we're always looking for original explanations for things, aren't we? In art. Science. Or when we're sitting chatting around a coffee table, for that matter. We all have a need to discover new, interesting, and amusing connections in life. But the truth is that there are obvious and ludicrous explanations for just about everything. Life is really pretty boring, we just don't want to admit it. [*laughter*] She saw her father in me. Well, well. [*pause*] But when it began to dawn on Ingrid and her parents that being a writer was not necessarily the same as being a best-selling author and a celebrity, having a writer in the family lost some of its charm. [*laughter*] Their interest in art didn't run very deep, you see. I mean, they liked to think of themselves as intellectuals, all three of them.

Ingrid and Rita are the sort of people who measure the success of a holiday by the number of museums and galleries they've raced through and Alfred was only waiting for the guy from *Dagens Næringsliv*, Norway's leading business newspaper, to call and ask what books he had on his bedside table, so he could mention some Hamsun classic, thus letting everyone know that he wasn't just a cynical capitalist but a man of flesh and blood.

MARIA: [*chuckles*] I see.

DAVID: In other words, for them a love of art and culture was just a pose really. And a totally unknown and almost unread writer like me was, of course, no use for that. They had expected more of me, you might say. Well, at first they thought it was just that I wasn't good enough at promoting myself and that was why I wasn't number one in the best-seller lists or gracing the front pages of the tabloids.

MARIA: Okay, now let me get this straight: Who exactly thought this? Ingrid or her parents or all three?

DAVID: Well, I suppose it was Ingrid who thought it . . . or wanted to think it. And that was the story she told her parents.

MARIA: And what happened when Ingrid realized that you were never going to be the writer she had hoped you would be?

DAVID: She stopped asking to read what I'd written. She stopped boasting about me to everybody and their uncle, she stopped encouraging me and supporting me and eventually she started to . . . well, in short, she let me know she had lost faith in me as a writer. But what disappointed her most of all, you see, was not that her dream of being married to a rich and famous author had been shattered, the worst of it was that she had chosen a man who didn't live up to Alfred's expectations. She wouldn't hear so much as a word about my writing when Alfred and Rita were present. She felt downright ashamed. And Alfred knew how to play on this, right? I don't know if Ingrid realized it, but her father kept trying to make her feel even more ashamed than she already did. Things improved slightly after Henrik was born, but prior to that he was forever bringing the conversation around to subjects that would put me in a bad light. For example, he might say: "David, you like soccer, have you ever thought of being a sportswriter?" Thus making me and anyone else who happened to be there think that I was no use as a novelist so maybe I should find something else to do, right? Preferably, of course, I should just find myself another woman. What he was really trying to say, obviously, was that I wasn't good enough for his little princess. [*laughter*] My princess . . . he still calls her that sometimes, you know. Christ almighty . . . Princess Ingrid!

MARIA: And how did you respond to all of this?

DAVID: Have you read Johan Harstad's *Buzz Aldrin*?

MARIA: No.

DAVID: It's a sort of salute to all those who've come in second. Buzz Aldrin was the astronaut who had to content himself with being the second man on the moon, right? Only moments after Neil Armstrong.

MARIA: I know.

DAVID: The point is that I began to act as though I wanted to be Buzz Aldrin, so to speak. I mean I would have loved to be rich and popular, obviously, as long as it didn't mean sacrificing my artistic ideals, but I pretended to Ingrid and her family that this was of absolutely no interest to me, you know? If any of them asked what I was working on, for example, I would describe the current project, whatever it happened to be, as much more offbeat and niche than it actually was. On one occasion I lied and said that *Dagbladet* had asked to do an interview with me, but that I had turned them down because I couldn't stand their smarmy tabloid focus on the private lives of their subjects. And as far as they were concerned, all of this was, how shall I put it . . . proof of my lack of ambition. And if there's one thing that antagonizes people who've been fed the capitalist ideology with mother's milk it's a lack of drive and ambition. They never said it to my face, but they were outraged and felt that I had squandered my talent.

MARIA: Have you lost your drive and your ambition?

DAVID: No. On the contrary, I would describe myself as being more than averagely ambitious. And not just as a writer. In other ways too, actually . . . well, I say ambitious, but I do like things to be done properly. I never use processed foods, I always cook from scratch, and I spend a lot of time and money on getting hold of good raw ingredients. It's the same with working out. I draw up a fitness schedule and keep a diary. So nothing's left to chance, right? I want to maximize on the hours I spend working out. That sort of thing. [*pause*] And this goes back, of course, to my childhood.

MARIA: What are you thinking of?

DAVID: Mom, of course. The fact that she was never happy with me as I was. The fact that she could never praise me unreservedly. That she was forever finding fault with me and correcting me and if I did anything wrong she would fly off the handle completely, go way over the top. Especially at those times when she was sick. But at other times too, actually. All of this left me feeling that it wasn't me she wanted, but someone else, you know. [*clears throat, pauses*] And . . . yeah . . . so I did everything I could to be the son she wanted me to be. The more useless she made me feel, the more obsessed I became with proving that I was good enough. I pushed myself further and further in one area after another . . . I mean . . . I still have a pretty strong competitive instinct, but as a child and a teenager it was unhealthily so. I simply had to be the best at everything. At school, on the soccer field . . . oh, God, even as a nine- or ten-year-old I was the sort of kid who would freak out and shout and swear at the referee for a wrong call. I simply could not bear to lose. And the fact that I've become such a . . . what shall I say . . . such a nitpicker, a pedant who drives everyone around me crazy . . . that is, of course, part of the same thing. Everything I did had to be perfect and this has . . . oh, I don't know, has somehow become ingrained in me. [*pause*] What?

MARIA: No . . . nothing. Go on.

DAVID: And all of this was, of course, exacerbated by my mom's refusal to tell me who my father was.

MARIA: Oh?

DAVID: Well, for one thing, I was convinced that she wouldn't tell me because he was a real no-goodnik and she wanted to spare me from knowing anything about him, right? But if you've got it into your head that you're the son of a man who is so bad, well . . .

unconsciously you also start to think that you're no good either, you know . . . like father, like son and all that. . . . And for another . . . well, my father, whoever he was or is, had never made any attempt to get in touch with me and naturally that also made me feel that I couldn't be worth very much. I tried, of course, to convince myself that he didn't know I existed, because if he did he would surely have tracked me down, but . . . well, it wasn't always easy to hold on to that thought.

MARIA: I can understand that.

DAVID: It was a bit like the time Mom tried to kill herself actually. That too left me feeling that I couldn't be worth much, not enough to go on living for, you know. We talked about this a while back, right? And . . . it didn't matter how hard I tried to believe Grandpa when he said that my mom loved me, but that she wasn't well and that was why she tried to kill herself, I was never really convinced. Or at least . . . I knew she loved me, of course I did, but . . . it . . . I don't know quite how to put this, but I felt there was a limit . . . that her love for me wasn't unconditional, if you like. [*pause*] And all of this filled me, you see, with a feeling of shame that I did my utmost to combat. And not without some success either. I mean, due to this variation on the "good girl syndrome," or whatever you want to call it, I excelled at school and on the soccer field, right? I was the youngest player ever to be picked for the Namsos A squad, for instance, I was only fifteen when I started training with the seniors.

MARIA: I don't know anything about soccer, but that does sound very young.

DAVID: It was. Too young. At fifteen you're not physically mature enough to train with grown men. Which is why I never had the soccer career I might have had. Training too much and too hard at such an early age, it's as simple as that.

MARIA: So you got sick of it?

DAVID: I started to have problems with my knees and my ankles. My body wasn't yet fully developed, you see. All that training had simply been too much for me.

MARIA: I see.

DAVID: But I wasn't sick of it. Far from it. It's no exaggeration to say that the day the doctor told me I would have to give up soccer was one of the worst days of my life. It's branded on my memory . . . I can still remember what I was wearing . . . white tennis socks with red-and-blue striped tops and a pair of Levis full of holes and tears that I picked at as I sat there with Mom in the doctor's surgery . . . and, not least, how appallingly lightly the doctor and my mom took the fact that I would have to stop playing. "There are lots of other ways of keeping fit," the doctor said, I remember. And Mom just sat there smiling and totally agreeing with him. How about joining the rowing club, she said, their jetty was just down the road from our house so I wouldn't have to bike all the way to Kleppen for training as I had to do for soccer. Do you see what I mean? They had absolutely no idea what soccer meant to me. They were both about forty I would guess and they saw everything from the point of view of a forty-year-old . . . to them soccer was just a way of staying slim and reasonably fit.

MARIA: While you saw yourself having a career in soccer?

354

DAVID: Yes. And it wasn't just a pipe dream either, it was a real possibility. But my mom didn't know anything about that, it wasn't like today, you know? Kids were left to their own devices much more back then, for good and ill . . . so there was no way my mom could understand what a huge loss this was for me, she had never seen me play, so she had no idea how good I actually was.

MARIA: Time flies.

DAVID: It does. But I'll see you Monday.

MARIA: Yes, see you then.

Trondheim, June 25th, 2006. Trouble with the lawnmower

I hear the chink of plates knocking together, take my eyes off the TV screen, and glance toward the kitchen, yep, just as I thought, it's Ingrid, she's emptying the dishwasher. I open my mouth, about to say that I was going to do that, then think better of it. I merely shake my head and give a little sniff, look at the TV again, try to concentrate on the film, but I can't, feel my annoyance from earlier in the day returning. Not only has she washed the bathroom and hallway floors even though I said I'd do it, and not only did she go to the supermarket herself even though I said I'd do that, now I'll be damned if she isn't filling the dishwasher. It's so typical, she's always so quick to do things she's either asked me to do or thinks I ought to do, and it really pisses me off, she does everything she can to create the impression that I'm a lazy jerk and that she does just about everything around here. Well, if that were true I could have overlooked this gentle hint to me to get off my ass, but it isn't true, there's many a thing that could be said about me, but I am not fucking lazy.

"God, I'm worn out already," she mutters, as if to herself, but still loud enough for me to hear, wanting to make sure I know how much housework she's done and how exhausted she is by it, I can tell. But I refuse to give her the attention she seeks, I just sit here, slumped on the sofa, staring at the screen and pretending to be too caught up in the film to be aware of anything she's saying or doing. "Right, well that's *that* done," she mutters, not giving up, angling for me to ask what *that* is, but I don't, and I won't.

Silence for a moment or two.

"Hm," I murmur, scratching my head, using the same tactic as her now, pretending to be talking to myself, but actually talking to her, emphasizing how engrossed I am, and she's getting annoyed now, I know she is, not only has she done all the chores she asked me to do, but she can't even make me feel bad about it and that infuriates her.

Silence again. Then she goes over to the veranda door and stands there. I can see her out of the corner of my eye, she's standing there looking out at the garden.

"Gosh, the grass has fairly shot up over the past few days," she says, supposedly still talking to herself, but this is actually her way of telling me that I could at least mow the lawn, I know it is. I don't say anything, keep my eyes fixed on the TV, act as though I'm totally focused on what's happening on the screen. "It's looking really messy," she adds.

"Yeah, yeah," I mutter, don't really want to start anything, but it just comes out.

"Sorry?"

"Relax, I'll mow the lawn," I say.

"Er . . . that's not what I meant."

"Yeah, sure," I say, not taking my eyes off the TV screen.

Silence for a couple of seconds.

"David . . . it wasn't, honestly," she says. "Just you finish watching your film."

"All right then, I will," I say. I know very well that's not what she means, but I take her at her word, smile at her as cheerfully as I can, then turn back to the TV and pretend to carry on watching, but now she's really annoyed, I know she is, she's furious with me for taking her at her word and acting as if I don't know that she actually meant me to do the exact opposite. I sit up, pick up my pen and notebook, and open it at the list of keywords I wrote down last time I saw *Fight Club*. I shut my eyes, purse my lips, and try to look as though I'm searching for the right word, sit like that for a moment, then do a little scribble to make her think I'm making a note of something important.

"It'd be great, though, if you could at least do it before Mom and Dad get here," she says.

I put down the pen and the notebook and look at her.

"*At least?*" I echo, grinning at her.

"What?"

"Ah, so what you were *really* trying to say was that I ought to switch off the film and go out and mow the lawn anyway."

She screws up her face the way she does when she's eaten something she doesn't like, I see the wrinkles appear as she narrows her eyes and turns up the corners of her mouth. She gives her head a little shake.

"See . . . you're *doing* it again . . . ," she says.

"Doing what," I say, pick up the remote control, and press Pause.

"What you always do when Mom and Dad come to see us. You've been like this all day."

"Like what?" I say, I've been dreading her parents' visit for days, but I frown, try to look as though I don't know what she's talking about.

She eyes me for a moment.

"Let me know when you come back, will you?"

"Come back?"

"Yeah, let me know when you come back down to earth, because I'm not finished talking to you," she says. I look at her, don't understand what she means for a moment, but then I get it, she's referring, of course, to the fact that I look as though I'm on another planet.

"My, my, aren't we witty today," I say. "But if there's anybody who changes character before your parents pay us a visit, it's not me, it's you."

"Oh, is that so?"

"Honestly, Ingrid, you've hardly sat down since you heard they were coming. I mean, there's nothing wrong with doing a bit of cleaning and tidying before they come, but you don't need to sterilize the whole fucking house. As far as I know, your parents aren't coming here to have their tonsils removed."

"There you go again."

"What do you mean *there I go again*?"

"Oh, forget it. But if you think I look harassed and run off my feet, why are you lying there on the sofa, watching a film, when you could be helping me?" she says.

"Lying on the sofa, watching a film," I repeat, raising my voice slightly. "You make it sound as though I'm doing this for fun. I'm working, for Christ's sake. I'm doing research!"

"Yes, but—er . . ."

"And anyway, I said I would wash the bathroom and hall floors and fill the dishwasher, but I hardly had a chance to draw breath before you'd done it all yourself. And as for all the other things you decide have to be done every time your parents pay us a visit, I freely admit that I don't feel like helping you with them. I can't be bothered moving heaven and earth to satisfy this need you have to show your parents how clever and conscientious you are."

"David. How can you say that to me?"

"Well—you've always been so desperate to show your mom and dad how perfect and how successful you are, Ingrid," I say. It's on the tip of my tongue to say "Princess Ingrid," luckily, though, I manage to stop myself, I know how mad that makes her.

"Oh, for God's sake! It's Friday, David. We always do the cleaning and tidying for the weekend on Fridays," she says. She stands there openmouthed, trying to look shocked. "Is something the matter?"

"There you go again!" I say. I stare at her, wait a moment. "But if you really want to know, then yes, Ingrid. This time there is something the matter. I'm trying to work, but you won't give me peace to do it."

"Oh, really. Well, I do apologize," she says. She turns on her heel, about to walk off, then she stops, turns to face me again. "It seems to me, David, that you can't cope with seeing how well I get on with my mom and dad."

"What on earth do you mean by that?"

"I think it reminds you that you don't have any family of your own. That you grew up without a father and that your mother died so young."

I look at her, grin.

"I know this may be hard for you to believe, Ingrid, but I wouldn't swap my family and my upbringing for yours for anything in the world."

"For God's sake, that's not what I said."

"No, but it's what you meant."

"No, it wasn't, not at all. What's got *into* you, anyway. Now you're just being mean, David."

"*I'm* being mean? What about you?"

"David. I'm guessing that anyone who has grown up without a father must feel that loss. And that anyone who has lost their mother must miss her. All I'm trying to say is . . . well, maybe for you that sense of loss is rekindled when you see me with my parents."

I raise my eyebrows, try to look astonished, sit like that for a moment or two, then give a little laugh.

"Uh . . . I'll refrain from commenting on that," I say.

"What's that supposed to mean?"

"Nothing."

And then, suddenly, it dawns on her. She doesn't say anything, but I can tell by her face, she glares at me, opens her mouth and shakes her head slowly from side to side. She feels like saying something hurtful now, feels like paying me back for being patronizing about her parents, it's written all over her, but she doesn't, she shuts her mouth and turns away, she's not going to risk taking this any further, I know her, I know how her mind works, it means so much to her for her parents to see her as happy and successful and she can't bear the thought of there being any friction between us when they're here. I pick up the remote control and restart the film, delighted to have had the last word, it's childish of me, I know, but I can't help it. After a moment or two I hear Ingrid open the veranda door and go outside, there's a faint creak as she steps on the loose floorboard, then silence.

"Don't tell me she's thinking about mowing the lawn as well," I mutter to myself. I wait a moment, then I press Pause, get up, and go over to the window. I watch her walk across the lawn to the far side of the garage. Fuck, yeah, she is, she stops, unwinds the hair tie from her wrist, and gathers her hair up into a ponytail, then she lifts the tarp off the lawnmower and pulls it out onto the grass, she's un-fucking-believable, she's doing her best to make me look like a layabout and herself as the tireless worker. "Okay, fine by me, sweetheart," I murmur, then I grin and shake my head. "You're not going to make me feel like a layabout, no matter how much housework you do and no matter how exhausted you try to look." I watch her as she tugs the cord to start the lawnmower, then I turn and go back to the sofa. I almost wish the sound of the mower had woken Henrik because that would have given me a good excuse to be mad at Ingrid, I could have told her off and asked her what the hell she was thinking. It's a low blow, I know, but I can't help it, I feel a sweet frisson of schadenfreude at the thought, I almost feel like waking Henrik myself and blaming it on the mower, but I can't, of course, I can't take it out on Henrik, that would be going too far.

I grab the remote control, go to switch on the TV again, then think better of it, instead I pick up my notebook and go through to the kitchen, it's so hot and I feel like having something cold, ice cream with peanuts maybe. People laugh when I say I love ice cream with peanuts, am I still living in the nineties, they ask. But it's so damn good, particularly when it's hot and I have the urge for something that's both salty and cold. I lay the notebook on the kitchen countertop and go to open the door of the freezer above the fridge but stop myself, it's a bit early in the day for a beer, but I would actually rather have a cold beer than ice cream, and besides, if Ingrid saw me drinking now she would be even more pissed off and I can't resist goading her just a little bit. I grin to myself as I open the fridge and take out a can of beer.

"I'll do what I like," I mutter. I pick the bag of peanuts out of the drawer, pour some into my cupped hand, and sling the bag onto the countertop, then I snatch up the notebook and go out onto the veranda. Ingrid is hard at it, mowing the lawn between the trees and bushes down by the gate, and she's obviously having trouble, there are so many roots around there and the trees and bushes are so close packed that it's difficult to get the lawnmower right in between them, I don't know why she bothers cutting that patch at all, but she says there are webcaps growing down there and she's worried that Henrik might eat them. He could never make it all the way over there on his own, though, so I don't buy it, she's only saying that because she doesn't want to admit how terrified she is that things won't look absolutely perfect, she's so fucking obsessed with appearances it's unbelievable. I toss the nuts into my mouth, hum softly, and try to look as cheerful as I can as I dust the salt off my hands, open the beer can, and lower myself into a chair, I'll show her just how unsuccessful her attempt to make me feel guilty has been. I swallow the nuts, take a big slug of beer, and let out a long *aahhh*, look at Ingrid and smile as I flick through my notebook. She's getting really riled now, I can tell by her body language, her abrupt, angry movements. She's heaving and straining and making really heavy weather of it instead of gently edging the mower between the bushes.

"Yeah, well," I murmur, grinning to myself. "I told you I'd do it, but if you don't have the patience to wait, then hell mend you."

She battles on for a while longer, but now what? The mower seems to have got stuck on some roots over by the black currant bushes, she's pushing and shoving and tipping up the front end, but it won't budge. Suddenly she gives it an irate yank. One second, two seconds, but uh-oh, what's this, there seems to be a problem, I see her lips move as she lets out a torrent of swear words that are drowned out by the drone of the engine, then she hunkers down next to the mower, something must have broken, because she's crouched there with her tongue between her teeth, fiddling with something.

I grin and shake my head, glance down at my notebook again.

Silence.

There's a loud bang as something heavy is thrown into the dumpster belonging to the people who're remodeling the second floor of the green house, it must be almost empty because I hear the metal sing out for a split second afterward.

Silence again.

Then I hear someone say: "Can I help you?" I look up and see Halvorsen standing there stripped to the waist, looking at Ingrid. He's usually so shy and diffident, that man, I don't think I've ever known him to speak to us before, but perhaps he spies an opportunity here to assert himself slightly. He's just about the only tradesman in the neighborhood so he probably doesn't want to pass up this chance to make a good impression.

"Oh, yes, could you?"

"Sure," Halvorsen says. He comes around the fence and onto our lawn, he's short and stocky with dispropor-tionately big hands. I watch him as he hunkers down and reaches those massive fists out to the mower, he looks like a crab.

"That . . . rod thing that the wheel fits on to, it fell off," Ingrid says. She glances across at me, smiling triumphantly as she gets up and stands back, leaving the problem to Halvorsen: this is a godsend to her, Halvorsen the trades- man turning up and sorting things out while I just sit here on my butt, watching and drinking beer, it makes me look every bit as lazy as she wants me to look. Not only that, but it also makes me seem rather unmanly, it makes me seem kind of inadequate and surplus to requirements, hence the triumphant smile, a smile that says she doesn't need me.

"Can you do something, do you think?" she asks.

"Yeah, yeah, we can fix this."

"Oh, that's wonderful," Ingrid gushes gratefully, laying it on thick. She's out to hurt me, I know she is, trying to make me look small by overstating Halvorsen's knight-in- shining-armor act, she's so, *so* happy that he has come to her rescue. I feel my hackles rise, look at her, and curl my lip. I have to go inside now, though, before Halvorsen no- tices me sitting here, that way this will stay a silent skir- mish between Ingrid and me: if he sees me sitting here, drinking beer while he helps Ingrid with the lawnmower, I'm going to look as small and ridiculous and unmanly as she wants me to look, and I don't want that, I won't give her the satisfaction. I place a hand on the arm of the chair, all set to get up, but too late, because suddenly Halvorsen looks up and straight at me. I feel myself growing hot and turning red as my eyes meet his, but he doesn't seem particularly comfortable with the situation either, he ob- viously hadn't been expecting to see me here and he looks confused and slightly embarrassed, he must feel that he has somehow trespassed on my territory. He looks rather as if he's been caught in the act of doing something much worse than helping Ingrid with the lawnmower.

"Hi," he mumbles, suddenly reverting to his old shy, diffident self.

"Hi," I reply.

Then we both look away, do it quite instinctively, he glances down at the mower, I gaze at my notebook, but this only makes things worse, the fact that we're both so quick to avert our eyes merely emphasizes the awkwardness of the situation, confirming as it does that we actually have good reason to be embarrassed and thus making it almost impossible to gloss things over and convince each other that this is all quite normal. I pick up my beer and take a sip, decide not to go inside after all, my cheeks are flaming, but I smack my lips contentedly and do my best to look as cool and laid back as I can as I put the beer down again. And why shouldn't I feel cool and laid back anyway? I'm angry with myself for letting it bother me at all, I mean, for Christ's sake, it ought to be just as natural for me to sit here while another man helps Ingrid with the lawnmower as for Ingrid to sit here while the same man gave me a hand. But it isn't. I like to believe that I think what I want and do what I want and that I refuse to be governed by outdated rules for how a man should behave, but it's not true. I mean, Christ, I'm sitting here blushing because another man is helping Ingrid to fix the lawnmower, and it's so fucking annoying, almost as annoying as Ingrid making me look like a fool by exploiting those same outdated gender stereotypes, how hypocritical can she be? Not that she's ever been one for taking to the barricades for women's liberation, she simply takes it for granted that there should be equality of the sexes in all areas and she can become highly indignant if she witnesses anything she regards as discrimination against women. And yet she goes and does something like this, it's so incredibly hypocritical.

"Trouble with the lawnmower?" I hear someone say. It's the chairman of the residents' association, he saunters over, pushes his sunglasses up onto his pink, shaved head, and regards Ingrid.

"Yes, but it's no problem, not with such a helpful handyman for a neighbor," Ingrid says blithely, doing everything she can now to make me look bad, making it sound as though I'm not particularly handy or helpful.

"Yeah, well, I can see how you might need that, living with an artist as you do," the chairman of the residents' association remarks, raising his voice and speaking loud enough for me to hear, trying to be funny and pull my leg a little bit, but I pretend not to hear him, I'm in no mood to laugh at his stupid artist jokes, so I sit here clutching my notebook and act as though I'm concentrating on reading my notes. "Wouldn't you say, David?" he says, even louder, but I still don't answer. I can't bring myself to meet their eyes, my cheeks are flaming and I just can't do it, they all know I can hear every word, I know they do, but I hide behind my notebook and try to look as though I'm totally engrossed.

"The great author seems to be in a world of his own," Ingrid says, the wry note in her voice designed to let everyone know they're absolutely right in assuming that I'm aware of everything that's going on.

Silence for a moment or two. Then they carry on talking,

chatting about one thing and another, laughing now and again, leaving me to sit there like a fractious child whom no one can be bothered paying any more attention to, that's how I feel too, feel the way I used to do as a kid when I went in the huff and Mom would say "let him just sit there and sulk." I hear Ingrid let out a loud peal of laughter at something that happened when the chairman of the residents' association and his wife were on holiday, she's trying to pay me back by appearing to be even happier than she is, I can tell, she knows what I'm like, the more bright and cheerful she seems, the worse I'll feel, so she's doing all she can to make me think she's in sparkling form, it makes my blood boil, anger courses through my veins. I reach for my beer and take another sip, leave a dent in the can with my fingers as I set it down again, I didn't mean to, I tensed my muscles without thinking about it and it just happened, I'm so angry. I see the chairman of the residents' association tip his sunglasses down onto his nose and stroll on.

"D'you have a star screwdriver?" Halvorsen asks. He gets to his feet and scratches his nose. He looks even shorter and more crablike standing next to Ingrid, who's so tall.

"Yes, of course, hang on a minute," Ingrid says and she walks off.

I stare at her, try to catch her eye so she can see how angry I am, but she doesn't look my way, maybe she realizes she's gone too far and needs to tread carefully now, maybe that's why she looks straight ahead as she heads for the shed, doesn't dare to antagonize me any more than she's already done, doesn't even dare to look at me. After a moment I lay down my notebook, pick up the beer can, and give it a little squeeze to straighten out the dent, then

I get up and go down the steps and onto the lawn. I stroll over to Halvorsen, don't stop to think, just do it. I have a huge, hot ball of rage inside me, but I smile cheerfully at Halvorsen.

"Can you fix it?" I ask.

He has hunkered down again and he glances up at me, then immediately looks away, clearly uncomfortable with the situation and possibly a little scared, maybe he's heard that I can be a bit unpredictable and prone to overreacting sometimes, I know there are rumors about me in the neighborhood and even if he doesn't have much to do with our other neighbors, he may have heard something on the grapevine, who knows—he certainly looks alarmed and uneasy, his eyes flicking back and forth as he tries to scrape the blackish-brown crust of old grass off the underside of the mower. I can't help having a little gloat, feel a little stronger too, somehow, it's as if the sight of him looking so uncomfortable makes me stand a little taller.

"Think so," he says.

"Great," I say. I take a sip of my beer, lower the can, and flash him a bright but cool smile. "Hey, you know what, there's something wrong with the faucet in our kitchen, it kind of seizes up sometimes, maybe you could take a look at that as well, while you're at it?" I say, nodding toward the house but keeping my eyes fixed on him. He doesn't answer straightaway, he's trying to figure out whether this question is my way of throwing down the gauntlet or whether I am actually asking for his help, but he can't make me out, I can tell by his face, he looks confused. "You being so handy and all," I add.

"Oh, well . . . I could always have a look, I suppose," he says. He raises one enormous hand, puts a finger with a blackened nail to his eye, and picks something out of the corner of it.

"Wonderful," I say. "Ingrid will be so pleased."

He smiles anxiously, nods hesitantly, and turns back to the lawnmower.

Then Ingrid returns.

"Do you hear that, Ingrid?" I say, looking at her as she hands Halvorsen a screwdriver with a black-and-yellow plastic handle, giving her the same bright, cool smile. "Mr. Halvorsen has just offered to fix the kitchen tap for us."

She doesn't answer immediately, merely stands there looking rather flummoxed, clearly not sure what to make of this turn of events.

"Oh, right," she says, then pauses. "Well, that's great," she finishes, trying to smile but still looking a little confused.

"Yeah, isn't it?" I say. I put the beer can to my lips and take another swig, look her straight in the eye, still smiling. "I'm going to sit down in the office and work for a while. I presume you'll pay him for his time," I say. I see Ingrid's face change color as soon as I say it, she knows what I'm implying, and her cheeks have gone bright red. "Awfully hot today, isn't it?" I say, smiling innocently and taking another swig of my beer.

Date: October 9th, 2006
Place: Fjordgata 69d, Trondheim
Present: Dr. Maria Hjuul Wendelboe, psychotherapist;
David Forberg, patient

MARIA: What have you done to yourself?

DAVID: Done to myself?

MARIA: Your hands?

DAVID: Oh. Nothing. I'm just a bit stiff. I've been spending too much time at the computer lately.

MARIA: And how's the novel coming along?

DAVID: Fine.

[*pause*]

DAVID: [*laughing*] I don't really like talking to other people about what I'm working on, you know? Not even my editor. I need the publisher to help me with proofreading and the jacket design and so on. But I have to keep the actual text to myself for as long as possible.

MARIA: Why is that, do you think?

DAVID: Because if I show it to anyone else too soon, it no longer feels like mine. I think most real authors . . . and artists generally, in fact, feel the same. They want to play God in the universe they create . . . I know it sounds idealistic, but for me this is absolutely vital. I've never understood people who go on writing courses or to creative-writing schools, for example. I could never dream of doing that. Even though I'm sure I could learn a lot in terms of technique. And all of this can be traced back, of course, to things that happened in my child- hood. You see, as a boy, well . . . in daydreams and in my imagination I could be whoever I wanted to be and not who Mom wanted me to be, so to speak. As I've said before, she let me know that I wasn't good enough, that I ought to change, become a different person, and my imagination provided a refuge from that, you know, a place where I could escape from all demands and pres- sure. And not just escape them . . . it's a kind of twofold thing, this, you see . . . because my imagination was also a place where I could invent a new persona for my- self, one every bit as great as I thought Mom wanted me to be, a place where I could compensate for my failings.

MARIA: Mm.

DAVID: So I gradually developed a tremendous need for and a pretty good gift for fantasy and invention.

MARIA: And you see a connection between this and the fact that you grew up to be a writer?

DAVID: Certainly. Or at least . . . I think I became a writer more by chance, really. It's not like I decided as a child that I was going to be a writer. I wasn't one of those four-eyes who wrote poems in secret, if you know what I mean. And I was no bookworm either. I've never been in any doubt that I wanted to do something creative, but I could just as easily have been a musician or a film or theater director, or a teacher come to that, doing something creative in my spare time. But at university I wrote a short story for a student literary magazine . . . and a guy from this publishing house happened to read it and liked it. And he called to ask if I had anything else he could read so I wrote another short story. Which he also liked . . . so he decided to include it in an anthology showcasing new writers. And one thing led to another, right? I began to feel a little more confident about my writing, so instead of doing a degree in social work I signed up for an introductory course in literature. And this introduced me to a milieu where writing and dreaming about being a full-time writer were more the rule than the exception, you might say, and then . . . yeah, then I started writing more and after years of trial and error a publisher expressed an interest in one of my manuscripts, and well . . . here I am. Thanks, in other words, to a great need to express myself, a modicum of talent, and a series of happy accidents.

MARIA: How many books have you actually published?

DAVID: Just the one novel. And another one out soon.

MARIA: It's not an awful lot.

DAVID: No, it's not.

MARIA: And yet you seem . . . how shall I put it . . . pretty secure in your role as a writer.

DAVID: How do you mean?

MARIA: Well, you refer to yourself as a writer as if it were the most natural thing in the world.

DAVID: I suppose that's because I consider quality more important than quantity. And as far as quality is concerned, I'm pretty sure I can legitimately call myself a writer. [*pauses*] He said modestly.

[*They both laugh. Pause.*]

DAVID: [*gasping*] Oh dear, oh dear. Sorry.

MARIA: Are you still having trouble sleeping?

DAVID: Yes.

MARIA: Have you done what we agreed you should do?

DAVID: Well, I've tried. I've been working out and going for walks, I've cut out supper. I go to bed at a set time . . . I probably lie too long in the mornings, it's hard to get up at seven when you've hardly slept all night.

MARIA: I'm sure it is.

DAVID: Maybe you could prescribe some other sleeping pills for me. Something a bit stronger.

MARIA: I'd like to see you work a little more on your sleep-wake cycle before I would consider doing that. If you can force yourself to get up early, it goes without saying that it will be easier for you to fall asleep at night.

DAVID: Okay.

[*brief pause*]

MARIA: And the nightmares?

DAVID: I dreamed about the killing at the weekend. The same dream I've had a hundred times before. The look in his eyes just before he keels over. The surprise and the horror in his eyes. The gurgling sounds. Yeah, you know . . . that was the first time in a while, though. . . . But I keep having the other dreams. The night before last it started with me playing for the Namsos boys' team. We were competing in the Scandia Cup here in Trondheim and we were staying the night in a class-room in some school and . . . we had all got into our sleeping bags and the coach reminded us that we were going to be playing at eight o'clock the next morning so it was time for lights-out . . . eliciting howls of protest, of course, from the boys who were lying around playing poker and blackjack. . . . It all seemed so real, you know? But suddenly I realized that I had turned into a snake. I . . . at first I didn't want to admit it. I told myself it was the sleeping bag that made me look like a snake. But when I went to pull down the zip, I found that there wasn't any zip. Then I noticed that my arms were gone . . . so I really *was* a snake.

MARIA: Mm.

DAVID: All the other boys were terrified, of course. It was utter chaos, with everyone shouting and screaming. And I was just as terrified, if not more. So I tried to get away . . . I shot off across the floor . . . wriggling and squirming . . . around carryalls and sleeping bags, mats, soccer uniforms, and empty soda bottles, and, yeah . . . with the coach in hot pursuit, trying to stamp me to death. But then . . . it was so surreal . . . suddenly I realized that my snake body was both a sleeping bag and a snake body, so to speak . . . so I crawled into the sleeping bag, down and down, deeper and deeper, until I couldn't go any farther . . .

[*pause*]

DAVID: And it was so warm and damp in there. The sides were kind of sticky. And right at the bottom there was a placenta for me to feed on. [*laughs*] Oh, Maria, honestly.

MARIA: What?

DAVID: I can read you like a book.

MARIA: Oh?

DAVID: But it was just a sleeping bag. From Norrøna, if my memory serves me right. And yes, it was a body too, but it was a *snake* body. Christ.

MARIA: Is this a ploy to avoid talking about your mother?

DAVID: A what . . . ?

MARIA: You're suggesting that I interpret your dream as a sign that you miss your mother. Then you go on to mock this way of interpreting your dream. You smile, to let me know what a Freudian cliché that is, right? And you're hoping this will make me feel so stupid that I won't pursue the matter.

DAVID: Oh, come on. I've just been sitting here going on about Mom. I've talked about her in almost every one of our sessions. Why should I balk at talking about her now?

MARIA: Yes, but your dream may not be about your mother, per se. It might be more about the mother figure and what that represents. Maybe *that's* what you'd rather not talk about.

DAVID: And what about the dreams I have in which I turn into other animals? How do those fit with your theory?

MARIA: David. Not many psychotherapists today believe that dreams have any particular significance. Not in Norway anyway. So I'm not really so interested in what your dreams mean. I do, however, find the way in which *you* interpret and feel about your dreams extremely interesting.

[*pause*]

MARIA: What are you thinking about?

DAVID: What you said. About what the mother figure represents. That it might make sense, after all. It's strange . . . you know . . . how that age-old distrust of priests persists. It's so deeply ingrained in people. I mean, when I was a teenager everyone around me saw Arvid as Namsos's answer to the bishop and stepfather in *Fanny and Alexander* and Mom as the somewhat pathetic mother. Okay, I'm exaggerating a little but still . . . they thought Arvid was very strict and domineering and wouldn't let me do anything and that Mom just stood by and let him boss me around . . . either because she thought he knew best or because she didn't dare to speak up. In fact, though, it was the other way around. Or no, that's going too far. But . . . Mom was certainly the more controlling of the two. She may have seemed like a very liberal mother, at least in my early teens when she gave me both freedom and responsibility, but as I got older and she found it harder to control me the way she had when I was little, she began to exercise power over me by playing on my emotions . . . usually by making a martyr of herself. She would try to make me feel bad if I didn't talk or behave as she wanted me to . . . she had a million different ways of doing this. And . . . at the time I didn't really know what was going on, you know. I just felt so guilty and so ashamed, but I didn't know why . . . or at least, I had a suspicion, of course, that it had something to do with Mom. Well, I usually did. But . . . I didn't know I was being manipulated. I remember one time . . . I must have been about fourteen, maybe fifteen, and I had opted out of a trip to Östersund in Sweden with Mom and Arvid in order to go to a festival in Mossjøen with a bunch of older pals instead. I was all packed and ready to go and then Mom looked at me with eyes that were almost swimming with disappointment, right? It was all she could do to whisper bye-bye. Anyway, the upshot was that I . . . well, I picked up my backpack and off I went, but then as I was getting into my pal's car I suddenly burst into tears . . . I wept and wept, I couldn't stop . . . and neither I nor my pals had any idea why. And it . . . it may be hard for anyone else to understand . . . I mean, a disappointed glance, a strangled "bye-bye" . . . it sounds so innocuous and yet that was all it took to demolish me completely.

MARIA: I don't think it's hard to understand at all.

DAVID: No, but . . . it was all so undramatic, you know. Although that's what's so effective about this way of controlling people, of course. Because with something as insidious, as subtle as this, although you may sense that you're being manipulated, you don't know for sure and that makes it impossible to challenge the person who's manipulating you, right? And often you think there must be something wrong with *you*. I mean, how crazy can you be . . . going to pieces just because your mother looks at you in a certain way.

MARIA: Mm.

DAVID: And . . . [*clearing his throat*] it's odd, really, but only now, as a grown man, do I see the link between Mom's emotional manipulation and the way I was in my teens. [*clears his throat again*] Because, well . . . I had to stand up for myself, you know? Otherwise, not to put too fine a point on it, I would have ceased to exist as an independent human being. And my way of defending myself was to shut off my emotions, as it were. Quite unconsciously I began to disconnect the instrument Mom played on. My conscience. My sympathy. I refused to be controlled by my feelings. So I eventually came to be regarded as a cold, hard young man. A cynic. I ran with a gang of petty criminals for a while, for example. I stole. Drank heavily. Got into fights . . . I did exactly as I pleased without any thought for the harm I did or the trouble I caused. Or no . . . I did think about it a bit. I felt bad about most of the stuff I was mixed up in, in fact. But I would never have acknowledged those feelings, I considered them a sign of weakness, and, as I say, I couldn't allow myself to be weak, if I did that I would be lost. This idea . . . or philosophy had become ingrained in me. And later, as I became more and more interested in art and literature, it also manifested itself in a deep loathing of any and all forms of sentimentality. Grand passion. Grand rhetoric. Bombast. Romance. I was allergic to it all. And still am, really. Anyway . . . I was reminded of this when you said a moment ago that it wasn't my mother, per se, that I was trying to avoid talking about. It could be that this profound contempt for frailty prevents me from admitting that I do actually need the protection and comfort that the mother figure represents. Maybe that's why I was so keen to distance myself from such an old-fashioned Freudian approach to interpreting dreams . . . because such an interpretation made me feel small and weak . . . do you see what I'm getting at?

MARIA: Mm-hmm.

DAVID: And maybe this was also partly what attracted me to May-Britt.

MARIA: How do you mean?

DAVID: That same contempt for frailty . . . for my own frailty . . . May-Britt is fifteen years younger than me and there's no doubt as to who is the dominant partner in our relationship, if I can put it like that. And hence it's easier for me to feel strong when I'm with her. While with Ingrid in many ways the opposite was the case: with her I was frequently confronted with my own inadequacy . . . and weakness. Because we were on a more equal footing, right? Same age, same experience, both university graduates, and so on and so forth. Well, actually, of the two of us she was in many ways the more powerful. You see . . . when I met Ingrid I had nothing. I had published one book, which sold about seven or eight hundred copies. So I was broke . . . and I was sick of being broke, I was worn out, drinking heavily. I longed for the nice, comfortable middle-class life I had spent years and so much time and energy on despising. You know: wife, kids, nice house, and a new Volvo in the garage. So when I met Ingrid, that was it, I was sold. Because she offered all of this, you might say. Not only did she want the same things as me, but the fact that Alfred was so wealthy obviously made it easier for us to get what we wanted. It took a while for Ingrid's business to build up to a point where she could draw a decent salary from it and I was earning next to nothing . . . so Alfred paid for a lot of the things we needed, you know . . . car, household appliances . . . and he gave us a cheap loan. And at first, yeah . . . I was happy, I really was. I felt as though I had reached my destination after a very long, hard journey. [*laughs*] I even admired Ingrid's rather haughty, snobbish, and slightly prim manner . . . I actually found it attractive, it seemed to emphasize the gap between us, made her seem unapproachable, almost unattainable and the fact that I had been able to win someone who was essentially unattainable made me stand taller, so to speak. It actually turned me on, that side of her, I remember. That she had hardly tried anything other than the missionary position and that she felt almost duty bound, if you like, to look appalled every time I suggested that we might do something a little more . . . how shall I put it . . . more daring. It made me even hornier. That she protested and was shocked, but still allowed herself to be talked into giving anal sex a go, for example, that little performance wasn't just a turn-on, it made me feel attractive and powerful somehow. That changed, though, to put it mildly. By the end, nothing annoyed me more than her prudishness. I . . . many a time I fucked her out of sheer anger.

MARIA: Against her will?

DAVID: No, of course not. She . . . I don't think she realized I was angry, she thought I was just really turned on. Which I was, obviously. But there was an element of punishment in it that . . . hadn't been there earlier in our relationship. The same went for the way I kept pushing her to go further and further, of course.

MARIA: Go further and further, in what way?

DAVID: Okay, well . . . sometimes when we fucked we would fantasize that Ingrid was having sex with other men.

MARIA: It's a common fantasy.

DAVID: Yeah, I know. But I wanted her to put the fantasy into action. I encouraged her . . . no, more, I would actually find myself pestering her to sleep with another man. I insisted. And I did this, of course, because I knew that Ingrid didn't *want* to be unfaithful to me, she was far too proper for that. And her propriety annoyed me so much that I always had the urge to provoke it, throw it in her face, test it.

MARIA: You touched on something similar when you were describing the difference between the world Ingrid came from and the one you came from . . . the contempt each class feels for the other.

DAVID: Ah, yes. [*pause*] And you? Where do you come from?

MARIA: David.

DAVID: Maria Hjuul Wendelboe. It reeks of the Conservative Party, the Masons, and the leafy suburbs. Wine with Sunday dinner and all that.

MARIA: [*laughing*] We're here to talk about you, not me.

DAVID: Aw, come on. I sit here session after session, sharing my innermost thoughts with you. Surely it wouldn't hurt you to let me know a *little* bit about you too.

MARIA: I don't quite fit that profile, I'm afraid. My family were Methodists.

DAVID: Are you a Methodist?

MARIA: Yes. Or . . . well, to be honest, I don't know. I'm in the middle of a difficult process, you might say.

DAVID: Are you considering leaving the church?

MARIA: Uh-huh. But we're talking about you here.

DAVID: Yes, I imagine that must be difficult. Particularly if your family isn't happy about it.

MARIA: David.

DAVID: Yeah, yeah. [*pause*] Oh, by the way, I received an interesting e-mail today.

MARIA: Oh?

DAVID: From an ex-girlfriend. [*laughs*] She had put an ad in the paper, with a picture of me, saying that I had lost my memory and needed help to find out who I was.

MARIA: Really?

DAVID: Yes. And she'd attached a document containing letters from people who'd known me at different times in my life. Who had obviously replied to the ad.

MARIA: Good heavens . . .

DAVID: I only had time to read a little bit here and there before I had to dash, so I don't yet know exactly what it's all about. But it was a good idea.

MARIA: It would be interesting to read it.

DAVID: Okay, well, I can forward the e-mail to you. I just have to read the whole thing first. To see whether it's fit for public consumption. [*laughs*]

Trondheim, June 25th, 2006. French or American?

I lay the manuscript on the office desk and get up. A wave of hysterical laughter rolls toward me from the television as I open the door, I shake my head and swear under my breath, I don't know why Sara always has to have it turned up so loud, it's impossible to be in the same house as her when she's got it as loud as that. I go downstairs, my right hand skimming the banister.

"Turn that down, Sara," I say, glancing at her as I go through the living room on my way to the kitchen. She's sitting in the armchair with her legs tucked up under her, gazing at the TV and eating ice cream from a little bowl, she makes no move to turn down the volume. I give a little grunt as I carry on into the kitchen, I'm sick and tired of her rebellious-teenager act: she turns everything, absolutely everything, into a fight. I get myself a can of beer from the fridge, pop it open, and wander over to the kitchen window, I ought to see about getting that pile of gravel raked out, I suppose, there's hardly any room for the car with it sitting there. I grab the bag of nuts off the counter, pour some into my hand, and toss them all into my mouth, stand there munching and looking out of the window for a minute, then I take a big drink of my beer, put the can down, and get the veal shanks, chorizo sausages, and the bag of carrots out of the fridge. I'd better get started on the dinner now if I'm to be finished by the time Alfred and Rita get here. It usually takes about three hours to make osso buco and they're due to arrive around six, as far as I remember. I open the corner cabinet, take out the cast-iron pan, and place it on the burner, glancing back at Sara as I do so.

"Turn down the TV, Sara," I say again, a little louder this time, but it does no good, she acts as though she neither hears nor sees me, doing everything she can to provoke and defy me. I'm about to ask her for a third time to turn down the volume, but I don't. Instead I go down the stairs to the basement, into the TV room, and pull out the decoder plug. I turn to go straight back upstairs, then think better of it: if I do that she'll know it was me who disconnected the cable TV and I don't want that, I can't face arguing with her right now, so I go into the utility room, open the freezer, and take out a loaf of bread, we have almost a whole loaf in the bread bin already, but there's slightly less chance of her suspecting me if she sees me bringing something up from the basement, so I take it anyway.

I whistle to myself as I go back up the stairs.

"The TV's gone dead," Sara says. She's sitting there pointing the remote at the television, clicking and clicking.

"Oh?" I say, looking at her and raising my eyebrows as I cut through the living room. "That's odd." I carry on into the kitchen. There's an apple lying on the countertop, not even half-eaten, only a couple of bites out of it and there's no question as to who's been at it, there's the clear imprint of front teeth with braces in the browning flesh of the fruit. I whirl around to face Sara. "How many times do we have to tell you not to help yourself to anything you can't finish?" I say, slamming the frozen bread down onto the countertop.

"What?"

"There's an apple on the countertop here with one, maybe two bites out of it!"

I hear her groan.

"Now, you see, I simply don't understand why we should spend money on food if we're going to chuck it in the trash instead of eating it," I say. "But perhaps you can explain that to me?"

"Rotten fucking TV," she mutters, not even answering me now, letting me know how little she cares by concentrating on getting the TV to work again.

"And by the way, I was planning to serve that ice cream for dessert this evening, so I hope you haven't taken more than one helping!" I say. "Because if you have, you'll just have to run down to the supermarket and get some more." I pick up the half-eaten apple and drop it into the trash can, she knows she's supposed to clear up after herself, but I can't be bothered nagging her anymore, I take a big gulp of beer and make a start on the osso buco. I hear Sara swearing to herself, then she gives up, bangs the remote control down on the table, and stomps off to her room.

Peace for a while.

Then I hear Ingrid come in from the veranda, sounds like she's out of breath from mowing the lawn, although I'm sure she isn't really, I bet this is just another act, to make me think she's worn out after doing a job that I was supposed to do. I take a sip from the beer can and set it down again, hear the soft pad-pad of bare feet on the parquet floor, but I don't turn around, pour red wine and marsala into the pot and turn up the heat to bring it to a steady simmer.

"Would you mind moving that bag of nuts?" she says, talking to me as if this is her kitchen and I'm only the hired help, her tone imperious, rather brusque.

I turn and look at her. It's on the tip of my tongue to say I'd forgotten His Majesty was on his way, but I don't, I merely grin and shake my head, then turn away again, to show her how ridiculously over the top all this fuss over Alfred is, it's nothing but an act from start to finish.

"For God's sake, David. He could die, you know."

"I knew he was allergic to nuts, but I didn't know it was that bad, I didn't think the sight of a bag of nuts would kill him. But of course," I say, picking up the bag and putting it back in the drawer.

Silence.

"Er, are you planning on drinking many more of those before Mom and Dad get here?"

I turn and look at her, frown.

"What?"

"I'm just wondering what sort of state you'll be in by the time they get here," she says.

I let my jaw drop slightly, to make it look as if I've never been so insulted.

"You don't need to look so surprised, David. I mean, it's not like it's the first time."

I feel the anger from before returning, am on the point of saying something about how you need to be drunk to get through a whole evening with her parents, but I don't, and I won't, because if I did, then I would be the baddie and I won't give her the satisfaction, so I don't say anything, just pick up the can, carry it over to the sink, and pour out the rest of the beer. White froth spills over the drain and spreads across the bottom of the sink and the pungent, acrid smell of beer fills my nostrils. Total silence. I shake out the last drops of beer and put the can down next to the faucet, turn to Ingrid, smile sweetly at her, then cross to the stove and turn down the heat.

"For fuck's sake," she mutters.

I turn around.

"Sorry?" I say, eyeing her quizzically.

She shakes her head.

"Nothing. But could you at least rake out that gravel before Mom and Dad get here? So they can actually park the car."

"At least? Well, I am actually in the middle of making dinner for them."

"Well, I thought maybe you could do it while the dinner is cooking. But never mind, I'll rake out the gravel as well."

"I'll rake out the gravel *as well*," I repeat with a scathing grin. "Oh, poor you, having to do all the things that I'm supposed to do."

She goes to say something, then stops, shuts her mouth, puts up a hand, and digs her fingers into her thick hair. She stands like that with her hand on her head, staring at the floor, looking more hurt and upset than angry now. She swallows once, then again.

"I don't know why it has to be like this. I want us to be friends, David," she says, giving a little sigh as she lowers her hand and looks up at me, sad eyed. She's afraid the tension between us will be so palpable that there will be no chance of dispelling it before her parents get here, I can tell by her face and her voice. She swallows once, twice. There's a part of me that wants to go on punishing her and

I almost say she should have thought of that earlier, but I don't, and I won't, I'm just as tired of being caught in this vicious, bitter cycle, I don't want to be angry anymore.

"I want us to be friends too," I say and I see how relieved and happy she looks as soon as I say this, it means so much to her that the atmosphere should be good when her parents get here. She eyes me gratefully, almost tenderly. I smile, it feels so good to shake off all this bitterness and anger. A wave of warmth spreads through me, a sense of peace.

"Sorry," she says.

"No, it's me who should say sorry," I say.

And she comes over to me, draws me to her, and buries her face in my chest and I nuzzle her hair, it smells faintly of rosemary. We stand like that, holding each other for a minute without speaking, then we pull apart.

"Hm, that smells so good," she says. She regards the pan of osso buco, juts out her chin, and kind of sniffs the air. I look at her and smile, it doesn't smell good at all, not yet, it smells of evaporating alcohol, she's only saying this to bolster the good mood, so to speak, I know.

"Yeah, it'll be good when it's done, I think," I say.

"I'm sure it will."

I get out the Parmesan and start to grate it, running my right hand steadily up and down and watching as the fine tendrils fall from the wedge of cheese into a little yellow heap on the chopping board that Sara made at school once.

"Is there anything I can do to help?" Ingrid asks. "Something that even I can't make a mess of?"

"Not really, no."

"Oh, thanks a lot!" she cries with a quick lift of her eyebrows, pretending to look offended.

"I didn't mean it like that," I chuckle. "But I only have

the gremolata and the risotto to do now. The osso buco just has to sit and simmer till it's done."

"No, no, it's okay, don't apologize," she says. She takes a feeding bottle out of the basin, unscrews the little plastic ring, pulls off the rubber nipple and puts the whole lot in the dishwasher. "I can put stuff in the dishwasher, though, right?"

"Idiot," I say with a little laugh as I tip up the chopping board and gently sweep the heap of grated Parmesan into a bowl. It feels so good to have broken out of that vicious, bitter cycle, to be friends, it makes me happy. "What time is it anyway?"

"Five o'clock."

"Right then, I'll go and rake out that gravel now," I say, doing a sudden about-face, saying I'll rake out the gravel after all, I didn't mean to say it, but I do—another instinctive step toward burying the hatchet, I suppose.

"No, it's okay. You can do it later," she says, furthering the peacemaking process by doing a similar about-face.

"I really ought to do it now if I'm to be finished by the time they arrive."

"They can park on the street for now," Ingrid says. "In one of the visitor spaces."

"It won't take long once I get started," I say.

"Yeah, I know, but why don't you do it tomorrow, instead?"

"Are you sure?" I ask, taking a pinch of Parmesan and popping it into my mouth.

"Yes, yes."

"Okay," I say, and swallow the Parmesan.

I pick up the bag of mushrooms, tip them onto the chopping board, and start to slice them. There's the odd little clump of black soil on a couple of the mushrooms, I brush this off onto the countertop and quickly inspect the rest, but they're all nice and clean, snowy white.

Silence.

Then Ingrid says: "I love you so much, David."

I turn and look at her, hear the jingle of the ice-cream van farther up the street.

"I love you, too."

"I want us to be happy together," she says.

"So do I, Ingrid," I say.

We stand there smiling and gazing into each other's eyes for a second or two, then we both turn away. I put the mushrooms into the dish next to the bowl of Parmesan, then go over to the sink, wipe away the glistening droplets of water that have gathered on the tap before rinsing my fingers—there's always a bit of condensation when the weather's hot.

"He managed to fix the tap then?"

"Gosh, yes, so he did," I say. I turn the tap on and off a couple of times to test it and, sure enough, it's fixed, as good as new it seems. I feel my conscience prick me as I turn off the tap again, I shouldn't have said what I did to Halvorsen, that was out of line. I turn, about to say this to Ingrid, but I don't get the chance.

"Oh, but he's so funny," she says with a little laugh. "It's maybe not right to call him simple, but . . ."

I regard her. This is her way of atoning for what happened in the garden, I realize that, she tried to make me look small and inadequate by casting Halvorsen as the knight in shining armor coming to her rescue and now she's doing the same again, only the other way around so to speak, trying to boost me by belittling Halvorsen.

"Ah, no, I don't think he's simple," I say as I bend down

and dry my hands on the dish towel hanging under the countertop.

"He said 'indegrients.'"

"He said what?"

"When we were in the garden . . . Joachim was telling us about his food-and-wine holiday in Tuscany and when we were talking about Italian cuisine, Halvorsen said 'inde-grients' instead of 'ingredients,'" she says, giggling. I look at her, I don't want to belittle Halvorsen, but I snigger anyway, she needs to make amends and laughing along with her is a way of helping her to do this.

Then I hear the front door opening.

"Hello," someone calls. It's Rita.

I take a deep breath and let it out quietly, so Ingrid won't hear me sighing. I feel myself bristle as soon as her mother walks through the door, there it is again, that sense of sul-len resentment that always overcomes me when I'm with Ingrid's parents. I try to fight it, but it's no use, it hits me anyway. I see Ingrid's face break into a big smile the mo-ment she sees her mother. I take another deep breath, mustering the energy to put on a smile, then I turn around and see Rita standing in the hall with a small potted plant in her hands. She looks like an aging movie star from the sixties, buxom but by no means fat, and wearing bright red lipstick and a pair of big sunglasses that she has pushed up onto her head.

"Oh, look, they're here already," Ingrid exclaims. She hurries over to her mother, lays a hand on her left shoul-der, and gives her a hug. "Hi, Mom," she says, rocking her back and forth before gently pushing her away and survey-ing her. "You look lovely."

Rita tilts up her chin, looking even more like a movie star.

"Ah, if only I didn't," she says in her rather husky voice.
"Oh?"

"Yes, because then people might understand how I'm really feeling."

"Oh, no, is it that bad?" Ingrid asks.

"No, no," Rita says. "I'm not great, of course, but I'm only saying that so you two will feel sorry for me. You know that!"

"Oh, Mom!" Ingrid says, laughing and shaking her head as if she despairs of her.

"This is for you, by the way," Rita says, handing her the potted plant.

"Thank you."

"You're welcome. I thought you could put it in the bathroom," Rita says and by *you* she means Ingrid, not us, as she always does when talking about anything to do with the house, as if this is Ingrid's domain. I've tried to explain to her that that's not how it works here, but it makes no difference.

"The bathroom?" Ingrid says.

"Yes, there's so much water energy in there, you see, and plants give off wood energy, so they bring balance and harmony to the room," Rita explains, and I feel myself bristle again. I'll have to pull myself together, I have to be a bit more tolerant, a bit more forbearing, I get just as angry and upset every time she starts spouting her eternal New Age, feng shui crap. "Just you wait, you'll soon start to feel much more serene in there," she says.

"Okay, well, I'll put it in the bathroom, then," Ingrid says. "But where's Dad?"

"Well, you know I can't carry anything, not with these hands, so that means more for him to do. But he's coming."

"I'll see if he needs some help," Ingrid says and she sets the plant down on the bureau and goes out to look for Alfred.

I smile at Rita.

"Hi," I say, going up to her. "Good to see you."

"Yes, all right, don't overdo it," she says, batting her eyelids and wafting the air with her hand.

I smile and try to look as if I find her amusing, but it doesn't quite work, all I can manage is a pained grimace.

"Are you suggesting that I didn't really mean that?" I ask.

"Yes, I probably am, I'm afraid," she says. She wriggles out of her jacket, takes Ingrid's hat off the hook, lays it on the shelf with one hand, and hangs her jacket on the hook with the other. She knows full well that I haven't been looking forward to their visit and she makes a liar of me by joking about it like this, she's challenging me to deny what she's saying about me, even though she knows it's true, thus making me seem like a conflict-shunning fool who'll go along with everything she says. I'm so tempted to play her at her own game and be just as blunt in return, I'm so tempted to usurp the role that she has given herself in this little charade and say no, you're absolutely right, I haven't been looking forward to your visit at all, in fact I've been dreading it. But I can't, because then she would tell me she was only joking, of course, and I would be left looking like an ill-mannered son of a bitch yet again.

Then I hear Ingrid and Alfred out on the steps, Alfred with his deep voice and distinct twang—he must have been living in Norway for going on thirty years but he still speaks Norwegian with a strong American accent. He makes some derogatory remark about men in electric cars and Ingrid laughs and says, "Oh, for heaven's sake, Dad!"

"So where's David?" Alfred asks.

"He's here."

"Really?"

"You sound so surprised."

"No, I just thought he must be away," he says. "What with that great pile of gravel in the middle of the driveway. There was no room for me to park."

My spirits sink another notch at this, I feel like retreating to the kitchen to be on my own for a little while, but I can't and there's no time either, because here they come, first Ingrid wheeling a small lilac suitcase, then Alfred with a blue cooler in one hand and a big black suitcase in the other. It's easy to see where Ingrid got her height from anyway, I almost forget how tall he is when I haven't seen him for a while, he must be well over six feet and with his slight stoop, hunched shoulders, and those long arms that he flaps about when he becomes animated he has always reminded me of a large bird of prey.

"Hello," I say.

"Hello."

"Sorry I haven't got that gravel raked out yet," I say. I don't want to say it, but I do. "I simply haven't had the chance."

"No problem. As long as you get it done sometime today," he says, as if it's he and not I who decides when I should rake out the gravel on my own property.

"Oh?"

"I'd prefer not to leave the car out on the street overnight. The things that go on out there—there's no telling what might happen," he says, then he thrusts the cooler at me. "Oh, and this is for you."

"Er, thanks," I say, taking it from him. "What is it?"

"Monkfish, cod, and a bit of halibut," he says. "One of my friends caught more in his net than he could eat himself. But he caught it yesterday so it needs to be eaten today. While it's still fresh. I thought maybe we could make bouillabaisse," he says.

I nod, look at him, saying nothing, don't quite know what to say, I'm fucking speechless. It's one thing to bring fish that Ingrid and I could freeze and have some other time, that would obviously be very nice, but to bring fish and expect us to have it for dinner this very day, without letting us know in advance, I mean, you just don't do that, it's downright disrespectful. I glance at Ingrid, she smiles uncertainly, eyes me apologetically. She knows exactly how I feel about this side of her father and she's worried that I'm going to lose my temper again, I can tell by her face.

"Osso buco tastes almost better the next day, doesn't it?" she says with a wan little smile, but I don't smile back.

"Yeah, maybe," I say.

"But isn't it a bit like lamb hot pot, that it's even better when the flavors have had time to cook in?"

"Probably," I say, then I turn and walk off, take the cooler through to the kitchen. I dump it on the floor, switch off the burner, and move the pan to the side, almost shaking with anger. I shut my eyes, take a deep breath, and slowly let it out, have to try to rise above this, it's just him, he's lived in Norway more than half his life, but he'll never be anything but a brash, arrogant American who's so sure everybody else would want exactly the same as he if they just thought about it. "Damn Yank," I mutter to myself.

"Oh, you've made a few changes in here, I see," I hear Rita say as they move into the living room, referring, I guess, to the fact that we've redecorated it.

"I know," Ingrid says. "We're not quite finished yet, but . . ."

I give a snort at this, we were finished over a month ago, but here she is saying we're not finished yet, in an attempt to beat her mother to it: Rita is bound to find something to criticize or make some suggestion as to how the end result could be improved upon and by saying it's not finished yet Ingrid gives herself the chance to counter any criticism by saying: Oh, yes, that's what we were thinking, we just haven't got that far yet. It annoys me, the way she's always so defensive, she's worked with fashion and design all her life and she's far more artistic than her mother, but still she's so defensive.

"Yes, well, I'm sure it will be eventually" is all Rita says. Not a word about how nice it looks, it hasn't been done according to those ludicrous feng shui principles she's started following in her own home, so I'm guessing she doesn't think much of what we've done, but that's not the point, she must know that Ingrid needs to hear her say we've done a lovely job, you'd think she could give her that much, it's her own daughter, for Christ's sake.

"Why don't you have a seat on the veranda while I put the coffee on," Ingrid says. "Or would you rather have a glass of wine?"

"I never say no to a glass of wine," Rita says.

"Oh, wine, please," says Alfred.

I lean against the kitchen counter, stand there waiting for Ingrid to come back into the kitchen, then I open the top drawer, take out the roll of plastic wrap, tear off a piece, and place it over the bowl of sliced mushrooms, then another to cover the bowl of Parmesan, want her to see me packing away all the food I had been planning to serve, don't know why, but it feels somehow satisfying, maybe because it highlights the fact that I did all that shopping and cooking for nothing, and because I hope this in turn will make Ingrid see that I have every right to be pissed off, I don't know.

"David, hey," she says softly.

"What?"

"Don't be mad, please. He's just trying to be nice."

"I know you think he's doing it to be nice," I say as I stow the mushrooms and Parmesan in the fridge.

"Think? Okay, so why do *you* think he's doing it, then?"

I turn and look at her, about to say something about him being a brash, loudmouthed Yank who thinks he can do whatever he wants, but I don't, and I won't, I've every right to be annoyed and upset, but I need to cool down now, I need to grit my teeth and get through this as best I can.

"It doesn't matter what I think," I say.

"David, hey. I know you were looking forward to giving them osso buco, but . . ."

I shut the fridge door a little more firmly than normal, making the jam jars rattle inside.

"Looking forward to giving them osso buco?" I say, raising my voice. I don't mean to, but I do.

"Shh," she says, putting her finger to her lips and eyeing me in alarm. "Please!"

"For Christ's sake, Ingrid, you talk as if I'm a little kid who's been looking forward to showing the grown-ups what I can do," I say, trying to keep my voice low, but not very successfully, so I reach out a hand and switch on the exhaust fan to mask the sound of my voice, the air in here is thick with cooking fumes so there's nothing suspicious about that, I should have switched it on a while ago, but I forgot. "I know you turn back into a little kid when you're with your dad, Princess Ingrid, but don't think I'm going to do the same. And just so you know: if it's to be bouilla-baisse for dinner today, then your father'll have to make it, because I'm not."

"David . . ."

"I mean it. I'm sick of being stuck in the kitchen."

"David," she says, imploringly now, terrified that her parents will realize something's up, she's not even mad at me for calling her Princess Ingrid. "I know you're offended, David. I would be too, I'm sure, but—look . . . can't we . . . ? Come and have a glass of wine with us. Please."

I almost say no, but I don't, I don't say anything, I hold her eye for a second, then look at the floor and shake my head resignedly to let her know that I'm seriously pissed off and don't much feel like having a glass of wine with her parents, but that I'm willing to do it for her sake. A second more, then she curls her hand around the back of my neck and gently tilts my head back with her thumb until our eyes meet. She swallows.

"I love you, David," she says.

"I love you too," I say.

We stand like that for a moment or two, then we both look away.

"Will you bring the corkscrew?" she says, smiling at me as she takes a bottle from the wine rack.

"Yep," I say. I open the drawer, hear the clatter of cutlery and other utensils as they slam against the back of it. I find the corkscrew, take it out, and away we go.

"So, how are you both?" Ingrid asks as we walk into the living room.

"Well, we hardly see each other, but I think your dad's doing all right, aren't you, Alfred?" Rita says.

Ingrid and Alfred laugh, letting her know that she's every bit as delightful and prima donna-ish as she likes to think she is.

"Yes, thank you, dear," Alfred says. "And you?"

"As long as I don't look in the mirror in the morning, I'm fine," Rita says. "Until my hands start to act up, anyway."

"Oh, my God, Mom," Ingrid says as she rips the plastic seal off the wine bottle. She looks at me and laughs, shaking her head, wanting me to laugh along with her at how wonderfully droll her mother is, I can tell, but I don't, I'm not in the mood, I just give a quick little smile as I hand her the corkscrew, then I cross to the cabinet on the other side of the room and take out four red-wine glasses.

"No, no," I hear Rita say. "We're absolutely fine. We're both very busy, but we wouldn't have it any other way. And you two?"

"Great, everything's great," Ingrid says.

"And business?" Alfred asks.

"Oh, it's going really well. I don't know if you remember, but I made a makeup bag and two handbags out of catfish skin a while back, a small one and a bigger one?"

"Yes, of course I remember."

"Well, we thought we'd priced them too high, but there's obviously plenty of money around because they've sold really well. And now an American chain has shown an interest in them as well."

"Wow. Well, what a clever girl, I must say, even if you are my daughter."

"Ah, but I had a good teacher," Ingrid says.

"Oh, well, I may have given you a few tips, but . . ."

"You taught me everything I know about running a shop, Dad," she says. "I wouldn't have been able to do any of the things I've done if it hadn't been for you."

"Oh, I don't know, I don't know," he says. I look at him, he's standing there, wagging his head and trying to look suitably modest, but he's not fooling anyone, he's lapping up every word Ingrid says, enjoying it even more because I'm here to hear it: there, you see, when it comes right down to it there's no one to beat Daddy, that's what he's thinking, or not thinking, maybe, but that's more or less how he feels, at any rate, I know it is. I hum to myself as I set my glass down on the table, try to look as if I'm not really paying attention, try to spoil his moment of triumph by pretending not to have heard a word of all this.

"And David has designed a website for us," Ingrid says as she works the corkscrew into the cork, talking me up a bit now as well, she probably feels obliged to after singing her dad's praises like that, feels she has to redress the balance a bit. "It looks great."

"Wonderful," Alfred says.

"Yes, good marketing is so important. And online sales is the way to go, you know," Ingrid goes on. She hunches over, trying to pull out the cork, but she can't. "Oh, bother . . . ," she says, then tries again, hauling on it until her cheeks turn pink, but it won't budge.

"Shall I get it for you?" Alfred says.

"Oh, no you don't," Rita says. "Let David get it. We don't want any heart attacks here."

"Ah . . . I'm not *that* decrepit."

She looks at him, raises her eyebrows, and sniffs.

"Uh-huh," she says.

Chuckling.

"We'll let David get it," Ingrid says. "To be on the safe side."

Alfred shakes his head.

"Talk about being put out of commission," he mutters. More chuckling.

"Here," Ingrid says, handing me the bottle.

"Is it a Bordeaux?" Alfred asks.

"Yes," I say and I hold out the bottle so he can read the label.

"We have a zinfandel as well, if you'd rather have an American wine," Ingrid says, eyeing her father inquiringly. Alfred wags his head from side to side.

"Oh, say yes, Alfred," Rita says. "We all know you prefer American wines."

"Well, actually I prefer French wines," Alfred says. "Although I'm not sure they're as good as they used to be." He looks at Ingrid, then me, waiting I suppose for us to ask him to explain so that he can say something about how disloyal it was of France to refuse to take part in the invasion of Iraq. I gather that a lot of Americans boycotted French wines after Chirac's statements and the decisions he made and it wouldn't surprise me if Alfred was one of them, although I don't know, even if he did lose a son on 9/11 and tends, therefore, to take any criticism of American foreign policy rather too personally, he's not as extreme as some of his countrymen, I don't think he's even a Republican. I regard him, manage a smile of sorts, I'm not going to ask what he wants me to ask, I can't face getting into a discussion right now.

"I'll get a zinfandel instead," Ingrid says.

"No, Ingrid, don't do that," he says. I don't know whether he means it or whether he's saying it purely for form's sake, but I'm guessing it's the latter, he makes no further attempt to stop her, at any rate. She takes the bottle of Bordeaux from me and disappears.

"Talk about a difficult, demanding guest," he says, looking at me and giving a little laugh, he's angling for me to deny that he's difficult and demanding, I know, but I don't.

"So how was the drive?" is all I ask.

Silence for a moment. He looks at me, saying nothing, obviously rather offended by my failure to protest and assure him that he's neither difficult nor demanding, I can tell by his face. He seems confused too, he probably hadn't been expecting this.

"Oh, all right," he says. "There was the odd RV home causing a traffic jam on the E6, but there was less traffic than I expected, actually." I look at him and nod, say nothing.

Then Ingrid returns with another bottle of wine.

"We can drink this one with a clear conscience," she says, smiling at Alfred as she hands me the bottle and the corkscrew.

"Oh, Ingrid, that really wasn't necessary, I was only pulling David's leg," he says, glancing at me, but I have my head bent over the bottle, apparently concentrating on inserting the corkscrew into the cork. This is just another attempt to draw me into a discussion but I pretend not to hear him, I can't be bothered discussing this with him, however much I might want to. I can't bring myself to say or do anything that might be construed as criticism of the so-called war on terror, I know how personally they take it, Rita in particular, but Alfred too. Usually I do my best to be open to other people's points of view, but he seems to take just about every objection to American foreign policy as an insult to Jonathan's memory so he always ends up feeling hurt or angry or both. And such a reaction is under-standable, of course, he and Rita were utterly devastated by Jonathan's death, so I get that, but still, it's hard to have a discussion about something that arouses such strong emotions and I certainly don't want to go there. I pull out the cork with a loud pop and fill our glasses.

"There you are."

They thank me and pick up their glasses.

"Oh, by the way, I brought the robe," Rita says.

"Oh, right," Ingrid says and immediately looks away. She starts toward the living room window, eyes wide, as though she has caught sight of something unusual in the garden.

"What is it?" I say.

"I thought I saw someone out there," she says, pushing the sofa a little to one side and going right up to the window, she looks right, then left. "But I don't see anyone now."

"That's odd," Alfred says.

Ingrid shakes her head as she pushes the sofa back into place, apparently just as puzzled.

"You really should get rid of some of this furniture," Rita says, nodding at the sofa. "When a room is as overfurnished as this one, it blocks the energies, you know. And that's actually one of the main reasons for many of the problems people have." There she goes, starting with all that feng shui crap again. I feel an immediate surge of indignation. I quickly pick up my wine glass, put it to my lips, and take a big gulp, hide behind the glass, so they won't see how ridiculous I think this is.

"Oh, really?" Ingrid says.

"And that mirror in the hall—you should hang that some-where else," Rita goes on. "All the fresh energy that flows in when you open the door is bounced back off that and out again. Leaving the air in here heavy and lifeless."

"Okay. Well, I'll have to do something about that," Ingrid says, nodding and smiling and actually looking interested, as though she has absolutely no objection to being lectured like this. I don't know how she does it, don't know how she can be bothered, I mean, I realize that Rita's neo-religious conversion has helped to fill the void left by Jonathan's death, but it's gone too far recently, the way she carries on now isn't just stupid, it's bordering on madness and Ingrid and Alfred should have told her that long ago. To do nothing when someone has become so embroiled in such lunacy is nothing but misplaced love, I don't understand why they don't do something, I don't know how Alfred puts up with her nonsense, he's normally so rational, so down-to-earth, I don't know how he stands it. But maybe he doesn't have the strength to set her straight. I've always seen Rita as a typical pampered rich-man's wife. As a young woman she was very attractive in an Audrey Hepburn kind of way and I'm pretty sure it was the money that persuaded her to say yes to Alfred, who's no oil painting, it has to be said. If that were true it would make it easier to understand why Alfred indulges her the way he does. What do I know?

"Actually," Rita says, "I've got a Chinese compass in the car, so I could help you finish off this room, if you like? To bring the energy flow in here into perfect harmony."

I glance down, put up a hand, and pretend to pick at something on my shirt, try to hide my face so they won't see how angry I'm becoming, do it quite instinctively: this is fucking incredible, not only is the bitch totally nuts, but she's acting as if I don't even live here, talking and carrying on as if I have no say in how my own house should look.

"Ah, so you just *happen* to have a Chinese compass with you?" Alfred says with a little laugh. "What a coincidence." He turns to Ingrid and she laughs too, they know that Rita had this all planned and evidently they both think it's sweet. I'm obviously the only one who feels this is way beyond the pale.

"Well, maybe not a complete coincidence," Rita says, flashing her prima donna smile and sipping her wine.

"No, but it's always good to get some tips," Ingrid says. "Isn't it, David?"

I knock back the rest of my wine.

"Absolutely," I reply. I give her a quick smile, then I set my glass on the table and wander out into the hallway. I have to get out of here before I say or do something I'll regret, I don't fucking believe this, how dare they, they think they can walk in here and do whatever they like. I go into the kitchen, take one of the wooden spoons from the earthenware pot on the counter, snap it in two with a dry crack, drop the two pieces back into the pot, go back into the hallway, and put on my shoes. I have to get out for a while, away from here, take a walk, get some fresh air, or maybe nip over to May-Britt's for a quickie, feel the need to punish Ingrid right now, and fucking May-Britt would certainly satisfy that need, it usually does.

Then Ingrid appears.

"The gloves are on the steps if you need them," she says, smiling at me, she doesn't seem to have noticed that I'm angry, I look at her, don't answer straightaway, I frown, what gloves? "The work gloves," she says. "I used them earlier when I was weeding the flower bed."

And then it dawns on me.

"What do I need work gloves for?" I ask, pretending not to understand.

"Aren't you going to rake out the gravel?"

"No."

Now she looks confused.

"Ok-ay . . . so where *are* you going?"

"For a little walk, I could do with some fresh air," I say, as if it's the most natural thing in the world, even though her mother and father have just got here.

"*Now?*"

"Yes."

"But . . . um, what about dinner?"

"I told you I was sick of being stuck in the kitchen," I say, shrugging and turning my palms upward. "I told you, if it's to be bouillabaisse for dinner, your father will have to make it, remember?" I say, still smiling and gazing at her as if I'm honestly wondering whether she remembers what I said. She opens her mouth, then closes it again, looking more and more confused.

"But David . . . you can't go *now* . . . we have guests . . . what am I supposed to say to Mom and Dad?"

Therapy session

Time: October 16th, 2006
Place: Fjordgata 69d, Trondheim
Present: Dr. Maria Hjuul Wendelboe, psychotherapist;
David Forberg, patient

DAVID: [*laughs*]

MARIA: What?

DAVID: You sound so surprised.

MARIA: I was surprised, I admit it. But go on.

DAVID: Well, as I say . . . at first being with her seemed to liberate certain sides of me, sides I had suppressed. Because . . . May-Britt's impetuous, free and easy, you know, she's adventurous, curious, and she likes to experiment, to explore. In all ways, actually . . . And naturally I found this exciting. I found it exciting to try new things in bed. I found it exciting to go with her to buy hash . . . and then go back to her place and smoke a joint. All of this, even being dragged to a karaoke bar by her . . . that she was so different from me . . . it made me feel alive. I used to tell her that too: I don't know where I've been all my life, I would say. But I gradually began to see that the very opposite was the case. I was in the process of losing myself, not finding myself. I continually caught myself doing things I really didn't enjoy. And I'm not talking here about being unfaithful to Ingrid, although the thought of that did bother me, of course. I mean more specific things . . . like going to a party with her friends. I pretended to enjoy it, I tried to convince myself that I enjoyed it, but I didn't. The thing is . . . the way they talked, the clothes they wore, the music they listened to . . . rap and hip-hop, you know . . . it all made me feel so old and that in turn made me . . . I was constantly being reminded of why I came to be in this situation in the first place. I was constantly being reminded that my affair with her was a way of trying to satisfy a longing to see myself as young, that this was in fact the midlife crisis we spoke about earlier. And so I began, in a way . . . to rebel. Oh, it sounds so silly. I hate to admit it, but I started acting like even more of an old fogey than I actually was. I insisted on listening to Radio P2 when she was in the car, no matter what was on: arts program, political discussion, or Folk Music Hour from the Jew's harp festival in Førde—whatever. And I would roll my eyes at young guys with their jeans slung so low you could see their underwear, you know? That sort of thing. And once, when she asked me to get her some chocolate, I bought her a Banana Cream bar. Knowing full well, of course, that this was the chocolate equivalent of peppermint candies or camphor lozenges. That did the trick, I tell you. Old folks' chocolate, she called it, and at first she was sure it was a joke, that I had another chocolate bar behind my back . . . [*laughs*] But she just found all of this charming. To begin with at any rate. And that simply annoyed me even more. Because I wasn't doing it to charm her. On the contrary, I wanted to make it clear that we didn't belong together, that I didn't need her, at least I think that's what I wanted to do. So my jokes became more and more caustic. I . . . oh, I behaved so badly sometimes that I blush to think about it. I made fun of her in front of her friends, I . . . yeah, well . . . and the thought that she might not be nearly as impetuous and free-spirited as I liked to imagine made me even angrier. Increasingly I had the feeling that she was making fun of me by going around flaunting her youth the way she did. In ten years' time she would be a plump, harassed new mother with cellulitis, an unhinged pelvis, and a dwindling libido. I knew it, right? I'd seen Ingrid go through that phase and I'd seen her friends go through it too. So to see May-Britt swanning around, taking her youth for granted when I knew that it would soon be her turn, well, that . . . for some reason that bothered me so much that . . . yeah.

MARIA: This is a very different account from the one you've given before.

DAVID: Well, things look very different now that we're no longer together. That said, though . . . from the day I met May-Britt and slept with her for the first time I think I knew that it would never work. But I tried not to think about that, I wanted to enjoy it for as long as it lasted. [*laughs*]

MARIA: You sound almost happy.

DAVID: Relieved, certainly. I'm glad the matter has finally been resolved. And that we both agreed it was all for the best.

MARIA: Might you also be relieved because you no longer need to be afraid you might hurt her?

DAVID: I never came close to hurting her, Maria.

MARIA: You've just been describing your growing anger.

DAVID: Maria, I've said it before and I'll say it again: I've learned my lesson, I will never hurt another person again, let alone kill anyone. No matter how angry I might be. [*pause*] I have to go soon.

MARIA: It's only eleven o'clock.

DAVID: I know, but May-Britt's going on holiday, she's leaving straight from work and I have to pick up my things.

MARIA: So when do you have to leave?

DAVID: She said she'd come and let me in during her lunch hour. So I'll need to leave in about five minutes, ten at the most.

MARIA: But . . . what about Susanne's project? All those letters! I'd been thinking that we might spend some time on that today.

DAVID: May-Britt will be away for two weeks. I have to pick up my things before she leaves. You know—my computer, my clothes . . .

MARIA: Yes, of course, but . . . it's just that I . . .

DAVID: So you've read the letters?

MARIA: Of course. And they're . . . they're so . . .

DAVID: They're quite fascinating.

MARIA: I don't know how to describe it, this . . . project. I've never heard of anything like it. Never. And you knew nothing about it?

DAVID: Not a thing. The ad saying I'd lost my memory was published on the fourth of July and I was out of the country at the time. I came home on the eighth or ninth or something like that, but I went off to the cottage the very next day so I didn't have time to read a single newspaper. I knew nothing about it until the package arrived in the mail on Monday.

MARIA: There's so much here for us to come to grips with. We'll have to talk more about it next time, but . . . what I'd really like to know is . . . how did you feel when you learned that Berit wasn't your real mother? And that you actually have family in Bangsund? A mother, a father, a brother . . .

DAVID: I wanted to find out whether it was true or not before I would allow myself to feel anything whatsoever.

MARIA: But both Paula and Marius wrote about this. And there's nothing to suggest that they had anything to do with each other.

DAVID: Surely you don't believe that what we've read is precisely the same as what was in these letters when they were sent?

MARIA: What do you mean?

DAVID: Well, Susanne has obviously tampered with them. Polished them. Rewritten bits. Added here and deleted there. [*pause*] Don't tell me the thought never struck you?

MARIA: Are you suggesting that Susanne wrote them all herself?

DAVID: Tampered with, I said. All of these letters are full of information that Susanne could not possibly have known unless she had spoken to or corresponded with these people, so I've no doubt that they did reply to her ad. And some of them probably wrote at length and in detail. But Susanne has deleted and inserted and embellished and rearranged. I know her style and her sensibilities so well, so I'm in absolutely no doubt about that.

MARIA: But why would Susanne go to the bother of doing that?

DAVID: Because she thought it would make the letters read better, I presume.

MARIA: But it also renders their content less true.

DAVID: You do realize she's thinking of having them published?

MARIA: No, that never occurred to me either, actually.

DAVID: Of course she is. Her revenge won't be complete until they're in print. And I can't see any publishing house issuing them as they were when she received them. The project itself, a staged case of amnesia, might well catch the interest of a publisher, but to have any hope of getting it accepted and published, she would need to rewrite the letters, improve upon them, and make them more readable.

MARIA: And how do you feel about the image of you presented by the various letter writers?

DAVID: I recognize a lot of it. Specific incidents, particular people and places . . . but if people think they know me and my life after reading what these individuals have written, they're wrong. Not just because Susanne has embellished their accounts and not just because their descriptions of me are riddled with projections, misrepresentations, misremembrances, lies, half-truths, and God knows what else, but also because hardly anyone who really knows me has written to give their version. My pals from my ten years at university, for example, or old friends and colleagues from the arts scene in Trondheim . . . none of them replied to the ad. Nor did any of my best friends from my years in Namsos. I played soccer until I was seventeen, for instance. I trained four times a week and played on the weekends, but there's nothing about that in any of the letters. Even though it was a big part of my life. The thing is, you see . . . that we all have a way of viewing the past through the lens of the present. And since everyone who wrote to me knew that I was a writer, that's what they've tended to focus on: how I came to be a writer. Which is why they all end up describing me as a typical artist and bohemian. But I wasn't, you see. Or, okay, yeah . . . I was that too. But when I look back on my childhood and adolescence, what I remember most is the soccer.

MARIA: And the people who could have described all that, why didn't they, do you think?

DAVID: It was a tiny personal ad, hidden among hundreds of others. So it's not entirely unlikely that some of those who could have written in simply missed it completely. And a lot of those who did see it must have guessed that it was some sort of prank. A joke . . . or an art installation, if you like. [*pause*] So it's hardly what you'd call a representative selection of sources. And not only that . . . those who did write to me also exaggerated the parts each of them played in my life. They give the idea that they knew me much better than they actually did. I mean, take Ole, for example. I had at least three, no four, better childhood friends than him, even though Mom and I lived in the granny cottage on his family's farm for a short time. Ole was the kind of guy I would have said hi to but wouldn't have stopped to talk to if I met him on the street. And Jon . . . well, we did have sex a few times, that's true, but honestly, from his letter you'd think we were both lovers and bosom buddies. The truth is that we occasionally ran with the same crowd during our second year in high school, that's all. But for Jon to give the impression that we were inseparable for three years, well, I mean . . . obviously that's because he's gay. I was his first homosexual partner, right? I was the first person with whom he dared to be himself, it's as simple as that. And once you know that, it comes as no surprise that he remembers and writes the way he does. But the fact is that he doesn't mean, and never has meant, as much to me as I did, and do, to him.

MARIA: It would have been interesting to speak to Susanne.

DAVID: I've tried to contact her, but she doesn't answer her phone or reply to my e-mails. I even went to her apartment. Twice, in fact. But it looked as though she had gone away. She's probably sitting in some hostel in South America.

MARIA: Do you think she's scared?

DAVID: Possibly.

MARIA: Does she have any reason to be scared?

DAVID: [*laughs*] You don't think I would do her any harm?

MARIA: Would you?

DAVID: For the last time, Maria: I've learned my lesson. You can relax. And anyway, I'm not even angry at Susanne. Not at all. The more I think about it, the funnier it seems . . . it's a brilliant hoax, actually. A huge practical joke. [*laughs*]

Trondheim, June 25th, 2006. An American invasion

I walk more and more slowly the closer to home I get, I really don't want to go back at all, I'm in a bad mood and I want to be alone, but there's no way around it. I flip up the latch and push open the gate at the side of the house, walk across the grass and up to the steps. The kitchen window is wide open, I can hear Alfred humming some well-known aria in there. He's doing the cooking, of course, self-appointed gourmet that he's become in his old age.

"Have you got the corkscrew out there?" he calls.

"Yes," Ingrid calls back from the other side of the house, it sounds like she's out on the veranda with Rita.

I shut my eyes, take a deep breath as I put my hand on the door handle, stand like that for a second gathering myself, then I press down the handle and step inside to be met by the lovely, delicate aroma of fish. I slip off my shoes in the hall and go through to the kitchen, hear the steady swish-swish of the dishwasher, otherwise all is quiet. I glance around: the trimmings he's used for stock are dripping into the sink from a colander and there are a couple of shreds of carrot peel on the floor, apart from that everything is spick and span. The bouillabaisse is almost ready by the looks of it. He hasn't added the fish yet, but the small chunks on the dish next to the stove won't need any more than two or three minutes, so he's probably been waiting till I got back before doing that. I get a glass from the cabinet, go to fill it from the tap, then stop, stare at the pot of bouillabaisse. The pack of table salt is right next to me. On the spur of the moment I put the glass back, pick up the pack of salt, flick open the little metal dispenser that serves as a lid, and pour salt into the soup. I gaze at the salt streaming out of the pack, but then it's like I suddenly come to my senses: what the hell am I doing, what the hell have I done, this is not right, I have to leave now, I have to get out of here before he comes back into the kitchen. I put the pack of salt back down exactly where it was, tiptoe into the hall, slip on my shoes, and nip out of the door again. I jog across the grass, open the gate, and step out onto the street, walk briskly for the first few yards, then gradually slacken my pace, my heart pounding so hard it hurts. I sit down on a road sand box with a rough black tar-paper lid, I need to calm down, need to act casual, no one saw me, no one heard me either, I'm sure. I shut my eyes, put a hand to my brow and run it back over my head, hear the rasp of hair being scraped across the scalp. I sit like that for a minute or two, breathing steadily—in and out, then I jump up and start to walk back, but wait, no, better to go around the block and come in from the other side, no one will suspect me of having been anywhere near the kitchen if I come in from the veranda. "Good thinking, David," I murmur to myself, "good thinking," then I turn and walk off in the other direction, feel the fear gradually loosen its grip on me and a gloating satisfaction take its place, I'm almost looking forward to getting home now. I cut through the gap in the hedge and stroll through the garden as non-chalantly as I can. The smell of cigarette smoke grows stronger and stronger as I approach the veranda, I put my hand over my mouth and give a little cough. Alfred has gone back inside, I see, but Ingrid, Rita, and Sara are still out on the veranda.

"Hi," I say, smiling at them, not too brightly, though, nothing that could be mistaken for anything but a perfectly ordinary smile—I mustn't seem too cheerful, have to act normal.

"Hi," Rita says. She's sitting there with her legs crossed and a cigarette in her hand.

"Did you get the saffron?" Ingrid asks quickly, not even taking the time to say hi, she's told her parents that I had to run down to the store to pick up saffron for the risotto for tomorrow or something like that, she's come up with an excuse for me walking out as soon as they arrived and now she's desperately trying to put me in the picture before I give the game away by mentioning where I've actually been. I look at her, all set to betray her little charade and show her up in front of her mother by pretending not to know what she's talking about, but I don't.

"Sold out, I'm afraid," I say.

"Oh, bother," she says, smiling at me, grateful to me for going along with her little lie, I can tell.

I come up onto the veranda, sit down with them.

"But *Mom*, why can't you drive me over to the party?" Sara asks. She picks up the tea bag from the saucer in front of her, twines the white string around the bag, squeezing it in the middle, and a trickle of tea runs onto the table. I open my mouth, about to ask her what she means by making such a mess, but I don't get the chance.

"Sara, I've had some wine," Ingrid says. "We've all had some wine."

"Okay, well, you'll just have to pay for a taxi for me!" Sara announces. She drops the tea bag onto the table with a little splat and sits back in her chair, arms crossed, pouting sulkily, she's so fucking spoiled it's unbelievable, it's downright sickening sometimes, I don't know why Ingrid lets her get away with it.

"I'll pay for a taxi, Sara," Rita pipes up. She tilts her head back, opens her mouth wide, and blows a smoke ring. I look at her, feel like saying something about it maybe not being such a good idea to reward Sara for talking and acting the way she's doing. Had it been Henrik, I would have, but not when it's Sara.

"You can come and sit down," I hear Alfred say. I turn around and look at him, standing there with his coathanger shoulders, hands on his hips and his upper half kind of stooping forward. The resemblance to a bird of prey is incredible, he looks like an eagle or a vulture hunching its wings.

"What are we having again—was it bouillabaisse?" I ask, pretending not to know what he wound up making, to make it sound even less likely that I've been in the kitchen.

"I had to improvise a bit with what I could find in the fridge, but yes, it's a sort of bouillabaisse," he says, making himself out to be something of an artist in the kitchen. It's a habit he's acquired over the past few years, presenting himself as a freewheeling cook, tasting and trying rather than relying on books and recipes in order to produce good food.

"Mm, I can't wait," I say brightly, to let everyone know I'm looking forward to dinner. I glance at Ingrid as I get up, she looks pleased and thankful that I've pulled myself together and am in such a good mood now, she looks at me and smiles as she picks up her wine glass and gets to her feet.

We go in and sit down at the table.

"It smells wonderful," I say.

"Mm, really good," Sara says.

"Now, there's bread there," Alfred says, "and rouille here." He nods to a little bowl of thick deep-yellow sauce.

"Lovely," I say.

"Right, well, help yourselves," Alfred says as he sits down, talking and acting for all the world as if he's the host and we're his guests and not the other way around, he's got some fucking nerve, American to the core. I study him, feel a little thrill of anticipation at the thought of what's about to happen, but I smile happily and smack my lips as if I'm looking forward to digging in.

"Thank you," we chorus.

I hear the faint scrape of chair legs being pulled in.

"By the way," Alfred says, "I noticed that you used a garlic press earlier on when you were making osso buco."

I eye him as I ladle soup into my plate. He's about to come out with some critical comment disguised as well-meaning advice or something of the sort, I know he is, that's him all over.

"Uh-huh," I say.

"You don't think that makes it a mite bitter?"

"Bitter?"

"Well, when you use a press, you release the juice, you see, and that can give a rather bitter taste. Or I think so anyway," he says, trying to make it sound as if this is a conclusion he has arrived at all on his own, although it's bound to be something he's picked up from a fancy cookbook by some celebrity TV chef, but it bolsters the gourmet image he's endeavoring to create. I bet he could never tell the difference, though.

"Oh, really? I didn't know that," I say. Usually it makes my blood boil when he carries on like this, but now I just grin cheerfully.

"It can be all right for cold sauces, but even with them it's better to chop the garlic," he says, continuing to lecture me, and I nod and smile and say, "Oh, really." I know what's going to happen as soon as we start to eat, so allowing myself to be lectured like this only serves to make my little performance all the more credible, and his downfall will be all the greater if he has first had the chance to present himself as the master chef and me as his apprentice. The prospect sends a gleeful shiver down my spine.

We start on the soup.

I glance at Alfred as he takes his first spoonful. He promptly removes the spoon again and sits there, mouth working. I don't think I've ever seen a face change color so quickly: a couple of seconds is all it takes for his mug to turn bright red. A great bubble of laughter wells up inside me at the sight, but I don't let it show, try to keep my face as straight as I possibly can as I taste the soup. It's absolutely inedible, so salty that it hurts my mouth, but I smile and try to look like I'm enjoying it, so the others will think I'm just being a polite son-in-law who would never complain about the food.

Utter silence.

"Ingrid, could you pass me the water?" I ask, although the carafe is as close to me as it is to her and I could easily reach it myself, but I want to alert everyone else to the fact that I need more water, thereby making them aware that they're not alone in feeling the soup is way too salty. I smile innocently at Ingrid as she fills my glass.

"Thanks," I say and take a big gulp.

Silence.

The veranda door is open. From farther down the street comes a loud bang, it sounds like something else being thrown into the dumpster from the second floor of the green house.

Silence again.

"Yes, well, we're all going to be nicely cured at this rate," Rita suddenly declares.

I look at her, almost burst out laughing, but manage to hold it in. Alfred doesn't appear to find this at all funny, he sits there, red-faced and fuming, staring at the soup.

"I don't understand it," he says, setting his spoon down in the plate. He crosses his arms and shakes his head in vexation. "I tasted that soup just before I made the rouille, goddammit, and it wasn't particularly salty then."

"That's odd," I say, pretending to be equally mystified. Ingrid and Rita are both sure that Alfred has simply added too much salt and if I talk as though he can't possibly be to blame for the soup being inedible they'll think I'm just trying to be a loyal son-in-law.

"Well, in any case, we can't eat it," Alfred says. He picks up his napkin, dabs his lips with it, and drops it into the soup. I watch as the paper immediately starts to soak up the liquid, a dark stain begins to spread, and the napkin is gradually drawn under as it gets heavier and heavier.

"Yes, it was rather, er . . . salty," Ingrid says.

I pick up my water glass. If we're to have dinner today, then clearly the simplest and most obvious solution is for me to finish making the osso buco, but it's not my place to suggest it, they're all going to have to come crawling back and ask me please to carry on where I left off when Alfred turned up with his damn fish, it may be childish of me but, hey, I'm not that big a man, I revel in the moment as I drink the last of my water and set the glass down again.

Pause.

"What about the osso buco?" Rita asks at long last. "That's ready, isn't it?"

I raise my eyebrows slightly and try to look as though it hadn't even crossed my mind that we could have the osso buco instead.

"Uh, yeah," I say, with a wag of my head. "But . . . well, would you like to have that?"

"Oh, yes, I love osso buco," Rita chirps.

Ingrid nods.

"Okay, but it'll take a little time, because I have to make the risotto and the gremolata first," I say, sounding almost as if I'm apologizing for the fact that they'll have to wait.

"Can you be bothered, David?" Ingrid asks.

"Yes, of course," I say, yawning and stretching a little: I'm tired, but I guess I could just about manage to spend a half hour or so in the kitchen, that's the message I'm trying to send, that I'll do it for them.

"Wonderful," Ingrid says.

"Would you like me to help you with it?" Alfred asks.

"No, stay where you are," I say, planting my hands on the table and pushing my chair back a little more, hear the scrape of chair legs again.

"Are you sure?"

"Positive."

"Okay," he says.

"And they all breathed a sigh of relief," Rita murmurs as she picks up her soup plate and pours her helping back into the pot. You can say a lot of things about Rita, but she does have a sense of humor and again I nearly burst out laughing, but I don't—Alfred really isn't in the mood for this, he gives Rita an astonishingly dirty look. My best plan is to carry on playing the well-mannered son-in-law.

"Oh, come on, Alfred!" Rita cries. "Can't you take a joke?"

And Alfred pulls himself together. He sniffs loudly and stares at the table, shaking his head.

"I simply don't understand how it can be so salty."

"Well, you obviously forgot that you'd already added salt and you've salted it again," Rita says.

I look at Alfred as I get up, he shakes his head again, but he doesn't seem to have a better explanation so he doesn't say anything.

"Okay, then I'll just take the chance to pop into the bathroom and get myself ready," Sara says. "I've got to be going soon!"

"In that case I would advise anyone with a normal bladder to get in there first," I say.

"Asshole," Sara says, glaring at me.

I give a little chuckle.

"Let me pour this soup down the toilet before you lock yourself in there, Sara," Ingrid says.

I take a sip of wine, then go out to the kitchen and make a start on the risotto. I take the bowls of sliced mushrooms, Parmesan, and onion from the fridge, get out a pan, and begin to fry the onions in a little olive oil, stirring them until they're soft and translucent and sweet smelling, then I get the garlic press out of the drawer, place two cloves in it, and hold it over the pan. I'm all set to squeeze the press when I hear Alfred's and Ingrid's voices, they're coming this way and if Alfred sees me using the press rather than chopping the garlic he's sure to say he detects a slight bitterness when he tastes it, I know he will, even if he doesn't notice any difference at all, and I won't give him that satisfaction. I draw the pan off the heat, winkle the garlic cloves out of the press, and drop it into the cutlery drawer, then I place the garlic on the chopping board and take out a knife.

I glance around casually as they come in.

"Just put the pot down there, Ingrid," Alfred says as he turns on the faucet and starts to rinse the dishes; globules of grease and the reddish remains of the soup slide off the plates and into the sink where they swirl and eddy a few times before disappearing down the drain. "I'll see to this," he adds.

"Okay, well, if you do that, I'll go and bring in Henrik," Ingrid says. "He's slept almost an hour more than he usually does."

Silence.

"Ah . . . so you don't use stock in your risotto?" Alfred suddenly pipes up.

"Huh?" I say, turning to him. He motions toward the pack of chicken-stock cubes lying next to the chopping board. He's just made a fool of himself by serving bouillabaisse that's been salted to death and yet he has the nerve to tell me how to cook. I know I ought to use proper stock instead of a stock cube, I usually do and I like to think that it tastes better, but still, it would befit him to be a little humbler, to say the least.

"Yeah, I forgot to buy things for stock, I'm afraid," I say.

He nods as he picks up another plate and holds it under the running water.

"Oh, a stock cube will do just as well, I'm sure," he says, giving me to understand that it's not ideal, but that he's magnanimous enough not to make a big thing of it, the risotto won't be as good with a stock cube, but it should be just about edible, that's what he's implying. He looks at me, smiles, then turns and exits the kitchen.

I pick up the chopping board and take it over to the stove, am about to brush the garlic into the pan, but stop half-way, no, fuck it, I'm going to press some more garlic and put that in, and Alfred will never know. I'm going to chuck the chopped stuff and use pressed garlic in both the risotto and the gremolata, and then we'll see whether he detects that blasted bitterness he keeps harping on about. I open the door of the cabinet under the sink, dump the chopped garlic into the trash can, then turn back to the counter, peel some fresh garlic cloves, press them over the pan, and scrape the pulp into the translucent onions, grin to myself as I do so. I pick up my wine glass, but it's empty so I open a bottle of Ripasso and fill it to the point where Alfred, Rita, and Ingrid would consider it vulgar—a feeble protest against all of their absurd middle-class conventions, but a protest nonetheless and I grin smugly to myself, almost tempted not to take a drink just so that the glass will still be as full when they come back into the kitchen, but I'm too thirsty for that. I take a big drink, put the glass down, and carry on with the cooking, put the osso buco on a low heat and make the risotto and the gremolata, I'm mildly tipsy already, I can tell, I'd better go easy on the alcohol, I didn't get much sleep last night and I've hardly eaten all day, so it'll go straight to my head. I open the drawer, take out the bag of nuts—I need to eat something, nuts may not help that much, but they'll at least take the edge off my hunger, because I'm starting to feel really hungry now. I take a handful of nuts and toss the whole lot into my mouth, dust the salt off my hands as I munch them.

Quiet for a while.

Then Ingrid appears.

"Will dinner be long?" she asks.

I quickly lean forward and hide the pack of nuts behind the granite mortar.

"It's ready," I say, turning to her and smiling, endeavoring to seem as relaxed as I can. "I'm just waiting for the hot water to run out, then we can eat."

She unwinds the white hair tie from her wrist and pulls her hair up into a ponytail, frowning at me as she does so, not sure what I mean.

"Sara *is* eating with us, isn't she?" I ask.

Ah, now she gets it, she closes her eyes and sighs.

"Oh, David, don't start all that again," she says as she pinches the hair on either side of the hair tie, lifting it closer to the top of her head and tightening and lengthening the ponytail. "And besides, Sara's out of the shower, she just has to put on her makeup and finish getting ready and then she'll join us," she adds.

"Yeah, well, she's already emptied the tank once today, so there might not have been that much hot water in it anyway."

"*Da*-vid!" she sighs, her shoulders slumping and her hands dropping to her sides.

"Oh, for heaven's sake, I'm only teasing you!" I say, in a slightly offended voice.

"Okay, okay," she says, blinking. "But I was wondering

whether we shouldn't just start. Mom and Dad have hardly eaten anything all day, they're both starving. And I don't think Sara would mind."

"Okay, well, if you take the risotto and the gremolata, I'll bring in the osso buco," I say.

And we go through.

"Dinner is served," I say, setting the pan of osso buco on the table. "At last!" I add, with a little dig at Alfred, hinting that we've been left to go hungry for so long because of his inedible bouillabaisse, but he doesn't seem to catch it, he's too taken up with Henrik. Rita is on her feet, holding Henrik and stroking his back and Alfred is standing behind her, acting silly, lifting the baby's chubby cheek slightly, then letting it go so that it flops and quivers gently. He laughs and murmurs something about what a lovely little boy he is, then does it all over again. I go through to the kitchen to fetch my wine glass and come back.

"All right, people, come and get it!"

"Thank you," says Alfred.

"Thank you," says Rita. She sets Henrik down gently on his blanket, places the baby gym over him and he promptly reaches up, groping for the little plastic figures.

"I hope it's okay," I say. I almost add: "Even if I did have to use a stock cube instead of the homemade variety," but I manage to restrain myself.

And then we all dig in.

"Delicious, David," Rita says.

"Glad you like it," I say.

"Very nice," says Alfred.

I look at him.

"It wasn't lacking a little in salt for your taste?" I ask. It just comes out.

A second's pause and then Rita and Ingrid burst out laughing, it was funny and they can't help it, I have a little chuckle as well, only Alfred doesn't laugh, he tries to smile and show that he can take a joke, but it doesn't quite work, he's clearly not amused.

"Sorry, Alfred. I didn't mean to rub salt in the wound," I say, chuckling again, it's a really awful, silly joke and I might not have laughed at all if Alfred hadn't gone into a sulk, as he so obviously has. A grown man sitting there sulking over such a little thing, I can't help but laugh. And Rita and Ingrid are laughing as well.

"Ooh, where do I get them from, one zinger after another," I say, laughing and shaking my head as I pick up my glass. "Well, cheers, people!"

They raise their glasses, drink their wine.

"What have you actually got in the gremolata?" Rita asks.

"Parsley, grated lemon rind, anchovies, and garlic," I say.

"It doesn't sound all that great when you describe it, but it's delicious along with all the rest. Isn't it, Alfred?"

"Hm, the gremolata is very nice," he says without raising his eyes.

"D'you really think so?" I say, looking down at my plate again as soon as I've said it, humming and grinning slyly to myself in a way designed to make him wonder what I'm grinning at. I can't help thinking of Tony Soprano when I do this, it's the sort of thing he might have done, a joke after his own heart.

"What?"

"So it's not bitter?" I ask, chuckling to myself as I spear a chunk of meat with my fork, I go to pop it into my mouth, then stop, lower my fork, and look at the others. "Only . . . I had actually chopped the garlic, you see, exactly as you said I should, so it wouldn't taste bitter. But then, once you'd gone, I tossed the garlic I'd chopped and used the garlic press instead. Simply to check whether there was something to it or whether it was just your imagination, you know?"

Alfred looks me in the eye for a moment, then he raises his brows, gives a little shake of his head, and carries on eating.

Silence.

I hear the scrabble of a bird on the gutter directly above the living room window.

Silence again.

"You didn't?" Ingrid gasps, looking at me and giving me a surprised and rather hesitant smile, a smile that says she's hoping I'll say no, no, of course I didn't.

"I only did it for a joke," I say with a little laugh and see her smile instantly fade. She sits there with her mouth open, staring at me in horror. "And anyway," I go on, "it's always interesting to find out whether it's true that a dish tastes more bitter if crushed garlic is used or whether we just think that because all those master chefs on TV say so." I glance around the table and give another little laugh. But no one else laughs, Rita and Alfred keep their eyes on their plates and quietly carry on eating and now Ingrid is eyeing me contemptuously. She holds my gaze for a second or two, then looks down at her plate, pink cheeked, and fiddles with her food for a little longer than normal before lifting the fork to her lips. She's embarrassed by me now, I can tell by her face, she thinks I've gone too far this time, they all do obviously. I don't fucking believe it, I don't see how this joke is any worse than the jokes about how salty his bouillabaisse was, Rita and I both made jokes about his bouillabaisse and daddy's girl Ingrid actually dared to laugh at our jokes, even though she must have seen that Alfred was not altogether happy with us teasing him. Possibly because the oversalted bouillabaisse could be described as an accident, while my little test exposed Alfred once and for all for what he is: a snob and a poser. Maybe that's why they think I've gone too far, what the hell do I know. There's silence, broken only by the soft rattling sounds from the baby gym, I stare at my plate, eat a little faster and chew a little harder than usual and suddenly I feel my cheeks starting to burn, shit, now I'm blushing as well, there's no fucking reason for me to blush, but I am and it annoys me. I sit for a moment and then I start to hum softly, do it quite instinctively, attempting somehow to ward off my embarrassment by summoning up and overplaying my don't-give-a-shit attitude, trying to behave as I imagine Tony Soprano would: sitting here blushing and smirking and humming while I wolf down osso buco and risotto.

Nothing for a few moments, then: "Wow, look at that lady!" Rita exclaims.

I turn and see Sara emerging from the bathroom, looking just about as awful as she did the last time she went to a party, she's wearing so much makeup she's almost unrecognizable, her face is totally stiff.

"What?" Sara says, looking at me.

"Nothing," I say, grinning. I shouldn't grin but I can't help it.

"What are you looking at me like that for?"

I give my head a little shake.

"Oh, it's just that . . . well, you look exactly the way you looked the last time you went to a party. And when you got up the next morning, you left your face on the pillow,"

I say with a strained little laugh meant to take some of the sting out of this barb, but it doesn't work, no one else is laughing, they merely sit there, stoney-faced.

"Would you . . . oh!" Sara cries, acting every bit as insulted as the reaction of the other three allows her to be, she knows they're on her side, so she pushes out her bottom lip a little farther, pouting as demonstratively as only an indignant teenage girl can. She stalks around the table, sits down, and proceeds to help herself in an ostentatiously aggressive manner.

"Don't mind him, Sara," Rita says. "He's just trying to hold back time."

I look at her, still grinning.

"Oh, really, that's possible too now, is it? There's so much we don't know, us non–New Agers," I say. She sticks her chin in the air, maintaining her haughty prima donna expression, but that hit home, she hates it when people make fun of all that New Age crap, so I know that hit home.

"No, David, it isn't," Rita says. "But that's never stopped anyone in midlife from trying."

"And what's that supposed to mean?" I ask.

"Well, anyone who has a midlife crisis is trying to hold back time."

"Ah, so I'm having a midlife crisis, am I?"

"You're quite evidently having a midlife crisis," Rita says. "Sara's makeup is a reminder to you that she's growing up and that in turn reminds you that you're getting old. That's why you get so upset and resort to making fun of her. You're scared of dying, it's as simple as that."

"Wow, so you're a psychologist too now, Rita? I didn't know that," I say with a strangled little laugh, trying to sound as though I'm enjoying myself and find this absolutely hilarious, but it doesn't really work, it comes out as more of a snarl than a laugh.

"Oops, I think I touched a sore spot there," she says. She takes a pinch of Maldon sea salt from the little ceramic bowl and sprinkles it over her veal. "Sorry, David, that's just how I am. All us O types are the same."

"O types?"

"Yes, people with blood type O. We're outspoken and self-assured," she says.

"Good heavens. I didn't know you were a Nazi," I say, grinning at her.

"What?"

"Wasn't it the Nazis who developed the theory of a link between personality and blood type?" I say. She puts down her knife and fork and stares at me, she's stung and she can no longer hide it, the haughty prima donna mask dissolves and her face seems to come alive. I glory in that sight, grin sardonically as I pick up my wine glass and take a drink.

"Do you know something, David? In Japan that link is common knowledge and generally accepted. There, if you go for a job interview, you're asked what your blood type is, dating agencies match people according to their blood types, and some kindergartens split the children into groups according to their blood type."

"Japan and Germany, weren't they allies during the Second World War? I seem to remember that," I say, taking an unholy delight in my own remark and smirking as I set my glass down on the table again. "What's my blood type, do you think, Rita?" I ask.

"A," she says without a second thought.

"Gosh, yes," Ingrid says, turning to me. "It *is* A, isn't it?" She turns to Rita: "How did you guess?"

"Most antisocial individuals are type A," Rita says.

"Rita," I say, "forty-eight percent of all Norwegians are type A."

"I know," she says. "And we all know what foreigners say about Norwegians. We're reserved, introverted, and when we get on a train or a bus, we always pick a seat as far away from other passengers as possible. Take a trip to America, for example, and you'll see what I mean."

I simply sit there staring at her for a moment.

"Er . . . Rita, are you serious? Are you really that gullible?" I ask, raising my voice slightly. I arch my brows, grin, and shake my head to emphasize my amazement that a grown woman could believe such a thing, how ludicrous that is.

"Oh, relax, David," Ingrid says, looking mildly surprised and giggling tentatively, attempting to smooth things over and convince everyone that we're having a lovely time, feelings may have run a bit high there for a moment, but it's all a good laugh, really, that's the impression she's trying to give.

"All things considered, I think I'm actually remarkably relaxed," I say. "I mean, I just found out that my mother-in-law is a Nazi."

"Stop saying that!" Rita snaps. "I mean it!"

"Jawohl!" I say, looking her in the eye for a second and grinning, then I lean over my plate, laugh and shake my head as I stick my fork in a piece of veal, no one else is laughing, they all think Rita's New Age theories are a load of bullshit too, but they seem to want to shield her from the truth, that's why they're pretending to take her seriously, but I'm damned if I'm going to play that game any longer, I refuse to conceal how unbelievably stupid this is. I pop the meat into my mouth, still grinning, chew briskly.

Silence reigns and then, all of a sudden, I feel my cheeks start to burn again, there's no reason for me to blush, but fuck, here I am, blushing again. I sit for a moment, then pick up my wine glass, I shouldn't drink so fast, I should take it a little easier, but I don't, I knock back the rest of the wine in one long gulp and set the glass down with a loud clunk, push back my chair, and get up.

"Where are you going?" Ingrid asks. "David?"

I look at her, smile stiffly.

"To the bathroom, to take a dump," I say. I know how crass and tasteless she finds language like this, neither she nor her parents can abide such breaches of style and etiquette and I see all three of them instantly recoil in disgust. I smile to myself as I walk off, I don't need the bathroom, I just need to get away from them, if I sit at that table a moment longer I'm liable to do something I'll regret, so I need to get out of here, need some time to myself, time to calm down. I push open the bathroom door and go in: it's like stepping into a sauna, I don't fucking believe it, Sara has forgotten to open the window again and it's so stuffy and steamy in here I can hardly breathe.

"Sara!" I yell, I know I shouldn't yell, but I do, I can't help it, I'm livid, but I sound almost jolly, I almost sing out her name.

"Yeah?"

"Could you come here, please?"

"What is it?"

"Just come here!" I say, drawing myself up and crossing my arms, a big smile on my face. The next moment I catch sight of something bobbing about in the toilet bowl, it looks like a wet wipe and a couple of Q-tips. If I've told her once, I've told her a thousand times not to throw wet wipes and Q-tips down the toilet, but she doesn't fucking listen, it's no use, I simply can't get through to her, it drives me mad, so it does, it drives me screaming up the wall. I clench my fists and shut my eyes, tense the muscles and squeeze them so hard it hurts, feel as though my eyeballs are being pressed back into my brain. I stay like that for a moment, then open my eyes again.

And here she comes. She gives me that studiedly languid teenage-girl look of hers, she's always the same, trying so hard to look as cool and blasé as possible.

"Yeah?" she says.

"You forgot to open the bathroom window again," I say, smiling, as if I'm doing her a favor by informing her of this oversight.

"Huh . . . ? Yeah, well, couldn't *you* have done it?"

"Oh no, no," I say with a little laugh.

"But you're *in* there, all you have to do is reach out your hand and open it."

"That's not the point," I say. "You'll never learn to do it yourself if I do it for you every single time."

"Oh, my gawd," Sara mutters. She marches straight past me and over to the window. "So I forgot to open the window, so what, it's not exactly a disaster," she says, flicking up the hasp and shoving the window open.

"Of course not," I retort. "The tsunami in Thailand was a disaster. The Holocaust was a disaster. There's absolutely no comparison. Although as far as the latter is concerned I'm sure Madame Göring in there would strongly disagree." I'm absolutely livid, but my voice sounds strangely bright and cheerful, it's like it's not even my voice. I look at her, smile pleasantly.

"Oh!" Sara cries, sticking her tongue out at me. She flounces past me, looking as if I make her want to throw up.

"Hang on a minute," I say. I point to the toilet bowl. "How many times do I have to tell you: Q-tips and wet wipes go in the trash can, *not* down the toilet. They'll clog it up."

"Yeah, yeah."

"Kindly don't say *yeah, yeah*. When you say *yeah, yeah* like that, you make it sound as if I'm nagging at you for no reason, but I'm not."

"No-*oo*."

I look at her, anger coursing through my veins, I feel as though my insides are melting and floating around in my stomach. I'm this close to opening my mouth and roaring right in her face, but I don't, I simply stand here, with this pleasant smile on my lips.

"Sara, dear, I'm well aware that I'm not your father, but I do pay my fair share of the bills in this house and hence I have the right to set some rules as to what you may and may not do here." I'm even calling her "dear" now, my manner becoming more and more amiable the angrier I get. "Remove the Q-tips and the wet wipe from the toilet and put them in the trash can, please," I say.

"You've got to be kidding."

"Nope," I say.

"They're down the toilet, no way am I picking anything out of the toilet," she says, her voice rising.

"Well, you shouldn't have chucked them in there then, should you?" I say, laughing shortly.

"I don't care, I'm not sticking my hand down the toilet, no way am I doing that."

"Ah, so you think someone else should do it for you, do you?"

"Oh, stop it, will you!"

"No, I won't, sorry," I say. I shut my eyes and shake my head, still smiling pleasantly. "Come on, Sara."

Her mouth falls open, as if she can't believe her ears, as if she simply cannot believe I mean what I'm saying.

"Excuse me—have you lost your mind?" she cries. "I am not sticking my hand down the *toilet*, it's gross."

"Well, you should have thought about that before you decided to throw things in there instead of in the trash can, which is only a couple of feet farther away," I say, keeping my tone soft and light. I'm seething inside, but I smile at her. "And anyway, you can use rubber gloves, there's a pair hanging over there." I nod to the yellow gloves hanging limply over the rim of the wash bucket sitting next to the cabinet.

Then Ingrid appears in the doorway.

"What's going on here?" she asks.

"He's trying to force me to stick my hands down the toilet," Sara howls, looking aghast at Ingrid.

"Huh?"

"I forgot and threw some Q-tips and a wet wipe into the toilet and now he's forcing me to take them out again."

Ingrid turns to me, she doesn't say anything straightaway, just stands there looking equally aghast. She opens her mouth, then shuts it again as if lost for words.

"Oh, right, so yet again *I'm* the one with the problem, is that it?" I ask, raising my eyebrows at her, still smiling brightly and that throws her, I can tell, that I seem so cheerful. She looks at me and frowns, she doesn't know what's got into me.

"Oh, come on, David," she says. "Of course she doesn't want to stick her hands down the *toilet*, she thinks it's disgusting."

"Oh, she does, does she?" I say in that soft, light voice. "Well, I suppose I'll have to do it then," and without more ado I take a step forward, bend down, and plunge my hand into the toilet bowl. There's a little splash and I feel the cold water close around my hand.

"*David!*"

"Yes?" I say, looking up at her, still smiling brightly as I grope around in the toilet water. She just stands there gaping at me, she thinks I've lost my mind, I can tell.

"What's the *matter* with you?"

"What's the matter with *me*?" I ask. How can she ask me that? I fish out the Q-tips and the wet wipe and straighten up, stand there smiling with toilet water dripping from my arm and hand. She just gapes at me, more convinced than ever that I've lost my mind and I rejoice at the sight, I hate their posturing and their snobbery, I hate all the middle-class etiquette, all the conventions, and I hate all the self-control and self-denial necessary to comply with that code of conduct. I hate it with every fiber of my being and it's so fucking wonderful to go totally crazy, to rebel against all they stand for, all they believe in, it feels so good and so right.

"She . . . she threw a wet wipe and a couple of Q-tips into the toilet, what's the big deal?" Ingrid says.

I look at her in feigned surprise.

"Oh," I say blithely. "Well, if it's no big deal I might as well put them back." I toss the Q-tips and the wet wipe back into the toilet, looking at her and smiling so brightly and broadly that my lips feel as though they're about to crack, mustering all the madness I can now. Ingrid doesn't say anything, she's speechless.

And then Alfred appears as well, stands in the doorway regarding us.

"What's going on?" he says.

"We're trying to clog the toilet," I say, beaming at him.

"What?"

"We're busy clogging the toilet," I say, as if deliberately clogging a toilet is a perfectly normal, everyday thing to do and he just stands there looking bewildered, also speechless. He looks at me, then Ingrid, then me again. "No, I don't know *why* we're doing it either. But then, as we know, common sense counts for nothing in this family," I say, getting in a little dig at Rita's unutterably stupid New Age theories while I'm at it, then I turn to Ingrid, still smiling. "Should I put any more in, do you think, or is that enough now?"

Alfred merely shakes his head and walks away.

"David, this isn't funny," Ingrid says.

"Oh, no?" I say.

"David. I . . ."

"Hang on a sec, just let me close this window," I say, and I step over to the window and close it. "I don't know who keeps letting all the steam out after they've showered. Don't they realize the bathroom will dry out if they do that?"

"David. Stop it!" Ingrid cries. "What's the *matter* with you?"

"Damned if I know. But I'm sure I'll be fine once your mother's plant starts to do its work," I say, reaching out and stroking the plant with my finger.

"Stop it, for fuck's sake!" Ingrid says, really shouting now.

I've never seen her lose control in front of her parents, but she looks very close to doing so now. She glares at me, but I'm not about to quit now, I give her a quick little smile, then lean to the side and look past her.

"Rita," I call merrily, almost singing out her name just as I sang out Sara's name.

"Yes?"

"How long d'you think it will take for your plant to re-dress the energy balance in the bathroom?"

"David." Ingrid says, lowering her voice again, almost whispering. She gazes at me with wide, grave eyes, her mouth slowly dropping open, she honestly has no idea what's got into me, she's genuinely shocked, she stares at me as if she doesn't recognize me. A moment and then I seem to come to my senses, as if whatever had taken hold of me suddenly loosens its grip, as if I've woken from one waking state into another, and I just stand there staring back at her, but now I have to give myself a shake, because this won't do—just because you're aware that you're act-ing like a madman is no guarantee that you are not, in fact, mad, so I really have to pull myself together now, I mustn't let this go any further, there's no telling what might happen if I do that. There's total silence, I nearly say that I was only joking, but I don't and I won't, not a living soul would ever believe that this was all just an innocent joke, it's so implausible that Ingrid could never even pretend to believe it. We stand there looking at one another for a moment, then I simply turn away and wash my hands, I can't think of anything to say, I'm suddenly very tired, feel myself starting to sag.

"Not so much as another drop of wine!" Ingrid snaps.

I turn and look at her. She eyes me sternly, she thinks

I'm drunk, she thinks it's the wine that made me say and do the things I've been saying and doing, but it wasn't, the drink may have gone to my head a little bit, yes, but that's not why it happened, it happened because they've been bugging me all day and I finally had enough, but for her to put it down to me being drunk is just a way of absolving herself and putting all the blame on me.

"Not a drop!" she repeats. There's no sign that she realizes how offensive her parents can be, it doesn't even seem to have occurred to her, she simply assumes that I've been acting as I have because I've had too much to drink. She locks eyes with me for a second or two, then turns on her heel and walks out. I watch her go: the straight back, the taut neck, and the ponytail bouncing in time to her firm step. A split second and then I feel my anger returning, but it's a different sort of anger this time, a heavier anger, something large and weighty seems to break loose and start to shift. I turn off the tap, dry my hands, and go back into the living room. It sounds as though Alfred and Rita are asking Sara how it feels to be Henrik's big sister, they're laughing and trying to look and sound as though everything's fine.

I sit down, my limbs heavy.

"Oh, my God, he's adorable," Rita coos, nodding at Henrik. He's lying on his back, gurgling and reaching eagerly for the figures on the baby gym.

"Isn't he?" Ingrid says.

"So, have you decided on a date for the christening?" Rita asks, eyes on Henrik as she says it. She gives it a moment, then turns to Ingrid and smiles. I look at the table, feel that heavy anger stir again, feel it rise up inside me. Rita knows very well that I don't want Henrik christened, she knows my stepfather was a vicar and that being brought up by him has made me proof against any sort of preaching or religious coercion, she knows I'm a dyed-in-the-wool atheist and the last thing I want is to enroll a tiny, unwitting infant in any church. I have nothing against Henrik joining a church when he's old enough to decide for himself, of course, but I would never cram a religion or a philosophy down his throat and Rita knows I wouldn't, that's exactly why she's asking, it's her way of paying me back. She talks as if she takes it for granted that we'll have Henrik christened and the moment Ingrid announces that I don't want him christened she's going to act all disappointed or huffy or preferably both, oh, yes, and she'll probably pretend to feel sorry for Ingrid, poor Ingrid, whose husband won't allow her to have her child christened. Ingrid swallows what she has in her mouth and gives her mother a quick smile, looking rather flustered now.

"Not yet," she says, bending her head over her plate again. I stare at her, what the hell is she saying: not yet? What the hell's that supposed to mean? She's talking as if we do actually intend to have Henrik christened after all.

"So where's it to be—Nidaros Cathedral?" Alfred asks as he picks up the pepper mill and holds it over his meat. I hear the soft rasp as he twists it. "Nidaros Cathedral, the eleventh of September, now wouldn't that be . . . oh, yes!"

"Oh, that would be wonderful," Rita says before Ingrid has a chance to reply, sounding much too enthusiastic, she's only saying that in order to cast me in an even worse light when it becomes clear that I don't want to have Henrik christened, I know she is, I mean how dare I deny her that pleasure, how can I be so cold, so heartless, that's the seed she wants to plant in our minds—in fact, who knows, she may even be trying to blackmail me into it, maybe she's stupid enough to think she can make me do what I know several of my friends have already done, that she can force me to chicken out and let my child be christened just to keep my parents-in-law happy.

"Yes, well, we'll see," Ingrid says, sounding more and more flustered, trying to dodge the issue.

"Oh, by the way, Alfred, I'd like a new sewing machine for my birthday," Rita says. "The old one's broken and I'll need a machine so I can take in the christening robe."

"Do you have to take it in?" Alfred asks.

"Oh, yes. Jonathan was a lot bigger than Henrik, you know, he was the spitting image of you."

"Hm," Alfred says, nodding. "I think we can afford a new sewing machine."

I look at them, not quite sure what they're talking about, but then it dawns on me, they expect Henrik to be christened in the robe Jonathan wore for his christening, fuck, they've got it all planned, they've already discussed the whole fucking thing with Ingrid, they've talked her into having Henrik christened, I realize that now, so that's the "robe" Rita was referring to earlier, I did wonder. That's why Ingrid was so quick to divert our attention, she hadn't seen anyone outside, she said that only because she didn't want to discuss the arrangements for the christening while I was there, she knows how opposed I am to having Henrik christened so she'd rather talk to me about it in private. She's probably told her parents not to mention the subject in front of me, but they pay no mind to that, of course. They know it's harder for me to refuse when they're here and that's exactly why they've brought it up. I stare at the table, anger coursing through my veins, my heart beating faster and faster. And it's no coincidence, of course, that Alfred suggested holding the christening on the eleventh of September, they're actually trying to pressure us into having Henrik christened by making it known that they would like his christening to also be a way of paying tribute to Jonathan. Their precious Jonathan, the hero who died in the terrorist attack on 9/11, they're making it known that they would like him to live on through Henrik, knowing full well, of course, that this will make it difficult, not to say impossible, for me to say no to having Henrik christened, I mean how can I refuse them something that would mean so much to them, that's how they want me to think, it's a fucking violation, an attempt by them to use Henrik as a means of fulfilling their wish to honor Jonathan. It's such a rotten fucking trick it's unbelievable.

"Oh, dear, I get all choked up just thinking about it," Rita sighs. She puts up a hand and wipes away a tear, she's fucking crying now, she'll do whatever it takes to make it hard for me to deny them what they want. "I don't dare to think what I'll be like in the church," she continues. "I'll probably howl my way through the whole thing." She gives a sad little laugh and wipes away another tear, it's unbelievable, she has no fucking shame, that woman, and neither does Alfred, now he's started as well, swallowing hard, clearly overcome. And I'm sure he is, they've never got over what happened to Jonathan and I realize this must be tough for them, but that's just too fucking bad, this is manipulation, it's a violation and I won't have it, I won't put up with it, it makes me so damn mad, I grab the wine bottle, fill my glass to the brim as if it were a glass of milk, eye Ingrid levelly, and send her a stony grin as I raise the glass and take a great gulp, I don't give a shit what she says

I can or can't do, I'll do what I like, I'll fucking show her, but she doesn't look at me, she doesn't dare to meet my eye, she gazes at her plate for a moment, then glances up at Rita and Alfred.

"Oh, by the way, David has a new book coming out in the spring," she says, abruptly changing the subject. She knows how angry all this christening talk makes me and she's probably hoping that talking about my new book will put me in a better mood, partly because—like everyone else—I like to talk about myself and my work and partly because it gives her a chance to boast about me to her parents.

"Oh, really?" Alfred says. He puts a hand to his mouth and gives a little cough, as if composing himself after his earlier display of emotion.

"How exciting," Rita remarks. She's acting as if everything is back to normal again, smiling at me now, both she and Alfred are smiling at me, partly, I suppose, because they think I've made a fool of myself and they want to help me regain my dignity, so to speak, and partly because they think their manipulative tactics are well on the way to succeeding. They've presented their plans for a christening without a word of protest from me so I imagine they're feeling quite relieved now, and not only that, they know that the longer we sit here and the better the mood around the table becomes, the harder it will be for me to put my foot down, which makes it all the more important to act as if everything in the garden is lovely again.

I take a big drink of my wine, let out a long, indignant harrumph as I set down my glass.

"So what's it about?" Alfred asks.

"It's hard to explain," I say and leave it at that, I don't

feel like talking about my book so I refuse to be drawn, but he's not to be put off.

"I've often thought that . . . as a writer you're in a unique position to address important issues," he says, biting into a piece of meat.

"But you think I'm not making proper use of that position."

He wags his head as he finishes chewing, making it clear that that is exactly what he means, he doesn't want to come right out and say it, but now that *I've* said it he can't really deny it, that's what that wag of the head is saying, Christ, he's got some fucking nerve. I look down at my plate, use my knife to nudge some risotto onto my fork, and pop it into my mouth.

"Well, I do wonder why there are so few Norwegian authors writing about the major issues of our day. We've been at war with Afghanistan since 2001 and with Iraq since 2003, we live under the constant threat of terrorist attacks, but hardly any of them are writing about that. Our democracy is under threat, our freedom is under threat, but the very ones who have a way with words, who could actually make a difference, they're not even getting involved in the debate. Now that I do not understand."

"Why do you say *we*?" I ask.

"Sorry?"

"Why do you say *we* when you actually mean the United States and Americans?" I say. "Whether you like it or not, nine out of ten Norwegians are against the invasion of Iraq. And what you're really asking, I guess, is why don't I express support for the US in my writing, right?" I know I have to watch what I say here. I know what a touchy subject this is for Alfred, Rita, and Ingrid, I know how personally they take it and how quick they are to construe any criticism of the US as criticism of and an insult to Jonathan, because seeing Jonathan as a victim of the battle between good and evil helps them to make sense of and derive some comfort from his death, and for anyone to question this view and argue that things aren't that black and white is tantamount to saying that he died in vain, that he was merely a random casualty rather than a victim of a battle between good and evil, and the inherent senselessness of such a thought is more than they can bear. But I'm damned if I'm going to take any of their bullshit either, my writing is the only thing in the world I care about as much as Henrik and Ingrid and if there's one thing I cannot abide it's people trying to tell me what I should or shouldn't write.

"Not at all," he says. His voice is cool and calm, but he's starting to lose his temper, I can tell, he lowers his knife and fork and looks me straight in the eye. "Let me ask you a question. Would you dare to write about Islam in a way you knew would offend fundamentalist Muslims?"

I consider him, initially uncertain how to reply, I'm not entirely sure where he's going with this.

"I don't know," I say. "The problem has never come up for me."

"I bet you anything you wouldn't dare," he says. "But the very fact that you don't respond with a clear and unequivocal *yes*, that you hesitate and have to think about it shows that democracy is under pressure and that the fight to safeguard freedom of speech concerns you. In fact, as an author, making a living from writing exactly what you feel like writing, I would say it concerns you in particular."

I eye him steadily as I lift my wine glass and take another swig, feel that heavy anger coursing through my veins.

"So this is not really about whether you agree with me or not," he goes on before I can answer. "What I'm trying to say is that this is the biggest, most crucial issue of our time and we all have a duty to take a position on it."

"Don't tell me what to write . . . ," I say.

"What?"

"Fucking Yank," I add under my breath, staring in fury at my plate.

Silence.

"David?" Ingrid says softly, sounding almost frightened.

"What did you say?" Alfred asks.

I place my knife and fork on the edge of my plate, rest my elbows on the table, and lean forward, look him in the eye.

"Let me ask *you* a question, Alfred," I say, throwing his own words back at him and mimicking his American twang. "Suppose I had been a victim of incest as a child and that as an adult I had used literature as a form of therapy, that I had written myself back to health, so to speak. In such a situation how do you think I would feel if someone were to tell me that unfortunately this topic wasn't important enough and that I really ought to write about Islamic fundamentalism or the climate crisis, or famine in Africa, come to that?" I say, my voice shaking slightly. I glare at him. He hadn't seen this coming, I can tell, he doesn't say a word, simply sits there staring at me, openmouthed. "Because, you see, I would take that as an insult, it would be like being abused all over again, in fact!" I say, my hand trembling with fury as I pick up my glass and take a sip of wine. "So, what I'm trying to say . . . *Alfred*," I drawl, echoing him again, "is that every writer has their own, often very personal, reasons for writing as they do and one should be extremely fucking wary of telling them how to write or what to write about," I say, my hand still trembling as I set down my glass. "Most people understand that," I say. "But not you, because you're an American and like most Americans you think you can do whatever you want whenever you want—yeah, and not only that, you actually think the people you order around value your input," I say, sneering at him. "You and Rita, you come waltzing in here . . . you try to dictate what we should eat and drink, you try to dictate how we should decorate our house, how we should arrange our furniture, you try to dictate whether and when our baby should be christened and . . . and . . . even the subject matter of my books, even *that* you think you can dictate. And then, to top it all, you expect us to be grateful to you. You simply assume that you always know best and that you're doing us a favor by telling us what to do, so you expect us to fucking well thank you, you expect us to bow and scrape and be polite, obedient guests in our own home," I say. "Just as the majority of Americans expect the Iraqis and the Afghans and the people of all the other countries they've invaded and destroyed throughout history to do."

"I was simply trying to get a discussion going, David," Alfred says. "I simply wanted to talk about a subject on which not all sane, sensible individuals may necessarily always agree. But you . . . there's simply no talking to you. You either sit there saying nothing no matter how much you might disagree with what's been said, dismiss it with some flippant or sarcastic remark, or blow your top completely . . . as if you want to scare us and put us off saying anything that might be in any way controversial."

I raise my glass to my lips again.

"Yeah, right, because you Americans are renowned for

being such good listeners, for talking first, shooting later," I say, grinning and knocking back the rest of my wine. I set the glass down on the table with a clunk.

"See, there you go again, resorting to sarcasm rather than having a decent discussion," Alfred says, still playing the brilliant conversationalist. It's so fucking grotesque: he's the most pompous, arrogant person I've ever met and here he is, making himself out to be the soul of humility. "And if you feel that Rita and I take liberties and try to tell you what to do, why don't you just say so instead of waiting until the mood turns sour like this?"

"You know why, Alfred," I say.

"No, actually, I don't."

"Oh, no, of course not," I say. I cross my arms and give a little snort, look him in the eye. "If it weren't for the fact that you paid for the house I'm living in and the car I drive, and that I could never be a full-time writer without your support, I obviously wouldn't have put up with any of the crap that I have put up with," I say with a wrathful grin, saying exactly what I think now, it's too late to turn back anyway.

"David," Ingrid says.

"What?" I say, sitting back in my chair with a jolt and flinging out my arm. "I thought the idea was for us to be honest and open with one another, I thought this was the time for a proper conversation," I sneer. I take a breath, then turn to Alfred again. "You're so self-righteous and so smug it's un-fucking-believable, you think people respect you, look up to you. That everybody wants to be like you. But what you don't realize is that people actually despise you," I say. "If you weren't the one with the money and the power, no one would give a shit what you said or thought or did," I say. I'm not entirely sure whether I'm talking now about Rita and Alfred or Americans in general—probably both, I mean there are clear parallels here: Rita and Alfred's behavior is a perfect allegory for American foreign policy, there are so many similarities that it seems almost contrived, concocted, too good to be true. And maybe that's exactly what it is, maybe I'm exaggerating how American Alfred and Rita are, maybe I view them in the light of my own prejudices against Americans, not to say in the light of my own thoughts on American foreign policy, maybe the writer in me has detected some parallels that are, nonetheless, real and maybe these have formed the basis for an allegorical way of thinking that has become deeply rooted in me and that I have molded most of what Alfred and Rita say and do to fit, maybe I've been wrong all along, what the hell do I know, I'm tired and I'm drunk and I can't be bothered thinking about it.

Silence.

"Now, who's for dessert?" I say, my voice suddenly bright and cheerful. I don't know where it comes from, that voice, it just comes.

Time: October 22nd, 2006
Place: Fjordgata 69d, Trondheim
Present: Dr. Maria Hjuul Wendelboe, psychotherapist;
David Forberg, patient

MARIA: You still haven't managed to get hold of Susanne.
DAVID: I didn't try again. She must be out of the country.
MARIA: What about the other people who wrote to you, have
you been in touch with any of them?
DAVID: No.
MARIA: Not even with your alleged biological parents?
DAVID: No. [*brief pause*] What is this?
MARIA: Oh, it's just . . . you seem so unfazed by it all. You
don't even seem particularly curious.
DAVID: Well, I am a little curious, of course. But it's not like
I'm losing sleep over it.
MARIA: I find that a little odd, to be perfectly honest.
DAVID: Find what odd?
MARIA: That you're taking this as lightly as you appear to be.
It doesn't fit with the image I have of you.
DAVID: Oh, really.

MARIA: David. You seem to have an answer to just about everything. It's quite amazing how quick you are to come up with an explanation for everything we talk about. No matter what the subject you have some theory to hand. And whatever you say, it always sounds so logical and so obvious.

DAVID: That sounds like a compliment, but I fear it's not meant to be.

MARIA: No, not really. You see . . . I'm usually wary of allowing my clients to put forward theories and explanations for their own actions and those of others and during our first sessions I did try to stop you when you started to do this. But I gradually began to see that this side of you could be a key to understanding rather than an impediment to it. So I let you carry on.

DAVID: And what conclusion have you reached?

MARIA: Well, for one thing, I'm often left with the feeling that you're trying to manipulate me. You seem to want to take over my role as therapist. You present one analysis or interpretation after another, leading me to think that you're determined to control everything that goes on in this room. That you're determined to control the image of yourself. And for that very reason I find it hard to believe that you can be so untroubled by the picture of you painted in the eight letters sent to you, letters that you are also convinced Susanne is planning to have published. It . . . it doesn't add up. [*pause*] And when you're at your most controlling, well . . . I'm often left with a sense that there's something—consciously or unconsciously—you're trying to *avoid*.

DAVID: And what do you think it is that I'm—*consciously or unconsciously*—trying to avoid?

MARIA: I'm not sure. But whatever it is, I think it's important in terms of understanding why you became a killer.

DAVID: Is that so?

MARIA: David, you've never said there were things in your
childhood that rendered you incapable of controlling
your temper, not directly, but when you attempt to put
all of your other problems down to your upbringing in
general and your mother in particular, I get the feeling
that you're trying to get me to say it for you. Let's say,
though—just for argument's sake—that you turned out
as you did for very different reasons. What I ask myself
is this . . . why is it so important for you to convince
me—and probably yourself—that it's all your mother's
fault? Is it because you need a clear answer but feel
that the real cause is too hard to talk about? Is it because you want to exonerate yourself?

DAVID: Don't ask me. You're the expert.

MARIA: I know this isn't easy to talk about, David. But it's
very important that we get to the bottom of this. The
first time you came here you were very low. You were
haunted by what you had done, you were drinking
too much, you were ridden with angst, and you were
hardly sleeping. And one of the first things I said was
that essentially our conversations would come down
to the question of what had brought you here. But if
we're to answer that, we can't get away with simply
saying that your mother taught you that you weren't
good enough and that this shaped you into an individual
who overreacts and responds with rage and violence to
the slightest offense. Or that your mother manipulated
you by making a martyr of herself and you defended
yourself by developing a contempt for weakness, which

eventually led to you becoming a killer—to name just two of the many theories you've been priming me to spell out for you. If I simply agree to endorse such theories, I'm only helping you to delude yourself. And if I do that, it won't be long before you're back where you were the first time you came here, I'm pretty sure of that.

DAVID: I don't think so.

MARIA: David, it's not at all unusual for us to form notions of the sort you harbor. There's not much anyone can do about their upbringing, so it's easy to fool yourself into believing that you can't do anything about the scars left on you by that upbringing either. And that saves you from having to do any work, from taking yourself by the scruff of the neck, giving yourself a shake, and actually doing something to change yourself. [brief pause] You know, I often feel that you . . . you're not nearly as certain of your own theories as you pretend to be. For instance, every time you start to talk about your mother and how she's to blame for the way your life has gone, you begin to cough and splutter, as if you feel guilty for what you're saying about her.

DAVID: I do. She was my mother, for Christ's sake. And I loved her, even if our relationship wasn't always an easy one.

MARIA: I realize that. But at the same time it seems to me that you say the things you do because you need a clear answer. It's as though having an answer matters more to you than the answer itself and deep down I think you know that . . . and this, laying more of the blame on your mother than you think she actually deserves, so to speak, I think that makes you feel guilty, that's how it seems anyway. [*pauses*] I'm worried about you.

DAVID: You don't need to be.

MARIA: Ah, but I think I do. Not least now that you have all those letters to think about.

DAVID: You don't need to worry, Maria.

MARIA: What's the matter?

DAVID: Nothing.

MARIA: No, there is something, I can tell.

[*pause*]

MARIA: David?

DAVID: Maria, I . . . I never killed anyone. [*brief pause*] I came to see you in order to do research. I'm writing a novel about a man who has committed a number of violent assaults and eventually kills one of his victims. It's . . . I don't know, like a combination of David Fincher's *Fight Club* and Dostoyevsky's *Crime and Punishment*, you might say. Set in a sated, decadent oil-rich Norway, the inhabitants of which are more dead than alive. I thought it would be a good idea to pose as a thug and a killer and get you to help me discover what factors in my own life could have caused me to turn out like my central character, some repressed experience or trauma, anything. As an author, to have a specialist like you involved in the creative process and then testify that what I've written is feasible and credible is particularly reassuring, as I'm sure you can understand. And I felt that by being on the inside, by posing as a killer undergoing therapy, I could gain greater insight than if I had merely interviewed you . . . and that this would, not least, lend a unique legitimacy to what I wrote. [*pause*] I'm sorry.

I know there's a long waiting list for an appointment with you and that I'm taking up time reserved for people with serious problems . . . it's terribly selfish of me . . . and for that I'm sorry. Truly.

MARIA: That's all right. [*brief pause*] What prompted you to own up to this now?

DAVID: I've felt like a fraud . . . or, how can I put it . . . I've felt bad about it for a while. And I can't bear to keep it hidden any longer. Besides, I think I have all I need now.

MARIA: Okay.

DAVID: Er . . .

MARIA: What?

DAVID: No, it's just that . . .

MARIA: Just what? Was that not the reaction you were expecting?

DAVID: Not really.

MARIA: So how did you expect me to react?

DAVID: Er . . . well, I suppose I thought you'd be hurt and angry and that you'd kick me out. I don't know. Not like this, though.

MARIA: Would you have preferred it if I were angry?

DAVID: Are you trying to tell me that you knew all along? Is that why you're trying so hard not to look surprised?

MARIA: Absolutely not. Your performance has been flawless and I've believed you from the word go. How many people knew about this?

DAVID: No one but me.

MARIA: Not Ingrid or May-Britt?

DAVID: No.

MARIA: Where are you living at the moment anyway?

DAVID: I . . . well, at the moment I'm sleeping on a friend's sofa. While I look for an apartment.

MARIA: Is there any chance at all of you and Ingrid getting back together, d'you think?

DAVID: That's . . . are you trying to confuse me now?

MARIA: Why would I want to confuse you?

DAVID: I don't know. But I'm certainly starting to feel a bit confused.

MARIA: Oh?

DAVID: Yeah—er . . . how come you're asking about Ingrid and me all of a sudden? I just told you, dammit—I came here to do research.

MARIA: Yes, I got that.

DAVID: So why are you carrying on as if nothing's happened?

MARIA: We still have a little time left. Besides, we've got to know each other pretty well over the past few weeks. And I care about you, you know. [pause] But you haven't answered my question. Is there any chance of you and Ingrid getting back together?

DAVID: It's . . . oh, I don't know. I haven't heard from her for a while.

MARIA: You "haven't heard from her" . . . but have you tried to get in touch with her?

DAVID: No.

MARIA: You know, David . . . the fact that you put the onus on Ingrid, that you leave it up to her to decide what will happen to you two . . . I think that says something very telling about you as a person.

DAVID: I just don't want to be the one who's begging to be taken back.

MARIA: But . . . I think I discern a pattern in all of this. Take, for example, the way you shy away from conflict.

DAVID: Shy away from conflict? I've fallen out with just about everyone I know lately . . . including you.

MARIA: Well, a bit maybe. But it's the way you do it. When you feel manipulated and put-upon by Rita and Alfred, you don't take it up with them. Instead you lose your temper and storm out of the house, only then to sneak back into the kitchen and drown the food they brought you in salt. Every single time it comes to a disagreement on something that really matters, you shy away from it, take cover, run away. You don't dare to take a stand and defend it, David. You don't dare to choose. [*waits a moment*] And as far as your relationship with Ingrid is concerned . . . well, it seems as though you didn't want to live with Ingrid anymore, but you didn't dare to end it, so you set out to get her to end it instead. You encouraged her to have an affair, you said and did things you knew would provoke her, and you kept trying to show her that you two weren't actually meant to be together. Take the time when you refused to let her hire a cleaner, for instance.

DAVID: Oh, for heaven's sake, I did that because I needed to make some sort of protest against the smug, middle-class culture she represented and to . . . show who I was. And that I was proud of my working-class background.

MARIA: But that in itself could be seen as a move to highlight how different you and Ingrid were. And that you weren't meant for each other.

DAVID: Oh, give me a break.

MARIA: You did the same to May-Britt. In her case you distanced yourself by exaggerating the difference in your ages. By acting old-fashioned and being impatient of her youthful ways. [*brief pause*] And . . . and as for all the details given and the assertions made in the letters, well, we see exactly the same thing there. It seems very likely that you do in fact have a biological family living not much more than a hundred miles away, David. A mother, a father, a brother! But it's been more than two weeks and you've done nothing to find out more about that. This too you shy away from. You hesitate. Wait. Hold back. [*pause*] And to say that you came here to conduct research . . . the more I think about it, the more certain I am that this was just a pretext, to allow you to receive therapy for problems you wouldn't admit to having.

DAVID: Oh, honestly, Maria. I have never killed anyone.

MARIA: I believe you. That's the genius of it.

DAVID: How do you mean?

MARIA: When you first came to see me, you knew that in these therapy sessions we would try to discover what could have happened in your life to leave you so full of anger that you killed a man for no reason. You also knew that any conversation regarding this question would bring you closer to an answer to your real problems. In other words, posing as a murderer in therapy for research purposes was a way of seeking treatment without admitting to the problems you actually have. Without, in fact, even having to admit that you're receiving therapy. Because that way it's as if it's not really you who's attending therapy. It's the character in your novel, right? *He* is responsible for what you say and do in these sessions. And this ties in, in a way, with your habit of always leaving the big decisions in your life up to other people, or chance, or whatever. You've opted out of your own life, David. You're scared of the consequences of big decisions so you relinquish control and offload responsibility onto others. And . . . well, take what just happened . . .

DAVID: Meaning?

MARIA: Meaning that you had expected a very particular reaction from me when you disclosed that you weren't a killer after all. You expected me to be hurt and angry and kick you out, you said. And that makes me think that you were trying to do the same with me as you did with Ingrid and May-Britt: you were trying, quite simply, to get me to end your course of therapy. Just as you got them to end their relationships with you.

DAVID: Maria, that's ridiculous.

MARIA: I don't think it's ridiculous at all. I think you're well aware that you need therapy, David. But I also think you're afraid of having to face up to what really ails you. And this ambivalence prompts you to do what you always do: leave it up to someone else to make the decisions. You want me to decide whether you should be in therapy or not. You choose not to choose. Always. And . . . and then there's your exaggerated rationality and your great need for control, the way you color-code shopping lists and are obsessed to the point of hysteria with the length of time other members of the family spend in the shower—such things are, I believe, primarily ways of compensating for having relinquished control in all the *key* areas of your life. [*brief pause*] You really have to come to grips with this, David. Before you slide even further into depression.

DAVID: Ah, so I'm depressed now as well?

MARIA: You have great trouble sleeping and you spend half the morning in bed. Your mood is generally low and you have a hard time seeing anything to cheer about in your day-to-day life; you're irritable, moody, and short-tempered, particularly in situations where you see those close to you leading what appear to be good, meaningful lives, because this brings you face-to-face with your own feelings of emptiness.

DAVID: Oh, honestly. On what do you base such an assertion?

MARIA: Take the anger you feel for Alfred and Rita. You talk condescendingly of Rita, the lonely stay-at-home rich-man's wife having undergone a personal crisis, and become positively aggressive when you describe how she found meaning through what you refer to as New Age crap. You're actually mad at her because she has found the meaning in life that you're so desperate to discover yourself. You're always trying to present yourself and Rita as being so different from each other, but to me the similarities between you are far more striking and interesting than the differences. And . . . the anger you display at their wish to honor Jonathan by having Henrik christened on the eleventh of September . . . in Jonathan's christening robe . . . I don't think that anger springs from your aversion to christenings as such, or not primarily anyway. I think it angers you for much the same reason as Rita's New Age theories. I think it angers you because you can see that they find meaning and comfort in the ritual of christening and because this reminds you that you're unable to find the meaning and comfort you seek in your own life.

DAVID: God Almighty, Maria. That is *so* far-fetched. It's the way they go about it that gets to me. Because I feel I'm being steamrollered.

MARIA: I see that. It fits with my description of you as being conflict averse, so that I believe. But I think it has as much to do with being forced to confront your own feelings of emptiness. All in all, well . . . I find the way you think about and talk about Alfred and Rita interesting, David. Especially your relationship with Alfred . . . I mean . . . Alfred and Rita lost their son in the terrorist attacks on 9/11. So they have experienced war and terrorism firsthand, it actually affected them, it touched them personally. And in many ways this jolted them out of their comfortable existence in what you just described as a sated, decadent oil-rich Norway. Alfred sold his clinics and resolved to devote the rest of his life to doing something worthwhile, right? There he was, a changed man, a man who wanted to make a difference. And not only that . . . after 9/11 he insisted on discussing politics with you. I remember you saying you could never be sure when he might try to draw you into a discussion. So it seems to me that what Alfred went through forced him to put his faith in discourse as a means to achieving resolution. And 9/11 was so awful that—for fear of something similar happening again—he instinctively came to believe in involvement, in words, in dialogue . . .

DAVID: Dialogue? The man wanted to bomb Iraq back to the Stone Age.

MARIA: That may be, but there's a difference, surely, between casual remarks he made in a conversation on international politics and the way he talks and acts at an interpersonal level. I mean . . . what he said about Iraq might simply have been an attempt to provoke a discussion with you. Or possibly just a rather careless observation, which you misunderstood. I don't know. In any case: if I understand you correctly, in his encounters with other people he is certainly much more willing to engage in discussion and dialogue than he used to be and this could be regarded as a response to what 9/11 did to him. Alfred has seen and felt the consequences of fanaticism, he has witnessed what obdurate individuals are capable of, how badly things can go when people are left in peace to create and immerse themselves in their own fictional universe. And he quite instinctively behaves in ways we associate with the opposite of fanaticism.

DAVID: To be honest I don't know where you're going with this.

MARIA: It seems to me that this side of Alfred offends you. I think . . . well, for one thing, I think this new Alfred offends you because he dares you to hold opinions on important issues. It's hard for someone as averse to conflict as you are to form—and, not least, to express—clear answers and definite opinions. And for another I think Alfred offends you because he's so . . . how shall I put it . . . because he engages with reality in a very different way from you. It's hard to explain, but witnessing the way in which Alfred has changed has, I think, thrown into relief and intensified an inner conflict you have always felt. You have a great longing for authenticity, David, but you also find it impossible to believe that any one thing is more authentic than any other.

DAVID: Okay. Now I get it.

MARIA: What do you get?

DAVID: This is your take on Susanne's version of me. You know: the romantic who hates romanticism.

MARIA: I may well have been influenced by her letter. I learned a lot about you from all eight letters.

DAVID: [*laughing*] Oh, for heaven's sake . . . you take tiny snippets from different parts of my life and cobble them together to form a theory that, on the surface, seems correct but is in fact pure fiction—just as Susanne and the people who wrote those letters did. Or as Rita does with her ludicrous New Age theories, for that matter. [*brief pause*]. Do you remember how I said a while back that Ingrid fell in love with me because she saw something of her father in me? I said this was true, but that it was also a trite, boring explanation for what brought us together, one that a part of me refuses to believe.

MARIA: Hm.

DAVID: We're always looking for unexpected and interesting explanations for things, I think that's what I said. We don't give a shit whether the explanation is true or not, so long as it's a good one. The same could be said of you when you sit here analyzing your patients. Me included.

MARIA: You're wrong about that. But you have a point, I grant you.

DAVID: A point? During the research for my new book I read about a serious study in which several different psychologists examined the same patients and arrived at the same diagnosis in only two cases out of ten.

MARIA: I know there are some disheartening studies out there. But they're some years old. And if you like I can show you other studies that indicate that things have improved since then.

DAVID: That's as may be. But it doesn't alter the fact that you could pick out any detail from my life and use it to confirm or disprove almost any theory whatsoever.

And hey . . . while you're at it, why not include the dreams in which I turn into an animal. They would slot perfectly into your narrative. After all, it's our ability to make choices that sets us apart from animals, right? If we elect not to choose, we cease, to some extent, to be human, so obviously that's what my dreams must be trying to tell me, that *that's* what's happening.

MARIA: As I say, I'm not so interested in the significance of your dreams in themselves.

DAVID: I'm simply trying to make the point that anything can be used to confirm or disprove anything. I . . . I think you were furious when I revealed that I'd actually been conducting research all along and that this whole therapy thing was a sham. You hide it well, but I think you feel you've been caught out, exposed, and that this . . . what should I call it . . . existentially inspired theory you've constructed on the basis of Susanne's letter is simply a desperate attempt to maintain the illusion that what you are practicing is science. But it isn't. What you do when you sit in that chair of yours is no more scientific than what everyone else does every fucking day. [*laughs*] Incapable of making important choices! Banal women's-mag philosophy, but hey, why not? It's trendy if nothing else.

MARIA: Now you're doing the same with me as you did with those letters, David. But just because everything is liable to fictionalization doesn't mean that everything is fiction. You shouldn't need me to remind you that the nineties are actually over.

DAVID: Meaning?

MARIA: I'm trying to say that what I said about you a moment ago is truer than all the other possible descriptions of you. [*pauses for a moment*] In fact I interpret that last statement of yours as a sign that what I said about you is correct. I don't know if you're aware of it, but you seem to have the idea that everything is fiction and that there's no way of getting at the truth—even when it comes to the question of your identity. And this makes it nigh on impossible for you to decide who to be and what to do with your life. You have no idea what's right for you because you have no idea who you are. You're falling apart, David . . . you're starting to break down into a string of situation-appropriate personas. And . . . and I think all those letters have left you even less sure of who you are. Receiving so many different versions of your life, so to speak, has affected you much more deeply than you are willing to admit. Which makes it all the more necessary for you to dismiss the whole lot as fiction. You try to convince me and yourself that you don't care what it says in those letters.

DAVID: Now, listen . . .

MARIA: But if you find it hard to accept the letters themselves . . . then think about the concern and compassion that lie behind them. Regardless of whether they've been edited by Susanne, the fact is that people who know you, or have known you, sat down and wrote long letters to you. They put a lot of time and energy into them, David, and they did it for *you*. And even if you choose to go on insisting that they are all pure fiction, I think you should at least be willing to accept the compassion invested in them. Because you are worth it, David. Even though you may find it hard to believe, you are worth it.

[*Pause. David clears his throat.*]

MARIA: Here!

DAVID: I don't need it.

MARIA: Take a tissue, David.

DAVID: It's not necessary.

MARIA: But I can see . . .

DAVID: [*raising his voice*] It's not necessary, I said. [*pause*] You know what, right now I feel a bit like Arnold Juklerød must have felt. Do you remember? That guy from Telemark back in the seventies who started out objecting to the closure of his daughter's school and was eventually committed to a mental hospital, diagnosed as paranoid, and condemned as a troublemaker? When he protested against the conduct of the psychiatric profession, well, they said, this wasn't because he had good reason to protest, no, no, it was a clear sign that he was suffering from persecution mania. And when I question your assertions about me, it can't possibly be because I actually have good reason to doubt what you say, no, no, it has to be because I'm some sort of nineties postmodernist, who's incapable of believing that anything is true.

MARIA: David! Don't back out now. We're onto something very imp—

DAVID: Now you're putting yourself above reproach, Maria.

MARIA: David. Listen to me. You have just acknowledged that those letters affected you deeply and that is the first real progress—

DAVID: [*raising his voice*] This is an abuse of power, do you realize that?

MARIA: Take it easy, David. David!

DAVID: Are you scared?

MARIA: Should I be?

DAVID: Oh, don't you just wish I would answer that question. Don't you just wish I would lose my temper right now.

MARIA: Why would I want that?

DAVID: Because that would provide you with even more proof that your theory is right. You hit a raw nerve and I snapped, right? No, Maria, you don't need to be scared. [*brief pause, wry laughter*] Maybe this choice theory of yours is actually a form of projection. Not so very different from that practiced by all the people who responded to the newspaper ad by writing to me. Maybe this is really about your problem with the Methodist Church . . . and whether you should break away from it or not.

MARIA: David. Please . . .

DAVID: [*more wry laughter*] In other words, what you've discerned is your own reluctance to choose, to make decisions, your own aversion to conflict.

MARIA: David. You *mustn't* back out now.

DAVID: But you're wrong, dammit! I'm no more afraid of making choices than anyone else. Simply choosing to conduct this part of my research and then to actually go through with it, that was such a big and such a crucial decision for me that that alone is enough to disprove your theory. Or . . . oh, I've plenty of examples of big decisions I've made. To have a child, for instance. Or . . . or . . .

[*Long silence. We hear David crying.*]

MARIA: You're not alone, David. There are a lot of people who care about you. And you're worth it.

DAVID: [*sighs*] Oh, dear.

MARIA: You're worth that concern.

The sun has just reached the front of the house and the crackling of frost on the paving stones glints up at us. I wheel the baby carriage over to the window and put on the brake with my foot, hear the faint rustle of a magpie hopping across the crisp, frosted leaves in the garden.

"We should let him sleep on, don't you think?" I say.

"Oh, yes," Ingrid says. She brings her hands up to her mouth, rubs them together, and blows on them a couple of times. "He sleeps much better in the fresh air."

I bend over the baby carriage, pull back a corner of the bunting bag, and peer in at Henrik. His pacifier hangs limply from the corner of his mouth. I try to slip it back in, but he curls his tongue and pushes it out again, once, twice, but then he accepts it. I wait a moment, watch as the pacifier works quickly in and out, then abruptly stops and stays glued to his lips. I tuck the corner of the bag in again, slip the little wooden toggle through the loop, and glance up at Ingrid. She sticks her hands in her duffle-coat pockets, hugs her arms to her sides, and hunches her shoulders, chittering.

"Brrr, that wind off the water is bitter," she says, hopping from one foot to the other. "They might not like having the window open."

"How do you mean?"

"Well, we'll need to leave the kitchen window open if we're going to let Henrik sleep on. So your mom and dad will hear him when he wakes up."

"Oh, Ingrid, please," I say.

"What?"

"Can't you just call them Kåre and Klara?" I whisper, no one can hear us, but I automatically lower my voice anyway. "It doesn't feel right to call them my mom and dad. I've only known them a few days."

"Sorry, David. I forgot."

I smile at her.

"I sometimes feel you talk like that because you want things to move a bit faster," I say.

"What's that supposed to mean?"

"Just that you talk as though we were a perfectly ordinary family because you want us to feel and behave like a perfectly ordinary family."

"You may be right," she says, smiling back. "But if I do it's only because I . . . I so want this to go well, David. For your sake."

I go up to her, gently stroke her hair back from her eyes.

"So do I. But if it's to go well, I think it's important that we don't fool ourselves into imagining that things are anything other than they are," I say. I press my forehead to hers and run my thumbs over her cold, rosy cheeks.

"I love you, David," she whispers, putting her arms around my waist. "And I'm so glad you decided to come back to us."

"I love you, too," I say. "And I'm so glad you asked me to come back."

We stand there gazing into each other's eyes for a few moments, then pull apart.

"Come on, let's go inside," Ingrid says. "We've got to be going soon anyway."

I let out a soft sigh.

"Oh, come on. It'll be interesting to see the rest of the plant," Ingrid says.

"I'm sure it will be. I just don't feel like going for yet another sail in the cold. I'd much rather stay here and help with the preparations for Halloween," I say. "Rikard's kids are going to make ghost pizza and blood jelly and stuff."

Ingrid laughs and shakes her head as we go up the stone steps, me first, her a little behind me. It's so bizarre, all this, to find myself in such a situation, it's so unreal, we've been here almost a week, but it's still hard to believe that this is actually happening. I open the door, go through the vestibule and into the hall, study the huge oil painting of my biological grandfather as I pull off my jacket and hang it on the coatrack. There is a resemblance, certainly, although it's not as great as Ingrid would have it, but she's so keen for me to feel connected to my birth family that she tends to exaggerate the likeness, I think—it's another attempt on her part to help me move on, so to speak. I appreciate what she's trying to do, of course, but it's true what I said to her a moment ago: if this is to work, it's important that I don't fool myself into thinking that things are anything other than they are, everything in me is telling me this. I take a step back, drop down onto the green velour sofa, and hear the squeak of tight springs giving under my weight. I sit there bouncing up and down for a moment, then bend down and start to untie my shoelaces. I hear Ingrid closing the front door and a split second later the kitchen door creaks open in the draft.

"It's got nothing to do with you personally," I hear Kåre

say. "All I'm saying is that it's hard to remain mindful of your responsibilities when you're so far removed from them."

"We're creating jobs down there," Rikard says. "Economic growth. Prosperity."

"To be honest I've been in business for far too long to buy that. We pay our workers next to nothing. And we don't pay any tax either! And, as if that weren't enough, we're ruining the local fishing industry, we commandeer waters they've been fishing for centuries, we pollute the surrounding area with salt, antibiotic residue, and all sorts of chemicals, and we're catching prawn spawn in a way that's endangering the fish stocks down there. I read somewhere that for every juvenile prawn we catch, we also catch fifty fish fry, which are then dumped."

"We abide by the existing regulations," I hear Rikard say as I slip my foot out of one shoe, there's a faint pop as my slightly sweaty heel comes away from the leather.

"Oh, I'm sure you do, but then again, there are next to no regulations down there," Kåre says. "To put it bluntly, we're doing things we know we shouldn't be doing. And it's easier not to think about your own ethical and moral failings when the people who suffer the consequences of these are on the other side of the world, because then it doesn't seem quite real, it's only a story. That's what I'm trying to say."

"Dad, this is the first weekend I've had off in God knows how long and I really don't feel like discussing this right now."

"But what we're doing now may come back to bite us later . . . did you know that the mangrove forests we cleared to make room for our scampi farm store five times more carbon on a per-area basis than ordinary rain forests?"

"All the same, I mean it's not that big an area," Rikard says, sounding a little tired and fed up. I put my shoes under the coatrack and get up, look at Ingrid, and smile as we head toward the kitchen.

"Yes, but when you know that any area we work will be destroyed by pollution within five to ten years and that we're forced, therefore, to keep moving around, then we're actually talking about a very large area," Kåre retorts just as I push the door open and look around it. They're over by the countertop, butchering the half carcass of some animal—a roe deer or possibly a stag, I'm not sure. Kåre is bent over the bloody side of meat, cutting out a fillet and Rikard is vacuum packing a haunch or something, he has just finished pressing the air out of the bag and now he's standing there glaring at Kåre. After a moment he catches sight of Ingrid and me.

"Christ, honestly," he says with a hasty laugh and a shake of his head, as if trying to conceal or at least make light of his irritation, trying to appear more exasperated than angry with Kåre. "Dad's suffering from elderly Conservative syndrome, he's become so radical in his old age there's almost no living with him."

"Radical!" Kåre snorts. He eases the tip of the knife under the silvery membrane around the fillet. "Although there's no doubt that I do agree with the Conservatives on most things," he adds. He makes a little incision, loosening the silver skin from the meat, then carefully peels it off with a faintly glutinous ripping sound. He smiles at me as he drops it onto the small glistening heap of trimmings and bone on the counter. I smile back, watch him as he bends over the side of venison, inserts the knife between two ribs, and slides it into the fresh, red meat. It's so strange, he and I are also less alike than Ingrid would have it, but no one could be in any doubt that we're father and son, we have the very same eyes, the very same mouth, it's weird to see an older version of oneself, so to speak. Mind you, this whole thing is so weird: to be here, with these people, under these circumstances, it's utterly unreal. "Is there anything we can do to help?" I ask.

"No thanks, we're nearly finished," Rikard says. He has just written "venison, shoulder, October 31st, 2006" on the vacuum pack and he straightens up and smiles at me as he puts the cap back on the black marker. "I thought we would leave as soon as we're done here, so if you want to change, you could maybe do that now."

"That's probably a good idea," I say.

Then I hear Klara say "Hi." I turn around, only now do I see her and Rikard's kids sitting around the dining table in the far room. Each of the children is working on a small pumpkin, concentrating hard, tongues between their teeth as they cut out the mouths, eyes, and noses, and Klara has just finished scooping out the insides of a larger one, she smiles at me as she picks up the bowl of pumpkin flesh, then she gets up and comes over to us. "Can you keep an eye on them while I get rid of this, Kåre," she says, glancing at him and jerking her head toward the cabinet under the sink.

"Get rid of it?"

"Now, now, dear, there's no need to shout," she says. "I'm right here."

"We don't throw out perfectly good food, dammit!" he says.

"Kåre, please. Not in front of the children."

"It'll do the children no harm to learn that you don't throw out food."

"No, but it doesn't do them any good to hear you swear."

"That'll make a lovely soup for this evening. To have before the venison. Or pumpkin pie, for dessert."

I look at him and smile. It's on the tip of my tongue to say that I could make soup for us to have as a first course this evening, but I don't get the chance.

"What?" Klara says, looking at Ingrid, who's standing there, mouth working, trying not to laugh.

"Oh, it's just that . . . it's exactly like listening to David. It's absolutely incredible. He charges around the house switching off lamps, turning down radiators, and . . . when we have prawns, I have to throw the shells out when he's not looking, otherwise he'll insist on freezing them to boil up for stock later."

"*Really*?" Klara gasps. She kind of sags in the middle and lays a hand on Ingrid's forearm. She gazes at her, wide-eyed and openmouthed for a couple of seconds, then she too starts to laugh.

"Women," Kåre mutters with a glance at me. He chuckles and shakes his head, but he actually looks rather pleased as he turns away and carries on butchering the side of venison, it's good to know he's glad to hear that there's a family resemblance, seeing that makes me glad too.

"I'll happily make soup for this evening," I say.

"Could you?" Kåre asks.

"Sure."

"There, you see, Klara," he says.

"Yes, yes, all right. Go ahead, gang up on me, why don't you," she says. She glances at Ingrid and laughs as she takes a roll of plastic wrap out of the top drawer, covers the bowl, and puts it in the fridge. Just then I hear the skitter of dog claws on the stone tiles in the hall.

"Did you remember to wash him, Marius?" Klara calls, spinning around as she pushes the fridge door shut, but Marius has no time to reply before the elkhound comes bounding through the kitchen door. Kåre has left a couple of meaty deer bones in the bowl under the counter and the dog makes a dash for it, looking neither to right nor left, and dives straight in, chomping and gnawing voraciously, growling low in his throat as he crushes the bones with his back teeth. Then Marius rushes in, still wearing his jacket, hat, and boots. He stomps across the kitchen at much the same speed as the dog, grabs the elkhound by the scruff of the neck with one hand and raps him on the nose with the other. He holds the dog like that, the tight grip on the dog's scruff drawing his eyes back into two narrow slits.

"Marius!" Kåre cries, shocked.

"Don't hit the dog!" Rikard snaps.

Marius doesn't say a word, he doesn't even turn around, he simply stands there holding the dog by the scruff of the neck and glowering at him. The dog still has the bone in his mouth, probably afraid that Marius is going to take it away from him because he gives a long, low growl, curls his mud-colored lips, and bares his teeth. Marius raises a hand, about to hit him again, but he doesn't.

"He doesn't listen," he says, letting go of the dog.

"Hey, he smelled the venison, what do you expect?" Rikard says.

"That's beside the point," Marius says. He doesn't look at any of us, his eyes flick from side to side as he turns and walks back out of the kitchen. I watch him go, what the hell was all that about, that outburst, was it a demonstration of some sort for my benefit? I've noticed how hard Marius tries to make it quite clear to me that he belongs here, he seems to see me as a threat and evidently wants to show me that this is his home in a way that it can never be mine. I've observed several instances of this and punishing the family dog in front of everybody is possibly yet another way of marking his territory, it's something I would never dare to do, something only one of the family can do.

Silence.

"You'll have to excuse him," Klara says softly, with a sad little smile to Ingrid and me. I raise a hand, shake my head faintly, and give her a similar smile in return, to show that I understand how difficult all this must be for Marius and that she doesn't need to say any more.

"It's not easy, and . . . well, he's always been a bit sensitive," she murmurs. She glances back at the children in the dining room, then turns to me again. "A mite highly strung . . . he was just born that way," she adds. I look at her as she pulls out one of the chairs at the kitchen table and sits down, is she trying to disavow any responsibility for Marius being the way he is? By saying that Marius has been sensitive and highly strung since the day he was born, is she trying to tell herself and the rest of us that she did the best she could, but that Marius was genetically disposed to be a bag of nerves, so to speak. Or is this perhaps an attempt to bond with me by reminding me that Marius is not her real son, thereby also reminding me that I *am* her real son, maybe that's what she's trying to do, maybe this is actually an instinctive attempt to get closer to me by pushing Marius away, yes, that has to be it, I get it now, and she sees that I do, I know she does because her cheeks suddenly turn pink, she's embarrassed, partly because she can tell that I feel uncomfortable and partly, I assume, because she feels bad about Marius. She loves Marius as much as she's always done and naturally she doesn't want to push him away just to get closer to me, she didn't mean to say what she said, it just came out, I realize that. I glance down quickly and put my hand over my mouth as if about to cough, use this as a pretext, to make her think I don't see that she's blushing, she might not feel so embarrassed if she thinks I haven't noticed.

"A few months ago he lied to his girlfriend and told her he had MS," Rikard says, placing another clearly labeled, sealed pack of meat on the countertop alongside the others. "And right after that," he goes on, "when he went on a trip to the mountains with some pals, he lied to them and said he was going to collect firewood, then he went down to a river with a huge waterfall just downstream, took off his shoes and left them on the bank, put his cell phone inside one of them, and walked off." He shakes his head and looks at me as if to say: Did you ever hear anything like it? "His pals thought he'd killed himself, right? Well, that's what we all thought. He'd left his car in the parking lot and everything. And when they got in touch with his girlfriend and it came out that he had MS, well, that clinched it, everyone was sure that was why he'd done it. But then it turned out that he'd walked all the way down to his cottage in Namsskogan. Marius denies it, but I think he planned the whole thing. That he actually did want to disappear. To go away and make a fresh start, maybe. Who knows."

"That's . . . ," I say, then I stop, I don't know what to say, so I simply stand there, looking at Rikard and slowly shaking my head.

"But he was found out when I called his biological father in Grong to tell him that Marius had killed himself," Rikard continues. "'Well,' he said, 'he's looking pretty good for a dead man, I'll give him that.' I asked him what he meant and it appeared that he'd just had a visit from Marius. And then we realized, of course, that he'd fooled us all and that he had to be staying at the cottage, right? It's not that far from Grong. Close enough for him to get there in that four-wheeler he keeps up there . . . and if you'd seen that place . . . we went to the cottage to pick him up and . . . well, it was quite a shock, I tell you. Have you ever seen one of those survivalist programs?"

"No," I say.

"Well, there are these TV shows in America about a bunch of pretty paranoid characters who're preparing themselves for various doomsday scenarios. They dry and can enough food to last for months or even years, they build water reservoirs equipped with all sorts of purification systems, construct weapons with which to defend themselves against intruders and, yeah . . . all that sort of thing. And that was exactly what Marius was doing at the cottage, it was absolutely . . ."

"He didn't have any weapons, though, did he?" Kåre asks.

"No, maybe not, but still . . ."

"Oh, come on, don't . . . ," Kåre says, resting the hand with the knife in it on the counter. He blinks slowly and shakes his head. "You make it sound as if Marius is a raving lunatic, but he's not. He's really a very bright, talented young man. He's kind and considerate and . . ."

"No one's arguing with that, Kåre," Klara interrupts,

sounding hurt. She looks hurt too. Marius is her son, she loves him and obviously she doesn't like to be accused of bad-mouthing him. That's why she's hurt, I realize that.

"But he's clearly struggling, Dad. He's . . ."

"Shh," Klara breaks in, putting a finger to her lips.

Someone's coming, I hear footsteps in the hall, turn to look at the door and a split second later Marius comes back into the kitchen.

Silence.

"Oh, don't stop on my account," he says. He knows we were talking about him while he was out of the room, he twists his lips into a tortured grin, his cheeks are pink, and he studiously avoids meeting anyone's eye. I feel so sorry for him, he's suffering so much it's incredible. He takes a wallet from a little basket full of keys, turns, and starts to walk away again.

"Marius, hey," Klara says.

Marius stops.

"Yes?" he says, his voice a little brighter than usual, a voice that's meant to sound nonchalant or something. He looks at Klara, tries to smile and look nonchalant too, but can't quite manage it. His eyes dart this way and that and he both sounds and looks so distressed, poor guy, it's awful to watch. When I read his letter, I got the impression that things were going better between him and the family, but it doesn't look like that at the moment, he seems to find it hard to believe that there's a place for him in the family now that I'm here, so he responds by trying to convince himself and the rest of us that he doesn't need a family anyway, it's a defense mechanism, I suppose, this must be his way of dealing with the threat, because he clearly sees me as a threat. I didn't get that impression from his letter, but seeing me with his mother, his father, and his brother, seeing that we're actually getting along very well and that we like one another, has evidently been harder and more hurtful that he had expected, he can barely stand to be in the same room as me. I'd been looking forward to talking to him, we've been living each other's lives, after all, and we have so much to talk about, but he keeps avoiding me.

"Can't you stay for a chat?" Klara says.

"Not now. There's something I have to do," Marius says, swallowing.

"Oh, what?" she asks.

"Hm?" He heard what she said, he's just playing for time while he invents some errand or other, I guess, hence that "Hm": he's trying to come up with an excuse because he can't bear to be with us.

"Oh, sit down, Marius," Klara says. There's an imploring note in her voice, an imploring look in her eye too.

"Didn't you hear what I said?" Marius says a little louder, still insisting that he's too busy to sit down with us, even though he must know he's not fooling anyone here.

"Yes, I did," Klara says, nodding and smiling stiffly.

Silence.

Then I hear Rikard sigh, he stares at the floor, arms crossed, and shakes his head, says nothing. Marius glares at him for a second or two, looking as though he's about to say something, but he doesn't, he only stands there for a moment, then wheels around and walks out.

Silence again.

I put my hand over my mouth, give a little cough.

"Well, shall we go up and get changed?" I say, turning to Ingrid.

"Yes," she says, smiling hesitantly.

"Great," Rikard says. "We'll leave as soon as you're ready."

"Righto," I say. I turn to Klara: "There's a bottle of formula on the countertop. In case he wakes up and is hungry."

She nods and smiles but doesn't say anything, that little scene with Marius has upset her and she may be afraid her voice will fail her, I don't know. I place a hand on Ingrid's shoulder, push her gently ahead of me out of the kitchen and into the hall, and suddenly there's Marius again, he marches straight past us and into the kitchen. I look around, still walking away, see Marius come to a halt right in front of Rikard.

"Well, at least there's one good thing to come out of all this, Rikard," he says. "You and I no longer need to pretend that we like each other!" Then he turns on his heel and exits the kitchen again, walks straight past us and out into the vestibule, without so much as a glance at us. A moment later I hear the front door slam. He's so troubled, that man, he's a total wreck, I need to talk to him soon, I need to explain that I'm no threat to him. I put my hand on the banister, set my right foot on the bottom step, then I turn abruptly and head back along the hall: I might as well have a word with him now, there's no point in putting it off.

"David," I hear Ingrid say.

"I'll be right back," I say.

"But we'll be leaving in a minute. Dav—"

I open the front door and go out onto the steps in time to see Marius emerging from the toolshed. He comes straight toward me carrying a screwdriver, a wrench, and a couple of bicycle tires.

"Marius," I say.

"Yeah."

"We need to talk."

"Talk away," he says. I look at him, such a smart-ass comment doesn't fit with his troubled, anxious manner and he knows it too, I can tell, his shoulders kind of slump and he looks even more anxious than before, he can't even meet my eye, stares at the ground as he covers the last few yards to the steps. He puts down the screwdriver, the wrench, and the tires, then reaches out a hand to a bike that's propped against the side of the steps, draws it toward him, and turns it upside down.

"Marius, you've nothing to fear from me," I say, then I stick my hands in my pockets and just stand there for a moment, waiting. It's cold, I press my arms tight against my sides. "But if you want me to, I promise I'll leave now and never bother any of you again." The words come out in a rush and I start to worry as soon as I've said it, I don't know if I'm capable of making the sacrifice I've just offered to make, I've known the family only a few days, but to leave now and never come back seems nigh on impossible.

He studies me.

"Why would you do that?" he asks.

"Your letter . . . and all the other letters . . . I don't know, but they did something to me," I say. "I'll be eternally grateful for everything that's happened to me recently. And when I think about the huge risk you took when you wrote to me, well . . . I owe you a lot and I would like to help you, that's all. Because I can see that you're having a hard time of it." It's strange to be talking like this, to be so open and honest, it feels so alien to me and yet absolutely right, these words come straight from the heart, they really do, even though I'm not sure whether I could find it in me to leave here.

"But even if you did leave, you'd still be here," he says. "And anyway, I don't want you to leave. I would never do that to Mom and Dad."

I look at him, so happy to hear him say this.

"You're a good person, you know," I say and it's strange to hear myself being so forthright, unwonted but good.

"Not everybody thinks that," he says with a rather wan smile, then he picks up the wrench, hunkers down, and starts to loosen the nut holding the rear wheel.

"Oh?"

He glances up at me, then turns back to the nut.

"Rikard's convinced that I got in touch with you just to get at him," he says. "He hates me for it . . . he simply can't understand how anyone would do anything they can't make money out of, he thinks everybody's as selfish as he is."

"Get at him how?"

He puts down the wrench, looks at me again.

"Well, now there'll be another legal heir," he says.

"Oh, right."

"I don't mean to scare you, but Rikard is quite . . . well . . . let's just say you'd be wise to watch your back."

I look at him, don't say anything right away, don't really know what to say. Klara, Kåre, and Rikard all warned me, they told me he can be a bit paranoid—more than once they've told me this and it's clearly the paranoid Marius who's speaking here, I've certainly never been aware of any hostility toward me on Rikard's part, anything but, in fact, he's been kinder and more hospitable than anyone might expect in such a situation. I put my hand to my mouth and give a little cough.

"Sorry," he says quickly. "I didn't mean to drag you into this whole thing between Rikard and me, it makes you uncomfortable, I can see that. But I . . . I just had to say it. So now you know."

I nod.

"I need to go and get changed, we'll be leaving in a minute," I say.

"Did you know he tried to have me committed?"

"Committed?"

"To the psych ward. He says I'm sick."

"Oh," I say, attempting to sound a bit more surprised than I actually am. I didn't know Rikard had tried to have him committed, but it doesn't really come as a surprise. I look at him and for the first time he meets my eye unwaveringly.

"Do *you* think I'm sick?"

I swallow.

"Oh, no . . . that's not for me to say," I stammer, but he knows I'm not telling the truth, he knows the thought has crossed my mind, I can tell by his face. He looks at me and smiles.

"That's okay" is all he says.

"I've got to go, but can we talk again later?" I ask.

He doesn't say anything, just glances up at me and nods, then turns to the bike again. I stand there watching him for a moment or two, then go back into the house, along the hall, and up the stairs. As I walk into the guest room, I hear the toilet a couple of doors down being flushed— Ingrid, I suppose, she's not in here anyway. I go over to the window, lean my hands on the sill, press my forehead against the pane, and heave a big sigh. The glass mists up and I smell my breath as it's thrown back in my face, warm and smelling faintly of coffee.

Then I hear Ingrid behind me: "How did that go?"

"Oh . . . yeah, he's in a real state. I tried to tell him he's got nothing to fear from me, but . . . I don't know." I pull away from the windowsill and flop down onto the bed, sit there bouncing up and down on the mattress for a moment. "I'm not sure it was such a good idea to come here," I say.

"Stop it, David," Ingrid says. She flips up the lid of her suitcase and takes out a red fine-knit sweater. "We can't even begin to imagine how difficult this must be for Marius. Anyway . . . you've done what you had to do. None of this is your fault."

I let myself fall back, fling out my arms as I hit the bed, lie there staring at the ceiling.

"I know, but . . . it's like a soap opera, this whole thing. So much emotion, so much drama. I feel like running away, shutting it all out."

"But you can't. They're your family. And you can't run away from your family, no matter how hard you try," she says. She strips off her T-shirt, drops it on the floor, and pulls the sweater over her head. There's a faint crackle of static and the fine hair of her bangs flies up and stays like that for a few moments, it glints in the sunlight falling through the bedroom window. "And it is wonderful, you know, we mustn't forget that."

"What is?" I ask.

"That you've been reunited, of course. After thirty-six years. Just look at your mom and dad. How happy they are to have you here."

"There, you said it again," I say.

"Said what?"

"My mom and dad."

"Yes, but—well . . . they *are* your mom and dad."

"Even so, I'd prefer it if you called them Klara and Kåre."

"You can't run away from it, David."

"You just said that," I say, putting my hands behind my head. "But, like I said, I need a little more time."

She nods, glances down, and unfastens her pants.

"Sorry," she says.

"No need to apologize."

She smiles at me as she pulls down her pants, lifts one foot and slips it out of the pant leg.

"So have you thought any more about what Rikard said yesterday evening?" she asks.

"What exactly?"

"About working for the company," she says.

"Aw, we'd polished off the better part of a bottle of brandy by the time he brought that up, Ingrid. So I think we should take it with a pinch of salt."

She slips the other foot out of her pants and tosses them onto her side of the bed.

"He didn't seem drunk to me," she says.

"Not drunk, exactly, but . . . for heaven's sake, why would he hire me as communications advisor?"

"Well, you're a writer. You're creative. Good with words. Articulate. I'm positive you've got exactly what it takes to be in promotion and image building," she says. She plucks her black woolen long johns out of the suitcase and slides one foot into them. "And besides, you would be perfect for it, the business sector has plenty of critics and you have . . . how shall I put it . . . the courage necessary to do such a job. So I, for one, don't find it at all strange."

"But Rikard doesn't know anything about that, he doesn't know me."

"Ah, well, he may have made a few inquiries, I suppose," she says with a sly little smile. Is she hinting that she and Rikard have been talking about me behind my back? Is that how I'm meant to interpret that sly smile, yeah, I'm sure it is. I push myself up onto my elbows, lie there eyeing her quizzically.

"Oh?" I say.

"I put in a good word for you. But I didn't say anything that wasn't true," she says, taking her black rain pants out of the case, she smiles at me as she puts them on. "Besides, I think he would have offered you the chance anyway. I mean, you're brothers, he has your best interests at heart."

I put my head on one side and breathe a little sigh instead of telling her again to use their names and not keep referring to them as my mom, my dad, and my brother, but it's lost on her.

"You should at least give it a shot, David," she goes on. "I mean it's a great chance to get a better idea of the company and how it works . . . from the inside and the outside. And there are bound to be opportunities for promotion once you learn the ropes," she adds. I look at her—I agree with her up to a point and if such an offer really were forthcoming there's nothing I would like more than to accept it, but at the same time it disappoints me and irritates me slightly that she can dismiss my writing so lightly, it sounds as if she simply can't imagine that I would rather write than work for the company, and that's actually quite hurtful, I mean, I've known her for years so it's no great surprise that she sees it that way, but still.

"Are you about ready up there?" Rikard shouts, from the foot of the stairs it sounds like. I get up from the bed, look at Ingrid as I take off my jeans and get my long johns and hiking pants out of my case. She opens the bedroom door slightly and puts her mouth to the chink.

"Just coming!" she calls, then she turns to me and smiles. "Ready?"

"Just a sec," I say. I do up my trousers, pull on my fleece, and grab my jacket off the stool. "There."

"I love you," she says, and then she leans forward and kisses me on the lips.

"I love you too," I say.

She gazes into my eyes for a second or two and smiles happily, then off we go, her first, me right behind her, I feel a sneaking sense of unease as we walk down the stairs, there's something about the way she's been acting lately, I can't put my finger on it, but she's always so chirpy, so perky, she's much more effusive than usual. I realize, of course, that the somewhat delicate and extraordinary—to say the least of it—situation that I, and hence she, have been thrown into has had an effect on her, but I can't help thinking there's a connection between the way she's acting and the fact that I suddenly appear to be heir to an unimaginably large fortune. That she's so anxious for me to bond with my biological family, that she insists on calling them my mom, my dad, and my brother even though I've asked her not to, and that she keeps reminding me of how incredibly alike Kåre and I are—is she doing all of this because she's eager for me to become a part of this family as soon as possible and thus secure my share of the estate quickly and without a fight, as it were? And the fact that she's so keen for me to join the family firm, that she takes a half-drunk Rikard on trust and puts in a good word for me, as she said, is that part of the same plan? I mean, maybe it's the prospect of all that money and wealth that makes her act the way she has been lately, maybe what I'm actually glimpsing here is her inner capitalist: like father, like daughter, you might say. I put on my boots, pull my hat and gloves out of my jacket pocket, put them on, and out we go. We walk side by side down the avenue and past the part of the laboratory we were shown around the day before yesterday. The smell of salt water, seaweed, and shore grows stronger the closer we get to the quay, it smells so good, it's the scent of my childhood, the scent of home somehow.

"Is there something the matter?" Ingrid asks.

"No."

"You're very quiet."

"It's nothing."

"Okay," she says, then she takes my hand. I'm not used to walking hand-in-hand with her, it's not something we ever do. I've never thought about it, but maybe it's because she's slightly taller than me and I would have to hold my hand a little higher than feels natural, I don't know. We walk out along the jetty and down the steel gangway to the biggest floating pier, it rocks in the swell and I have to do a little shuffle as I step onto it to keep my balance. It's not really the weather for going out in a boat, the water's choppy even this far up the fjord, I hear the sea crashing over the huge rocks on either side of the jetty only then to be sucked back out. The pennant on Rikard's boat cracks in the breeze and farther out the waves are whitecapped. I'm glad we're not going out beyond the skerries, although in a boat as big as this it would probably be all right, even if not particularly comfortable.

"Come on, come on," Rikard says, he has already started the engine and he's standing in the cabin doorway, looking at us. "We have to be back before dark."

We clamber on board, Ingrid first and me right behind her.

"Could you cast off and pull in the fenders?" Rikard asks me, pointing to the mooring lines. I nod, untie one line, then the other, wait till he has pulled away from the pier, then haul the three fenders over the side and onto the deck. I go to join Rikard and Ingrid in the cabin, then change my mind and instead just pop my head around the door. It's nice in there: the floor, walls, and most of the fittings are of some dark wood, probably oak, and it's remarkable how well this goes with the burgundy upholstery on the chairs and benches and all the gleaming brass fittings.

"I'm going to stay outside for a while," I say. "I feel like getting a bit of sea air." They don't reply, just nod and smile back, then face front again. I shut the door, climb the ladder to the top deck, and park myself on one of the seats behind the windshield, sit there, scanning the steel-gray waters of the fjord. The roar of the engine fills my head, it must be a hell of a powerful engine, we're moving much faster than I expected, at any rate. I place my hands on the rail, shut my eyes, and hang on tight as the boat shoots forward. But what if my reconciliation with Ingrid is also part of her plan? I hadn't really been expecting her to ask me to come back to her, but what if she was motivated by the thought of money and wealth? I mean, she already knew what had happened to me when she called, I had told her about the newspaper ad and the letters and that the people I had always believed to be my mom and dad might not be my real parents. I didn't say anything about my alleged biological mother and father being rich, it's true, but I mentioned their surname, and that they lived in Bangsund, so a quick Google search would have told her that. I open my eyes, swallow. I don't know, of course, but I wouldn't rule out the possibility that the thought of the money made it easier for her to initiate our re-union, it's an awful thought, there's something greedy and calculating about the whole thing, and however understandable it may be, however human, it makes it hard for me to believe that she loves me as much as she says she does. Since I returned home she could not have been more attentive, she says "I love you" umpteen times a day, she kisses and hugs and touches me in situations where she would never have done so before and now, sud-denly, she wants us to hold hands as well.

I grip the rail a little harder as the boat rolls and plunges over a run of slightly higher waves, try to keep my seat but it's impossible, I bounce up and down in time with the waves, letting out a little "ow" every time my tailbone hits the plastic. It lasts only a few seconds, then the sea is calmer again. I shut my eyes and tilt my head back, sit like that for a minute, then open my eyes and let out a little grunt of exasperation: I had made up my mind to let all that go, I had made up my mind that I would have to learn to trust that most of the time people are actually telling the truth, that there isn't always some hidden meaning for me to uncover, but here I go again, shit, I'm so sick of myself, I don't want to be like this, I mean there's nothing wrong with a healthy dash of skepticism, of course, but thinking like this is no good for me or for those around me. And anyway, what if it's not Ingrid but me who's the greedy one, what if it's my own selfishness I'm glimpsing here and not hers, maybe deep down I don't want to share my good fortune, maybe I'm scared of los-ing control of the inheritance that appears to lie in store for me and maybe that, in turn, is why I'm beginning to suspect Ingrid of wanting to get her hands on what's mine, maybe I'm simply becoming tarnished by the prospect of money and wealth.

"Hi," Ingrid says.

I turn to look at her and she smiles at me as she comes up the ladder.

"Hi."

"Rikard says we're not far from Otterøya now," she says, sitting down beside me.

"That's Otterøya over there," I say, pointing to the steep, wooded headland visible between Kvarvøya and Brannøya.

"I'd love to see the place where you grew up," she says. "Your childhood home."

"It's on the other side of the island. I could ask Rikard to take a swing around that way, it's not far. Look," I say, pointing to the other side of Lokkaren Fjord. "Over there, that's Merraneset. And there's Gullholmstranda, Gullholmen, and Kattmarka," I go on, moving my finger from one spot to the next. "We went there a lot when I was a kid . . . well, after I moved to Namsos, that is . . . we used to play there, and go swimming, camping, held our first parties there, and, yeah . . . all that. And over there," I say, pointing to a little red cottage over at Selnes. "That's where we stole our first boat engine."

She smiles roguishly and arches one eyebrow almost flirtatiously.

"What?" I say.

"Oh, it's just that it's kind of exciting to think that I'm living with a real bad boy. Quite a turn-on, in fact."

"Mm, that bodes well for tonight," I say, smiling roguishly back at her, let my eyes linger on hers for a moment, then turn and look across to Lokkaren again.

We sit quietly for a while, then: "I've decided to trust you, Ingrid," I burst out.

Her hat has slid down over her eyes, she nudges it back up. "What?"

"I've decided to trust you."

She says nothing for a second, obviously not quite with me, she looks puzzled, but pleased too.

"I see . . . so does that mean you didn't trust me before?"

I shrug.

"I think . . . it's just a way of saying I love you," I say, eyeing her levelly, unsmiling, and she sits there with that slightly puzzled but pleased look on her face. Neither of us speaks for a few moments, then I turn away again, glad to have said what I just said, I feel lighter somehow, clean, I don't really know why. I've said "I love you" so many times before, of course, but possibly never with such conviction, maybe that's why. I look across to Lokkaren, I can make out the remnants of the old ferry landings on either side of the inlet, God knows how many times Mom and I took the ferry across there, before the bridge was built at the end of the seventies. I remember being really scared of one of the men who worked on the ferry, he was so stern and imposing in his overalls, smoking his roll-your-owns as he directed cars and people on and off the boat, but he may well have been just an ordinary guy who felt small and insignificant in all other ways and compensated for this by lording it over others when he had the chance.

"Shall we go inside," Ingrid says. "It's a bit chilly out here."

"Okay."

We climb down the ladder and join Rikard in the cabin.

"Come and have some coffee," he says.

"Ooh, coffee sounds wonderful," Ingrid says. She peels off her gloves, cups her hands around her mouth, and blows on them. "Brrr."

"There're mugs in that rucksack," Rikard says to me, with a nod toward a black-and-red rucksack hanging over one of the chairs. I pull off my gloves, take two mugs from the rucksack, grab the thermos off the table in front of the banquette, look out toward Survika as I sit down, and unscrew the cap.

"Do we have time to take a run past my old childhood home, do you think? It's not far from here. Just around that point and down a bit," I add, motioning out of the window as I pour coffee into one mug and hand it to Ingrid.

"Sure," he says.

"Great," I say. I pour coffee for myself, put down the thermos, and curl my hands around the mug, feel the warmth spread through my fingers. I take a sip and stand there looking out of the window, watching the landscape of my early childhood unfold before me: the bare rocks appearing and disappearing in the rough gray sea, the islets with their clumps of juniper trees, dwarf birches, and small pines blown sideways by the wind whipping down from Folda and along Namsos Fjord. And the scattering of houses and cottages on Otterøy itself, of course. There are a lot of new buildings since I was last here, one tract of summer cottages after another has sprung up, all over the island apparently. Well, cottages—but what passes for a cottage nowadays would have been described as a villa thirty years ago, so I don't really know what to call them. There certainly seems to be plenty of money around, you can tell from these properties: there may not be too many single-family homes here, but a lot of the old houses appear to have been extended and given dramatic face-lifts. When we were kids, the house where Eva lived was just a standard seventies catalog house, but now it looks like a palace: the front has been completely redone and two new wings have been added, with acres of glass and the sort of oriel windows that always remind me of *Dynasty* for some reason.

"You see the woods up there, below that stretch of scree? That's where we had our Indian camp," I say. I think of telling her what it was like to be a little Indian from Otterøya, but I decide against it, there are so many memories, I wouldn't know where to begin. I take a sip of coffee. "That's where I grew up, on that headland."

"Amazing," Ingrid says.

I smile at her, try to look cool and unaffected, but I feel my pulse quicken as we round the point and slip into the bay where our old house lies. It's so weird, I haven't been back here since I grew up. I helped to clear out the house after Grandpa died, but that must have been the last time. I don't know why I've never taken a trip over, I've almost nothing but good memories of this place, so it's not that, I just never got around to it. I swallow, it's so strange to be here, it feels both familiar and foreign, I know every nook and cranny of our old house and yet it's so much smaller than I remember. I feel a bit like the central character in Hamsun's *Victoria*, returning to his parents' home after many years in the city and being struck by how small the miller's house is.

"Is it that white one there?" Ingrid asks.

I don't say anything, just nod, not taking my eyes off the house. Rikard slows down even more, the drone of the engine fades to almost nothing, and we glide quietly up to Grandpa's old jetty. Only now do I see how dilapidated the house is, the roof is green with moss and has sunk in the middle, the windows are broken and someone has sprayed the word *dick* on the wall facing the water, it even looks as though there's been an attempt to set fire to the porch, there are black, sooty trails where flames have licked the walls. I swallow again, no one has lived here since Grandpa died and it has become the sort of hangout I remember from when I was thirteen or fourteen and living in Namsos: abandoned, derelict, slightly out of the way, the kind of place frequented by teenagers looking for somewhere private where they can do things they don't want the grown-ups to know about; where some kids will run riot, some seize the chance to smoke their first cigarette and have their first drink, to read porn mags or feel up the only girl they know who's willing to be felt up. I sip my coffee, consider asking whether we could go ashore for a little while, then think better of it, there are so many memories attached to this place and I would rather see it alone, I don't quite know why, I just would. I'd like more time to look around, it'd be better to take a drive over before we go back to Trondheim. I lower my coffee mug and run an eye over the farm. The barn door has come loose and dangles lopsidedly from the top hinge, yellow grass and spindly aspens have grown through the planks of the deck where we used to sit in the summer, and the big cherry tree my swing once hung from has been uprooted and has toppled backward onto Grandpa's old HiAce—the car has lost its wheels and the tree seems almost to have pressed it into the ground when it fell, it looks really funny.

"Oh, my God, look, there's somebody over there," Ingrid

says, pointing. She gives a little laugh: "I nearly jumped out of my skin."

I look where she's pointing. There's a man down on the shore with his back to us, only a few yards away. He's wearing a black-and-blue snowsuit that blends with the rocks and the hillside behind, rendering him also invisible. He's gutting fish on a board set on a large rock. After a moment the man turns and peers at us, the gaunt, chalk-white face is framed by the black hood and at first glance he resembles an older version of Death in Bergman's *The Seventh Seal*. Holy shit, it's old Uncle Albert. I thought he died years ago, but it's him, no doubt about it. Grandpa would have been ninety-one now had he lived, so Albert must be in his late eighties. He stares at us, he never did like strangers and he certainly doesn't seem to have changed in that regard.

I open the biggest window, hook it back on the hasp, and stick my head out.

"Hi, Albert."

He doesn't reply.

"Don't you know who I am?" I ask.

"Should I?"

"It's David, Erik's grandson."

"Aw, Christ. I thought it was the warden. I didn't recognize you right away."

"Yeah, well, time leaves its mark, you know," I say.

"Eh?"

"Time flies," I say, a little louder.

"Aye, it's goin' by faster and faster," he says. "We'll soon have no time for anythin' but chopping down fuckin' Christmas trees."

I laugh. "So how are you?"

"Aw, mustn't grumble," he says.

"You're looking great, anyway."

He considers me for a moment, then snorts and grins.

"Aye, the specs fair steam up when I walk into a room full of women," he says, and he lifts another pollack out of the bucket and slaps it onto the chopping board. I laugh and shake my head, he hasn't changed in that regard either, old Albert, that's just how he and Grandpa and their cronies used to talk and joke when I was young and it does my heart good to hear him. I shoot a glance at Rikard and Ingrid: Rikard's busy plotting something on the GPS and Ingrid is just standing there smiling politely, she doesn't look as if she finds Albert the least bit funny, she thinks he's common, I suppose. I turn back to the window, in time to see Albert slit open the belly of the fish, rip out the guts, and toss them into the water, only inches away from the boat. A split second later a great black-backed gull dives down out of nowhere, snaps up the entrails, swallows the lot in one big gulp, and rises up again in a gentle arc.

"I think we may have to move along soon," Rikard says. "It gets dark quickly these days."

I nod, turn, and see Albert chop the head off the pollack and toss this too into the water. There's a little splash and the next instant I hear the gull screech, it's worked out what's going on here and it swoops in again from the other side of the bay.

"We have to go now, Albert," I say, smiling at him. I'd like to stay and talk to him some more and I almost add that I might pop over to see him soon, but I don't get that far.

"Ach, I wouldn't have paid the fine anyway," he says.

"Huh?"

"I'm ninety," he says. "I've never worn a life vest in my

life and I'll be damned if I'm goin' to start now." He sticks his hand into the bucket and pulls out another pollack, lays it on the board, and starts to clean it. What the fuck, he still thinks we're the wardens, didn't he hear what I said?

"It's not the wardens, Albert," I say. "It's me, David, Erik's grandson."

He eyes me for a moment or two, then lifts his chin the way people often do when something finally dawns on them.

"Ah, so it is," he says. "I didn't recognize you right away."

I just look at him—shit, the man's fucking senile, I didn't realize it at first, but it's obvious now.

"Yeah, time flies," I hear Ingrid giggle, repeating what I said to Albert only moments ago, bringing our conversation around in a loop, as it were, in an illustration of Albert's senility. Behind me I hear Rikard laugh—well, it was quite funny so I can see why he's laughing, but I'm not laughing, there's something painful about all this and I can't bring myself to laugh. Besides which, I'm rather annoyed at them for laughing.

"Bye, Albert," I shout.

No reply. He doesn't even look around, merely raises a hand in farewell, holds it over his head for a second or two, then carries on cleaning the fish. Rikard reverses a little as he brings the boat around to starboard and I stand there gazing through the porthole in the door, slowly swiveling to the left until the stern is pointing landward and the bow aiming out into the fjord, never taking my eyes off Albert and my childhood home.

There's a little jerk and then we start to move.

"Is it far to the plant?" Ingrid asks.

"No, no," Rikard says.

I simply stand there, watching Albert and my childhood home grow smaller and smaller, until Albert is gone and the house is just a tiny dot. I give it a moment longer, then turn and look across to Jøa, am about to say something about the realm of Olav Duun and *Odin in Fairyland*, but I don't get the chance.

"So, communications advisor?" Ingrid says, harking back to Rikard's job offer. They must have been discussing it earlier on when I was outside, it sounds like it anyway, from the way she's talking, it sounds as if she's taking up where they left off. "I understand that it involves promotion and image building. But more specifically . . . ?"

Rikard gives a little wag of his head.

"Well, that particular department has a wide range of responsibilities," he says. "The job involves writing press releases and information sheets, drafting speeches when the occasion calls for it, acting as spokesman for the company. And then there are our websites, of course. They've been neglected for far too long and I think we need to initiate a project to redesign them fairly soon. I see that as a good place for you to start," he says. He turns and smiles at me, then faces front again. "If you're at all interested, that is?"

"I'm sure you would have a lot to contribute, David," Ingrid says.

"But I don't have the relevant experience or the right qualifications," I say.

"We have people with experience and the right qualifications already," Rikard says. "We're looking for people from other backgrounds, with another sort of ballast. Someone who can think outside of the box. And you would be given proper training in all the working of the firm, of course."

"Hm," I say, looking at him and smiling, still not sure why he's making this offer, maybe Ingrid's right, maybe I could do a good job here, I actually think so too, but Rikard has no way of knowing that, so there must be some other reason for this move on his part. I don't think she's right, though, when she says he's doing it because we're brothers and he has my best interests at heart, I mean he knew about me for years but never got in touch, so that doesn't seem very likely, yeah, what do I know, maybe he's offering me this job because he wants me on his side from now on, maybe he's afraid I might use my clout as an heir to the company to put a spoke in his wheel and this is his way of making me his ally, maybe this is simply a sop to me to keep me happy and possibly even to teach me to think like him and follow the same line as him on the running of the firm. I gather that Kåre doesn't approve of some of the things Rikard and the other members of the board are doing so maybe Rikard is afraid I might turn out to be a rival and serious contender for the ownership and, hence, control of the company when the time comes. Or maybe he's simply jockeying for position. Because it's not necessarily the case that an estate is always equally apportioned in such settlements. As far as I know the law requires that each heir receives a minimum share of the estate, but other than that Kåre can choose to favor whomever he deems best equipped to assume owner-ship, so maybe Rikard is actually afraid of being sidelined. Although, if that were his thinking, surely it would be more sensible not to let me have anything whatsoever to do with the company. In that case surely the obvious thing would be to get rid of me. And maybe that's what he's plan-ning to do—plenty of people have killed for a fraction of the assets we're talking about here, so who knows, maybe Marius was right when he warned me earlier, maybe that wasn't Marius the paranoiac talking after all, maybe I have good reason to be wary of Rikard. I look at him, feel a sudden ripple of unease because, well, maybe I am in danger—it sounds unreal, but it's not entirely unlikely. So perhaps I should turn down his offer, to prove that I don't pose any sort of a threat, it's actually quite tempting to say yes, but maybe it's best not to have anything whatsoever to do with the company. Oh, fuck, I've got to stop this, it's no use, I mustn't think like this, it's fine that I'm entitled to inherit something and it's fine that Kåre is critical of the way Rikard runs the company, but for fuck's sake, that doesn't make me a serious contender for the top job. Rikard was born and raised to succeed Kåre and I know nothing about running a business, the mere thought that he might regard me as a rival is ridiculous. Unless it's Ingrid he's worried about, maybe that's it, she's the daughter of a business magnate and entrepreneur and she's shown herself to be an adept businesswoman over the past few years, so maybe he sees her as the biggest potential threat, maybe he's afraid that she'll exploit the situation and use me to gain control of the whole concern. Oh, but no, this is no use, I mustn't think like this, I need to stop speculating and stick to what I actually know.

"There it is, over there," Rikard says suddenly. He points to a cluster of tall, round, brightly lit silos on the other side of the bay.

"It looks like a palace," Ingrid says.

"I've never thought about it, but so it does," Rikard says. Pause.

Then: "I think I'll give it a go," I blurt.

Ingrid and Rikard turn to me, but neither of them says anything.

"I'll take the job," I say. "I wouldn't mind trying something new.

"That's great!" Rikard says, although I don't know if he means it, he's smiling, but he's taking it pretty calmly, he doesn't look exactly overjoyed.

"Oh, I'm so glad," Ingrid says, trying to play it cool but not succeeding very well, she gazes at me for a second, eyes glowing and lips compressed, as if she's struggling to stop herself from cheering out loud, then she takes my hand, turns, and looks out toward the fish vaccine plant. She doesn't say a word, merely squeezes my hand, to emphasize how happy she is, I suppose, and I'm happy too, happy and relieved, but I'm also apprehensive and a little daunted, not that I think I have anything to fear, because I'm pretty certain I don't, I think it's more the idea of embarking on something so different that I find daunting, this is a new and unknown world after all. It's unbelievable really, that I should have wound up here, in this situation. I mean, when you think about it, it's absolutely unreal, pure fairy tale.

CARL FRODE TILLER is the author of five novels—the last three forming *The Encircling Trilogy*—and four plays; all of them are written in the distinctive language of Nynorsk ("new Norwegian"). One of the most acclaimed Scandinavian authors of his generation, Tiller has received multiple prizes, including the EU Prize for Literature and the Nordic Critics Prize, and his *Encircling Trilogy* has been twice nominated for the Nordic Council's prize.

Tiller was born in 1970 in Namsos, Norway. He now lives in Trondheim with his wife and three daughters. He was, until recently, a member of the rock band Kong Ler.

BARBARA J. HAVELAND is a leading translator of Norwegian and Danish fiction, drama, and poetry. Other Norwegian writers translated by her include Henrik Ibsen, Jan Kjaerstad, and Linn Ullman. She lives in Copenhagen.

The text of *Encircling 3: Aftermath* is set in Trump Mediaeval and SansSemiLight to a design by Henry Iles. Composition by Bookmobile Design & Digital Publisher Services, Minneapolis, Minnesota. Manufactured by Friesens on acid-free, 100 percent postconsumer wastepaper.

Also available from Graywolf Press
The groundbreaking first novel in *The Encircling Trilogy*

The audacious and daring opening novel in *The Encircling Trilogy* begins the story of David's search to recover his identity after suffering from amnesia. When he places a newspaper ad to ask his friends and family to share their memories of him, three respond with letters: Jon, his closest friend; Silje, his teenage girlfriend; and Arvid, his estranged stepfather. Jon's and Silje's adult lives have run aground on thwarted ambition and failed intimacy, and Arvid has had a lonely struggle with cancer. Each has suspect motives for writing, and soon a contradictory picture of David emerges. Whom should we believe? Or do they all hold some fragment of the truth?

Praise for *Encircling 1*

"What makes this novel, the first of a trilogy, extraordinary is the suspense: like the best mystery novels, it transforms the reader into an obsessive gumshoe—though, in this volume, at least, David's identity is a question with no definitive answer." —*The New Yorker*

"A beautiful meditation on the subtler ways we fail each other, our quieter forms of grief. . . . It's thrilling to know two more books will arrive to tell its story." —*USA Today*

"[An] impressive and ingenious novel. . . . [Tiller's] authentic voices consistently entrance and intrigue." —*Star Tribune* (Minneapolis)

Also available from Graywolf Press
The suspenseful second novel in *The Encircling Trilogy*

With steadily growing suspense, Carl Frode Tiller's carefully scored polyphony of voices continues to piece together the fractured identity of David, the absent central figure of *The Encircling Trilogy*. To remind David of the memories he lost, three friends write about his childhood on the island of Otterøya: Ole, a farmer struggling to save his floundering marriage; Tom Roger, a rough-edged and violent outsider; and Paula, a former midwife harboring an explosive secret. Filled with questions and answers that stay tantalizingly out of reach, *Encircling 2: Origins* is an exhilarating look at how identity is influenced by our friendships, and a thrilling continuation of *The Encircling Trilogy*.

Praise for *Encircling 2: Origins*

"Intense and psychologically acute. . . . Bombs dropped in the final pages ensure hot anticipation for the final installment." —*Booklist*

"An incomparable intellectual escapade. . . . [*The Encircling Trilogy* leads] to an inescapable conclusion: identity is not a monolith but a collage—an odd, overlapping, contradictory collage, impossible to reconcile." —*Los Angeles Review of Books*

"A moving, complex portrait. . . . [*Encircling 2*] gets at the uncomfortable truth: though we may view ourselves as the heroes of our own stories, we're little more than supporting players in everyone else's." —*Words Without Borders*